Front ...sion

Leonie Rogers

FRONTIER INCURSION

This is a work of fiction. All the characters and events portrayed in this book are fictional, and any resemblance to real people or incidents is purely coincidental.

Hague Publishing
PO Box 451
Bassendean Western Australia 6934
Email: contact@haguepublishing.com
Web: www.haguepublishing.com

ISBN 978-0-9872652-5-8
Cover Art: *Frontier Incursion* by Emma Llewelyn

Typeset Garamond 11/12
Printed in the USA by CreateSpace

Dedication

THIS book was a long time coming. The fact that it has finally arrived is due to the encouragement of a number of people. To Andrew, at Hague Publishing, thank you for taking a punt on a complete unknown! To Emma Llewelyn, who created the most beautiful cover art, thank you so much. Your ability to divine what is inside my head has been truly remarkable. Mum and Dad, who kept safe my early poetry for so many years - thank you! My test readers, Sandra Langley, Marguerite Walsh and David May; a very special thank you for the time spent working your way through all of those typed pages, and in Dave's case, multiple emails. My husband Mal, whose faith never wavered, and whose enthusiasm has been boundless, and Lachlan, who read the very early version in various bits and pieces and snippets, and then managed the building of a web page. My final, and very special thank you is to Briana, who enjoyed reading this book so much that I had to keep writing it. Briana has read this book more times, and in more forms, than anyone else. All I can say to you is - "I love you Grubsy!"

Chapter 1

SHANNA tapped one foot as she waited outside the Records Precinct. *Where on earth was Kaidan this time?* she thought, standing on tiptoes to peer over the jostling crowd. She chewed the end of one of her braids impatiently. He knew that students of the same family always stood together during the ceremony – they'd talked about it on the road into Watchtower just that morning, when they'd arranged where they'd meet.

She scanned the groups of students hurrying past, one by one leaving their small groups to join with family members, before hurrying through the old Storm Shelter's entrance. She could just see the stone archway; at this distance, the stonework simply looked decorative, but up close, the light coloured stone was worked with sequences of images that marked the three hundred years of human settlement on Frontier. On either side of the archway, the names of the heroes of the last three centuries were carved deeply into the polished stone walls. She bounced with impatience, beginning to feel irritated.

***

Kaidan accelerated again, sliding around the corners of the stone buildings of Scholars' Precinct in his rush to arrive before the ceremony began. The imposing façade of the thick stone walls towered above him, the heavy blocks of light coloured stone gleaming in the late afternoon sun. The long, rectangular, two-storey structure that heralded the Records Precinct squatted sturdily at the end of Scholars' Avenue, its lack of decoration and small windows hinting at its original purpose as a safe haven from the wild weather and marauding native fauna of Frontier. Dust puffed up from his boots as he saw the last few students ahead of him disappear around the corner. He knew he shouldn't have stayed in the classroom, but that last maths problem had just been so fascinating ...

Kaidan glimpsed his sister's trademark braids as a uniformed group of final year students cut in front of him, and dodged quickly around them, judging to a nicety the slide required to cut the corner. Knowing how late he was, he took off towards his sister with a spurt, and ran full tilt into Master Cerren – the mathematics and navigation teacher – his shoulder impacting the Master just below the sternum.

The short, greying man was knocked flying, grey robes flapping as he cannoned into a group of final year students, who just managed to catch him before he ended up on his back in the dust. Kaidan paused panting, completely aghast at the near disaster he had almost visited upon his favourite teacher. As the other students carefully stood him upright, one of the girls gently brushing his robes to straighten them, Master Cerren could be seen to be struggling to regain the breath that Kaidan's shoulder had driven from his body.

"Master Cerren, I'm sorry," gasped Kaidan, "Truly, I didn't know you were there! I'm really, really sorry!" Embarrassed, he felt himself blush hotly. He hated that he seemed to blush at the slightest provocation, his face growing hot enough – he felt – to boil water. There was a silent pause, punctuated only by Master Cerren's gasping inhalations, while the final year students looked carefully at the ground, and Kaidan felt like he might emit steam any second. Master Cerren finally drew enough breath to speak. He ran his hands through the grey fringes of hair over his ears, dusted the bald dome above and straightened his now very rumpled grey scholars' robe, before looking Kaidan firmly in the eye. He paused again, clearing his throat and drawing his brows down, before beginning sternly.

"Young man, when I set you to study the forces of motion and angular momentum today, I was not expecting you to use me as a test subject!" He frowned at Kaidan for a few seconds, before his eyes suddenly twinkled, and the frown vanished into a grin. One of the final year students suppressed a giggle, pointing at Kaiden's stupefied expression. It took him several moments of panicked emotion before he belatedly caught on, and grinned through yet another fiery blush, muttering "Sorry sir…"

"It's all right lad, no real damage this time, just a little bit of bruised ego and a good lesson learnt – please don't travel at that speed in this kind of crowd again." He winked. "Now, I believe the young lady making faces from behind Master Andra over there is, like yourself, in a hurry to get to the ceremony. I suggest you join her."

"Thank you Sir," he whispered in a slightly strangled voice, hoping fervently that his face would stop imitating a sunset. And still trying to gather himself walked off at a much subdued pace towards his irritating sister.

Shanna punched his arm as he arrived. "Where have you been? You're so late. I was just about to go in without you." Without waiting for an answer she pulled her brother towards the Storm Shelter entrance, and they clattered down the two tiers of steps together. As they entered the dimness, lit only by tall candles evenly spaced down the sides, Shanna murmured to her brother in a slightly more friendly tone. "You know, that was one of the funniest things I've ever seen. You should have *seen* your face when you ran into Master Cerren! I could feel the glow from over here." Shanna dropped her pace, slowing it to one that more suited the solemnity required by the occasion. The large hall was filled with the Masters and Students of Watchtower, grouped as families, all standing.

"Yes, well, you don't have to turn up in his class next week, do you?" Kaidan whispered crossly, "How am I ever going to live that down?" He was still mortified, and felt another blush rise as he and Shanna took their places with only moments to spare.

"Sssshhhhhhh! It's beginning," Shanna whispered, as the candles were abruptly extinguished, shaking her head at her brother in warning."When this is finished, you're going to tell me why you were so late!"

In the darkness, the assembled Masters and students stood, as Master Florentine began the familiar words that signalled the beginning of the question and response litany for the Day of Remembrance Ceremony.

"Just over three hundred years ago, our forefathers began the task of learning to survive on Frontier." He cleared his throat and continued.

"Where did they come from?"

"From the Federation of Races," came the response from massed voices.

"Where were they going?"

"To a new home, of hope."

"What happened to the dream?"

"It was changed by a trial of fire."

Master Florentine lit the first candle, and its glow gently spread across the front of the hall, illuminating the darkness and the Master, standing solemnly by the ranked candles.

"This is the Candle of Remembrance for the dead." The assembled crowd bowed their heads.

"We honour their lives and sacrifices."

The assembly lifted their heads and quietly responded.

"We honour them."

He lit the second candle. "This is the Candle of Endurance."

"We remember their courage, on a world full of fear, standing together to survive." Arms were linked throughout the assemblage, and Shanna linked hers with her brother and those on either side. She felt her annoyance with Kaidan's lateness lessen, as she remembered the history of her people, and the trust that they'd needed to develop in each other, just to survive.

He lit the third candle. "This is the Candle of Sanctuary."

"We remember that our forefathers completed the first town wall." Two of the youngest students each laid a piece of rough stone at the base of the candle, and then returned to the waiting ranks.

"This is the Candle of Promise."

"We remember the pledge of our forefathers to the precepts and rules of life on Frontier." Two of the most senior students laid two heavy books of law at the base of the candle.

He lit the fifth and final candle. "This is the Candle of Hope."

"We look towards the future," the massed voices spoke in unison. "When we once again regain the stars." Shanna heard Kaidan's voice join hers, and as they spoke the litany, she wondered as she did every year, whether that hope might ever become reality.

Master Florentine looked solemnly at the students assembled before him. "One day, we hope to regain the stars. But today, we continue to honour the memory of our ancestors. We remember in thankfulness their resourcefulness and inventiveness, and pledge to continue their work, making a home here for humans, and exploring and caring for this world that we have been given." He raised one hand and the students mirrored him. "We pledge that we will work towards this aim, dream that one day we will regain the stars, and agree never to forget those who came before. We will keep a moment's prayerful silence."

The student body stood quietly in silence, and then, as the Master lowered his hand, sat to conclude the yearly remembrance ceremony.

***

The shadows slowly lengthened as Shanna and Kaidan walked through the crowds of students recently released from the Day of Remembrance Ceremony. Shanna flicked her gold-streaked brown braids over her shoulders and settled her backpack straps more comfortably.

"Race you!" she said, as she elbowed her brother in the ribs in order to be first through the gates of the precinct.

"Shove off Shanna!" Kaidan complained, making a grab for the braids flicking enticingly along in front of him. After his earlier collision, he was a little unsure about racing his sister, but her irritating behaviour was needling him, and he swung his own backpack over his shoulders, and jogged quickly to catch up to his sister, long legs in their heavy boots smoothly making up the few strides that separated them.

"Got you again!" she laughed as she ducked away, beginning a breathless chase around their fellow students, packs bouncing, legs flying and dust spurting at every sliding turn and twist. They both laughed as Shanna punched Kaidan's shoulder when he finally caught up and continued laughing as they made their way steadily towards the merchant precinct of Watchtower.

They paused briefly at a baker's shop and purchased the two loaves of fresh, grain-laden bread that their mother had requested, and a small fruit bun each for the walk home.

"Here, hold this." Shanna tossed her bun at her brother while she carefully stowed the bread in her backpack, making sure her books were stacked at the bottom to avoid squashing the yeasty loaf. Kaiden contemplated the wisdom of taking a bite out of his sister's bun, or possibly licking the sweet glaze on top. He decided on the bite. And dodged her retaliatory hand, dancing out of the way as she attempted to retrieve her bun.

"You are so annoying today!" She finally caught him, and landed another wallop on Kaidan's shoulder. "And what made you so late?" Kaidan rubbed his stinging shoulder.

"Maths."

"You were nearly late because of *Maths*?" Shanna shook her head. "You're such an idiot sometimes, Kaidan."

Kaidan tossed her bun back to her. She frowned and shook her head, as she regarded the bite mark.

"Late because of Maths, and now you've bitten off the best bit!"

"Yeah well, you shouldn't hit so hard," Kaidan said. "Let's get going. Dad'll be waiting."

Straps buckled up, the two wound their way through the merchant's quarter, zigzagging the maze of streets and bypassing tempting stalls of fascinating goods, before descending the knoll upon which Watchtower perched. The odd wagon of goods lumbered past, hauled by large placid horgals, their feathered hooves contrasting oddly with the scale patterns on their four sturdy legs, while their long necks and lavishly lashed eyes peered curiously at passers-by.

Shanna laughed at the large chestnut that snuffled at her braids as it plodded past, hooting gently with surprise and twitching its pointed ears, as they flapped under the breeze from its nostrils. Its driver tapped its round rump gently with his cane to redirect the beast's attention to the roadway, and waved at the two siblings.

"Adlan's waiting at the gates for you two."

"Thanks Hodan!" Both picked their pace up as the streets steepened, the merchant quarter gradually giving way to terraced dwellings interspersed with tall, yet sturdily constructed guard towers. Shanna and Kaidan walked down the last slope towards Watchtower's imposing gate as the sun lowered towards the horizon. Just inside the gates, their father, Adlan, waited, accompanied by two of the home starcats, Moshi and Boots. The two starcats were enormous felines with darkly silky smooth coats, violet and blue eyes, and enormous paws. Their black coats exhibited the characteristic glowing tidal marks of their breeding lines.

Moshi butted his huge black head against Kaidan's hip, the indigo marks on his rump and shoulders glowing slightly with affection as he angled his head for a caress. Boots purred deeply in his throat as he raised one heavy paw to poke gently at Shanna's hand in a bid to encourage her to pat him. Shanna obliged, the cat leaning his heavy head into the caress.

"Hi Dad."

"A good Remembrance Day Ceremony?" Adlan asked as they walked through the gate. Shanna rolled her eyes at her father, and related the afternoon's episode. As she described Kaidan's impact with Master Cerren, Kaidan felt his face flush bright red again.

"You're lucky it was Master Cerren, and not one of the other teachers," Adlan said, raising his eyebrows.

"Hmmm, yes," Kaidan placed his eyes firmly on the road as it wound down the hill and snaked its way through the greenery before rising again towards the ridge line that housed Hillview.

"Actually, he'll be out visiting us tomorrow," Adlan went on, "He's looking for another starcat to replace Prince." Prince had been the old Master's constant companion until his recent death at the venerable age of twenty five.

"You can meet him and escort him in, Kaidan. Just make sure you do everything at a walk…" He quirked an amused eyebrow as Kaidan sighed.

As the sun set, they climbed the last steep rise to Hillview, the family home and starcat breeding lodge. The squat stone frontage was set directly into the low hill, flanked by the fenced and shuttered breeding cavern on one side, and the individual cat caves on the other.

Both Moshi and Boots flicked their large triangular ears forward, tidemarks glowing happily in the rapidly gathering dusk. A soft chorus of almost subliminal melodic greetings, rolled out from the family starcats. All three family members replied with soft greeting whistles, before entering the warmly lit interior of the house, hanging their backpacks on brass hooks set into the stone wall by the front door.

Janna looked up from the large pot of thick soup she was ladling into bowls on the heavily loaded kitchen bench. She pushed her long, dark hair back impatiently with one hand and looked up at her family as they came through the front door, deep blue eyes smiling a welcome. Starcat training aids mixed with collars and harnesses vied with stacks of paper and the family's dinner for room, and Janna absentmindedly elbowed aside a jar of dried meat treats as she placed the pot onto the tiled top.

"Evening all," her musical voice welcomed them. "A bit late tonight?" As the two starcats undulated over to mats in front of the fire, Shanna put the bread on the waiting board and the family settled around the bench automatically making room for the bowls and plates. A superlative starcat trainer and cook, Janna had long ago decided that she could live with a little chaos on the kitchen bench. Shanna pushed aside a pile of paperwork.

"Don't move that too far, Shan, it's the paperwork for tomorrow, and you know I can't find the things I need if you tidy up. I have a system!"

"And if we move anything, you won't be able to find the important stuff, I know, I know." Shanna carefully made sure that the stack of paper was clear of her soup bowl, but close enough to where it had been for her mother to locate.

"Smells great Mum, I'm starving!"Kaidan took a deep sniff of the steam rising from his bowl.

"Bottomless pit," she said fondly, "No seconds before the rest of us finish; and try and slow down, there's no need to inhale it." They paused to give thanks for their food, and then began to eat. Adlan sliced the bread and slid the board into the middle of the family.

"So, tell me, how did the day go?" Janna enquired again. Adlan grinned, and related the tale yet again, while Kaidan attempted to control his rising blush, again unsuccessfully, and then promptly changed the subject.

"Has Sabre had her kittens yet?"

His father frowned, sighing slightly, breaking off a piece of the bread and dipping it into the soup. "No – and this is the second litter she's been overdue with – mind you, she's getting on a bit now, so perhaps we should consider whether this should be the last one. Anyway, she's never had any problems, so I think at the moment we'll just sit tight and wait for her."

"Can I go and see her later Dad?" Shanna queried, "I did promise her I'd drop in every day."

"You and your starcat conversations!" Her mother laughed, gesturing with the filled soup ladle towards Shanna's bowl. "More soup?"

Shanna grinned at her mother. "You know they understand every word I say." She scraped around her bowl with her spoon and then held it for Janna to ladle more soup into it. Kaidan quickly slurped his last spoonful and held his out too.

"Don't forget you're on dishes young lady." her father said, "And before you go to bed, your Mother and I have a few things to discuss with you. Kaidan, you're on cat feeding."

After washing and drying the dishes, Shanna opened the side door into the breeding cavern and left the house. Grabbing a shielded lantern off the shelf, she lit it, the warm light illuminating the breeding cavern. Shanti, a large grey female with violet tidemarks, lay reclining on her cushions watching her six adolescent cubs gambolling around her, chasing tails, batting toys and mock wrestling with each other. She raised her head and greeted Shanna with a rumbling purr, as her offspring paused briefly in their play. "Hello Shanti, glad to see those little monsters aren't wearing you out too much."

She walked quietly towards the far side of the cavern, where a large, very pregnant, black starcat reclined in a woven basket filled with blankets, tucked into a recess in the cavern wall. Although normally one of the house cats, Sabre preferred to spend the few days before her cubs arrived in the peaceful privacy of her cavelike corner. The other cats in the cavern knew to respect the distance that Sabre required.

"Hello most beautiful of starcats," Shanna pitched her voice low and quiet. Sabre stirred, her violet eyes glowing as she lifted her head to regard the visitor, revealing the first of her new cubs tucked neatly beneath her chin. As Shanna approached, she produced another, the nearly three kilo cub wriggling and mewing wetly in the dim light, "Clever girl, Sabre!" Shanna backed away and settled quietly on a cushion near the cavern wall on one side of the labouring cat.

An hour later, a soft-stepping Adlan appeared, just in time to see Sabre gently nose the final cub towards its first meal. Her great violet eyes regarded him quietly above the eight fat, feeding cubs. She gave a soft chirping purr, arranged her tail neatly around the cubs, and laid her chin on her forefeet with such an enormously self-satisfied expression that Adlan and Shanna chuckled softly.

"Well, I should have known she'd wait for you to be here – she hasn't had a litter without you watching since you were born. " He paused and smiled, "Your mother and I have decided that one of these will be yours. We want you to watch them carefully for the next three months, and then you can choose."

"I can? I'm ready?" Shanna's voice was almost breathless – there was a lot of responsibility in owning a starcat, and knowing her parents' strict requirements for prospective starcat owners, she was feeling both excited and a little humbled that they felt she was ready for individual ownership. However, her own starcat was something she'd coveted for a long time, and she began running her eyes speculatively over the cubs feeding from their mother.

"That's one of the things we need to discuss tonight. Have you finished out here? Your Mother's waiting near the fire."

After one last check of the cats, father and daughter walked together to the front entrance of the breeding cavern, looking out across the fenced runs at the spectacular vista. The cultivated front pastures of Hillview overlooked the verdant green forest of the plateau, and dimly in the distance, the northern mountains raised their craggy tops towards the sky. One of the reasons the family was able to live safely outside the walls of Watchtower was the presence of so many starcats. Even the largest of predators hesitated to enter a starcat pride's territory.

The dark sky was speckled with a myriad of stars. Father and daughter paused, as always, to savour the spectacular view. Very faintly in the distance, a few of Watchtower's lights were visible. As they turned to re-enter the house, Adlan regarded his daughter fondly.

"One day we'll return to the stars," he murmured.

"Maybe one day they'll find us." Shanna replied in their evening ritual.

They turned as one and headed inside into the warmth of the house.

Above, one of the stars detached itself from the others, heading on a southerly trajectory. Unnoticed by the pair, it maintained its steady course for a few moments, and then descended below the southern horizon.

Chapter 2

INSIDE amongst the warm firelight, Janna was putting the final touches to a starcat harness for one of the youngsters she would be working with the next morning. Over by the front entrance, Kaidan looked up from placing two large bowls of food on the floor and then whistled quietly in two tones. Two large black forms padded over towards him, sat, and looked steadily up at him.

"Who's hungry then?" Kaidan queried. Both cats lifted their right paws, purring loudly. He immediately gestured towards the bowls and they each pounced on a bowl, tails flicking gently as they ate.

"I'm off for a wash and bed now, if I've got to be up early tomorrow to meet Master Cerren." Kaidan hugged his mother and father, gave his sister a mostly friendly poke, and headed towards the tiled bathroom off the hallway.

Adlan raised a hand. "Night, mate – I'll call you just after dawn for breakfast." There was a sigh as Kaidan closed the bathroom door.

Over by the fire, Janna and Shanna had drawn up squashy chairs and foot stools and settled down with hot drinks, warming their toes in front of the embers. Boots wandered over, grunted comfortably, and lay down between the two of them, his heavy head leaning on Janna's legs, while Moshi had already curled up in front of the fire, fastidiously washing his face and whiskers. Adlan sat opposite, absently toying with a tooled leather, harness strap.

Janna placed her cup on a low table next to her, and sat slightly more upright in her chair, provoking a slightly grumpy look from Boots, who had just managed to get properly comfortable.

"Shanna, have you put any thought towards your future?" Janna asked. "A few weeks ago, Dad and I were approached by a number of your teachers. They've suggested that you're ready to move into your specialisation years, and after some discussion, your father and I think we agree. We'd like to know what you think."

Shanna sat silently for a few moments, staring into the fire, startled thoughts chasing themselves through her head as she contemplated her mother's words.

Her father smiled slightly. "We know this has come to you earlier than expected."

Shanna nodded – specialisation usually occurred sometime between the ages of sixteen and seventeen, and was a gradual progression for a class of students, generally occurring over a full twelve months. She was just fifteen, and hadn't expected to be thinking about her future for at least another year.

"I'm not sure what to say. Or think for that matter – it's really not something I've given a lot of serious thought to – I thought I had at least another year to settle into specialisation." She sipped slowly from the mug in her hand and was slightly startled when Moshi paused in his grooming to slurp her other hand with his rough tongue. He bumped her hand again to remind her to pat him, ducking his head to make it easier to reach his favourite spot on the left cheek, while his purring gave her enough space and composure to look up at her mother.

"Why now Mum?"

Janna grimaced slightly. "Your current teachers have decided that you've learnt as much as they can teach you in the pre-specialisation setting. You've always been in the extension classes, but again you've always worked ahead – as you well know. They're beginning to worry that your fertile mind might start thinking up other things to do if you're bored, things that are not necessarily strictly educational. Along the lines of your recent horgal dung prank, perhaps." Shanna's face attempted to rival her brother's. She had believed that her parents, along with everyone else, were still mystified as to the originator of the delivery of horgal dung that had somehow ended up underneath a particularly stuffy teacher's study window. She quickly changed the subject.

"But Mum, I've not really thought seriously about anything except following on here – with the starcats and you and Dad." Shanna was a little concerned. "What else would I do?" She loved learning, but the family's starcat breeding business had always seemed to be a logical extension of her life.

"Lovey, there's many things you can do other than join us here at home! You don't need to limit yourself, or ignore your talents and gifts, just to stay here because you think we expected you to." Adlan was leaning forward earnestly, leather strap forgotten on the chair arm next to him.

"We'd love you to stay here if that's what you want, but it's not taken for granted at all. Not for you and not for Kaidan either, when the time comes for him to choose. The family business is all well and good, but it may not be where you want to be, either now, or even later. Your mother and I didn't start our lives training starcats, you know, we both specialised in other things before settling to this." He leaned back again. "Don't be in a hurry to make up your mind right now. Take a few weeks to think things over, talk to your teachers – have a good look at your options, think about your skills and the things you love, and then we'll see."

Shanna looked up from Moshi, who had surreptitiously draped most of his huge black body across her and the chair during the conversation, effectively preventing her from getting up, as most of his considerable weight was relaxed comfortably – for him – across her lap. He was a past master at the sneaky lap snuggle, and his purr was rumbling comfortingly through her body while her thoughts raced.

"Do I really need to make this decision so soon? What about leaving all of my friends? What will they think? What –" Shanna broke off abruptly. It was hard enough being clever at the best of times, easily understanding in seconds what took some of her fellow students weeks, and friends had come slowly during her school years. She didn't relish the idea of beginning again with a group of complete strangers, and she worried that she'd lose the few friends she felt comfortable with.

Janna smiled. "I know it's hard, but it really is time, kitten – you need to do this – we know you've been bored at school lately, and you can't just mark time for the next year. Some of your friends might not understand, but the real ones will. Take time tonight to enjoy the idea of that cub, and then have a good think about what you might like to do over the next few weeks. Remember that you can talk to us anytime, if you need to, but this, in the end, must be your own choice." She looked over at her husband. "We'll go to bed now – early start tomorrow. Don't stay up too late, and give that cat a shove if he gets too heavy."

After her parents departed, each dropping a kiss on the top of her head, Shanna remained in front of the fire, staring idly at the embers, as the lantern finally guttered and died. Moshi remained draped across her, while Boots slunk quietly off in the direction of Kaidan's bedroom. A few moments later there was a grunt from Kaidan, and a sleepy murmur, which suggested that Boots had managed to claim enough room on Kaidan's bed for him to be comfortable for the night.

Moshi simply sighed, violet eyes closing slowly, and settled more heavily across Shanna's lap as thoughts chased themselves one by one through her head. Images of starcats interspersed with Frontier's seething jungle life, lashing wind and rain, faces of friends, and the view of the Thunderfall cascade hurtling over the edge of the plateau to plummet towards the verdant forest below.

Thoughts of Sabre and her cubs brought a slow smile to her face, which was then extinguished by thoughts of various professions she'd never given much thought to. Healer? Militia? Advocate? Baker?

She didn't know what to think, and after an hour of staring into the dying embers, she heaved a sigh, poked Moshi in the ribs to move him and headed off to bed, thoughts still cycling round and round inside her head.

***

Several hundred kilometres south of the plateau, the slowly moving star disappeared into the forest canopy in a flare of landing lights. Routine scanning sensors on board had noted the heat traces of congregating organisms on the plateau during the flyover, while the insectoid crew scanned the surrounding vegetation at their chosen landing site more thoroughly for potential threats. A brisk command, and the star ship settled heavily to the ground, wisps of smoke from crushed vegetation rising lazily towards the stars. The plateau could wait. There were no telltale traces of high technology. In the meantime, the surrounding area would be subdued, and made fit for Garsal habitation.

Chapter 3

KAIDAN grunted and wriggled out from under the heavy weight of the sleeping Boots. The starcat sighed and then stretched out more comfortably across the bed, tail draped over the edge and trailing onto the floor.

"Coming Dad," Kaidan muttered sleepily, as he dragged on shorts, boots and shirt, and then ran a comb quickly through his hair. The smell of fruit porridge wafted through into his room, hastening his preparations, as his ever hungry stomach gurgled impatiently. Unfortunately in his haste, he stumbled over the long black tail twitching near his feet. A pained grumpy "Meh," sounded from the bed, as Boots complained about the cruel abuse to his furry appendage.

"Sorry Bootsie, keep it out of the way next time." He swiped a conciliatory hand down the cat's flank, and was rewarded with a sighing purr.

The porridge was warm and filling, chunks of plump dried fruit adding flavour to the morning cereal, as the family slowly congregated around the bench. Kaidan noticed dark circles under his sister's eyes and wondered what had caused them. He wisely decided, as she yawned and propped her head in her hand to eat her porridge, that he would wait until she was more awake before asking her what was going on. His father had told him about the cub Shanna would be choosing, but that would only have provoked excitement in his sister, so there must be something else bothering her. He was, however, too wary of early morning sisters to wish to pry when she was half asleep, and then wondered how grumpy she might become later when he decided it was time to prise the information from her.

"Kaidan, you'll need to groom the weanlings and the trained cats first thing, and then prepare the display arena for Master Cerren's visit." His father said.

Kaidan nodded. He always felt a bit like a militia recruit at sixth day breakfast.

"Shanna, you're on breeding cavern. See if you can get Sabre to allow you to handle her cubs. We all know that the earlier they're handled the better they'll be after weaning."

Shanna removed her head from her hand, rocketed to her feet, clicked her heels and stood to attention.

"Yes sir! Dad sir!" Her father, as he had reminded her the previous night, had actually specialised in the Militia, before settling to starcat breeding when he married Janna.

The effect was slightly spoiled by Moshi sitting heavily on her left foot and wrapping his tail around both their feet, effectively providing her with a pair of furry boots ringed in glowing purple.

"And you and I Sergeant-Major, will feed and water everyone else before we all tidy up this mess." Janna saluted her husband cheekily with her spoon, and then had to scrape a smear of porridge off her right eyebrow. Adlan smiled and raised his tea mug to her.

Kaidan gathered the grooming tools and the arena rake, and then headed for the young starcats in their individual dens. There were four ready to be sold on as basic trained, general purpose companions. He greeted them with soft whistles and experienced appreciative rumbles in return. Like all the Hillview starcats, they had soft, smooth, dark coats, with tidemarks in shades of blue or purple, glowing in response to the starcat's emotions. Josen's cats were usually ruby or scarlet toned, and he'd seen only one emerald toned cat, as none of the breeders in the Watchtower region had breeding pairs that threw greens. All of the Hillview cats had tones shading from electric blue through the spectrum to violet. An hour later, the shining coats were adorned in decorative leather harnesses, and the trained cats were sitting placidly at stay outside the display arena.

Kaidan then went into the breeding cavern, to Shanti's cushioned abode, her six cubs still snoring around her in various attitudes of complete relaxation.

"Big day, little beauties," he murmured. Some starcat owners preferred the challenge of training their own cub from scratch. This, however, was certainly not recommended for the faint hearted. A well trained starcat might appear placid, but a young starcat required very careful training, as misplaced leniency could result in an out of control, hundred kilo juggernaut, intent on self-gratification. Adlan and Janna only sold cubs to carefully selected customers, and Master Cerren was well known for his spectacularly trained feline companions. He might well choose a cub today.

Each cub was groomed while their mother carefully oversaw Kaidan's every move, from the gentle brushing and trimming of over fluffy ear tips, to the fitting of comfortable colour coded collars and soft leather training harness.

Over the other side of the cavern, Shanna had managed to coax Sabre into allowing her to gently handle the new cubs. Kaidan strolled quietly over, leaving Shanti's cubs with their mother for another few moments. He could see that the new cubs were spectacularly marked, vivid violet and blue tidemarks glowing in unique patterns across each cub's back and flanks. Two of the cubs bore the highly sought after ear tip tidal marks, with one of the young males exhibiting a series of spiral tidal marks up each leg, and another young female had beautiful indigo tail tip markings.

"Nice litter." He murmured appreciatively to his sister as she placed the little female back into the basket with her mother.

"They surely are." She certainly wasn't volunteering any information to her brother, as she rose to her feet and walked over to Shanti's waiting cubs with

Kaidan. Attaching leather leads to the cubs' harnesses, they each walked three of the cubs over to the holding pens around the arena, trying to avoid tangles as the bouncing cubs frisked in the early morning air.

"Have you picked yours yet?" Shanna looked up, surprised, as Kaidan's query reached her ears.

"Dad told me while you were out last night with Sabre, that you were getting a cub." He was envious, but realistic as well. After having grown up in constant contact with starcats he understood that thirteen years of age was much too young for such a tricky task as handling a potential natural disaster.

"Not yet." Shanna replied. "I've three months until they're weaned. They were only born last night! You can help me, if you want."

Kaidan grinned, surprised at her generosity.

"Thanks Shan, I shall give you the benefit of my amazing experience, and wonderful insights into starcat behaviour and breeding," he said smiling. "Now I'd better go and wait for Master Cerren, and then later you can tell me what's really bugging you."

He smirked at her startled expression as he jogged out of the gate, down towards the roadway at the bottom of the hill, accompanied by Moshi and Boots who had finally decided to stagger out of bed. In the distance, a small dust cloud was visible, gradually resolving into a horgal wagon with Master Cerren perched upon the front seat next to Hodan. Kaidan attempted to get his rising blush under control as the balding, grey haired Master waved cheerily at him, but the image of himself striking Master Cerren full-tilt kept intruding on his self control. Moshi poked him with one outsized paw to gain his attention as the wagon came to a halt and he remembered his manners abruptly, welcoming the wagoneer and Master to Hillview.

"Come on up with me to the house for a few refreshments, Master, before we show you who's available. " Kaidan hoped fervently that his mother had remembered to remove the starcat debris from the bench for the visit of such a well-known scholar. He held his hand out to assist Master Cerren to alight from the wagon. The Master smiled his thanks, but leapt down lightly, attired today in utilitarian trousers and shirt above walking boots.

"Hodan, you can put your horgal in the front paddock with ours – there's plenty of water and fodder in the troughs, and Shanna will bring you something to eat and drink if you'd like to meet us at the arena."

"Thanks Kaidan, he'll appreciate the break and a chance to feed – and I won't be unhappy either." Hodan grinned at Kaidan and turned the horgal towards the house paddock. It snorted softly as the gentle wind brought the sudden smell of starcat on the breeze, but didn't balk at entering the paddock as the two Hillview horgals snuffled greetings.

Kaidan beckoned Master Cerren towards the front door, where his father waited to welcome them into the dwelling. With a subtle hand signal, Kaidan motioned to Moshi and Boots who promptly separated and lay down either side of the door. Master Cerren smiled appreciatively and entered the house with Adlan and Kaidan.

After the Master was served with refreshments, Adlan began the business at hand.

"We have a number of starcats at hand for your perusal, Sir, both weanling cubs and basic trained youngsters, along with a variety of demonstrations for you to view, and then you can take your time to meet them all. Both Janna and I are familiar with how well trained your Prince was, and we know that you're well aware that choosing a starcat is a mutual decision – a decision made by both yourself and your new cat. So I think we can dispense with the usual introductory information session. We're able to begin anytime you wish." He smiled at the Master.

"Yes, the day my Prince and I chose each other is still one of my fondest memories!" The old scholar's eyes misted slightly in remembrance, and then he rose after firmly placing his cup on the bench, and giving his greying head a small shake.

"Shall we start?"

"By all means, Janna has the cats down at the arena, and we have some comfortable seating ready for you. She'll put the older starcats through their paces, and then the weanling cubs. Have you any preference at this point?"

"Not at all, I thought that I'd just watch and and then take things as they come." As Master Cerren stood Adlan gestured courteously towards the door.

Down by the arena, Shanna and Kaidan perched themselves in vantage spots, ready to assist their mother as required. Demonstrations like this occurred on a fairly regular basis at Hillview, and they were well practiced assistants. Janna had decided to show the ready trained cats in a group, and then demonstrate their individual strengths. The younger cubs had only very basic training, and would be shown after their more experienced fellows. After that, Master Cerren would meet and greet any that had taken his eye.

"Jay, Socks, Bouncer and Flip, come!" Four handsomely harnessed starcats appeared by Janna's side in a flash, each sitting neatly with its tail curled over its front feet. Janna demonstrated the basic commands taught to all starcats – sit, drop, come, stay, stand and wait. She then demonstrated the four cats' response at a distance, to both whistle and hand signals, as the four starcats flowed gracefully around her in a complex weaving pattern, their brightly glowing tidemarks showing their enjoyment.

Shanna sat watching the display almost absently. She'd spent hours lying in bed the night before, unable to sleep. She loved living at Hillview, with her family and their cats, and the unexpected discussion with her parents had rocked her comfortable world to its foundations. Her parents and brother were such a solid, dependable part of her life, and until now specialisation had sat nebulously in the future, not yet close enough to disrupt the ordered pattern her life had revolved around. Apart from being completely unprepared for the conversation she'd had the previous night, Shanna had become anxious – she didn't know if she was ready to move away from the predictably comfortable life with her family, the secure place she inhabited with her friends, and the ordered days of school life.

The promised cub was something she'd longed for for years. But its advent was now tarnished by the unknown. How could she care for a cub if, for example, she decided to become a baker? Not that that was likely, but how was she to raise a cub if she had to live in a house or student accommodation that didn't allow starcat cubs? Master Cerren applauded vigorously at the end of the group display, and Shanna started from her reverie, checking that her equipment was properly organised. Master Cerren was very obviously appreciating not only the sheer beauty of the display, but the skill required to train the cats to such a superlative level.

Janna then put each young cat individually through its paces, each cat demonstrating its particular strengths. As the four youngsters waited at one end of the arena, Janna motioned to Shanna and Kaidan, who readied the extra aids.

"Jay, Hunt!" Shanna released a marmal into the arena. The small furry creature's tufted ears twitched and its pointy nose wriggled as it caught the starcat scent. The violet toned black cat dropped, almost merging with the dust as he settled to absolute stillness. In an almost unseen blur of movement, he appeared face to face with the marmal, and froze to absolute stillness again, his gaze fixed intensely upon the small, furred creature's eyes. The marmal stood stock still, pinioned by the big cat's glare, and completely unable to move, yet seeming strangely unafraid.

"Release!" The cat blinked, and the marmal hurtled back into the safety of the carry box Shanna had waiting.

"Well done, big boy." Janna said, scratching the cat's cheekbone as he preened. He returned to the line of youngsters obediently, and Janna called the next cat forward.

"Socks, hide!" A dark grey female with blue points, slipped silently from Janna's side, moving with such silence that her foot falls were completely unheard. She gradually faded herself from view, so completely that she appeared invisible, even the faint shimmer that normally marked a starcat's presence had disappeared. Within thirty seconds, she appeared to have completely vanished from the arena. From the side of the arena, Kaidan and Shanna could see the Master's head sweeping from side to side, trying to detect Socks, turning first one way and then the other, as he listened for the slightest noise and attempted to catch the shimmer.

"Socks, up!" To Master Cerren's great startlement, a large purr sounded in his left ear, and a set of whiskers swam into view. Shanna and Kaidan chuckled at the starcat's sense of humour as Socks returned obediently to Janna. Master Cerren laughed along with them, nodding his head at the big grey as she settled beside Janna.

"Bounce, climb!" Bounce blurred his way up a tall pole at one end of the arena and then at Janna's command, leapt to an identical pole at the far end, finishing his acrobatics with a sliding flourish down the pole.

"Flip, guard!" Kaidan, dressed in a padded suit, attempted to attack his mother with a wooden stave. Flip dropped under the whirling stave, then leapt on Kaidan from behind in that startling burst of starcat speed, seemingly appearing out of nowhere. Slightly winded, Kaidan picked himself up off the ground as Flip positioned herself in a guard posture in front of Janna.

As the four starcats lined up neatly next to Janna, Master Cerren and Hodan applauded vigorously. Janna waved the four youngsters towards Shanna, who dropped them neatly in a line to watch the young cubs, giving each cat an appreciative rub in its favourite spot.

The cubs demonstrated their basic training, neatly sitting, dropping and coming to Janna's commands before she released them to play in the arena. They gambolled happily together, playing with the various training toys the siblings dropped for them.

Janna beckoned Master Cerren into the arena to meet all of the starcats, and Shanna set the four older cats to wander as they wished, allowing them to meet the stranger on their own terms. Choosing a starcat was a mutual event – a human might show a preference, but the cat usually had the final word. Over the years, humankind had learnt that a starcat who wanted someone in particular could not be diverted. Master Cerren strolled amongst them, intermittently smoothing an appreciative hand down a silky coat, or tossing a toy for the weanlings to chase, while murmuring to Bounce and Jay who approached to look him over. He whistled gently and the cubs bounded over to him, attempting to chew his shoe laces, almost tripping him over in their enthusiasm. As he staggered slightly, there was a gentle growling noise, and the cubs paused in their play, stepping back slightly as a large body inserted itself firmly in front of them. Socks gently separated Master Cerren from the cubs, butting his hand with her head in order to draw his attention to her, and brightening her vivid blue tidemarks. She nudged him again, and purred loudly. Master Cerren laughed, running his hands over her head, automatically seeking out the itchy spots all starcats loved to have scratched, along their cheeks.

"And here I thought I might never find someone to replace Prince – but how could I resist the attentions of such a beautiful lady – her pick up lines are impeccable! I don't think there's going to be much more to sort out, except her price." He looked down at Socks, as she purred yet again, violet eyes glowing. Master Cerren dropped his hand onto her head again, and they strolled up together to the house with Janna and Adlan to begin the bargaining.

Shanna and Kaidan returned the young cats and cubs to their living quarters, and returned to the arena to tidy up.

"So Shan, what's up?" Kaidan queried his sister as she threw a training toy into the crate he was holding.

"Nothing," she replied, avoiding his eyes.

"Don't kid me Shan, you should be *bouncing* over the idea of having your own starcat, and you've barely even mentioned it. You obviously didn't sleep well, so what's bothering you?"

His sister sat with a thud on the ground, drawing her legs up and resting her chin on her knees. Kaidan joined her, idly sorting the training gear into neat heaps as she sighed, and finally decided to come clean. At the end of her explanation, he whistled softly.

"You're worried about what everyone else will think, aren't you? And you don't know what to pick either, do you?"

She sighed heavily. "Yes, you're dead right on both accounts." Kaidan quite understood her dilemma, he'd had a few of the same issues himself – liking mathematics too much, being tall for his age and not always fitting in with his peers. Living out of town meant that contact with school friends was not as frequent as he would have liked either. Good friends were hard to come by, and alienating them by progressing faster through the standard levels at school was something he tried to avoid, but it was hard work making sure he wasn't sticking out like a sore thumb. And he knew he hadn't really succeeded in camouflaging himself that well either.

"I'll still like you – mostly! Well, as much as any brother likes his sister!" He gave his sister a thump on her shoulder, "And the good friends will be OK." He tried to sound more certain than he felt, and mentally reviewed a list of professions in his head, wondering what he'd choose when the time came.

"Thanks Kai," she sighed again, heaved herself to her feet, and hefted the crate. "We'd better get this stuff put away, I can see Mum waving from the window."

***

Several hundred kilometres away, the first of the slaves ventured off the Garsal ship, and began the slow job of clearing around it. Each wore a bright orange band locked around each ankle, bearing a tracking device. Deep in the vegetation, a loud rustle sounded and a deep grunting roar echoed through the forest. Fear shot through them.

Chapter 4

SHANNA heaved her aching body off the practice mat, and staggered to her feet yet again.

"Enough." Master Peron clapped her on the shoulder. "Go and get clean, then you can come and see me before you go home." Shanna staggered gratefully off down the corridor to the bathing room, shedding her sweaty practice clothing and settling slowly into the warmth of the large bath in the female change rooms. Eight weeks ago, she had finally decided on her chosen profession. She had applied for and been accepted into the Scout Corps.

The first six weeks had passed in a haze of physical and mental exhaustion. She had always excelled in school, but so had the other five recruits, and she was a full two years younger than the youngest of them. Her worst fears about her school friends' reactions had mostly been realised, and she was feeling lonely, tired, and unsure of whether she had made the right choice. All of her current classmates had been in the same student year and had known each other prior to donning their Scout recruit uniforms. They were a tight-knit group, and she, the outsider. They were tolerant of her presence but that was as far as it went, and she was unsure of how she might change this. Assuming she made it through the probation period, the three years of Scout Training looked like a very lonely road.

She swished her hands through the warm water. To make things worse, she was still a bit on the short side in comparison to the others, and on the first day of training, to the unconcealed amusement of the other five, she'd had to walk around in the smallest sized uniform available, with the sleeves and legs rolled up. She knew she'd looked ridiculous. Fortunately, skills learned to create starcat harnesses proved transferable to clothing, although the finer points of tailoring had come from her father.

Being younger and shorter had made many of the physical challenges harder. The obstacle courses had taken her longer than any of the others, as she'd heaved and scraped her way up the taller obstacles. In strength conditioning, Shanna had simply struggled. Three days into the first week, she'd almost not made it out of bed due to muscle soreness. Luckily the walk into Watchtower from Hillview had loosened her up, so that she was walking nearly normally by the time she reported to Scout Compound for the day's training. It seemed that she'd been aching for days. Fortunately size made no difference in the endurance tasks, and in that area at least, Shanna had held her own.

Accustomed to memorising facts easily, Shanna had found the sheer quantity of information she was expected to process daunting. Hours she had previously devoted to sleep in her comfortable bed had been spent sitting memorising the duties and obligations of the Scout Corps. She dreamt the regulations now, and every morning on the walk in to Watchtower feverishly revised the chapters she'd studied the night before.

Sighing softly, she undid her braids and then ducked under the warm, constantly circulating water of the bath, allowing the sweat that had been stinging her face and scalp to wash away. Reaching to the edge of the bath, she grabbed a handful of soapleaves and rubbing them in her wet hands, used the frothy result to shampoo her hair. She resisted the urge to simply soak there for an hour after rinsing, remembering Master Peron's instructions, and climbed tiredly from the hot water. She dressed in a clean uniform, bundling the dirty one into the basket at the end of the row of lockers.

Shanna had felt reasonably well prepared, if a little young, for entry into the Scout Corps. Right up until her first lesson. Now, she felt constantly exhausted and as though she was furiously paddling in a wildly flowing body of water. She felt as though she might never master even the basic skills of a bottom rank scout. What had seemed an adventurous and exciting career that she was already partly equipped to begin, had proved much harder than anything she had ever contemplated.

Leaving the change rooms, she went left down the corridor, up a flight of stairs to the second storey, and along to Master Peron's office where she knocked politely on the door.

"Come in," the Master said, and still feeling her aches, Shanna took a seat in the tall backed chair in front of the desk.

"Well, Shanna, six weeks you've been with us. How are you feeling about the Scouts now?"

Shanna paused, trying hard to sit tall and ignore the aching of her abused muscles, while gathering her scattered thoughts to make some form of coherent answer. She knew that the first six to eight weeks were probationary and that some Scout candidates were gently let go in that time. This was likely to be yet another test.

As a fully qualified Scout, she would be a member of one of the most highly trained and respected service groups on Frontier. Even a basic bottom rank scout, was expected to be able to navigate flawlessly through Frontier's uncharted regions, journey for days living off the land, identify and cope with any kind of predator or lethal vegetation, and be able to examine, test and catalogue any unknown species. In addition to those skills, a Scout had to be able to survive Frontier's violent cyclonic storms if away from settled areas, cope with any kind of terrain, and most importantly have a rapport with and be able to train starcats, the Scout's constant companion and lifeline. The last requirement was the one that had set Shanna's feet towards a career with the Scout Corps. Scouts were highly educated, well known to be innovative, intelligent and brave, and were highly respected in the wider community.

"It's harder than I expected, sir." She had learnt early on that the Scout Masters did not take well to anything other than truthful directness. A few early attempts to brush off queries about her physical state when she was totally exhausted had met with sceptical silence, followed by a dressing down. Used to succeeding easily, Shanna was feeling miserable at having to admit to what for the first time in her life, felt like failure. Master Peron drew his eyebrows together, and looked at Shanna across his wooden desktop, leaning back in his leather chair.

"You're very young for this Shanna, however you're not the only one to have been admitted to training at a young age since the establishment of the corps. You are aware that your time up until now has been probationary, and you know that you have been constantly assessed over this period." He sat forward. "Know now, that a Scout's training will challenge any candidate in every facet of their life. And know now that even a graduated Scout never stops learning." Master Peron steepled his fingers, looking seriously at her, and Shanna nodded – was this his way of letting her know that she wasn't going to make the grade? Her self doubts bubbled to the surface again and she tried to prepare herself for the gentle let down. After six weeks of association with Master Peron, she knew that he would be kind, but firm.

"During their training, every junior member of the corps works with a mentor until graduation. We use the first six weeks to assess each candidate, and decide who will mentor them, or to ease them out gradually into a more appropriate career choice." He smiled.

"Resign yourself to the fact that for the next three years, you will be spending a lot of time with me, as the council has decided that I will be your mentor." Shanna collapsed against the back of the chair, almost not believing what she was hearing. "One of the most important things you will learn as a Scout is the ability to go beyond the barriers of normal human endurance. Our early training is designed to weed out those who will never learn this."

Shanna listened incredulously, realisation gradually dawning that she would be able to continue with her chosen training and then with some chagrin, that the sore muscles were probably only going to get worse and that she would somehow have to get to know her classmates, even if they didn't want to know her.

"Thank you, sir!" Her voice was fervent, and she broke into a smile, determining privately to figure out some way of getting the older cadets to accept her. Peron grinned back at her, and pushed his chair backwards.

"Bring your starcat when you return tomorrow." Shanna stared at the Master Scout incredulously.

"How did you know that I'm choosing a starcat today, Sir?"

"You already know that all Scout recruits need a starcat partner, and it's something we discuss with each candidate's family during the probation period. When probation ends, each recruit chooses their first starcat partner, and then training proceeds for the pair together. A Scout without a starcat is only half a Scout, and we like to train both of you together. There may be a few things that even *your* parents haven't taught you that a starcat can do." He smiled again, eyes twinkling. "As part of our routine arrangements, I contacted your parents a couple of weeks ago, and they'll be bringing a group of weanlings in tomorrow, along with another breeder from east of Watchtower, for your candidate class to meet. They also told me that they had promised you a cub around this time and agreed to time your choice with the end of the probation period, to fit in with your training should you be selected to continue on." Master Peron paused and regarded Shanna for a moment.

"There's something I wanted to discuss this with you today, before the choosing process. Most of the candidates will not have your level of experience in handling the weanlings, and will probably not really know what to do with them. They may also be a little miffed that their cats may come from your family holding." She nodded and almost sighed again, stifling it before it escaped.

Master Peron gave Shanna a considering look.

"Another aspect of our program of which you may not be aware, is that a normal part of a Scout's training is to be trained by their fellow candidates. All of you are talented and experienced in different areas, and that is part of what makes you all so valuable as recruits. Therefore each of you in turn will be instructing the others in some aspect of your training – the things you have learnt from your families, and your studies. Tomorrow you will begin instructing your fellow students in starcat handling and training." Shanna's heart gave an enormous thud, and appeared to turn over inside her chest – training her class when she was already the outsider! Training your own starcat was different to helping your very experienced parents with the family business, let alone instructing others at the same time.

Master Peron's eyes were compassionate as he said, "You'll be the first of your group to become a temporary trainer. Unfortunately you are also the youngest, and the others may make this a little more difficult for you than it normally would be." Shanna realised that the Master was not unaware of her issues with the other students, and there was sympathy in his expressive green eyes. "In the normal scheme of things, there would have been no warning for you, simply a statement on the day; however, because of your youth I am allowing you one day to consider how you'll go about tomorrow, and you will begin your period of instruction immediately after the choosing. All right, off with you now. I'll see you bright and early tomorrow with the starcats, in the outdoor arena." He dismissed her with a wave of one hand.

Shanna hastened out of the office, head spinning, and went down the stairs and out into the main corridor. One of her classmates was exiting Master Dano's office just down the hallway, his face alight with joy.

"I take it you've passed your probation too, Verren?"

"Oh yes, and starcats tomorrow!" Verren was a tall, dark young man, who had demonstrated a most useful ability to treat the minor contusions and injuries that had plagued the new candidates. After her discussion with Peron, Shanna had a sneaking suspicion that Verren would shortly be instructing his fellow cadets on basic medicine and first aid. Both his parents were medics. She had always enjoyed his company, even if he did tend to treat her as if she was about twelve years old. He was at least friendly and had always been polite to her.

"Have you had a starcat at home, Verren?"

"No, but some of my extended family do, and I've always got along well with them." He displayed a look of enormous longing. "The cubs are so cute! Anyway, got to meet Taya in five, see you!" He headed towards the exit, striding quickly. Shanna followed more slowly, contemplating how someone who thought starcat cubs were "cute" was going to cope with the very blunt reality. They *were* very cute to look at, and they did play very enthusiastically, so maybe that's all Verren had meant – the whole wide eyed, big pawed, fluffy tail stage was very endearing. It just didn't necessarily translate to biddable... It was going to take her some serious effort to get the essentials over tomorrow, if Verren was anything to go by. Her head buzzed with all kinds of strategies and potential problems, first amongst them how to get her fellow classmates to take her seriously.

She pushed through the double doors of the Scout Hall and then wended her way towards the front of the records precinct. On the way, she encountered Master Cerren who beckoned her over, Socks sitting comfortably at his feet. Theirs was a truly happy partnership, although, and Shanna grinned in recollection, some of Master Cerren's students had not enjoyed the advent of Socks quite as much as the Master had. He thoroughly enjoyed Socks' ability to conceal herself so effectively and then pop up without warning, and he had begun to use her as a kind of special teachers' aide. He would tell her to "Hide", whispering a distracted student's name into her ear, and then five or six minutes later he would get the mischievous starcat to pop up behind the misbehaving student's back and breathe heavily on their neck. Some of the previously underachieving students' grades had improved spectacularly since the advent of Socks. She seemed to enjoy the trick as much as the Master did.

"I hear you'll be choosing your starcat today, Shanna."

"Yes Master Cerren!" She grinned, almost bouncing at the thought, and firmly pushed the anxiety caused by her imminent teaching duties down. "Hello Socksy!" Shanna greeted the starcat at Master Cerren's side. "I hear you've become quite the teaching assistant!"

Master Cerren's eyes crinkled with amusement. "And what an assistant she is! Ah, here's Kaidan. Off you go. I shan't keep you from the moment any longer!"

Kaidan and Shanna walked off together, waving at Socks and the Master, Shanna trying to contain her news until they were outside the main gate of

Watchtower, shoving down the sudden resurgence of anxiety that twisted her stomach into a knot as she contemplated her teaching role.

"I wonder how Master Cerren knew I'm going to choose tonight?" She puzzled to her brother. He tossed off the query impatiently.

"So, who are you going to choose tonight?"

Shanna frowned, her forehead furrowing. There was a slight dilemma she hadn't mentioned to anyone at this point, but she had finally decided that she was just going to wait and see how things panned out that evening. Surely there was no point worrying at this time. "I'm not sure," she admitted.

Kaidan frowned, then remembered his own news. "I'm starting archery next week! Hopefully I'll be better at archery than I was at wrestling... Oh well, can't be much worse!"

"Hah! Have fun," Shanna said. "*I've* got to instruct my cadet class on starcat training after they choose tomorrow! And for the foreseeable future!"

"You are so sunk, Shan! You are so *dead* when the rest find out!" was her brother's comforting response.

"Thanks so much, little brother!" He grinned and elbowed her in the ribs gently.

"You'll be OK. You know heaps. Once they get over their first day or two they'll figure that out." Shanna wasn't so sure. After six weeks with the other cadets, she was positive that they weren't prepared to take her seriously. They continued their journey home after meeting their father with Boots and Moshi at the gate, with Kaidan intermittently having another dig at his sister about the next day's repercussions.

"Don't worry too much," Adlan advised, "If you have any problems to start with, give them one day of ignoring your advice, followed by one night alone with a starcat cub, and I suspect things will sort themselves out. You should know – as you're one of them – that these students are meant to be bright; hopefully the majority of them will actually use those brains." The advice was practical, but it still didn't stop Shanna from worrying. Her father dropped his arm around her shoulder gently.

"Just concentrate on enjoying tonight's choice young lady – your mother has your favourite dinner all cooked to celebrate!"

Janna was waiting outside with Sabre by her side as they arrived home. The beautiful starcat had her tidemarks gently glowing in welcome. She nudged Shanna with a cold nose and then stalked regally off into the breeding cavern with the family following in her wake.

"You'd think she knows exactly what's going on, wouldn't you?" Kaidan murmured.

"I'm not so sure she doesn't, to be honest." Janna said. "You should have seen her making those cubs spruce themselves up this afternoon!"

"You'll have me believing that they understand us too, if that kind of thing keeps happening!" her husband said.

"Perhaps not all of them, but Sabre has had a special bond with Shanna for as long as I can remember – they were born the same day, after all, and sometimes I used to find Shanna and Sabre curled up asleep together, tucked in with Sabre's mother Ebony. Occasionally I felt that Ebony and I were raising twins – one with fur and one without..." Janna laughed and she and Adlan entered the cavern hand in hand.

Inside the breeding cavern sat Shanna's dilemma. She'd observed and worked with all of the cubs on a daily basis since their births. She'd got to know the cubs well – and they were all spectacular examples of exactly what a starcat cub should be. Each of them showed personality and intelligence – there wasn't a dud in the whole litter. And then she had to giggle slightly as she realised that Sabre had somehow lined them up as if showing them off, and was keeping them neatly arranged with the odd warning growl.

"Will you look at that," Adlan whispered to his wife. "I'll bet you two nights washing up she picks Storm." His wife leaned into him smiling.

"You'll lose," she whispered back as Shanna approached the waiting cubs. "My bet's on Twister."

Unlike a prospective client, who usually met their starcat for the first time on choosing day, Shanna and the cubs knew each other well. There was no need for displays of obedience or agility or showy tricks, just the need to choose each other.

Shanna walked up and down the line several times. Then she stood and simply looked at the cubs.

"What's taking her so long? I thought she'd have figured it out ages ago." Kaidan asked his father quietly.

To the surprise of all, Sabre rumbled gently and six of the cubs backed away from the line, and sat neatly behind their mother leaving the other two sitting alone. She then looked at Shanna with her violet eyes shining and ducked her head, tidemarks pulsing in complex patterns.

Shanna deliberated. Her problem was simple – she knew she wanted Storm, *and* she knew she wanted Twister. She was also certain that both of them wanted her, however, her parents had promised her one starcat, not two. No-one had two starcat cubs at once. Breeders like her parents would sometimes have two cats as companions, but they were not generally the same age. The two cubs were both staring brightly up at her, violet and blue ear tip tidal marks glowing, and violet eyes sparkling, both oddly intense.

Janna, Adlan and Kaidan couldn't take their eyes off the bizarre behaviour of the starcats and Shanna. In all their years of watching humans and starcats bond, they'd never seen the mother cat involve herself at all. Normally, only the cats and the prospective partners interacted. Minutes passed and still Shanna had not chosen.

Finally, Shanna turned to her parents despairingly, turning her back on the waiting cats.

"I can't choose! What on earth am I to do?" Tears ran down her cheeks with the intensity of her emotions.

Janna opened her mouth to speak, and left it hanging there as Sabre, with an almost human eyebrow raise, hummed briefly at the two cubs. As one, they headed for Shanna, each leaning heavily on a leg, and then sat firmly on her feet. Sabre gave a satisfied chirrup, rounded up the other cubs and returned to her cushions, blinking her great eyes at the tableau.

Shanna's family regarded each other without words, and then Adlan laughed. "Well, that seems to be that, I don't think Sabre takes returns."

His wife nodded. "Well, she certainly knew what was going on, but I think I'm going to have to revise that chapter on choosing, in the new manual. It looks like you now have two cubs, Shan. I'm also thinking that you might be a wee bit tired by morning though...." Janna knew exactly what the night would bring, as young starcat cubs were generally quite active at night, and would certainly be testing Shanna's ability to be the boss as they worked out their new relationship. "Let's eat."

"Kaidan, you can stop standing there with your mouth open, and give your sister a hand with the food bowls. Bring Storm and Twister in, Shan, and we'll see how they go in the house. Hopefully after tomorrow, Sabre will be back inside again too. We'll just wait and see how many cubs go, and any who don't can move into the adolescent cavern. Besides, it's not a bad idea for the cubs to have their first evening inside without their mother keeping them in line for you." Adlan grinned. "You're going to have your hands full, young lady."

Shanna looked down at the cubs, and put a hand on either head, and then whispered, "Love you boys." Realising she was dripping tears on the two upturned heads, she wiped her face, and then with a hand signal, put the cubs at heel and entered the house via the side door.

Inside, Boots and Moshi lounged indolently in front of the fire, bellies turned to soak in the maximum heat. Kaidan was banging food bowls around and Janna was serving up roast lamb. Shanna took Storm and Twister over to the fireplace, and bade them sit. Boots stirred himself, stood, and then deliberately peered into Storm's face from about two millimetres away. Moshi got slowly to his feet and then did exactly the same thing to Twister. Both young starcats held their ground, and then slowly leaned away from the older cats, while attempting to stay sitting where Shanna had placed them. Unseen by Storm, Boots stealthily lifted a paw, and then gave the young cat a quick poke, just enough to unbalance him and tip him over. With an amused "Meh," Boots then strolled over to where Kaidan had placed the four food bowls and sat. Moshi was a little less subtle; Twister got a quick smack across the face that knocked him over, followed by a heavy footprint in the tummy as Moshi meandered over to Boots.

Kaidan giggled, and then signalled to the older cats to eat. The two young cats struggled to regain their dignity, while the whole family attempted to straighten their faces, and then Shanna walked them over to their bowls. Kaidan, in typical younger brother fashion, had placed their bowls in between Moshi and Boots' bowls. Shanna sat them, and then motioned to them to eat. Both gave her quizzical looks, and then looked at the bowls. Boots had finished his food and had decided to sit and wash while the young cats ate. He was too well trained to blatantly attempt to eat more than his fair share, however he was quite prepared to try and bluff the younger cats out of their dinner.

With a sigh, both Twister and Storm dropped to their bellies, and crawled to the bowls, eating lying down, ears twitching and eyes flicking towards the adult cats. Shanna laughed

"Well, you two are braver than some I've seen."

"Come and eat", Janna called, and the family sat down to the savoury roast lamb dinner to celebrate.

***

At the Garsal ship, forty slaves laboured to construct a strong fence, yet again. Over the past three months, several hundred had died, sacrificed to prevent Frontier's predators from damaging the colony ship. Several Garsal patrols had set out to survey the immediate area: none had returned. The Overlord had ordered the current crew out earlier that day. Finally the laser fence was almost complete, and yet again the throbbing roars of the predators could be heard on the breeze, and the sweating slaves worked faster and faster. The commander would order them out to defend the gaps with their bare hands if they didn't complete the last section before the scaled monsters arrived. Anjo ran to flick the switch and turn their safety on and the scarlet bars of light flicked into existence just as the first monster cleared the greenery. Garsal slave masters herded the exhausted slaves back inside the ship, to lock them in their pens as the first scaled monstrosity hurled itself into the threads of light and then staggered back with an ear splitting roar.

The Garsal Overlord transmitted an assembly call throughout the ship, and the crew gathered for review. When at last the muted roars of the monster outside the fence line ceased, the alien lifted its front appendage.

"Tomorrow we begin our survey again, and tomorrow we begin the hive." He turned and motioned to his underlings. "Assemble a construction crew from amongst the slaves." Striding towards the command level, he began composing the notification he would send to the Matriach, safely sequestered with the other female Garsal in their private quarters. His plans for the new residence had met with her approval. She would be pleased that the construction would finally begin.

Deep in the bowels of the ship, Anjo clutched his thin rug around him, huddling closer to his exhausted companions, holding desperately to the thin hope of survival.

Chapter 5

KAIDAN and Shanna hitched Spot the horgal to the wagon, and then loaded the unpartnered starcat cubs in their crates onto the wagon bed, ready for the journey into Watchtower. Shanna attempted to stifle a large yawn as she tightened a harness strap on the wagon shaft, and then followed it up by rubbing her eyes. It had been a busy night, attempting to settle the two young starcats and beginning to accustom them to inside living with their human partner. She had previously assisted her parents with housetraining young cubs, but that had been only one at a time. Two cubs certainly meant twice as much trouble as far as indoor training went. Despite taking Storm and Twister outside for a nature call prior to attempting to go to sleep, it seemed that one or the other had needed to go out again about once every two hours thereafter.

In between the outside trips, Shanna had attempted to encourage less playing and more sleep. First, Storm had felt he needed to pounce on Shanna's toes every time she breathed heavily, and then Twister had decided to attempt to live up to his name and wrestle the bedclothes into a whirlwind. Persuading a starcat to sleep other than exactly where it wanted to had been the bane of every starcat owner for the last three hundred years. No-one Shanna knew had managed to ban them from the bed, however the trick was to teach them to respect the bed's owner, and at least share the space reasonably equably. In many ways it was easier to teach complex hunting or hiding skills than appropriate night time behaviour. In short, it was the same problem experienced by any kind of cat owner over many millennia, just multiplied by more kilos of cat.

Her night had continued in that vein until the early hours of the morning when the tired cubs had finally given in to her (exhausted) patience and gone to sleep, one on either side of the bed, heads resting on her legs. She had woken a couple of hours later at dawn, to find them actually draped across her – fortunately weanling starcats were only a mere thirty kilograms or so – and still snoring dreamlessly. That constant patience and perseverance was what she would have to impart to her fellow students. She hoped she was able to keep it up herself.

"Are we a little bit weary, Shan?" Kaidan patted her shoulder, mock sympathy on his face and then dug her in the ribs with his elbow. "I heard a bit of the ruckus last night. Guess you didn't get much sleep."

"Sleep? What's that?" said Shanna ruefully. "I'm sure it'll get better, but two is definitely a challenge. When it's your turn for a cat, make sure you only end up with one. Hope I don't fall asleep today in training." Kaidan laughed at his sister's ongoing yawns.

Adlan and Janna appeared, starcat harnesses and collars draped over their arms. Janna beckoned Shanna over and handed her two handsome leather harnesses, Twister and Storm's names carved into the leather.

"You'll need this too." Adlan handed over a full backpack to his daughter. "Master Peron has asked us to explain that as of today, you'll be lodging in the Scout barracks for the next six months. Apparently it's felt that the less time you have to think about the sudden change, the better. Your classmates' parents will be explaining the same thing to their children right now."

Shanna felt as though the world had just dropped out from underneath her. There just seemed to be too much change in her world right now. Her brother looked stricken.

"Don't worry, you'll still be able to see me intermittently at school." Shanna felt a sudden need to reassure Kaidan. "When will I see you two?" She looked at the tears gathering in her mother's eyes.

"The rules are quite strict Shanna – about once every three weeks until you finish the six months. Your father and I had no idea what Scout training actually entailed before you started. We'll miss you, but be sure we'll think about you constantly. And we will see you again in three weeks, and we'll send notes in with Kaidan. That's allowed." Janna blinked furiously.

Adlan cleared his throat. "At least we'll have this morning before we need to say goodbye properly, which is more than most of your classmates."

He slung the last of the equipment into the wagon and then hopped onto the driver's seat, reaching down to assist his family up one by one, and then prodded Spot down the road towards Watchtower. Now feeling extremely apprehensive about the next few weeks, Shanna decided to make the most of the few hours she had left with her family for the foreseeable future.

"Well, come on Kaidan, if this is the last time I get to hear your stupid jokes for the next few weeks, you'd better get a move on and bore me silly until we get in to town." She swallowed past a suddenly large lump in her throat, and feeling her mother's hand on her knee, dredged up a soggy smile.

After dropping Kaidan off at Scholar's precinct (Kaidan even coped with being hugged by his sister in public), Shanna, Adlan and Janna proceded to the Scouts' Compound. On arrival, Shanna hugged both her parents, trying to convey in hugs what words seemed inadequate to express, then resolutely hefted the heavy pack and called Storm and Twister to heel. "Love you both," she said.

Her parents both smiled. "Love you too, Shan."

Shanna waved as she turned toward the main building. She had a feeling that it would be better to explain the presence of not one but two starcats, as early as possible.

Fortunately it was still early, and the corridors were mostly deserted, and to her relief, none of her fellow cadets were in evidence. Only a couple of Masters and a few older scout recruits were about, all giving Shanna curious glances for the two cats trailing at her heels. For their part, the two weanlings paced quietly, only glancing around intermittently as unfamiliar noises caused the violet and blue tipped ears to twitch.

Outside Master Peron's door, she deposited the heavy pack on the floor, leaning it up against the cool stone wall, and knocked briskly at the door, feeling somewhat apprehensive about her reception.

"Come in," came the command.

She entered the room and went to stand before Peron's desk, the two cats sitting neatly at her heels, one on either side.

"Excuse me sir, but I need to explain a couple of things." Peron eyed the two starcats seated by Shanna and raised his eyebrows quizzically as he regarded the three of them.

"I believe you probably do – explain both of them," he said, motioning to her to sit in the same chair as the day before. Somewhat encouraged, Shanna began to describe the events of the previous evening.

"And so you see, sir, that there's not much I can do about having two – and I know how it looks right now, but I will take good care of them, and I know it'll make things even more awkward with the others, but....." Master Peron folded his hands and leaned forward, elbows on his desk, looking at Shanna consideringly.

"I can see that you will indeed simply have to have two. I've not met anyone who has been able to say no to a starcat's choice, and having met Sabre myself I wouldn't argue with her either." He smiled. "It is an unusual situation, but not really a problem that cannot be overcome, and may one day be quite advantageous. I'll explain the situation to the other Masters, and you can explain it to your fellow classmates today as you begin their instruction in starcat care. Use it as an object lesson if you wish. I suspect that after tonight, any envy on their behalf will be a thing of the past. And I must say you do look a little tired today." His look of sympathy was heartfelt, if slightly tinged with humour. "I well remember my own first time with a starcat cub! Off you go now. You'll find your room on the ground floor on the second corridor. Second one on the left. Leave your pack there and go directly to the arena."

"Thank you, Sir."

Somewhat relieved, Shanna rose to her feet and went to locate her room. It was an unexpectedly large space although sparsely furnished with a bed, shelving for clothes and books, a desk, and a number of large mats. There was a small wash and toilet facility in one curtained off alcove, and a fireplace with two old, but comfortable looking saggy chairs sitting in front of it. There was a small supply of cut wood to one side. She deposited her pack on the bed while she looked around the room. Storm and Twister took the opportunity to poke their noses into every nook and cranny, and to bounce happily on the bed. Fortunately it was a large one. There was also a door next to a large window, leading outside to the main compound area and training arena. Checking quickly in the mirror, Shanna made sure her uniform was spotless and that she was as neat and tidy as possible, stuffing a few necessities into her thigh pockets, before she called the two cubs to her, opened the outside door, and walked towards the arena.

She could see her parents chatting animatedly with Josen, another starcat breeder, at the far end and gave them a little wave, but she could see four of her five fellow classmates assembled at the near end with their mentor Masters in attendance. The other two Masters were waiting nearby.

A door closed behind her, and Verren hurried out of the next door room, smoothing his dark hair. She turned around and smiled nervously at him; he smiled back, right up until he noticed the two starcats next to her. His smile faded, and he grunted in surprise, the expression on his face closing down quickly.

"Morning," Shanna said. There was a pause. "Looks like we're the last to arrive." Still, Verren said nothing, then nodded curtly and motioned towards the arena.

Great, thought Shanna, *Good start! And it's only going to get better when they all find out who's teaching them after the choosing*. She had hoped that Verren's friendliness would act as a buffer for her. It looked like she was wrong.

In the arena, the other four students were watching them approach. There was some fairly obvious nudging and whispering as Shanna and Verren approached the group.

"Fall in." Master Lonish commanded, and the students hastened to obey, Storm and Twister padding obediently, but very obviously, behind Shanna. "As you know, this morning you will be choosing starcat cubs. Some of you have some experience with adult cats, and some of you have limited experience. We know that all of you will be acceptable to the starcats, or you wouldn't be here. I will tell you right now, that starcat cubs are a completely different prospect to work with than the adults that most of you have previously encountered. You will have all the expert help you need, but you must be prepared to be flexible, patient, good humoured, and willing to lose a lot of sleep over the next few weeks. That is *one* of the reasons that you are now living here at Scout compound."

Master Lonish strolled to the end of the line where Shanna stood – as the shortest, she was always the end of the line. "Today begins a new lesson. You will all take turns as instructors over the next few months, in the subjects that you have expert knowledge in. Today after your choosing, Shanna will be instructing you in starcat care and training. Her family breeds starcats, and today some of you may choose, or be chosen by, cats that they have bred. She will be available for expert advice and assistance and will formally instruct you and your cats for two hours per day for the next six months. I suggest you listen to her. As you can see, she has already chosen her own cats."

Five pairs of eyes stared shocked at Shanna, who attempted to meet their gaze without flinching too much. She could feel hot colour rising in her cheeks, understanding belatedly exactly how Kaidan felt much of the time.

"She will also explain later today exactly why she has two starcats – I understand the tale is quite amusing." Master Lonish flicked a reassuring grin at Shanna. Master Peron must have used the time she had spent sorting her room out to fill the other Masters in, as he seemed quite unperturbed about the whole thing. The other students were a completely different matter, however. Verren still wore his closed look. Taya, one of the other two female students, was looking like a thunder cloud; Amma simply looked shocked, while Ragar and Zandany looked as though they'd both eaten something that disagreed with them. Shanna attempted a conciliatory smile. It came off a little wobbly.

"While any other student is teaching, you will award them the respect you would give to any Master. Do I make myself clear?" Master Lonish was suddenly stern.

"Yes sir." Most of the cadets at least tried to school their features into the appropriate expression, but Taya continued to glower as she mouthed the words.

"All right then, go up to the other end of the arena now, and we'll get the choosing underway. Shanna, you and your cubs can join the Masters over there." A number of the resident Masters were in attendance at one side of the arena, seated on benches.

At the other end of the arena, the three starcat breeders had their charges sitting neatly in front of them. Apart from the six that Janna and Adlan had brought with them, there were another four starcats in front of Josen, all handsome, well developed cubs. His cats showed reddish tones to their tidemarks, distinguishing them from the Hillview cats, which were always blue or purple toned.

Storm and Twister had behaved extraordinarily well all morning, however, on seeing their litter mates, their tidemarks had begun to flicker slightly in the well known warning tones of potential mischief. Shanna sat them, pulling a handful of treats out of one pocket and two feathers out of the other one. Knowing starcat cubs as she did, she was well aware that it was time for structured play right now, or there would be completely unstructured disaster instead. She blocked Storm's first attempt to gambol over to his littermates with a feather trailed across his nose as a distraction and began tickling the two cubs.

In the centre of the arena, the handlers were demonstrating the basic commands all weanling starcats learnt, as the students watched the cubs covetously. Shanna could tell that each of the students was itching to call one of the cubs their own. Each cub was run up and down in front of the students, with the well schooled masters sitting on the sidelines making informed comments about each cub, and then, to Shanna's slightly shocked ears, making bets about who would pair up with whom. Three of the Masters had adult starcats seated next to them and the others had well behaved youngsters. One was catless and watching the weanlings avidly. With a jolt, Shanna realised that all of the adult cats were well past the flush of youth, and into their old age. Two of them bore major scars, and the third walked with a limp marring his grace. It was not until then, that the danger that Scouts routinely operated in really struck her. She looked at Storm attempting to bat the feather she was teasing him with, and Twister who was trying to catch his in his mouth, and felt horrified that something might actually hurt them one day. Hard though the first six weeks of training had seemed, it was obviously nothing compared to what might be waiting in the real world of the qualified Scout.

With a start, Shanna brought her attention back to the centre of the arena, where the handlers had released the starcat cubs to play and were beckoning the five students in to interact with them. Already it was easy to see who had interacted with starcat cubs previously and who had little experience. Ragar was allowing two of the cubs to play fight with his hand, intermittently tickling their bellies and allowing them to mouth his fingers. On the other side of him, Amma was staggering as three of the little monsters tugged at her bootlaces. Verren was absolutely entranced, as one of Storm and Twister's litter mates wormed her way towards him on her belly, batting her eyelashes captivatingly. She rolled on her back in front of him, then without any warning at all leapt straight into his arms. He lifted his head, spitting dust as he found himself lying on his back under thirty kilos of starcat cub perched on his chest. Cirrus settled herself purring, and Janna grinned at him.

"I think you're chosen young man."

Zandany had fallen for a common starcat trick, and had ended up with his bootlaces tying his ankles together, a small starcat on the end of each pair. He also ended in the dust, while further over, two of Josen's cats were happily bouncing between Taya's legs as she attempted to help Verren up off the ground.

It was happy chaos, with the Masters exchanging money as pairings were made. Shanna tried not to eavesdrop too much, but was amused as she realised that Master Lonish appeared to have come off rather well. Ragar paired with another of the Hillview cats, the young male with the spectacularly marked legs, whom Janna had dubbed Sparks for his engaging nature. Taya was happily paired with Spinner, one of Josen's cubs, and Zandany was obviously completely besotted with Punch, his litter mate. Amma had spent the most time watching the cubs – when she wasn't staggering from shoelace tugs – and finally ended up sitting surrounded on the ground, while the tail patterned female, Spider, yet another of the Hillview cubs, sprawled relaxed in her lap.

The breeders handed out harnesses to the new starcat owners, and demonstrated how to fit them, then rounded up the other cubs and went to the other end of the arena to pack up.

The catless Master, whose name Shanna didn't know, strolled down to chat with Josen, Janna and Adlan.

"Cadets, fall in!" Master Peron's voice was loud and startling, and the student Scouts hastened to obey. Shanna bolted off the bench, calling Storm and Twister to heel and fell in with her cubs at the end of the line, or more correctly, where the end of the line would have been, had there been a line.

Utter chaos ruled. Students unaccustomed to starcat handling forgot to call their cubs to heel, and ended up in the line without their cats. Starcat cubs who although well trained to the basic commands by experts, recognised lack of expertise and ignored commands that sounded uncertain. Three of the cubs were wandering the arena exploring; Zandany was hotly pursuing Punch under the bench seats, and only Ragar and Shanna had managed to fall in properly at all. Verren, Amma and Taya had realised that their cats weren't with them and had left the line, and were all calling their cubs at once. Verren was yet again knocked to the ground by Cirrus, who obviously felt that the proper place to be was in his arms. That was definitely going to have to change before she reached her fully grown weight of around 100 kilos or more.

Peron beckoned to Shanna.

"You're on. Get control now, and then you have your class for the next two hours. We'll see you all at lunch." He nodded to the other Masters, and they all filed out of the arena, most trying to hide grins. The three older cats stayed behind, lazily observing the chaos.

Shanna looked round wildly, and decided that the chaos needed to be stopped immediately. She whistled piercingly in the ascending tones that her parents taught each cat to hear, as soon as they were handled, hoping fervently that Josen used the same system. The cubs immediately paused and sat, exactly where they were. Shanna gave thanks that Josen obviously did use the same system, and then changed the tone of her whistle, to the food call, which set all the cubs bounding towards her. Delving into her pocket she produced rewards for all the cubs, simultaneously beckoning their new owners towards her.

"Right, let's start with the basics." She cleared her throat and attempted to use the firm tone her parents always lectured in, rather than the slightly strangled squeak that had first popped out. She'd heard her parents' introductory lectures to prospective starcat owners so many times over her fifteen years that it was second nature. She began. "No matter what happens, you are always in charge of your starcat – always."

Five sets of eyes looked at her with various expressions.

"Never forget that they are there, never take their company and obedience for granted, and never, *ever*, offer a starcat violence. Starcat partnership is earned, not a right, and they will only obey those they respect, even when they are perfectly trained. You will need to be firm and patient and consistent."

Shanna spent the next fifteen minutes attempting to impart things she took for granted, realising only as she spoke, the amazing amount of knowledge her parents had passed on to her that she had simply absorbed as a routine part of her upbringing.

After that, she began revising the basic commands and hand signals that all the cubs knew, explaining what tone of voice was appropriate, and how to convey approval and reassurance to the newly paired cubs. Towards the end of the lesson, she saw some of the expressions of her fellow students begin to change, as Storm and Twister bore out her comments when she used them to demonstrate. At the same time, she attempted to privately evaluate her classmates' early responses to their cats.

She used the final fifteen minutes before lunch to explain why she had two cats. At the end, Amma queried her.

"And you managed a whole night with two of them? I'm exhausted already." She gave a rueful grin, and looked around at the other four students who were regarding Shanna with much greater respect, although Taya was still obviously unhappy with a much younger teacher, no matter how much that teacher knew.

Shanna laughed, and said, "Now you know why I have bags under my eyes. Just wait until tonight! Take one of these treat bags to put in your pockets and let's go to lunch. Now before we move off, remember to call your cats to heel, don't forget to make them sit and then drop, in the dining room, and do *not* feed them table scraps – no matter how much they beg. And they will…"

✳✳✳

At the Garsal ship, three of the large predators prowled outside the laser fence as the slaves commenced the preliminary excavations for the new hive. Inside the ship, Anjo huddled in his pen, shovelling down the slave slop and pulling the thin rags of his blanket around him. Each time the Garsal guard went past, he counted silently under his breath.

Chapter 6

KAIDAN nocked the arrow, raised his bow, drew back until the string touched his lip and then released, all in one smooth movement. The arrow thudded solidly into the very centre of the target, one hundred metres down the range. He attempted to control the grin that had seemed permanently attached to his face since commencing archery several weeks previously. Generally well known for the ability to calculate anything mathematic in his head, Kaidan had not until now excelled at any of the more physical activities on the general curriculum. It wasn't that he *couldn't* do things, but an overactive imagination sometimes meant that he was overcautious when boldness was important.

For some reason, applied mathematics became instinctive as soon as he had a bow in his hands. It didn't seem to matter whether there was wind or sun in his eyes, or even a moving target, it was almost like a metronome was ticking away inside his mind, directing the actions of his body. After only a few weeks' practice, his skills were growing at an amazing rate. Smoothly nocking a second arrow, he sighted again, this time aiming for one of the smaller targets below the one he'd just hit. The arrow flew true yet again, landing with a satisfying thump in the small straw target.

"Nice shooting Kaidan," Master Dinian called across the range, "OK, bows down now and pack away. Kaidan, come and see me after you've tidied up." Kaidan unstrung the bow and began to pack away the quiver and arrows, before walking over to where Master Dinian perched on a small bench at the side of the range.

"Well, young man, you've certainly seemed to be enjoying yourself these last few weeks." Kaidan was completely unable to contain the grin stretching itself across his face.

"Yes, Sir!"

"I'd like you to commence an extra session with the older students, three times a week in the morning, before your regular classes. While you're young, we want to explore your abilities to their fullest extent. Will that suit you? I know you live outside Watchtower, so you'll need to make sure you're able to get into town earlier. Go home, talk to your parents and let me know tomorrow."

"I'm sure I'll be fine, but I'll check and let you know, Sir." Kaidan could hardly wait to meet his father at the gate, and had to remind himself to keep to a steady pace as he walked through Watchtower that afternoon. Fortunately the spectre of Master Cerren hurtling through the air was enough to restrain his desire to jog. By the gate, the familiar tall figure of Adlan waited, accompanied today by Boots and Sabre, who had finally been relieved of all her cubs.

"Dad, Dad!" Kaidan yelled as he bounced the final strides to his waiting parent. "Guess what?"

His exciting news poured out of him as he patted the two starcats and they walked off down the road towards home.

"So, Dad, can I? I mean, is it all right if I head in an hour earlier to school? Do you and Mum mind the earlier rising to take me?"

His father chuckled as he pretended to take his time to consider.

"That'll be fine, but we'll be taking the extra time out of you in work, you realise!"

He smiled down at his excited son, pleased to see Kaidan enthusiastic about something other than mathematics and extremely bad jokes.

Within a few days, Kaidan had realised that all his inborn talent was going to take quite a bit of honing to match the older students. Some of the more gifted students were able to hit moving targets using short bows, while performing an astonishing set of gymnastic moves. Others were able to run, string their longbows on the run, and launch a series of shots at targets well above them, while dodging small sandbags thrown at them by other students.

He practiced at home on days off from school and during the lunchbreak, when he would shovel his food down as fast as possible and then make a bolt straight for the archery range. He found a kindred spirit in another of his classmates, Balto, who also excelled at archery. Hours and hours of practice later, after blisters had developed and then become hard callouses on their hands, the two of them began to attempt some of the gymnastic moves he so admired. Under the tutelage of the senior students he threw himself onto the soft mats placed at the sides for practice over and over, desperate to learn the balance skills necessary for success, his normally instinctive caution pushed to the back of his mind in his enthusiasm. As a result, he was beginning to regularly sport a variety of bruises.

One morning practice, when he finally managed a full sequence of run, roll, shoot, run, roll, shoot, hitting each target squarely, he was startled to hear a pair of hands clapping as he turned to walk back and put his practice gear away. At the side of the range, Shanna and her two starcats stood waiting for him. Hastily stowing his equipment, he jogged to where she waited, one hand riding easily on her hip, and Storm and Twister greeting him with soft purrs and head butts.

Obliging the two cats, now approximately half grown, he regarded his neatly uniformed sister with pleasure. He was particularly pleased that she had seen him succeed, rather than fail, in his attempt to master the complex move. He hugged her tightly, and then let go, slightly embarrassed that he had let her know he was actually missing her.

"I thought we'd get to see you sooner than this, Shanna, wasn't it going to be about every three weeks?"

"Yes, well, apparently that depends completely on whether the masters think it's a good idea or not, and that depends on not just how I'm going, but how all of us are doing."

Shanna grinned wryly at her brother and then motioned to Storm and Twister as they smooched around their ankles, ear tips glowing happily.

"Well, Storm and Twister are coming along nicely, and I'm looking forward to working with them on a few extra things shortly, but a few of the others are having a little more difficulty than they expected. And because I'm so much younger, it's taken them a while to begin to listen to me." She sighed. "The masters have made a certain standard of starcat behaviour a condition of our first home leave. None of us are allowed to go home until all the starcats are night trained, and reliable in basic training."

Kaidan raised his eyebrows at Shanna.

"So how much longer, do you reckon? And why are you here with me now?"

"There's just one cat to sort out now, so hopefully not too much longer – *if* I can get Taya to listen to me. At the moment if I say one thing, she immediately does another..."

Shanna sighed heavily again. "I have special permission to come this morning, so that you can let Mum and Dad know. I'm sure they've been expecting me way before now." His sister's face seemed tired, and her usual sparkle was dimmed.

"It's OK Shan, I'll let them know, and I'm sure that Taya'll learn to hear you. Her cat must be driving her mad by now!"

"That's the bit I don't get," Shanna shook her head, "Spinner's going to be such a great cat, if she ever starts to train him. And it's been over six weeks since she's had a full night's sleep, so you'd think she'd stop being stubborn and start to at least try and sort things out; but no, she just won't."

She sighed yet again, and looked at Storm, who was nudging her gently with his nose.

"Anyway, I've got to get back now, so give my love to Mum and Dad, and hugs to all the cats, and keep this one for yourself." She hugged her brother again much to his surprise, called Storm and Twister to heel, and plodded off towards the Scout compound.

"See you Shan, soon, definitely soon." Kaidan called, wishing he could help shake some sense into silly Taya. It surprised him that he was starting to actually appreciate his older sister. He stood looking after her for some minutes before he shook himself and went off to his next class, jogging to catch up with Balto, waiting for him at the edge of the archery field.

It was another two weeks before Kaidan saw Shanna again. He was again at morning archery practice when he saw her silhouette appear against the early morning sky. She was apparently practicing a complicated starcat drill, as the two cubs were not apparent, yet Kaidan could see her flashing hand signals. He approached Master Dinian for permission and then moved to the edge of the range, unstringing and then racking the longbow he'd been practicing with. He looked around to see where Shanna had got to just before exiting the range, when he heard a sudden "Woorrrooo" from behind him. Spinning about, he got a face full of starcat whiskers, some of which managed to go up his nose, and came face to face with Storm and Twister, who had obviously been sneaking up on him, guided by Shanna's hand signals. He could hear his sister's giggle from behind a small tree on the edge of the range, and stalked over to it.

"Typical sister!" Kaidan and Shanna had a long history of playing practical jokes on each other, and Kaidan could foresee a long list of starcat aided jokes that he was going to be the butt of. It was definitely time to be planning something special for Shanna's first home leave. He would need to think on it, and make sure it was detailed enough to mitigate the presence of two starcats. He was going to need to be much more creative than he would have previously. Maybe Balto could help. He often had interesting ideas.

"Hi Kaidan." Shanna was still giggling. "What do you think of the boys' ability to sneak, eh?" Kaidan made an appropriately impressed face, gesturing broadly in appreciation.

"Next time, tell them not to stick their whiskers up my nose, Shan. I really hate whiskers up my nose – Boots used to wake me up like that all the time. Yuck! Hey, how's icky Taya going?"

Shanna perched on one of the benches surrounding the arena.

"Well, I think she's finally desperate enough for some sleep, so I'm hoping she'll start doing some listening." She changed the subject abruptly. "Anyway, I just dropped by to let you know I'm hopeful, and to get you to ask Mum and Dad for some of their special whistles, as I'd like to teach the guys a few tricks with the silent whistles while the rest of us wait for Taya to get her act into gear."

"OK, no problem, can do. Have you got much time for a chat today?"

"Sorry Kai, have to get right back, but I'll catch you again soon. I hope." Shanna and the two smug starcats turned and headed off, waving. At least she seemed a little more cheerful this time around.

***

When she was out of sight, Shanna dropped her cheerful expression, and let out a long, drawn out, sigh. Sensing her depression, the two starcats moved closer, one on either side, pressing their bodies against her legs. Despite what she had told her brother, Taya was still ignoring her suggestions, and in addition, she was dreadfully homesick. The first couple of weeks in Scout Compound had been exciting, full of new experiences, and the challenges of training her cubs. Then the reality of Taya's attitude had begun to take the gloss off the newness. She wished she could go home and ask her parents' advice, or at least feel their arms giving her the hug she so desperately wanted. The other girl had become more than just a training problem – she was abrupt to Shanna to the point of rudeness, and dropped casually demeaning comments disguised as humour, on a regular basis.

Despite the good results the other four recruits had shown from following her advice, Taya persisted in attempting to train Spinner without assistance from Shanna, or more accurately, not train him.

Spinner was a sleek, intelligent starcat, with a distinct stubborn streak. He was desperately in need of proper handling if he was to be trained to the high standard that the Scout Corps expected of their starcats. Shanna felt she was fast running out of time for Taya to develop the appropriate relationship with her cub. She had tried suggesting, she had tried waiting, she had tried getting the other students to make suggestions, yet Taya remained recalcitrant. She never argued in class, or blatantly ignored Shanna, yet her attitude bordered constantly on the unacceptable. After a few sleepless nights, the other students had quickly come to realise that Shanna really did know what she was talking about, and had slowly begun to treat her as one of the group. Apart from Taya, Shanna finally felt that she was beginning to fit into her cadet group, and the starcat training, far from alienating her, had been the catalyst – except where Taya was concerned.

As she walked back to the Scout compound, Shanna decided that she had tried everything possible except outright commands to Taya. She had hesitated to order the others to do as she was suggesting, preferring them to respect her as an instructor in order to get them to comply. With everyone except Taya, it had worked.

With her heart sinking towards her boots, she walked through the arena entrance, deciding to gamble everything on one last plan. In the arena, she laid out a number of pieces of equipment and then sat down to wait for the others, readying herself for what she expected would be an unpleasant morning.

The other students filed in, and she gestured them towards the centre of the arena. Taya was still showing dark circles underneath her eyes, and yawned loudly and rudely, just before Shanna commenced her introduction.

"Right, we've covered all the basics and begun some of the more complex skills over the last few weeks. I thought today we'd try a little test to see how our youngsters are going. You can see I've arranged a kind of obstacle course around the arena – we're going to set our cubs at a stay, and then retreat to the other side of the arena and guide them through the obstacle course to us." She paused briefly as the others made exclamations of surprise, the expressions varied from eagerness to apprehension, and on Taya's part, pure panic.

"What do we do if they can't quite manage it?" Amma was apprehensive, but also excited. Her cub, Spider, was agile and bright, and thoroughly enjoyed challenges, but occasionally still became overexcited. The others nodded in agreement.

"Don't worry. I think you'll be surprised at how far they've all come. You all have your treats with you?" There were nods from four of the students. Taya didn't meet Shanna's eyes.

"All right, set your cubs at stay over here, and then we'll go to the other side of the arena."

Shanna hand signalled to Storm and Twister, who immediately dropped to their bellies in the stay pose. The others did likewise, joining Shanna at the far end of the arena. Spinner took several steps towards Taya, before she hurried back and propped him into the appropriate posture with her hands.

On the other side of the arena, Shanna gathered the students around her.

"I'll take Twister through first, so you can get an idea of the course, and the cubs will have a chance to see what you want them to do."

With a quick whistle, she gained Twister's attention. A hand signal sent him hurtling towards a pole set into the ground and a finger flick sent him up it. She had him pause at the top, then leap to a platform several metres away, before dropping him to his belly to crawl under a pegged down cloth tunnel. After the tunnel, hand signals again sent Twister to lope through a row of short upright poles, bending in and out between them. At the end, Shanna whistled and the starcat hurtled towards her, coming to a sliding halt in front of her and sitting expectantly. She rewarded him immediately with a small food treat and his favourite head scratch, before motioning to him to sit behind the group.

"Righto, who's next?" Shanna looked around expectantly, expecting Ragar to step forward, but Verren beat him to it, smiling happily.

"That looked like such fun! Cirrus will just love trying that!"

"All right then, let's see how she goes." Shanna stepped back as Verren whistled confidently to Cirrus. She hurtled off towards the pole, and was up it in a flash, and then over to the platform. She dropped happily to her belly, and then wriggled into the cloth tunnel, negotiating it successfully, and then bending easily between the poles. At Verren's whistle, she sped towards him then launched herself exuberantly into the air to land in his arms. At around fifty kilos, this proved to be a bit much for Verren who ended up winded on the ground. After a few moments he managed to inhale enough air to stagger to his feet, coughing and brushing dust from his uniform.

"Thought we'd managed to stop that – I think I'd better keep working on that as a priority. She's not a delicate little thing anymore..." His classmates were rolling around on the ground laughing uproariously at him, as he sent Cirrus to sit with Twister.

Ragar sent Sparks efficiently around the course, as Shanna had expected. He'd had quite a bit to do with starcats, as evidenced by the first day, and he and Sparks had quickly developed a workmanlike partnership. Amma and Spider performed admirably, the excitable starcat becoming slightly distracted inside the cloth tunnel, using her paws to fish around the edges as if some small prey might be lurking there, but then regaining her concentration when Amma whistled. Zandany had a little trouble convincing Punch to jump to the platform, but he performed the final portion of the course with such spectacular speed that he drew a spontaneous round of applause from the students.

Shanna held her breath, and then motioned Taya forward. Her trained assessment of Taya's Spinner suggested that the cat wouldn't make it up the pole, let alone through the rest of the course. Taya paused, and then whistled to gain Spinner's attention. She signalled the starcat to the pole. Spinner looked at the pole, and looked at Taya, then sauntered slowly towards the pole. There was insolence in every stride, and Taya signalled impatiently again. He deigned to break into a lope and finally arrived at the pole. She signalled the cat to commence the climb up the pole. The starcat cub looked directly at his owner as his tidemarks began the telltale flicker of mischief, then he bolted over to the group of finished cats and lay down. Angrily, Taya called his name and signalled to him to head back to the pole. He staggered lazily to his feet, wandered back to the pole and lay down yet again, this time with his back to Taya. She whistled in vain, while he stubbornly remained lying down. The other students began to look anywhere but at Taya, shifting uneasily as she began to angrily call Spinner to order. The big cub then decided to sit up and begin to wash his paws. At that point, Taya lost her last shred of self control and took several angry steps towards the cub, fists clenched, with the obvious intention of dragging him bodily towards the pole before Storm blocked her way.

"Stop right there, Taya!" Shanna signalled Storm to sit in front of the other girl. "What do you think you're doing?"

Taya ground her teeth and raised her voice. "I'm about to make that cat do as I wish him to!" Her face was flushed with anger.

"You are not going over to him while you're in that frame of mind." Shanna threw caution to the wind. "You have not listened to a thing I've said in the last two months! You have deliberately ignored my teaching. You have not attempted to train your starcat, and you are in grave danger of making him completely untrainable. And you know why? Because you simply won't take direction from someone younger than you! This is your last chance with your starcat Taya. Today you have to decide whether you will do what I tell you, or I will arrange to have Spinner sent back to Josen before you ruin him." Shanna had no idea whether she had the authority to arrange anything of the sort, but she thought that the other girl was probably as ignorant as she.

"You have no right to tell me what to do!" Taya was almost spitting in her anger. "You're just an upstart little twerp!"

Shanna took a deep breath.

"I may be an upstart twerp, but I'm an upstart twerp who knows starcats. You have a simple choice – you can either knuckle down and start learning, or you can give Spinner up. You have two minutes to decide." Taya attempted to move towards Spinner, but at Shanna's signal, Storm again herded her back.

"You've no right, no right at all!"

"On the contrary," a voice spoke from the stands of the arena, as Shanna spun around in astonishment. Master Lonish was seated there with Masters Peron and Yendy, Taya's mentor. "I told all of you that you must treat each other as you would a Master, when they are instructing. Taya, Master Yendy tells me that he has spoken to you at length about this very subject. Shanna is right. Now is the time to choose. You have no other options, today you not only choose whether you keep your starcat, but also whether you choose to remain in the Scout Corps. There is no argument to be mounted, your starcat has demonstrated everything we need to know about your current attitude. If you choose not to learn, then Spinner will be sent back to Josen, and you will have chosen to leave the Corps."

There was a sudden silence. The other students looked heartily embarrassed at being present for such a public ultimatum. On the other hand it was a sobering lesson of the cost that pride might have extracted from each of them.

Taya paused, her shoulders heaving with the intensity of her emotions. She stood rooted to the spot, glancing from Spinner to Shanna in an angry agony of indecision.

Master Lonish stood, and took a step towards Taya. "Choose!"

Taya bowed her head, There was no friendliness there, but only grim determination, and anger.

"I will do as she says, then, and stay."

"You have made a wise choice for today, but rest assured that we will be watching carefully to see you continue appropriately. A choice for expedience is no true choice unless you come to believe the principles you are taught." Master Lonish sat again. We will stay and watch, and see how you progress." He waved his hand at Shanna for her to continue. Shanna cleared her throat, nervous again suddenly about teaching in front of so many Masters.

"In that case Taya, we will start from the beginning with the basics."

***

At the Garsal ship, the slaves laboured day and night on the digging of the new hive. The laser fences kept the big predators away from the ship, but it was still hazardous and a number of slaves had perished after encountering some of the more dangerous vegetation inside the compound. Anjo laboured along with the others, obsessively watching the Garsal guards, calculating schedules and trying to memorise time counts and procedures.

The Garsal had begun to learn methods of combating the jungle's ferocious inhabitants, and had started to send ground exploration parties further and further from the ship. They now had an idea of the terrain within twenty kilometres of the ship. As the hive was slowly dug, the slaves began to expand the area inside the laser fence.

The sequestered females on the ship were becoming impatient, and the Overlord had received a carefully worded message from the Matriarch querying when they might move into more appropriate accommodation. The unloading and construction of the smaller exploratory vessels had begun at last, which meant that he had been able to reassure her that the appropriate resources to commence the interior of the hive were much closer to being sourced. It would only be a matter of weeks until the smaller Garsal ships took to the air, and this planet could then be properly surveyed.

Chapter 7

SIX weeks later, the precursors of the storm season were evident in the atmosphere. Ripped banners of high cloud streamed in the upper reaches of the sky, with fitful breezes blowing through the trees high on the plateau. Each year, the storm season started the same way; humid, warm weather preceded the telltale cloud marks in the sky, and then within a few weeks the first of the great cyclonic storms would spiral in from the ocean on the western plateau border, bringing destruction in their wake. The Frontier settlers had learned to understand the planet's changeable weather over the several hundred years of their enforced settlement and began their early season preparations as soon as the horsetail clouds appeared in the sky, stowing any loose equipment safely where the enormous winds were unable to pick it up and turn it into a lethal missile. Roofs were checked for possible leakage, and all were thoroughly examined for instability or previously unnoticed damage from prior storm impacts.

Out at Hillview, Adlan, Janna and Kaidan checked the dwelling and the outside structures thoroughly and made sure that there was sufficient food and emergency stores available should torrential rain make the roads impassable. They also made sure that their emergency signal flags and equipment were in good working order and easily accessible. Communications during the storm season could sometimes be limited in the aftermath of the enormous cyclones, but regular patrols to all the outlying areas would be undertaken by the local Militia, Scout Corps and civic groups that serviced the Frontier settlements in the event of any storm impact. Early disasters had necessitated the development of efficient assessment and recovery procedures.

At the Scout compound, Shanna and her starcat pupils were working on search and rescue skills, teaching their now three quarter grown starcats how to track, seek out trapped victims, and assist in rescue operations. Over the past six weeks, Taya had followed most of Shanna's instructions in starcat training to the letter, with only a few omissions. Spinner was now responding nicely to directions, although he still had a reasonable way to go before he would approach the skills demonstrated by the other cats. Spinner's improvement however, had not been mirrored by an improvement in Taya's private behaviour towards Shanna. Her in-class and public behaviour was impeccable, yet in private, Taya constantly dropped put-downs and sarcastic comments. She was Shanna's blot on an otherwise enjoyable horizon.

With her starcat classes going well, Shanna was able to throw herself fully into the lessons she and her fellow students were given by the various Masters: in unarmed combat, rope skills, tracking, botany, zoology and navigation, and as she had suspected, in basic medicine, from Verren. Verren had proven to be a capable and compassionate instructor, with a deep knowledge absorbed during his upbringing now suddenly useful in an unexpected context. There had been a number of practical sessions in the wilder areas outside the area of Watchtower's influence, and after the storm season the group would be venturing off the plateau into the true wilds of Frontier, an area known simply as "Below." They were also to start constructing their own survival gear. There were no hard and fast rules about what they were expected to carry, and the Scout Corps provided only the framework for their basic kit, expecting each individual to find out what worked best for them. Shanna had spent a fair amount of time in the outdoors around Hillview, and therefore she had a reasonable idea where she'd like to start in terms of her kit. Even so, she figured she'd do a bit of observing on the field trips with the various Masters, and then adapt her kit with what she considered were the best bits of everyone else's.

Shanna smiled as the growing starcats finished another retrieval drill, this time inside a classroom where she had concealed small objects. They had worked hard for the better part of an hour.

"OK, enough for now guys, time for a bit of starcat fun." She hitched one eyebrow at her fellow cadets. "All work and no play makes starcats really bored, and that is not conducive to having a peaceful day, or a night where we actually get to sleep! So, it's time for hide and seek!" Her classmates looked slightly puzzled. "Set your cats to stay, here, and then follow me outside."

They did as she requested, looking slightly puzzled, and then gathered outside in the hallway. Shanna beckoned to them and tiptoed to the far end of the corridor.

"Have you all been practicing with the whistles I gave you a few weeks ago?" They all nodded. "And have you brought them here with you?" Again everyone nodded. She lowered her voice to a whisper and beckoned her classmates closer. "Right, time for all of us to go and hide somewhere in the building, then when you're nicely hidden, blow your whistles in the signal you've been working on for 'come'. And then just wait. Hopefully we'll all be found without too much trouble. When they've located you, head back here, and then we'll finish up."

"Why are you whispering?" asked Amma, whispering as well. There were a few quizzical expressions on her fellow cadets' faces.

"Because you can never be sure exactly how much they understand, and I don't want them to have any idea what we're about to do." replied Shanna, still *sotto voce*.

"You're kidding aren't you?" Taya was openly sceptical. "You don't really expect us to believe that?" Her tone was scathing.

Shanna opened her mouth to reply, but was beaten to it by Ragar.

"I wouldn't be too sure if I were you." My uncle swears his cats understand much more than we give them credit for. And sometimes Sparks seems to know what I want before I ask him."

"Well, I don't think they do." Taya's voice was rising, and the others could read the warning signs that she was about to settle in for an argument.

"Look, this isn't the time or the place Taya," interjected Verren, "And the cats have been waiting for quite some time now. Shall we get started?" He raised an eyebrow at Shanna while Taya shut her mouth with a snap, levelling a glare at him. Shanna nodded.

"We'll talk about this later, Taya." She tried to keep her tone even. "Let's not push our luck with a long stay now. Let's go!"

"Woohoo!" Ragar bounded off up the corridor.

The others looked at each other, grinned, and then dispersed rapidly in different directions. Shanna hurried off up the steps to the second storey, where she had decided to conceal herself in an old storage area full of various bits of equipment. After ascending the steps two at a time, she jogged around the corner into the long corridor, through a number of interconnected rooms and then into the storeroom, where an old empty chest was concealed behind a pile of discarded practice rope. She lifted the lid of the chest and crawled inside, dropping the lid, leaving just a small gap between the lid and the chest. An old piece of leather served to stop a complete closure, giving her a small gap to look through. She then pulled her whistle out of her pocket and blew. In various locations within the building, the other five students were doing exactly the same thing.

Seven adolescent starcats pricked their ears one by one, and then bolted out of the door of the classroom where they had been waiting patiently. There was a fair bit of sliding as each cat attempted to be first out of the door to find their partners, along with a few growls and raised paws. Three immediately galloped off to the far end of the corridor at a run, and the other four hurtled straight up the steps to the second storey. The three cats heading to the end of the corridor skated on the smooth tiled flooring as they skidded to take the turn to the left towards a long series of classrooms. Unfortunately, Master Lonish and his aged starcat, Samson, happened to be turning the corner at the same time, but from the other direction. There was a loud growl, and the younger cats all attempted to move out of the way at the same time, which resulted in a spectacular pile up. The three of them rolled over in a kind of starcat snowball, which burst through a partially closed door and into an office where a number of older cadets were working together on storm season plans. The starcat snowball knocked their table flying, separating the stunned felines who then hurtled back through the door before thundering off to find their partners. The cadets picked themselves up off the floor and peered bemusedly out of the door at the departing tails. Their own starcats had heard the incoming commotion and prudently moved themselves out of the firing line.

At the top of the staircase, four starcats all headed in the same direction, straight down the major corridor. Master Peron took that moment to decide to head down to the refectory for an early lunch. He opened his office door, walked out into the corridor and ended up straight in the path of the oncoming rush. With that amazing starcat ability to react, Storm flew over the top of him in a prodigious leap, Twister managed to somehow slip between his legs, and Spider and Punch went to either side. The Master was spun around in the commotion, and managed to come to a halt facing four fast retreating tails, which then split off in three different directions.

Inside her chest, Shanna could hear the sound of rapidly approaching starcat paws – and she made a mental note to work on stealth at some point in the future. There was a pause in the footfalls as the two cast around in the adjoining rooms until they picked her scent up. There was a quiet "Merrow", and the soft but heavy padding of adolescent starcat paws and, through the crack, Shanna saw the door of the store room swing open.

There was a flurry of shoving and glowing starcat bodies as they both realised her scent ended at the chest at the same time, and then Twister began to nose at the lid. Shanna stifled a giggle, and watched the two cats puzzle out how to get to her. A clunk sounded, and the chest rocked, before a pair of paws inserted themselves underneath the lid of the chest and shoved. The lid lifted and two smug starcat faces peered at her, whiskers bristling and ear tips glowing happily. Shanna giggled again before she levered herself out of the chest to hug both of them.

Gathering the two purring starcats to walk at her heels, she exited the store-room to encounter Master Peron in the corridor, pacing up and down.

"What on earth are you doing?" He demanded. "I was just about knocked flying by four starcat tornados, and I hear that three others almost destroyed a storm preparation meeting downstairs!" Shanna had never seen Master Peron even slightly agitated before, and was a little startled to hear him sound so displeased. Her two starcats chose that moment to decide she needed a little protecting, and both inserted themselves between the master and herself. This did not actually help matters, judging by the frown that appeared on the Master's forehead. Shanna could feel one of Kaidan's whole body blushes beginning.

"I'm sorry sir, we were just practicing calling the cats with our silent whistles, and getting them to seek us out – they needed a little bit of fun after all the heavy training. I didn't realise they'd cause so much chaos in their enthusiasm, Sir." She attempted to be properly apologetic, realising that she had failed to think ahead about the consequences of letting seven young starcats loose inside a building, moving at potentially high speeds. She attempted to be conciliatory. "We'll do that exercise outside if we do it again, sir." Master Peron looked at Shanna from under lowered brows, and grunted.

"It wasn't a very wise choice of venue young lady, even if it was a useful exercise. Have a bit more care from now on when you plan your activities, please.

Another episode like today's and you'll have to be penalised a home visit. Remember, a Scout *always* considers the consequences of his or her actions, preferably in advance. " He motioned for her to continue back to the classroom, a frown still in place on his normally cheerful face. As Shanna, somewhat chastened, disappeared down the stairwell, Master Peron let out a breath and finally gave way to the laughter he had been at pains to suppress while attempting to lecture his young charge.

At the classroom, the rest of the class was waiting, most with slightly downcast expressions on their faces. Given Master Peron's reactions, it was relatively easy to figure out the cause. Shanna sighed.

"Sorry guys, I didn't think about the chaos we could cause. Master Peron caught me upstairs, and has suggested we don't do this exercise inside again..."

Verren laughed as the others sniggered.

"I bet he did!"

"But we were all found by our cats!" Ragar patted Sparks' upturned head, and grinned unrepentantly and then the others joined in, eagerly describing how fast and clever their cats had been. Even Taya had a smile on her face for once.

***

At the Garsal ship area, three small, almost completed aircraft were dragged out from under the cover of the colony ship. A few more days would see their commissioning and the beginning of the Garsal expansion across the planet. There had been a heavy toll on the slaves. The Overlord was becoming more and more impatient at the restrictions the large and fearsome fauna had placed upon the usual fast expansion of a colony. The hive caverns had reached a crucial stage. With the major excavation work almost complete, it was imperative that the colony expand in order to find the requisite resources for the interior work. Until then, there would be no breeding, and no population expansion.

Anjo had almost completed memorising the guard movements. He had confided in no-one. It was never possible to completely trust another slave, as it was well known that there were informers among them – cunning people who traded information with the Garsal for more rations, or simply to prevent a loved one on a home planet from being lifted offworld into the many slave ships. He kept to himself, he watched, he counted and he waited. He had absolutely no idea what he would do if he found himself able to escape, and he could only wonder how long he would evade the predators that continuously prowled the fenced perimeters of the area. Hope for survival on an unknown world was small, but there was no hope at all as a Garsal slave.

Chapter 8

KAIDAN and Shanna walked home together, alone on the road for the first time in their lives. Shanna's two starcats, now at three quarters grown, and well on the way towards being fully trained, were considered safe enough for the relatively short trip from Watchtower to Hillview. It was rare for any of the larger beasts to venture this close in to settled areas, yet the odd incident still occurred, often enough for caution to be necessary. Despite enjoying their parents' company, Shanna and Kaidan were revelling in the chance to be independent of adult supervision. Realistically, Janna and Adlan had recognised that in a few short months, Shanna at least, would be venturing far beyond the safer areas of the plateau, into almost completely untamed areas of Frontier. Such places were considerably more dangerous than the walk between Hillview and Watchtower, and it had seemed silly to insist that she still required parental supervision for the walk from town to home.

At last the Masters had decided that the new class of students had earned a home leave, and thus Shanna was heading home for the first time in nearly fourteen weeks. Taya's slow progress still rankled, and Shanna couldn't help feeling that she could have handled things differently. She shook herself internally and deliberately changed the direction of her thoughts.

"So, pretty good with a bow now little brother?" Shanna had been watching at the archery range again that morning as her brother had demonstrated his phenomenal accuracy on moving targets.

"I'm improving a bit, but I've still got a way to go until I'm as good as the others!" Shanna raised her eyebrows incredulously – she couldn't believe how accurate he was.

"Really Shan! Look, I know I can be good at this, but I've got a lot of work to do yet. You've never seen the older students." Kaidan knew he had talent, but was under no illusions about how far he still had to go after working with those older students in the morning sessions. The first few had been quite humbling. "Mind you, it's great fun, and I'm really enjoying the challenge. Although sometimes it's pretty painful after practice sessions – I don't think I've ever been this constantly sore and stiff!" Shanna nodded with an understanding grin. As the weeks had passed, she had toughened up considerably, but she was still sporting the odd bruise from the practice sessions on the mats.

"We can take turns whinging all the way home if you like, and then see who can get the most sympathy from Mum and Dad – what do you reckon?"

Kaidan grinned and poked Shanna's arm.

"You're even growing muscles – I think they're bigger than mine..." He flexed his arm muscles to show them off, and she punched him back.

"And you've grown. I'm sure I was quite a bit taller than you last time we walked home." She measured his height with her hand. "It's been a while I suppose."

The two continued on their way, with Twister walking in front, glowing ears twitching at the sounds from the vegetation by the side of the road, and Storm behind, nose sniffing the air, and violet eyes watchful. As the sun began to lower in the afternoon sky, the two cats became slightly restless.

More horsetail clouds had begun to streak themselves across the sky, coloured dramatically by the lowering sun, and Kaidan looked at the sky critically.

"What do you think about the weather, Shan?"

Shanna looked at the two starcats, both obviously more restless than when they had started out. She, too, was concerned at the gradual changes. "I'd say we're in for a storm in the next day or two, but whether it's just a precursor, or a true cyclone, I'm not sure. Let's get a move on, home's not far."

She hummed reassuringly at her starcat friends, and they quieted slightly as they picked up their pace.

The welcome lights of home appeared at the top of the hill as the sun continued to sink towards the horizon, the clouds becoming more and more dramatically coloured. Storm and Twister pricked their ears, as the spicy odour of other cats wafted on the slowly gathering breeze. Shanna hefted her backpack on her shoulders.

"I hope Mum and Dad like the bread I've brought home today, I actually made this lot. I never knew Scout training would involve cooking. We had to make this in an outside oven that we built ourselves."

Kaidan looked skeptically at her. "You mean I've got to eat something that *you* cooked?" He grimaced, having previously experienced some of Shanna's cooking.

"You think I'm bad? You should try Verren's food then… I've actually improved, but he thinks his cooking's great already!" Shanna shuddered in remembrance.

They turned into the driveway, and walked up towards the house where it sat snugly back into the top of the hill. Apart from taking advantage of the natural caverns for starcat breeding, the recessed house was sited for maximum safety from the violently devastating storms that had taken such a toll in the early days of Frontier life.

"Shanna!" Janna almost flew through the door, with Adlan following at a more sedate pace. As she was enveloped in a hug from her parents, Shanna felt like she never wanted to let them go. There were greeting hums and purrs emanating from the fenced starcat caverns as the sun sank below the horizon in a flurry of vivid colours.

The four of them finally entered the dwelling, Storm and Twister following the babble of happy voices. The welcome smell of a spicy simmering dinner was wafting from the stove. Waiting in a row were Boots, Moshi and Sabre. Storm and Twister, following Shanna inside, were brought up short by the three adult starcats, who were sitting in a line in front of the fire, observing the two youngsters coolly. Although Storm and Twister had spent one night inside with Shanna, Hillview was not really their home, as they had then spent the ensuing formative weeks in Scout Compound.

Sabre, as oldest and longest in possession of the house interior, sat slightly in front of the two males. Despite being Sabre's cubs, it was immediately obvious to the family that there were no concessions about to be made in the pecking order, and it was up to the two cubs to work out their status. The Hillview family paused in its dinner preparations in order to watch the showdown, which was likely to be highly entertaining.

Sabre grunted softly, as Storm and Twister approached. Boots yawned insolently, showing all his teeth and an enormous pink tongue as his lips peeled back. Moshi snorted softly through his nose, and regarded one large paw, extending his claws one by one as if inspecting them.

Twister, always the more impetuous of the two, disregarded the warning signs, twitched his ears, and decided unwisely on the direct approach. He strolled directly up to the older cats to take a comfortable position in front of the fire. Shanna shook her head, and decided not to watch. Storm, the more cautious of the two cubs had obviously decided that discretion was the better part of valour, and dropped immediately to his belly.

With a flick of her tail, Sabre signalled Boots and Moshi, and they pounced heavily on Twister, who ended up on his back with Boots sitting his whole weight across the young starcat's belly. He kicked out with his hind legs, and was rewarded with a heavy whack across the nose from one of Moshi's large paws. Fortunately, he had decided to sheath his claws. Another wriggle, and another whack, and Twister shook his head, violet eyes slightly unfocussed. With another final whack across the nose, Moshi and Boots allowed Twister to struggle to his feet. Sabre growled slightly, and he dropped immediately to his belly and rolled over again. Storm wisely crawled all the way to the older cats on his belly, and then dropped his head to his paws and "Woorooed" gently.

The older cats allowed him to crawl over to the edge of the warmth from the fireplace and resume an upright posture. Twister attempted a conciliatory little hum, and was ignored for the next few moments, while the three older cats casually turned their backs on him. Fortunately, this time he was wise enough to remain lying where he was. Finally Sabre looked over her shoulder, grunted, and Twister was allowed to crawl over to the far side of the fire.

"Should I look, now?" Shanna had decided that in the interests of starcat dignity, and her current relationship with the cubs, it was more appropriate for her to avoid watching the unfolding drama.

"Yep, it's all sorted now." Janna giggled slightly. "I don't think Twister will make those same mistakes again. Some cubs just think they're all grown up before they're ready. Storm is certainly a much wiser youngster at this stage."

"Hmmm, yes, I'd figured that one." Shanna sat herself down, and then bolted back to her pack to drag out the bread she'd so laboriously baked herself. "Hey mum! Here's my own bread!"

"Are you really sure it's safe, Shan?" Kaidan was still not keen on eating something his sister had baked.

"Be brave young man, I'm ... mostly sure that it's pretty safe, I mean they wouldn't let our potential new Scouts poison their families and each other would they?" Adlan enjoyed poking fun at his children. "Someone go and get my hatchet, and we'll cut it!"

The rest of the evening passed in a happy blur, as the family had their first meal together in months. Shanna felt that she hadn't talked so much for ages. Finally the meal was over and they retired to the fire, starcats happily lounging around them as they chatted for several more hours before retiring to bed. Shanna spent the evening basking in the warmth of the easy, familiar companionship of her family.

The following morning dawned red and cloudy, the wind whipping its way through the trees surrounding the hill, with clouds now ripped to tatters in the sky above. Adlan roused early and called the others out of bed after one look outside at the glowering dawn. The starcats were all restless, vocalising worriedly to each other.

"Storm's brewing guys, and it looks like a big one." After a quick breakfast, the family began storm preparations in earnest. Although Shanna was due back at the Scout compound the following morning, she knew that there would be no problems with being late if a cyclone was the cause. The enormous storms would sometimes linger for up to twenty-four hours, with dangerous winds and heavy torrential rain lashing the surrounds. All travel under such conditions was out of the question, and Shanna knew that the standard procedure in this situation was to assist her family prior to the arrival of the storm, and then return to the Scout compound when it was safe.

Food stores and emergency water supplies were checked, and extra firewood stored in the breeding caverns. First aid supplies were set out, and the signal flags arrayed in the living room area for quick set up should the need arise. The two horgals, Spot and Fluffy, were penned in a corner of the breeding cavern and all the adolescent cats and breeding females were also safely secured inside. The marmal hutches were carried across into the cavern and sited towards the back, the inhabitants a little anxious in the presence of so many starcats. Its access directly from the dwelling made it an ideal safe house for the starcat pride. Shanna and Adlan then installed the metal storm shutters at the outside access to prevent the expected wind and rain from intruding into the cavern.

Kaidan and Janna dropped the storm shutters down over the narrow windows at the front of the house, and then secured them tightly, slotting drop bars across them. A check of the outside fences and gates followed, making sure they were shut and that there was no debris lying around anywhere, ready to turn into a dangerous missile.

"I think we're just about done, Dad," Kaidan called. The sky had darkened dramatically as the family finalised their preparations and took shelter inside with the house starcats. The wind had begun a steady rise as the trees started to sway under the pressure of the gusts and early rain. Great fat drops were splashing into the dust as Adlan closed the door and Janna lit several covered candle lanterns. Warm light bathed the interior of the house, and the five starcats with their tidemarks glowing gently, settled themselves, tails curled carefully over their feet, near the fire's embers. A gust from the rising winds blew ash out of the fireplace, and Kaidan quickly damped the embers with a bucket of sand, and then poured another bucket of water slowly over the top, completely extinguishing the fire.

"Right, lunch before we settle in I think." Janna headed for kitchen bench, and began cutting slices of bread, spreading them with soft cheese and chutney. Kaidan took the big kettle off the back of the stove, where the fire was safely contained in its metal box, and poured hot tea into four mugs. Outside, the noise of the wind had begun to rise rapidly, the gusts now howling loudly. There was the sound of heavy rain pouring in torrents. Adlan went to the side door and peered into the breeding cavern. A multitude of steadily glowing tidemarks greeted him with a chorus of muted humming, along with a couple of snorts from Spot and Fluffy. The shutters were holding against the wind, although the sound of the rising gusts was distinctly louder in the cavern.

"Well, let's settle in family." Adlan sat comfortably on one of the soft couches by the fire, patting the seat next to him for Janna to snuggle in beside him. Kaidan and Shanna settled on the floor, Storm and Twister snuggling into Shanna, and Boots taking up his usual head-on-lap position with Kaidan. The wind howled louder and the family prepared for a long wait.

***

Several hundred kilometres away, the Garsal pilots settled into the seats of the three finally completed flyers. They finalised their checks and lifted slowly into the air, hovering briefly as the pilots tested their controls. Below, the waiting slaves trudged back into the colony ship. The three ships lifted above the trees, and turned north, intending to overfly the life signs picked up in the initial descent.

Chapter 9

THE wind howled around Hillview, gusts roared, and tumbling debris was sent end over end to impact on the fencing around the property. Inside the house, the sound of the wind was somewhat muted, but the wilder gusts still caused the outside wall to vibrate and bow. Pounding rain was audible, and intermittently the sound of trees uprooting and branches snapping could be heard above the wind. Occasionally, the front wall of the house would shake under the impact of flying wreckage, and the sounds of the impacts rose as the wind speeds escalated.

The huge storm system spiralled in from the ocean, trailing devastation in its path. Native vegetation, long immured to the intermittent storms, bent and swayed to the wild winds, curving almost horizontal before springing upright again. Introduced species fared variably; those that had hybridised with native species, flexed and bowed with the winds, while those that still retained most of their original genetic makeup tended to break, rather than bend, as the gusts pushed them beyond their ability to recover.

Wind and rain caused damage across a wide area of the southern portion of the plateau, outlying structures in more exposed areas suffering the most. The human population tended to take shelter in larger centres when enough warning occurred prior to the storm's arrival, but most communities had local storm shelters for anyone who was unsure of the safety of their home. The Hillview family could have taken shelter inside Watchtower's walls, however their snug dwelling, built by Janna's great great grandparents as one of the first satellite dwellings near Watchtower, had survived many major storms, and they routinely chose to sit the storms out at home, emerging afterwards to assess any damage and begin the cleanup.

***

The three Garsal aircraft assumed an arrowhead formation and headed north towards the plateau that was their assigned target. Weather scanners showed an intense storm spiralling in from the ocean. The pilots had flown in many atmospheres, and many weather conditions. They noted the disturbance impassively, but continued on their way north, implacably heading towards the plateau and entering the outer area of the storm system. Previous experience had shown that native inhabitants of colony planets could be a valuable source of new slaves, or potentially, food. The attrition of slaves in the early weeks of settlement on this new planet had left the Garsal short of manpower for their projects and it was imperative that they replenish their stocks so that the hive could be completed on schedule.

***

The wind reached its peak ferocity, howling in continual gusts around the Hillview dwelling. Adlan went through the side door into the breeding cavern to check on the two horgals and the starcats. Spot and Fluffy stirred restlessly, tossing their heads and snorting as he moved towards them. Kaidan appeared at the door.

"Need a hand Dad?"

"Yes, Kaidan, could you go and get some feed for the horgals? Hopefully they'll settle down if they're eating."

Kaidan grabbed a bale of fodder, and heaved it over to the two horgals, who harrumphed as their frightened attention was diverted by the smell of the hay. The storm shutters vibrated under the force of the enormous winds, clanging and banging as yet another gust howled outside.

The starcats were grouped together by the far wall of the cavern, snuggled in baskets and curled on cushions, their great violet eyes regarding Adlan and Kaidan levelly. Blue and violet tidemarks in various shades and patterns, glowed dimly through the gloom as the two walked over to check on them. They were greeted with purrs and hums from the cats, and several of the females stood as they approached. Kaidan and Adlan moved from cat to cat, gently running their hands over the smooth fur of their large heads.

They replenished the water bowls and checked the one litter of cubs that were still with their mother, before assessing the security of the storm shutter at the front of the cavern. There were a number of large dents in the metal doors, but they were holding securely, vibrating as the intermittent gusts moaned around them. Some water had been driven in around the edges by the force of the winds, but the elevated position meant that most of it simply pooled at the front of the cavern before trickling slowly outside.

Inside the house, Janna had checked the starcats' water bowls, begun a large pot of soup on the back of the stove in the kitchen, and was now checking the front of the house. Shanna assisted by beginning on the opposite side of the house front. The rear of the dwelling was built completely inside the hilltop, which meant that the only really vulnerable area was the front of the house. There were a number of water leaks around the windows and door frame, but all were relatively small and easily contained with rags. The storm shutters were holding well, and there appeared to be no structural damage. By then the storm had been raging for six hours, and the light visible through the cracks around the edges of the shutters had begun to fade into darkness. The cyclonic winds showed no sign of abating, and indeed seemed to strengthen as they all finished their safety checks.

Storm and Twister had watched Shanna through her series of checks, and then followed her as she went down to her bedroom to collect a book on botany to study as the storm blew on outside. It was always hard to sit doing nothing through a cyclone, and Shanna had learnt from long experience that trying to sleep was almost impossible. Apart from the howling of the winds, the constant impacts on the storm shutters kept jerking her awake from the edge of sleep. It was easier to give up on resting and attempt to study something useful instead. When Adlan and Kaidan returned from the breeding cavern, the family again gathered around the cold fireplace, each with a lantern to allow them to pursue their chosen pastimes.

Outside, rain pounded and slashed horizontally through the air as the wind clawed at the vegetation and grasped at manmade structures.

*****

The wedge of Garsal ships punched through the outer edges of the storm and into the more turbulent spirals of violent winds. They bumped and bounced as the pilots fought the controls of the small craft. Undeterred they continued to arrow north towards the plateau, wind intensity growing rapidly as they penetrated further into the storm. It wasn't long, however, before the pilots began to feel the first stirrings of alarm as their aircraft began to buck and toss more violently as the crosswinds of the storm rose in velocity. The orders of their superiors were never to be disobeyed, though – while disobedience cost status, a successful mission might mean a recommendation from the Overlord to the Matriarch. A number of recommendations, and their chances of becoming breeding males became much greater. They drove onward, deeper and deeper into the storm, until all that existed was the fight against the storm and the drive to obey. Suddenly, the storm spun the right hand wingman into a rocketing spin. He spiralled out of control to the east, swallowed up by the violently swirling clouds. The scanners showed the blip of the aircraft for a few more moments, before it vanished off the screen.

The other two Garsal continued forcing their craft through the typhoon, the small craft flipping and yawing continuously. The navigation instruments became useless as the titanic force of the storm took total control.

*****

The eye of the storm passed over Hillview in the middle of the night, and the sudden silence as the wind dropped was almost deafening. Janna stood up and walked to the front door with Adlan, unsure how long the eye would last. It wasn't often that the eye would pass directly overhead, and the time until the other side of the eye wall impacted and the winds began again was extremely variable. They quickly unbarred the front door, and both cautiously walked out into the suddenly calm night. Shanna and Kaidan followed, with the house cats spreading out in a fan behind them. The four quickly began an inspection of the outside of all the storm shutters under the flickering light of the candle lanterns, checking for weaknesses and potential leaks or hinge damage. There was marked denting of all the shutters, the winds had flung many missiles at the heavy metal, some obviously sharp, judging by the shapes of the impact marks. Around the front of the house, they could see piles of debris and the vague shapes of damaged fencing in the gloom.

Janna eyed the sky, looking for the edge of the eye wall approaching. Directly above them a few stars were speckling the clear patch of sky, but visible from the northwest was an approaching band of cloud.

"Are you all finished?" Janna's urgency jerked the heads of the other three quickly around and they left off their examination of the outside of the building, looking at the eye wall that Janna was indicating with her hand.

"OK, back inside again. " Adlan whistled the three Hillview starcats, and Shanna called her two into the house. They re-barred the house door, and with large bowls of soup in hand, retired to the dead fireplace. Outside, the wind began to rise again, blowing from the opposite direction, and the vegetation began to toss in the gathering breeze.

***

The remaining two Garsal pilots continued to fight their craft through the violently tossing clouds, lashing rain, and crashing winds. They were completely disoriented, their navigation systems a mess of blinking lights and chaotic readouts. The lead pilot lost control and dropped into a sharp dive before being tossed sideways, plummeting downwards through the clouds, to spear into the vegetation below. The final craft continued to bounce and flip through the sky, finally hurtling through a wall of cloud into a sudden peace. He had one glimpse of a towering cliff face before he smashed straight into the rock wall, the craft crumpling on impact, one wing breaking off and spinning skywards. He began a slow tumbling fall into the vegetation far below.

***

Hours later, the winds finally started to abate, the larger gusts came less and less frequently, and the impacts on the outside of the storm shutters began to diminish. As the winds dropped, the rain seemed to increase with the sound of trickling, then pouring, and finally an audible thundering. On the northern side of the Hillview property was a creek, which was normally a minor tributary on the river that ended in the Thunderfall cascade outside Watchtower, an enormously spectacular waterfall that plummeted in a series of falls down the southern face of the plateau.

Donning wet weather gear, Adlan unbarred the storm shutters to do an initial assessment of the damage from the storm, and the rate of rise of the creek.

"Wait here you lot, no need for all of us to end up dripping wet, I'll go and do a quick check of the outside of the house and see how much the creek's come up. I'll take Moshi with me to make sure we've no extra visitors." Occasionally after storms of this magnitude, some of Frontier's less friendly wildlife would be swept into more settled areas, posing a hazard to the residents. He whistled Moshi, who obediently came over to the door, an expression of distaste on his large feline face, ears twitching as he watched the rain falling outside the door. He looked pointedly at the unlit fire, before striding out into the pouring rain with Adlan.

"I'll light the fire, now that the wind's dropped," said Janna, with a grin, "Can you two start bringing a pile of firewood into the house from the cavern?"

"OK," Shanna said. "Do you want us to do another check on the horgals and cats while we're there?"

Her mother nodded, as she began to stack kindling and shavings in the cold hearth, before bringing a coal from the stove to light the fire. "Kaidan, go and grab a few towels as well, your father and Moshi will be drenched by the time they get back, and I'd rather not have water tracked everywhere."

Shanna went into the breeding cavern, Twister and Storm in tow, to check on the horgals, and then the other starcats. Now that the storm had begun to abate, the horgals had settled happily down and were both dozing, legs folded underneath them, peacefully chewing their cud. The starcats were still grouped together, but the young cubs were beginning to play under the watchful eyes of their mother. There was plenty of water available for them, so Shanna contented herself with briefly reorganising a few piles of bedding before moving to the corner where the firewood was stacked. She hefted a good armful and then walked back to the side door of the house, pushing the door open with one foot. She could hear the rain continuing outside, and the roar of the creek steadily rising. Depositing the armload of wood in the basket by the fire, she decided to go back to the firewood stack in the cavern for a second load, just as Kaidan deposited the towels by the front door.

"Creek's getting louder." Kaidan and Shanna knew that the creek was well down the hill from the house, but if it rose too far it would cut the road to Watchtower, effectively isolating them and their neighbours from the town. Isolation was not too much of a problem, as most of the out of town properties were reasonably self-sufficient, and prior to the onset of storm season, all would have ensured that they had adequate supplies in hand.

The siblings stacked the basket full as the lighted fire began to lend a cosy glow to the room, and the rain continued to pour down outside. It was late afternoon, and Kaidan pulled the soup pot over the heat on the stove as Shanna readied a jug of hot tea. There was a sudden sound of stamping feet and door rattling. As the door opened, Moshi shook himself hard, spraying water all over Janna and the towels she was attempting to hand to her husband as he removed his waterproofs. Muddy water flew in all directions as the huge starcat flicked each paw before strolling through the front door. Adlan growled and Moshi looked somewhat abashed, and then carefully moved over to allow him inside. Janna shook her head, tossed two of the damp and slightly muddy towels to Adlan, and then motioned to her children to assist her to dry Moshi before he managed to spread the wet any further.

"Well, we've lost a few fences," Adlan's voice was somewhat muffled as he towelled his hair, "And about half a dozen of the fruit trees are down. One of the outbuildings is underneath the big frondan tree down in the bottom paddock." He paused to remove his very muddy boots before he moved further inside in his socks.

"The cavern storm shutters have suffered quite a bit, and I think we'll have to get a smith out to sort out a few of the more major dents, and the left hand hinges look a bit iffy. Apart from that, we've come out of things fairly well – as far as I can see in this weather. We'll know more tomorrow when the rain settles a bit. The creek's come up far enough to cut the road, so it'll probably be a day or two until you two can head back into town."

"Figured that," Kaidan was philosophical, as Shanna nodded. "At least we can give you a hand cleaning up over the next day or two." Moshi was purring loudly, as the towels soaked up the water marring his sleek coat, and he wriggled luxuriously as Shanna and Kaidan finished drying him.

"One other thing," Adlan paused, his face serious, "I'm pretty certain there's a staureg around – I found what looked like its prints down by the fallen trees, but they were washing away pretty fast. Moshi certainly thought something was around while we were down there, but he settled as soon as we turned back towards the house. It may just be passing through, but no one is to go out alone or without at least two cats." Staureg were one of the larger sized predators on Frontier. They were stealthy trackers and bloodthirsty killers, prone to taking livestock or attacking unwary humans. They were not often seen in the more populous areas, but anything was possible in the aftermath of a big storm. Neither Kaidan nor Shanna had actually seen a staureg, but both were familiar with the tracks, as they were standard learning for all children in the early stages of schooling.

"All right then, let's get settled, have something to eat, and then get a bit of sleep before tomorrow. I know none of us slept much last night, and tomorrow will be a big one, rain or no rain." Janna gave a final swipe to Moshi as he wandered over to the fire and settled himself with a large grunt.

The following morning, the rain had abated to a drizzle. After feeding the cats and horgals, still safely inside the breeding cavern, the family prepared to go outside, donning rain gear, heavy boots, and assembling hand tools.

"Shanna, you're with me, bring Storm, Twister and Sabre. Janna and Kaidan will be taking Boots, Moshi and Shanti; and Kaidan, I'd like you to make sure you have a bow at hand wherever you're working today. Make sure your cats are on guard, and if anyone sees any sign of the staureg make sure you signal. If we locate it at any point, the other pair is to get all the trained cats from the house and then we'll stalk to kill." Adlan was serious. An adult staureg this close to the house and the town was a major danger, not only to them, but to anyone it came in contact with. Thanks to a multitude of starcats, they were the best placed in their area to remove the beast without having to claim help from Watchtower – help that would probably be more useful somewhere else, in the aftermath of the storm.

Adlan and Shanna called their cats, and then headed for the downed frondan tree leaning on the damaged outbuilding in the bottom paddock. Janna and Kaidan stumped off through the mud and down the hill towards the damaged fences on the southern portion of the property.

"Guard." Shanna directed the three starcats with a quick hand signal, and they spaced themselves out in a triangle around herself and her father. Donning heavy leather gloves, father and daughter set about removing some of the superficial foliage of the massive tree leaning on the roof of the outbuilding. Five hundred metres away, Janna and Kaidan set their cats around them and began to straighten fence posts and clear debris away, stacking it in piles for easy collection later.

The four of them laboured away, slowly clearing the debris of the storm. Around them, the six starcats stood, alert for any hint of danger, ears pricked, noses twitching, and tidemarks glowing gently.

"Hold it steady Kaidan, I've almost got it." Janna poised the sledgehammer, before bringing it down hard on the top of the post, driving it back into the ground and raising it for another blow. Kaidan steadied the post again, carefully making sure his hands were well below where Janna's sledgehammer would strike. Again she brought the large hammer thudding down on the post, seating it deeply to make sure it wouldn't budge in the sodden earth.

From the north, there was a sudden call of alarm. "Staureg! Get the cats!" It was Adlan.

Janna and Kaidan sent Boots, Shanti and Moshi bounding towards him, and then bolted for the house. Kaidan stringing his bow as he ran, making sure that he still had the heavy bladed arrows close at hand in the hip quiver. As Kaidan stood on guard by the front door, Janna hurried to the side door, calling the young cats and two older females by name to assist. "Pancho, Shandy, Jay, Bouncer, Flip, Argon, Flash!" She left only the mother with the young cubs and two very old males in the cavern, "Heel." Janna knew there was no point sending the cats out aimlessly until she could see what was happening.

Down in the bottom paddock, Sabre, Twister and Storm had flicked their ears, suddenly alert, deep, rumbling growls coming simultaneously from the three throats as they scented the smell of staureg. The trees outside the paddock provided a good cover for any hidden predator, and the staureg had been lurking quietly, watching the small human and cat figures, until a change of wind brought its scent to the guarding cats. The scaly reptilian beast lumbered towards Shanna and Adlan, who immediately swung behind the outbuilding. Sabre, Twister and Storm had dropped into crouches, the two younger starcats flanking their mother, as she prepared to spring. She growled deep in her throat and began slinking forward towards the thundering carnivore, its dorsal ridges swaying from side to side. At a hiss, Storm slunk right and Twister left while Adlan called his warning to Janna and Kaidan.

Peering cautiously around the edge of the outbuilding, Shanna directed Storm and Twister to flank the beast further, trying to angle them into its blind spot, as Sabre began to increase her speed towards the staureg. It hesitated slightly as the wind changed yet again, bringing the starcat smell to its nostrils. Sabre, however, did not balk. She sprang, claws outstretched, as Storm and Twister leapt from either side at the same time, teeth and claws and fury launched in all their ferocity at the assailant. From the top of the hill, Boots, Moshi and Shanti arrived, forms blurring with the speed of their run. As quick as thought, Shanna flicked a signal at the three cats, who separated and attacked the whirling staureg from different points. Storm was flung from the staureg, landing heavily and rolling, before launching himself back into the fray. Sabre hung grimly onto the staureg's neck, claws embedded in the creature's tough, scaly skin, as the five other starcats darted and tore at it.

As Janna and Kaidan reached the bottom paddock, they were stunned by the size of the beast – it was easily the biggest Janna had ever seen – and was snarling and whirling ferociously inside the ring of cats, Sabre now attempting to straddle its back. Janna sent the other seven cats in to circle and dart, trying to hamstring the beast, as the first five again launched themselves at the staureg's body. They clung grimly to its hide, sinking their claws deeply into the scaly skin. It lurched and swung its heavy spiked tail from side to side, while starcats dodged and flowed under and over it. As Sabre tried for the beast's throat, it swung violently, desperately trying to avoid the cats around its back legs, and she was flung heavily to the ground, tumbling through the other cats and opening up an escape route. The staureg dipped its head and charged, Sabre directly in its path.

Kaidan raised his bow, pulling one of the heavy bladed arrows from his quiver, sighting carefully in an attempt to access a clear shot at the beast and avoid the starcats.

"No Kaidan," Adlan shouted from behind the outbuilding. "You'll hit one of the cats!" Ignoring his father, Kaidan continued to sight carefully at the charging beast, his stomach churning at the thought of any of the family's cats killed or severely injured by the rampaging beast. Twister jumped again at the staureg, and clung with his claws, sinking his teeth into the looser skin at the creature's neck.

Shanna drew her breath in sharply.

The beast became more and more desperate, lashing out frantically with clawed feet and spiked tail as it thundered towards the gap in the ringing starcats, while Sabre staggered to her feet, desperately limping around to face the reptile.

Kaidan loosed his arrow as the beast swung its head, attempting to avoid a lunge from Boots. The arrow flew straight and with a thud, sank deeply into the staureg's eye. It spasmed and the starcats struck. Two hamstrung the roaring beast, collapsing it still thrashing onto the ground, and exposing its softer underbelly and throat. Its life was quickly ended under the combined attacks of the rest of the starcats.

Shanna called the cats off as Kaidan lowered his bow, exhausted and trembling, and then ran and hugged her brother. Janna joined Adlan, slipping her hand into his, soberly regarding the huge predator that the cats and Kaidan had brought down. The rain had stopped, its departure completely unnoticed during the struggle.

Chapter 10

THE following morning the water level in the creek slowly began to lower. As Shanna gently examined the various abrasions, contusions and cuts sustained by the starcats, she looked over at her family. Storm lay upside down on the floor of the house, his head comfortably pillowed in her lap as Shanna gently rubbed an aromatic cream into his foreleg.

"I should probably get back to Watchtower as soon as the creek is far enough down."

Her mother looked up from a particularly nasty scrape on Sabre's leg.

"Are you sure you really need to go so soon?"

"Well, I was initially meant to be back there yesterday, and storm recovery is part of a Scout's job, even for those of us who aren't fully trained. I need to report in as soon as possible. Sorry Mum." Shanna understood her mother's reluctance to see her depart; part of her still wanted to be home with her family, and she had no idea how soon she would be able to come home again after such a storm. The time with her family had been so short.

"I'll send you messages with Kaidan, and you should be able to drop in on me if you're in town, now that we're past the first few months with the cubs. I can check on the neighbours on my way, and then send any assistance needed if they've got more problems than they can handle." Not all the neighbours had properties with such natural advantages as the Hillview caverns or were fortunate enough to have actually built their dwellings inside a hill.

"Well, given yesterday's drama, I think we'll send two of the older cats in with you, and you can send them home when you reach Watchtower's gates," Adlan said seriously. It was unlikely they'd see another staureg – this was the first staureg he'd seen in the flesh for over twelve years, but there were any number of dangers that could have been brought in by the storm.

"OK, who will I take? I guess Sabre will be staying here to recover?" she said, knowing her parents' starcats would be perfectly able to make their own way home from Watchtower. Fully trained starcats were perfectly capable of homing skills, and would probably not even be seen by any other travellers on the road. By themselves, they chose to move almost invisibly, and as fast as possible. She was also aware that her own two, although growing rapidly, were not yet fully trained, and a large predator would be too much for them to handle alone.

Janna considered for a moment, gently stroking the fresh-smelling cream into the long graze on the starcat's leg, while Sabre purred appreciatively.

"Take Moshi and Jay. Moshi's completely reliable, and young Jay can do with the experience Moshi can impart on a solo trip. Send word back to us if any of the neighbours require help, and we'll go and assist them. Thanks to you two we're well under control here, and if we can help sort the neighbours out, it's a few less jobs for Watchtower."

"I'll be gone as soon as the creek's down then. I'll go and set my pack up after I've finished here." Shanna finished with Storm and began to apply the salve to Shanti's abraded shoulder where she'd caught a glancing blow from the staureg's spiked tail. The wound looked clean, but she wanted to be sure.

"Can I take some tins of this salve with me Mum?"

"Take anything you need love, we've plenty, and we've a couple of other things your father and I thought might be useful as well." Janna straightened up and looked meaningfully over at her husband. "Actually, I think we've got something for both of you tucked away; we'd thought to wait, but I think you've earned it." Adlan nodded, and smiled at his son.

"That was a most impressive piece of bow work yesterday young man!" Kaidan felt yet another fiery blush begin to rise up his neck. Shanna laughed.

"Now you've made him all embarrassed again." The blush rose higher, and Kaidan felt as if his ears were about to catch fire. While he was relieved with the way it had turned out, there'd been one awful moment just after he'd loosed the arrow when he'd doubted his aim completely. A vision of the enraged staureg, egged on by his irritating arrow and trampling his family, flashed across his mind and he resolved to practice even harder at the morning sessions.

"OK, I think we're done here." Adlan placed the tin of antiseptic salve on a shelf, and then he and Janna hurried down the hallway to their bedroom, reappearing shortly with a number of objects. In front of Shanna, they placed a new, beautifully crafted knife, complete with a number of attachments and a neat leather case which would enable her to attach it to her uniform belt. It had with it a small box, which when opened, revealed a small blue stone on a chain, glowing gently and illuminating the living area. Both Shanna and Kaidan gasped, and Shanna looked quickly up at her mother with a query in her eyes. Occasionally the settlers would find glow stones like the one on the chain, generally in river beds, but they were very rare, and treasured by those who owned them, handing them down from generation to generation. Shanna had seen the stone only a few times, and knew that it had been in her mother's family for many years, carefully passed on from mother to daughter.

"You're old enough now, and it will be useful to you when you're Scouting. Here, it just sits in its box. I really don't use it as I should." Janna undid the chain and fastened the stone around her daughter's neck. "This is to show you how proud we are of the difficulties you've already faced in the last few months, and how proud we are that you've stuck to the training program." Her eyes looked suspiciously shiny as she stepped back to admire the glowing stone. Shanna's hands trembled slightly as she tucked the sturdy chain inside her shirt.

"Thanks Mum, Dad. I'll take good care of it."

Their father stepped forward to Kaidan, taking a beautifully crafted bow from behind his back and placing it gently in his son's hands.

"Master Dinian spoke to us a few weeks after you began your archery training. He believes you have a rare talent. More than that, he believes that you have demonstrated exceptional dedication to practice, and a work ethic second to none. We're very proud of how hard you've worked, and we had thought to reward you at the end of the year with this bow. Yesterday's events showed us that you deserve it now. The starcats would have eventually taken the staureg down, but not without more injuries. Your shot made it possible for the cats to finish the beast quickly."

Kaidan took the bow, and ran his hands down its sleek length, feeling the silky smoothness of the seasoned wood, hefting it gently and appreciating its perfect weight – it had obviously been handcrafted to his exact measurements (with a little growing built in, judging by the length).

"It's beautiful. I'm not sure what to say, but, thank you. And I'll keep practicing really, really hard, every single day!" Kaidan was barely able to get the words out, as his hands slid up and down the length of the bow's satin finish.

"Well, you can start by helping your sister pack, and then you can feed the horgals." Obviously being the owner of a spectacular bow didn't excuse you from your normal jobs. Shanna and Kaidan went into Shanna's room to pack her gear, both carrying their gifts. Shanna banished her brother briefly in order to change into her Scout uniform, and then began to lay out her gear on the bed, assembling a variety of things she felt might be useful.

"Can you go and get a tin of salve, a tin of pain cream, some woundseal, and two of the small cat kits, please?" Shanna carefully placed her waterproof liner inside her pack, and then began packing a variety of spare underwear and socks, warm wear and waterproof wear, and a few various necessities that had occurred to her in the course of their introductory training. In the outer pockets, she carefully stowed her firemaking gear in its waterproof pouch along with her navigation equipment. When Kaidan returned, she placed the cat kits in easily reached pockets, and the various small tins inside her pack. Mindful of the weight, she hefted the pack to make sure that she hadn't overloaded herself for the journey back to Watchtower.

"Thanks Kai. I'm relying on you to keep Mum and Dad up to date on how I'm going and I'll try and fill you in as often as possible. Hopefully I'll be home on the three week schedule soon. I expect it depends on how things go over the next little while." She slung the pack on her back, adjusting the straps to sit comfortably and making sure the water bottle was easily at hand. Her new knife was already sitting neatly in its pouch on her belt, and she could feel the glow-stone on its chain under her shirt.

It seemed that she was forever saying farewell to her family without knowing exactly when she'd be back, and she realised that home, although always "home", was slowly becoming less and less the place she actually lived. It was a strange feeling, and the knowledge that her relationship with her brother was also beginning to change felt a little weird. He had always been a great friend, but still her little brother. Now, she was beginning to regard him with more respect as she watched his dedication and persistence in both his studies and his new found archery skills. It was a little odd, but she was enjoying the new independence, and the adjusted relationships. The one cloud on her horizon continued to be Taya, and she had no idea at all what to do about the ongoing issues. It appeared that she would simply have to wait and hope things worked themselves out. She let out yet another of the sighs that were always provoked by thoughts of Taya. At least she was now listening to Shanna as far as the basic nuts and bolts of starcat training went. Spinner was now progressing reasonably steadily, but there was still something not quite right in the relationship between the older girl and her starcat. Shanna resolved to give the matter some more thought and then firmly pushed Taya out of her mind as an unnecessary distraction.

Farewelling her parents and brother, Shanna whistled Storm, Twister, Moshi and Jay, and then strode through the gate and out onto the main road. The creek had subsided to a crossable level, and Shanna and the cats forded it easily where it crossed the road. They walked briskly down the road towards the nearest neighbour on the way to Watchtower.

An hour later, Shanna turned in towards the gates of Watchtower. The guard on duty beckoned her over.

"All Scouts and cadets are to report directly to Headquarters, you're needed for Storm recovery duties."

"Shall do. I've checked in at all the homesteads between here and Hillview, and apart from some superficial damage they're all fine. None of them have requested any assistance." Shanna paused, "There was a staureg driven in on the storm at Hillview, but we dealt with that yesterday."

"Really? What happened?"

Shanna shook her head. "Dad and Kaidan will be here in a day or two. You can get all the gory details from them. I'd better get to Scout headquarters."

She ran her hands affectionately over Moshi and Jay and slotted a message for her parents into Moshi's collar and turned them for home. Moshi paused a moment, and glanced briefly at Storm and Twister, humming firmly, and then vanished into the undergrowth, the younger cat echoing his every move. Shanna watched fondly as the two cats vanished into the vegetation, their glowing tidemarks fading from view into the masking green. She waved at the guards and walked briskly through the gates.

Arriving at the Scout's Headquarters Shanna was directed to the arena, and after dumping her pack near the seating, she joined her fellow cadets with a murmured greeting. Over the next two hours, the arena filled while the cadets exchanged storm stories. Master Lonish took the centre after a quick assessing head count, signalling for silence.

"There are a number of damaged settlements at the edge of the plateau, which require assistance. We will be sending you out in teams, for specific tasks. Please assemble in Patrols and classes."

The assembled Scouts and cadets fell in as requested, starcats obediently sitting at the heels of their owners, awaiting orders. Shanna's cadet class assembled at the very back of the group of ten Scout Patrols. At any one time, the various sections could be posted anywhere on the plateau, or surrounding wilderness. The Frontier Scouts were responsible for ongoing exploration and also for patrolling the settled areas that bounded on wilderness areas. Each of the three major settlements usually had around one hundred and fifty active Scouts servicing both the town and surrounding areas. During major storms the Scouts would take shelter in the nearest settlements or safe areas. They were well trained to observe the weather signs, and interpret them, in order to avoid being caught in unsafe situations while travelling. Part of Shanna's training would include the safe areas built in the charted areas of the wild, and how to survive storms when away from manmade shelter.

Each Patrol consisted of ten Scouts, including the Patrol First and Second. The entire Scout Corps was led by a council of nine Masters, each specialising in one aspect of Scout training, with an elected First Master, who was then part of the Settlement Council. Most of the Masters were older men and women with many years of experience in their craft, but age was not necessarily a prerequisite, as wisdom and skill were the major criterion for selection. A number of the Masters would at any one time be actively patrolling. Cadets were not generally assigned to a patrol until their final six months of training. The command structure was deliberately simple, as Scouts were chosen from the pick of the applying students, and rigorously trained in decision making and survival. They were all expected to be able to deal independently with the unusual and complicated situations that would regularly challenge them in their duties.

Master Lonish deftly divided the patrols into two larger groups and one smaller one, which included the first years. The second and third year cadets were spread amongst the five patrols that would be assisting with the post cyclone flooding. They moved off to be further briefed by Master Vandos. He dispatched the second large group, consisting of four patrols, to Master Kenwell to assist with search and rescue activities. Shanna's class glanced quickly around; apart from Patrol Ten, they were the only Scouts left in the centre of the arena. Master Lonish noted their restlessness, and quelled it with the briefest of glances.

"Patrol Ten, you and the first year class will be investigating a disturbance reported by the residents of Thunderfall Cascade during the storm. Apparently there was some unusual noise during the brief period when the eye passed over. We need to exclude the possibility that anything dangerous has moved into the area while fleeing from the storm. The residents have been informed to stay indoors until you have cleared the area." Master Lonish paused, and then looked directly at the cadet class, briefly wrinkling his brow at them.

"Cadet Class, you will be under the control of Patrol First Spiron. Each of you will be paired with a Scout for the duration of the operation. You will give your Scout the full respect due a Master. You will obey any command they give you, without hesitation, and to your fullest ability. This is a learning opportunity, and you are fortunate to have it. Do not waste it." He turned his sternest gaze on them one by one, and then handed them over to Patrol First Spiron before heading back over to confer with Masters Kenwell and Vandos.

The Patrol First strode to the front of the assembled cadets. His eyes lingered briefly on Shanna and a small frown crossed his face as he looked at her, shorter and younger than the others, and with one too many starcats, and then he paused briefly before calling his Patrol out one by one and assigning them to the younger cadets.

"Nelson, pair with Verren. Karri, you're with Zandany, and Arad, you'll be with Taya. Challon, take Amma; Sandar, you can have Ragar. Allad, you'll take on Shanna." Shanna wondered how he knew all of their names, as she'd never seen the tall Patrol First before. The allocated Scouts fell in beside their named cadets. Shanna found herself standing next to an enormous man in his mid thirties, whose starcat was unusually patterned with deep green glowing tide-marks. The large female starcat blinked lazily at Storm and Twister, her eyes glowing deep violet, and each swayed slightly backwards under the intensity of her cool gaze.

"All right, listen up now. I want you packed for travel and assembled back here in thirty minutes. Perri, Barron and Kalli, go and collect extra travel rations from the quartermaster. You others, make sure the cadets are packed up properly and not overloaded. Dismissed." Spiron turned away, heading for the barracks, trailed by his cat, a large blue marked male with spiralling tidemarks on his tail.

Allad motioned Shanna towards the barracks, his moustache twitching, and his starcat eyeing her two, who walked slightly closer to her heels than was normal. As she collected her pack from the side of the arena, Allad eyed her up and down consideringly.

"You're a bit on the young side, if you don't mind me mentioning it." Allad regarded Shanna from under his rather bushy blond eyebrows. "And you have two starcats." With a sigh, Shanna realised that she was going to have to explain why she had the two cats again and again, in her career as a Scout. Obviously Patrol Ten hadn't been in Watchtower recently or they would have known how young she was, and the reasons for it. As they walked to the barracks, Shanna began to supply Allad with both answers. At least she was learning to be brief about it.

In her room, Allad directed Shanna to empty her pack and change into her field uniform. The field uniform was tougher than the regulation cadet issue, and designed to blend into the foliage of Frontier. When she emerged from the bathing area dressed in her field clothes, he was examining the contents of her pack which he had spread out all over her bed.

"Good idea," he grunted as he examined the cat kits and first aid equipment she had brought from home. "Now, you'll want to pack a little differently and you'll need to add just a couple more things which I'll get from my room shortly." He demonstrated how to fold and roll her belongings so that they fitted more easily, and then rearranged a few things to make sure that they were more easily accessible. When he collected his own pack from his room, he handed Shanna two small containers. One contained a strange smelling paste, much like that of the pungo tree, and the other, a multitude of compartments, all with different coloured pigments in them.

"For masking your odour, and concealing yourself as required." Shanna investigated the contents of the containers and then deposited them in her pack. The two then hoisted their packs and proceeded together towards the arena. Shanna's cats continued to regard Allad's warily as she paced queenlike next to him, completely ignoring them.

"My cat's name is Satin, and if yours take a step out of line, she will mention it to them – so be prepared for it. I'm hoping you're not the kind of cadet who coddles their cats." His mobile eyebrows raised and lowered, and then he went on. "I expect you to jump when I say jump, and keep your cats under control at all times. I also expect you to ask when you don't know – I can't abide cadets who sit quiet in ignorance and remain that way. If you have any problems, tell me, don't let them fester. Don't touch anything you don't know about and make sure you look where you're walking."

"Yes Allad." Shanna took a deep breath and tried to remember exactly what he'd said, frantically filing it away in her head. Despite the youth of her starcats, she had confidence in her training of them, and looked forward to continuing their education on this trek. She suspected that she would probably have more difficulties on this trip than her two cats would, which was somewhat daunting if she thought too long on it.

Back at the arena, she and Allad lined up just behind Verren and Nelson, the cadets exchanging glances of supressed excitement. *Our first operational activity!* was the shared thought. With the six cadets, the full patrol now numbered sixteen, larger than any of the other patrols in the arena. When they had all assembled, Spiron left Masters Lonish, Kenwell and Vandon and fronted the patrol. With a quick gesture, he indicated that Perri, Barron and Kalli should provide the cadets with travel rations and show them how to stow them in their packs, and then the Patrol moved in neat order to the Southern Gate of Watchtower. They had an hour's walk on the main road before the patrol would turn onto the smaller road leading to Thunderfall Cascade. They would be several hours on that road. With a slight shiver, Shanna realised that they would be travelling at night for part of that time. She had never travelled at night before; despite three hundred years of settlement on Frontier, the early loss of life, inclement weather and extraordinary wildlife had restricted human expansion, and it had taken all of those three hundred years to establish just three major settlements. Frontier yet remained an untamed planet, and while travel at day was generally safe with sensible precautions taken, travel at night was only for the most skilled or alternatively, the particularly foolish.

While on the main road, the patrol maintained only a loose formation, the trained Scouts using the time to assess the new cadets and their starcats. At the beginning of the trek, Spiron had each cadet send their cat out and around the patrol to a series of hand signals. Shanna held her breath during each manoeuvre, knowing that they were, to a large extent, assessing her training of the other cadets. It was a somewhat unnerving experience. Fortunately all except Taya's Spinner, performed well, and even Spinner was only somewhat hesitant as Taya had to reinforce her hand signals with voice commands. Spiron had watched, eyebrows raised, as Shanna sent her two out simultaneously, but in separate directions, so that they flanked the patrol on opposite sides. He said nothing. Allad only grunted as the two youngsters moved out smoothly and returned promptly on Shanna's signals. When she returned to the big scout's side, he turned his head to her as they walked.

"So you've been training cats with your parents for a while?" his mobile eyebrows lifted enquiringly.

Shanna nodded.

"For as long as I can remember. We've three housecats, and a few other breeding pairs, and Cirrus, Spider and Sparks come from the same litter as Storm and Twister. Master Cerren's Socks is from an earlier litter this year."

Allad continued to ask her questions about the family business as they walked. He'd heard of her parents' starcat stud, but he hadn't met them, although he had met quite a number of their cats during his time in Watchtower.

As they turned off towards Thunderfall Cascades, the sun sank below the horizon and dusk deepened rapidly. Spiron directed the patrol to form into a more defensive array. He sent the Scouts who were unencumbered by cadets out on point and rear guard with their starcats, and then had the cadets and other scouts send their starcats out to flank them. As the night darkened, the triple moons shed dim light over the road, allowing the patrol to move steadily towards the hamlet at the very edge of the plateau. There was little talking, the cadets were too unsure of themselves to initiate conversation, and the Scouts were clearly discouraging it. Shanna wondered if it was yet another way of assessing the new cadets. Four hours later, after uneventful travel, the dim lights of the village came into view.

By then, the cadets were tired, and Shanna's legs were beginning to complain, however the regulars of the Scout patrol appeared to be as fresh as when they had set out, swinging along easily. Shanna felt that the young starcats had performed well, and relaxed somewhat as they walked down the main street, knowing that none of the cats had disgraced themselves, and by extension, her training. Spiron directed them straight to the village hall, where they were to be accommodated for the time it took for them to assess the unusual sounds and ensure that no large predators were loose in the area. The village appeared essentially intact, although all around them were indications of the effects of the storm. As yet, there were few signs that the villagers had begun the post storm cleanup. Shanna really appreciated for the first time, the relative freedom that a large number of starcats had provided her family.

"Two hour watches, on the standard roster. Cadets, enjoy your last night of full sleep, tomorrow you'll join your Scout on their rostered watch." Spiron's eyes twinkled slightly, softening his rather stern features.

They settled into the hall, bedding down in neat rows with their starcats. Shanna ended up at the end of a row near the door, adjacent to Amma.

"How are your feet Shan?" asked Amma, wincing slightly as she removed her boots, wriggling her toes.

"Well, no blisters, but they're feeling the distance a bit," Shanna replied. She rubbed the soles of her feet as she changed into clean socks for the night, carefully rolling up the dirty pair and stowing them in her pack. "But I'm tired! What time do you think it is?"

"Midnight perhaps?" hazarded the other girl. She turned to Taya on her other side. "What do you reckon Tay?"

"No idea really, I'm going to sleep." She rolled over, back turned to Amma and Shanna. Amma rolled her eyes slightly, and Shanna smiled slightly, realising that the trip might have some positive effects on her relationships with at least some of the other cadets, or at least she hoped so.

"Night Amma."

"Goodnight Shan." Amma lay down with a slight thud, one hand rubbing wearily over Spider's head.

Shanna slid wearily into her bedding, feeling the hard boards of the hall floor underneath her. Twister lay down at her right hand side, angling his head for a caress, as Storm leaned heavily on her legs on the left, purring as he wrapped his tail neatly around his length. Rather than distracting her, the two large weights were comforting and warm, and she fell asleep almost immediately.

***

The wreckage of the Garsal aircraft lay crumpled at the base of the plateau. Occasionally one of the instruments emitted a dim green or red light that played a slowly dying glow over the shiny carapace of the dead pilot. At the Garsal ship, the communications technician attempted yet again to contact the three craft that had disappeared off his scanner shortly after they penetrated the storm. The dying remnants of the cyclone had just moved over the encampment, and although the winds had abated somewhat, they were still strong enough to howl loudly through the barrier fence. Drenching rain was pouring down outside, pooling in the entrances to the newly dug hive, and seeping in trickles down into the lower levels.

Inside the slave pens, Anjo listened to the noises penetrating the hull of the ship. He now knew enough about the Garsal's movements to effect an escape from the ship, but he despaired of learning enough to survive by himself outside the safety fence, and had no means of removing the tracking bands from his ankles. The repeated attacks by the large scaly beasts had left him all too aware of the difficulties he would face should he venture into the wilderness alone, and the onset of the massive storm had brought home the realities of life on an uninhabited planet. Living amongst the Garsal was a constant struggle to simply survive, but life amongst the wildlife of this planet would be even more difficult, if not impossible. Completely dispirited, Anjo counted the seconds between the guard patrols by habit, sinking deeper and deeper into despair.

Chapter 11

SHANNA was poked awake by a booted foot, which nudged her in the ribs. She struggled out of the haze of sleep, completely disoriented, barely aware of her surroundings and trying to wriggle out of her bedding. She was hampered by the weight of two heavy starcats on her lower body. Twister grunted slightly in protest.

"Come on lazy! Up and at it, no time to lie around!" Allad's voice seemed awfully loud as she struggled out from under Storm and Twister, until she realised that his mouth was only centimetres from her ear. As she staggered to her feet, hair sticking every which way out of its braids, she could see that it was still dark. All around her were recumbent sleeping bodies with only Sandar on watch, sitting on the front steps of the village hall. Storm and Twister raised sleepy heads and regarded her briefly before returning to the untidy mess of sleeping gear behind her. Behind them, Satin stood unnoticed. She watched the two young cats sleepily place their heads back on to Shanna's bedding, and then gave each a swift whack across the hindquarters that rocketed them out of the bedding and facing her in a flash. She looked disdainfully at them, deliberately turned her back and strolled off to sit behind Allad, who made no attempt to hide a grin.

He spoke quietly. "Come on Shanna, we're on breakfast. I hope you can cook. There are a few supplies here from the Cascades people, so after you've stowed your bedding, you can cook breakfast for us all." He regarded her from under his eyebrows again. "Send your cats out with Satin. She'll show them where they can hunt at the edge of the village and keep them out of trouble. While we're on active duty, the cats forage for themselves."

Shanna knuckled sleep from her eyes, collected Storm and Twister with a gesture, and then sent them to sit with Satin. They sat very correctly and bolt upright, to one side of her, violet eyes fixed firmly on her face, as Allad gave her the hunt command. Shanna told the two youngsters to follow Satin, watching curiously as they walked meekly behind the older cat.

"She's certainly got them under her paws." Shanna said amused. Satin was very much like Sabre in temperament, and the two normally exuberant young-sters were certainly learning to watch their step with her.

Allad chuckled quietly. "You've done a very good job with the two of them so far, but there's nothing quite like a trip with Satin to show a couple of youngsters the real ropes of a Scout's life. Come on over to the hearth, and I'll relieve Sandar while you cook breakfast." Shanna followed Allad over to the hearth, hastily replaiting her braids and tidying her clothing as she did. At the hearth, Allad indicated containers of porridge, dried fruit, and cooking pots, and left her to get on with the job. Cooking wasn't her strong suit, and Shanna had a brief flashback to some of Kaidan's more pithy comments, but she wasn't too bad at porridge. Her finished product was somewhat stodgy, but at least it was hot, filling, and reasonably tasty. Over the next hour as the rest of the scouts roused, each sent their starcat out to hunt before filing over to the hearth to collect a bowl of porridge and a hot drink. As Shanna moved to tidy up the dirty bowls and pots, Allad stopped her with a quick movement.

"If you cook, you don't clean. Leave that for Ragar and Sandar, and come and make sure your pack is sorted and ready to go; we may be sleeping rough tonight."

After everything was sorted out to Spiron's satisfaction, he divided the patrol into two sections. Nelson and Verren, Sandar and Ragar, and Allad and Shanna were placed in one group with Spiron and Perri. Barron, the patrol second, took the other cadet and Scout pairs as well as Kalli, making two groups of eight.

"Barron, you and your team are to patrol the village, door knocking each dwelling before moving your search out into the surrounding paddocks and cleared areas. My team will patrol the edge of the forest as far as the edge of the plateau, and then we'll meet back here in no longer than four days. Barron, if you find anything, send a message to me with one of the cats." Spiron hefted his pack. "Make sure that anything unusual is reported immediately." He directed Allad and Shanna to the front of his group to take point, and indicated that Perri would take the rear as they moved off towards the edge of the village. Behind them, Barron was dividing his group into pairs to begin door knocking. Shanna looked enquiringly at Allad, wondering what she was actually meant to be doing at the front of their small group.

"Send your cats to either side of Satin, Shanna, and direct them to be on watch." Allad gave two swift gestures to Satin, and she accelerated to the very front of the group as Shanna directed Twister to the right and Storm to the left. Storm's blue ear tips glowed gently as they twitched at the various sounds around him.

"Now, watch and learn from Satin. She'll direct your youngsters as she sees fit until it's our turn to flank." Shanna was completely intrigued with Allad's cat. The starcat was in the prime of her life, unusually coloured and impeccably trained, and had her two young charges completely under control. A slight flick of her head and Twister, deep purple tidemarks glowing, moved further to the right; a slight rumble, and Storm ranged further forward, eyes scanning and ears flicking back and forth.

"Where did you get Satin, Allad?" Shanna asked. She had only seen one other green tidemarked starcat, and that had been Master Cerren's old Prince - she'd never had the opportunity to query the Master about his origins.

"She's from Starfall." He was referring to the first human settlement on the plateau, several hundred kilometres from Watchtower and much further north. "She was bred by the Nandie family, whose cats throw greens every couple of generations. I was posted there a number of years ago when my original starcat died, and Satin chose me before I even knew what was happening. I used to visit the Nandie's and assist with the selection of young cubs for each new cadet class, and I woke one morning with her on my bed. She'd abandoned her mother, snuck into the guest room and then simply refused to leave me." He scratched his nose. "She was a handful to train I might add, but she's the best educator of youngsters I've ever seen, and very special in a number of ways as you'll discover." He smiled smugly, privately amused. "Now, young lady, let's attend to *your* education. You can name each new species of plant we walk past on our way to the edge of the forest, and then you can demonstrate your tracking skills." Shanna began frantically to dredge all her botany study from during the cyclone to the front of her mind. Absently she noted the starcat positions, and then began dutifully to name plants, explaining their lifecycles, properties and dangers as they encountered them. Within half an hour, she was aware that she had a long way to go before her knowledge even approached Allad's apparently encyclopaedic memory. As they entered the edge of the forest, she began to point out tracks of various animals, how old they were and how big each beast was.

"Try and be silent as you walk - watch me." Allad demonstrated which vegetation to avoid in order to move more quietly. "If you pound through the bush like a staureg, then you will observe nothing and simply make yourself a target for some large beast. Listen always to your starcats – never disregard them, they're your lifeline out here and even more when you go Below. We can converse up here, but if we were Below, we'd need to talk only at need, and then very quietly, and use hand signals wherever possible."

"What's it like Below?" Shanna was curious – all of Frontier's current human inhabitants lived on the Plateau, but part of a Scout's job was to explore for more habitable areas, and that meant going 'Below' to the lands below the plateau - completely untamed wilderness and mostly unexplored. Allad looked at her silently, considering his words.

"It's like nothing you've ever experienced. It's wonderful, astounding, so vast you feel like you'll never explore all of it, and it draws you back time after time. It's also terrifying." His eyes were far away, and abruptly he gestured to Shanna to keep moving. "You'll be down there soon enough." He continued to lecture her as they navigated further into the wilderness area, and began the circle around Thunderfall Cascades. The starcats were sent to scout ahead and circle around the half patrol, eyes watchful, ears twitching. Shanna and the other cadets attempted to emulate the silent glide of the Scouts through the bush, with varying degrees of success. From the corner of her eye, Shanna could see each of her classmates being lectured by their Scout.

As Shanna intermittently stumbled her way into unexpected holes or stood on twigs which then snapped loudly underfoot, she would lift her head to find one or another of Spiron's patrol watching her with an amused expression on their face, and she became hotter and sweatier every moment. Two hours later, Allad directed Shanna to bring Storm and Twister around to the left flank, and Verren and Nelson moved up to take their place. As they moved towards the flank, Cirrus, and Nelson's starcat Glutton, fanned out in front. Allad continued to grill Shanna quietly as they moved deeper and deeper into the forest, until the vegetation was so thick that visibility was minimal. Shanna began to feel apprehensive as the light dimmed to a twilight green. She took several nervous glances around, appreciating for the first time what she was actually doing – hunting for the maker of an unknown noise in an unknown area. Of course, she thought, it might be absolutely nothing, but then the image of the staureg at Hillside flitted across her memory and she swallowed slightly, feeling her skin prickle. The patrol concentrated harder, each Scout sending his or her starcat silently back and forth in its assigned place around their human companions. Occasionally one would come to a silent point, and the patrol would stop, investigate whatever had alerted the cat and then continue on. Each time, Shanna would feel her heart rate accelerate slightly and her breathing quicken. The light waned as they wound further and further into the bush. They stopped briefly at midday to eat and rest.

"Shanna, show me where you think we are," Allad said, beckoning Shanna over to where he had his map spread out. From the corner of her eye, she could see Verren and Ragar also attempting to estimate exactly where they were, and plot it on their respective Scouts' maps. Without visible landmarks, just the thick vegetation, Shanna had to rely on glimpses of the sky, estimations of distance, and her compass. Distracted during the earlier part of the journey by Allad's endless questions on botany and tracking, and her attempt to move silently, Shanna had neglected to pace herself and also to commit the earlier visible landmarks to memory. After ten minutes of frantic work, she tentatively indicated a point on the map to Allad. He snorted slightly, one of his mobile eyebrows lifting, and then with a shake of his head walked over to Nelson and Sandar. The three Scouts conferred briefly, and showed the results to Spiron, who grinned wryly and sauntered quietly over to the three cadets.

"Well, having seen your results, I suspect that should the rest of us perish in the bush, the three of you will then remain lost until something eats you - that is, unless one of your starcats is already good enough to guide you home." He assumed a stern expression. "None of you have managed to place us within three kilometres of our actual location. Lesson one in real time navigation: observe, observe, observe. Lesson two: pace at all times until you learn to do it unconsciously." He looked at them consideringly. "You'll each spend time with me this afternoon and tomorrow navigating. You'll be solely and wholly responsible for getting us to the edge of the plateau tomorrow night. We'll be moving completely to your direction. Now, go to your Scouts, get them to show you where we are, and this afternoon we'll be under your direction. Ragar, you'll navigate first." Shanna saw her fellow cadet start, and nod nervously.

The three returned to their Scouts, somewhat chastened.

"So, you want to know where we are then?"Nelson placed the map on a convenient stump, and indicated a spot well to the north of Shanna's estimation. She shook her head. Despite their stealth, and the thick undergrowth, they'd travelled considerably further than she'd thought. They were almost directly north of Thunderfall Cascades, and had a long way to go before they circled further to the east, and then south of the village to the edge of the plateau. "The three of you can sit over there for the next fifteen minutes to sort out your plan for navigating us. Don't forget to set your cats to guard." Nelson crinkled his brown eyes at the three, indicating a spot near the edge of the clearing where they had paused. The three cadets walked over to the indicated spot and then eased themselves tiredly to the ground, grinning ruefully at each other as Verren flattened the map on a layer of dead leaves and grasses.

"Where did you two have us? This was my estimation." Ragar pointed to a spot further west than Shanna's, and Verren indicated a part of the map west and north of that again. "Well, now that we know that navigating in the wilderness is a bit more challenging than on paper or in settled areas, how are we going to avoid getting everyone lost?"

"I vote we chart a course now, and that we keep comparing notes on where we think we are." Verren sighed heavily. "That is between the botany lessons, quick quizzes and instructions on silent movement....not to mention the stumbles in the holes and the tripping over the logs...."

Shanna echoed his sigh. "I think that's a really good idea. I didn't even con-template precise navigation in the middle of all of that." She pulled a twig out of her hair and dropped it on the ground.

"Me neither," Verren made a rueful face, "I feel completely incompetent right now. Working together might reduce the errors. Theoretically we're all really good navigators – as long as we concentrate...or at least I thought we were!" They began to work on a probable path to the edge of the plateau, each calculating the course and bearings, and then cross checking the other two's calculations. Fifteen minutes later they felt reasonably sure they might know where they were going, but not entirely sure that they would get there.

"On your feet! Time to move out." Spiron's soft call jerked them off the ground and Ragar swallowed, gathered up his map and rough workings, and walked somewhat apprehensively to where Spiron waited.

As they began to work their way (silently) through the bush, starcats ranging around them, Shanna attempted to keep track of direction, distance and speed of movement. Allad began quizzing her again almost immediately, intermittently interspersing his questions with tips on real life navigation, and her head began to reel from her attempts to multitask while answering his questions. Four hours later, just as the sun began to set and the humid air to cool, they came to a halt in a clearing near a low rock face which had a small cave at its foot. Allad sent Satin into the cave to investigate and with a glance at Allad, Shanna sent Twister and Storm in after her.

"If you're able, always find some kind of shelter when you're out in the bush. There are no weather issues now that the cyclone's passed, and this is a reasonably well settled area, so we're probably pretty right. But given the noise heard during the eye and the fact that we know a staureg penetrated as far as Hillview, it never hurts to be cautious." Satin poked her nose out of the cave, chirped softly at Allad then stood aside for Storm and Twister to exit. To Shanna's horror, Twister was limping slightly and she hastened over to check him out. There was a long spine in his front right paw, which she recognised immediately. Fortunately it was not from a poisonous creature but from a cavechidna, a relatively harmless creature that had as its defence a number of spiny quills that it was able to shoot from its back as it attempted to burrow away. The impulsive Twister had probably scented it and then chased the creature, which had used its only defence as it attempted to elude him. The spine would need to be removed and cleaned as soon as possible to avoid infection.

"Right, we'll be stopping here for tonight. Shanna, attend to your cat, Ragar, come and show me where we are, and Verren, you'll be navigating in the morning. Perri, you take first watch after we've set up in the cave, followed by Allad, then Nelson; I'll take the next and then Sandar, you finish up. Verren, you're on cook duty."

Shanna grimaced slightly, as she'd tasted some of Verren's cooking on a previous occasion. She hoped he'd improved. Depositing her pack on the ground, she pulled the cat kit out, unrolling it on top of the pack. Twister was sitting in front of her, occasionally attempting to bite the quill in his paw. Without any prompting, Satin sat in front of him and fixed him with her compelling stare, and to Shanna's surprise, he immediately stopped trying to bite the quill and simply sat still, paw in the air. She shot a quick glance at Allad, who grinned back at her. Working quickly, Shanna pulled her knife from her belt pouch, opened the pliers attachment and gripped the quill firmly. Holding the paw with one hand and the pliers with the other, she applied a deft tug to the quill and removed it. She placed it to one side on the ground, then hastened to clean the wound with antiseptic salve, finally sealing it with the woundseal she had so fortuitously brought from home. Allad oversaw every movement, nodding in approval at the workmanlike way Shanna had doctored Twister, and making a few suggestions for the next day's care. She finished by rubbing Twister's large head comfortingly, scratching his cheekbones and jaw. With a quick glance at Allad for permission, she then gravely thanked Satin for her assistance and at the big cat's subtle hint, scratched her face as well. Her green tidemarks glowed brightly and she collected Twister and Storm with her eyes as Allad gave her permission to hunt. Shanna sighed softly – it seemed that she'd managed to pass at least one of the big Scout's tests, but then she began almost immediately to worry about her turn to navigate the next day.

Over by Spiron, Ragar appeared to be sweating heavily as he finally placed his finger on the map in the position that the three of them believed the patrol to be currently located. Intermittently, during changes in patrol position that afternoon, the three cadets had briefly compared direction, distance and speed information with each other. Fortunately none of them had produced wildly differing calculations to the other two. The other Scouts had shot knowing glances at each other during each contact, the odd one smirking slightly. Spiron did not correct Ragar at all, simply nodded and then sent him off to attend to his starcat, leaving the three cadets sweating with the realisation that they would have no certainty from the other Scouts about whether their navigation was accurate at all. Shanna fleetingly wondered if the search for the disturbance was to be handicapped by a lost patrol, but reasoned that if they were too badly off track, the experienced Patrol First wouldn't hesitate to notify them. Or at least she hoped so.

"Come and eat." Verren waved his spoon over the pot he had simmering on the smokeless fire in front of the cave. Unfortunately Shanna and Ragar caught a whiff of his culinary efforts as they settled themselves, backs to packs on the ground, exchanging worried glances. It smelt as though Verren's cooking had perhaps worsened. Resignedly they handed their bowls to him, knowing that a Scout ate whatever was provided, as food could be scarce in the wilderness and there was a finite amount able to be carried on your back. Their worst expectations were realised. On the other side of the fire, Spiron could be seen poking the contents of his bowl suspiciously, while Allad had taken a couple of sniffs of his, and was regarding it with surprised horror. Perri was holding her nose while eating as fast as possible prior to taking her watch, and Nelson and Sandar were simply incredulous. Verren looked around cheerfully, completely oblivious to the effect that his cooking was having on the others.

"More, anyone? There's just a little left if you'd like it." Disbelief was on every face. Shanna had privately thought that perhaps Verren's sense of smell and taste was a little impaired. Now she was convinced, or perhaps he just never ate his own cooking. He seemed surprised that no-one was taking his offer up. Spiron's eyebrows were vanishing into his hairline, and he spoke with incredulity in his voice.

"You actually think we'd like some more? What on earth did you do to that perfectly good dried meat and vegetables?" Verren looked a little hurt at Spiron's tone and waved his hand at his pack.

"I just added a little touch of herbs here and there during the simmering, although I'm never quite sure about the proportions, so I always experiment a bit. My Mum always says that a recipe is only to be improved upon." Allad nearly choked at this amazing statement, while around them,was disbelief on every face. Shanna stifled a giggle.

"You can't possibly be serious! This is disgusting!" Verren looked slightly hurt. "Verren, fortunately you've been paired with the best cook in the Patrol. Nelson, from now on, this cadet is *never* to be left to cook unsupervised. You'll drill him in cooking techniques every day until he can produce something fit for human consumption. If he can do this to pre-prepared food, I can't imagine what he'd manage with foraged food." Spiron shook his head in amazement, then sat heavily down and stared into his bowl. "Well, no good wasting what was once perfectly good food..." Resolutely he picked up his fork and began to slowly eat the contents of his bowl. The others shuddered slightly and followed his example. Shanna decided that Perri's example was a good one, and held her nose before shovelling the rest of the food down as fast as possible.

Entering the cave some time later to lay her bedding out, Shanna looked around carefully in the light of the small shuttered lantern at the back of the cave to make sure she would avoid the cavechidna burrow. She found it towards the rear of the small cave, just to one side of the lantern, and placed her bedding on the other side nearer the front, mindful of the coming watch schedule. Allad entered shortly after, with Satin and Storm and Twister following, and advised her to get to sleep as early as possible.

"Come on boys," she beckoned to her two cats. "Time to rest for a while." Storm nudged her hand gently as he and Twister settled themselves around and upon her, and the three of them settled down with mirrored heavy sighs.

Surprisingly, she slept again almost immediately despite the aching feet, and her apprehension about the next day. Several hours later, she roused as Allad stirred next to her. Moving as quietly as possible, she gently touched Storm and Twister awake, signalling them to move out of the cave ahead of her. She grinned to herself as they moved quickly from her bedding; this time Satin had no need to move them along. Outside the darkness seemed thick and impenetrable, with only a few stars visible in the gaps amongst the dense foliage. Very dimly she could see Perri sitting on a rock, her starcat Spangles, red toned tidemarks almost invisible, lying next to her. She and Allad moved quietly towards Perri, who stood and whispered.

"All mostly quiet, although a herd of weldens went through an hour or so ago. They didn't notice us." Perri's quiet tone was matter of fact, although Shanna didn't think that weldens were particularly matter of fact. The large omnivores were prone to sudden stampedes and had been known to consume almost anything in their path. Allad indicated that Perri should go and rest, and then motioned for Shanna to precede him towards Perri's rock.

"OK Shanna, talk quietly and infrequently if you're on watch with someone else. Your cats don't need to range out from you, but they do need to dim their tidemarks. We need to become effectively invisible. We're not out here to make a noise and attract unwanted attention, but simply to make sure that our fellow Scouts can sleep in safety. We do that best by watching and listening. The only reason to give the alarm is if you are certain that they're in danger. So set your cats to watch and then sit still, keep your eyes moving, and listen quietly." Allad gestured to Satin, who lay down beside him, and gently ran his hand up and down her smooth dark coat. Her tidemarks dimmed immediately. Shanna sat next to him on the rock, following suit, with Storm and Twister lying within reach of her hands. The darkness seemed to increase, and Shanna had to work hard not to start at every odd sound. Sleeping securely in a cave surrounded by others, with someone else on guard, was very different to being the person on guard outside the cave, even if you were with a highly skilled Scout who had years of experience, and three starcats to help you. All Shanna's lessons about the inimical fauna of Frontier played through her mind as she sat tensely in the darkness. Realising that in a couple of short years she would be doing this alone, didn't help. She felt completely inadequate to the task before her, imagining every sound was a staureg and every rustle another herd of weldens. An hour into their watch, the three starcats tensed, getting silently to their feet, ears pricked and noses scenting the air. Allad leaned forward, hand on Satin's back, listening intently, while Shanna's heart rate increased. Faintly through the air came the sound of something large moving through the vegetation. He placed a hand on Shanna's arm, cautioning her against movement or sound. Silently he sent Satin into the surrounding bush. She vanished without a sound and, under Shanna's hand, Twister made a slight movement as if to follow. Quickly she signalled both starcats to remain where they were. The sound of movement increased, and suddenly Satin was by Allad's side again. She was looked up at him and then sat again, completely unconcerned, and Allad rose to his feet, drawing Shanna with him. He spoke directly into her ear.

"Follow me silently. Leave Twister here on guard, and set Storm to follow Satin." He and Shanna crept silently to the edge of the clearing, Shanna's heart pounding furiously and noisily within her chest while she attempted to avoid stepping on anything crunchy. The rustling of the vegetation increased and Allad motioned for Shanna to crouch with him behind a large rock. The starcats dropped obediently to their bellies. A dim light appeared in the vegetation, and Shanna almost gasped. Sliding sinuously through the trees and vegetation was a starlyne. The starlyne was legendary on Frontier - and rarely seen. In the early chaotic days of settlement, it was believed that some of the starlyne's quirky Frontier genes had merged with those of the large domestic felines brought on board the original colony ship, eventually producing the first starcats. Coming through the bush was a softly glowing, enormous, sinuously furred creature. It was gracefully undulating its long body between the trees, large eyes taking in everything before it, a soft violet glow emanating from its sleek coat. The starlyne wound its long body between the great tree trunks, amazingly quiet for a creature of its bulk. Shanna could see the sleek fur gleaming, and the small forelimbs used to manipulate objects were neatly folded beneath the creature's neck. There were no hind limbs. The settlers had never seen a starlyne corpse; where the creatures went to die was a mystery that had perplexed the human inhabitants of Frontier for the three hundred years of settlement. The creatures rarely left tracks, and when tracks had been found, they were so minimal that it was almost as if the creature had lightly brushed the ground in its passing, leaving no clues to how a starlyne actually moved. Early settlers had been fearful of its resemblance to the enormous serpents of legends from their home worlds, and it had taken a number of encounters before they realised that the starlyne was never an aggressor, unlike the even larger tornado serpent - a highly dangerous, lone predator several times the size of the starlyne.

Shanna suddenly realised that the two starcats had vanished from next to them and alarmed, tugged at Allad's arm. He pointed in front of them, as Satin and Storm walked deliberately out into the forest in front of the starlyne. It paused in its slide through the vegetation and lowered its immense head to the two cats, appearing to spend some time in silent communion with them. Their tidemarks glowed brightly, blending with those of the starlyne as the three held each other's gaze, then the starlyne raised its head, looked directly at Shanna and Allad crouched behind their rock, and glided off into the vegetation. The two starcats returned to their partners and the four then moved silently back to the rock, where Twister sat steadily on guard in front of the cave. Shanna sat silently again on the rock with Allad, the sounds of the forest suddenly much less threatening with the passing of the starlyne. She made to whisper to Allad, but ceased at his quick head shake and they sat silently for the rest of their watch, Shanna pondering over the amazing encounter. When they changed over with Nelson and Verren at the end of their shift, Allad's whispered handover to Nelson included an incredulous gasp from Verren and a nod from Allad, before he and Shanna ducked into the cave and back into their bedding.

"We'll talk about this tomorrow, Shanna, you need to sleep now." Allad's low voice was firm, as Shanna opened her mouth to let out the myriad of questions that had rolled around her brain during the silence of their watch. Storm and Twister lay down with Shanna, leaning their heavy heads on her middle, and with the vision of the starlyne before her eyes she deliberately relaxed her body, gradually drifting comfortingly into sleep, as her tired body overruled her wondering mind.

The next morning, Shanna's first question almost exploded out of her as the Scouts gathered around the fire for their morning repast. "So what were the starcats doing?" she demanded.

"No one's really sure," replied Spiron, "But that's what happens every time – the starlyne arrives, the cats commune, and then the starlyne goes. If one of us attempts to join in, the starlyne is gone faster than you can believe." He shrugged. "Most of us have encountered them at some time or another, but that's the first starlyne encounter I know of on the plateau for some time." The discussion continued as they finished their morning hot tea, with Verren and Ragar enviously questioning Shanna for every detail she could remember.

"It was just…I don't know… It was like they were greeting an old friend," she stammered as they pressed for more details, "And it was just glowing – you know, how the cats' tidemarks glow – but… I don't really know how to describe it any better than that!"

Allad grinned at her "That's just about the standard explanation really. I've seen more than most – it's like Satin attracts them actually, but the last time was two years ago and we were Below – you remember Spiron?"

The Patrol First nodded, and drained the dregs of his cup.

"There were about three encounters within a few months that year. Sometimes we'll go years without seeing a starlyne, and then every Patrol will have an encounter in the same month. Despite three hundred years of life on this planet, they're one of the species we know very little about, and how we'll ever learn any more I'm not sure. We don't see a starlyne unless it wants us to in my opinion." He wiped his cup out and replaced it in his pack. The more experienced Scouts were inclined to feel that the presence of the starlyne suggested that there would not be any large predators around Thunderfall Cascade, which then raised the question of what could have caused the noise heard during the eye of the storm. Spiron decided that they would continue their planned patrol, but then search the plateau rim in case of unstable rock falls or edge crumbles. He quirked an eyebrow at Verren as they hefted their packs, preparatory to moving off.

"I hope your navigating is better than your cooking. Lead off Verren." They proceeded quietly through the dense bush for the whole morning, encountering nothing worse than a number of carnivorous plants concealed behind some rocky outcrops. At the midday meal, Spiron again gave no indication to Verren whether his navigation was adequate, simply nodding as he had to Ragar, before they stopped to eat.

"And now for the last of our new navigators," said Spiron, "Shanna."

He motioned to Shanna to direct them on their way. She took a deep breath, nodded, and took her place next to him. She felt intimidated by Spiron's silent presence by her side, he was not inclined to talk to her as much as Allad, preferring to suddenly question her about complicated aspects of starcat training and medicating, and his starcat paced silently beside her as she sent Storm and Twister out to flank them. Strangely, since his encounter with the starlyne, Storm was more inclined to take the lead from his usually more impetuous brother, moving confidently through the vegetation, blue tidemarks glowing smoothly.

She concentrated on navigating as accurately as she knew how, and several hours later, to her hastily concealed surprise, they reached the rim of the plateau almost exactly as the three cadets had planned. As she looked around, checking visible landmarks and taking a final back bearing, Shanna estimated that the three of them had navigated to within approximately two hundred metres of their anticipated arrival point. The patrol, still surrounded by their ever watchful starcats, had all emerged from the forest into the lower vegetation at the edge of the plateau. According to Shanna's positioning and map, they were now well to the east of Thunderfall Cascade. Spiron's plan called for them to begin to survey the edge of the plateau, searching for possible rock falls or unstable edges as they went, while continuing to look for signs of anything else that may have caused the disturbance. The Patrol First gave her the first smile since the previous day as the three cadets almost collapsed in relief. The other scouts each gave a thumb's up, grinning at them all, and Shanna, Ragar and Verren celebrated by back slapping each other vigorously.

"Phew, looks like we can do it if we concentrate – glad I wasn't the only one navigating though." Verren was openly relieved, as an error by any of them would have landed the Patrol in the wrong place on the edge of the plateau, no matter how flawlessly the other two had navigated.

The sun was still about two hours above the horizon, so they began the rim walk, pausing every now and then on outcroppings which allowed them to better survey the rock faces below. Shanna marvelled at the view from the plateau edge – Below was spread out in an amazing panorama of mysterious green before her and she had to avoid being distracted by imagining what she might eventually encounter when she was finally allowed to go there. As the sun began to set, Perri, scouting ahead with Spangles, signalled that she had found a place to camp for the night. Wincing slightly, Spiron directed Nelson to supervise Verren at the cook fire. Shanna devoutly hoped that Nelson's constant guidance was going to be enough to counteract Verren's desire to "improve" upon recipes. When the call to come and eat came, the patrol passed their bowls with some hesitation to Nelson to dish up. Fortunately Nelson had managed to keep Verren mostly on track with the dinner, and it was all at least edible.

"Better, better," was Perri's comment, "At least I can eat it without holding my nose!" Prior to sleeping, Spiron directed the Scouts to send the starcats out in twos and threes to hunt.

Settling down to sleep surrounded by starcats and Scouts, Shanna felt as though she was finally getting a sense of some of what it really meant to be part of a Patrol. It was clear there was much to learn, but she felt that she had a much better sense of where her training was heading. Finally, she allowed herself to ponder on Below – what it might be like, what kinds of animals she might encounter. She shivered slightly with excitement, pleasurably mixed with a small tingle of fear.

***

Twelve kilometres ahead, a chunk of alien metal protruded from a large scar on the edge of the plateau. Below, dimly seen through the vegetation, were areas that had been stripped bare of greenery as the Garsal aircraft had bounced on protruding rocky outcrops. The local flora and fauna had kept clear of the alien craft, and the forest surrounding the edge of the plateau was strangely quiet. Down below, the instrument lights slowly dimmed for the last time, fading into darkness, their jewel like glints no longer twinkling through the vegetation.

Chapter 12

THE wind sighed through the trees on the edge of the forest near the plateau rim, riffling the low grasses before whining gently around the rocks perched on the very edge and cooling the early sweat on Shanna's forehead. Satin, Storm and Twister were flanking the patrol, confidently picking their way through the edge of the trees, and ranging on command into the bush as requested. Ahead, Sandar and Ragar were on point, starcats pacing a hundred metres in front of the patrol. So far the edge of the plateau had appeared completely intact with no rock falls or unstable edges. The native vegetation had been barely disturbed by the ferocity of the storm, adapted perfectly to the vagaries of its natural environment.

The beauty of the vast expanse of Frontier visible from the plateau rim was almost overwhelming as Shanna worked on constantly surveying her environment, attempting to commit significant landmarks to memory and make sure she was navigating accurately. In the extreme distance, she could see what appeared to be peaks of mountains covered with snow. The centre of the plateau contained a number of peaks high enough for snow, but Shanna had never actually seen it. She lived in the hope that as a fully qualified Scout, she would one day travel far enough to experience the wonder of such a thing. Below beckoned quietly to her.

As they walked Shanna turned her head to ask a quiet question of Allad, but was hushed by his sudden hand signal. The rest of the patrol had stopped and were all listening intently. Shanna suddenly became aware of the silence emanating from the surrounding bush. Spiron signalled, and the patrol melted swiftly into the undergrowth. Shanna attempted to emulate Allad's silent movement as they concealed themselves in a rocky depression, gesturing to her starcats and watching as they faded completely out of sight. They remained motionless, listening to the intense silence as the moments passed one by one. Again Shanna's heart rate began to accelerate. Ten minutes of silence later, there was a quiet whistle from ahead and Spiron rose gracefully from just in front of Shanna and Allad, signalling the others to reappear and move forwards quietly and with caution. With a sweeping hand signal, he indicated that they should send their starcats ahead in a search pattern. They complied, and the three cats reappeared, loping forward noiselessly and disappearing in the direction of Sandar and Ragar. They then began to glide forward as silently as possible. Shanna envied the almost effortless way that Allad and the other Scouts moved, attempting to copy his smooth, almost catlike movements as he slid from cover to cover. Up ahead, there was another slightly louder whistle. Spiron motioned the others out of cover, slipping into a smooth jog towards the now visible Sandar. Allad and Shanna jogged after him, arriving shortly behind, joined by Verren and Nelson with Perri bringing up the rear, her starcat ranging as rear guard. Sandar had set the five starcats in a semicircle just in front of where he and Ragar were concealed behind a large rock formation. The absence of wildlife noise was eerie, as they peered out from behind the rocks. In front of them, a large chunk of what appeared to be a strange dark metal protruded from the disrupted edge of the plateau. It was around two metres in length, and judging by the jagged edges, had broken off something larger. There were protrusions and shiny insets on one edge, and various wires trailed from the broken off end.

There were no obvious signs of inimical animal or plant life in evidence, and for some minutes the patrol sat hidden, silently watching. Shanna watched with them, wild thoughts chasing through her mind. The metal looked like nothing she'd ever seen before, matte rather than shiny. The starcats were curious, but not overly anxious or cautious about the metal embedded in the ground in front of them. They stayed unmoving for several minutes, then there was a short, cadenced whistle and Spiron and Perri moved out from behind the rocks, cautiously approaching the metal object. The others joined them in carefully spaced groups of two, Shanna remaining unmoving until Allad beckoned her forward. "What do you think it is?" Perri was openly curious, reaching out to cautiously touch the smooth coolness of the dark metal with one brown fingertip, while Spangles paced steadily around the group, alert to any danger

"I have absolutely no idea." Spiron knelt and tentatively fingered one of the shiny insets on the edge, running his hand over one of the protrusions which terminated in a cylindrical barrel. Allad lifted his bushy eyebrows and then called Satin to come forward. She sniffed the dark metal, sneezed abruptly, then hummed deeply at Allad with a disgusted expression on her feline face, green tidemarks darkening in distaste. She turned her back and stalked several metres away before sitting and washing her face vigorously with one large paw. Shanna wondered at the cat's expression.

"Well, I don't think she's particularly impressed with whatever put that there." Allad wrinkled his forehead. "I expect that's the sound that Thunderfall Cascades heard during the storm, but the question remains, how on earth did it actually get there? It's obviously speared into the edge from the air somehow." Shanna thought furiously, nothing she could think of could explain what Allad was suggesting and her mind kept veering from one wildly implausible explanation to another. For some moments the Patrol simply investigated the metal object from all angles, puzzled expressions on their faces, until Spiron shrugged his shoulders and indicated for them all to gather and sit, starcats on watch around them.

"Alright, ideas please – no matter how wild or improbable."

"Do you think that we've somehow been ....*found*?" Verren's voice was quietly tentative. There was a sudden silence, as the Scouts contemplated the implications of the cadet's suggestion. The human inhabitants of Frontier had arrived as the result of an intergalactic colony ship crash. Over three hundred years previously, their ship had suffered a malfunction when attempting to exit a wormhole on their way to settle a new colony planet. The colony ship had plummeted onto the surface of Frontier, suffering major damage and stranding the colonists. The inimical wildlife and enormous cyclonic storms had caused devastating losses until the surviving colonists had managed to fortify a small area of the plateau. Although the memory of their origins had been meticulously preserved and treasured, the possibility of actually being found more than three hundred years later was slowly fading into a dream as the generations passed. In reality, despite preserving the knowledge of their origins and placing an enormous value on education, the settlers were more and more focused on spreading out across Frontier and beginning to develop their own unique, planet based skills and technology, gradually moving away from the concepts and practices preserved in the archives. The long term aim had always been to regain the stars, but in recent years this had become a matter of contention in some parts of Frontier society.

The silence lengthened as the Scouts continued to contemplate the implications of Verren's suggestion. Shanna remembered her quiet conversation with her father just a few months previously as they had looked at the night sky, and now here was the actual possibility that someone had found them. More questions raced through Shanna's head – If someone really had found them, then what had happened to them? Was the metal just a piece of something larger, or was it the whole thing? Was it actually a spacecraft, or a smaller exploratory craft? If it was just an exploratory craft, then where was the main craft? And if it wasn't either, what *was* it, and where had it come from? The questions went on and on, circling round inside her head until Shanna was almost dizzy with the number of them. She tried to recall the drawings of spacecraft that all students on Frontier had been shown as part of their early education.

Spiron tapped his thigh with one hand, and then came to an abrupt decision.

"We need to notify Barron immediately, send a message to Watchtower, and then we need to continue to investigate here and attempt to discover as much as possible about whatever has occurred. I think that this looks as though it's a part of something much larger, and that means we need to locate the larger portion. Perhaps there's someone out there who needs help. Perri, you're to take a message to Barron, detailing our location and what we've found. Tell him to bring the rest of the patrol straight here, and then I want you to continue directly to Watchtower as fast as possible and alert the Masters as to our suspicions. Tell nobody else of what we've found at this stage. Call Spangles in, and leave immediately. " Perri nodded, called Spangles, and then vanished swiftly into the bush. Shanna's now constant calculations of their location suggested that Perri would be able to reach Thunderfall Cascades within twenty-four hours, as they had now travelled far enough west to be within a day of closing their circle around the village. Of all the things she had expected to learn in the aftermath of the storm, this was the most unlikely.

"Allad, you and Shanna set your starcats to scent tracking. See if they can find any more pieces of metal like this. Nelson and Verren, you can search out a location to set up a semi-permanent camp, and hunt for fresh game and forage for some edible plants. Sandar and Ragar, I want you two to continue another few kilometres west, looking for any more impact sites. I'm going to take a closer look at whatever it is we have here. Nelson, make sure you set the camp up as close as possible to here, as long as it's safe."

Shanna and Allad called their three starcats over to the metal object. Shanna indicated to Storm and Twister to smell the metal. Both sneezed almost immediately, showing the same disgusted expression that Satin had, whiskers twitching violently. She wondered what the metal smelt like to the cats – she could detect nothing particularly unusual about it herself.

"Right, let's send them out in a standard sweep to see if they can pick anything up." Allad said, and Shanna signalled her cats to join Satin. When they came up with nothing, they widened their search, sending the starcats zigzagging in overlapping patterns across the area

Reasoning that the object had impacted the edge of the plateau during the cyclone and that any debris may well have been flung around by the wild winds, Shanna directed Twister up some of the nearer trees and had him leap from tree to tree, while scenting. Her forethought was rewarded shortly thereafter, when he let out a loud hum, poking at something caught in the foliage of a tree a short way inside the treeline. It was another jagged piece of metal. As the day wore on, Shanna and Allad had assembled a small pile of similar pieces from the surrounding vegetation. None were very big however, appearing to be just smaller pieces of the object embedded in the side of the plateau. Even when placed together, it was clear that they were part of something still larger. Shanna shook her head as she attempted once again to imagine what they might have come from.

As the sun set, the patrol gathered together in the campsite that Nelson and Verren had established in one of the rocky outcrops. A small fire was tucked away in a small recess formed by the rock face, with several small marmals spitted over it. As Shanna seated herself, the smell of the roasting marmals wafted towards her and her stomach rumbled. Several starcats were on the edge of the firelight finishing off their evening kills, while those not eating were lounging close to the fire, washing themselves fastidiously. Spiron's cat, Fury, was perched high in the outcropping keeping watch.

"Well, it seems definite that whatever crashed into the plateau during the cyclone is now in at least more than one piece," said Spiron, "All we've found are smaller fragments, and they're only in a small localised patch of forest just near the original object. It was hard to tell, but the view from the edge of the plateau looks like the rest has probably come to a stop somewhere below the plateau."

"So what do we do now?" asked Allad. "It'll be another day before Barron gets here, and at the earliest it will be several days before anyone else can be here."

"Do we really want to do anything else at this stage?" Nelson asked. "I mean, shouldn't we just wait and keep an eye on things until someone from the council arrives?"

"I'm not so sure that we have time for too much waiting, to be honest." Allad said.

"So what do you suggest?" Sandar said. "Don't forget we've got three cadets with us - and first years to boot."

"I think that we need to look further to find the rest of the artifact, whatever it might be. It seems most likely to me that it's a portion of some kind of flying craft, and the more I think about it, the more likely it seems that we have been found!"

As Allad leaned forward, Shanna exchanged an uncomfortable glance with Ragar and Verren. She was surprised that the discussion was so frank.

"Let's just think for a moment!" Spiron raised a hand. "We really have no idea at this stage who or what may have been in that craft. I, like Allad, believe it is some kind of flying craft. From what I can remember from some of the older texts that I studied when I was a cadet - and that is longer ago than I care to remember," Allad snorted "The piece on the rim looks very much like a wing from some of the flying craft illustrations preserved in the Scholar's precinct archives. But can we really be sure that whoever was flying it was looking for us or is even human? Remember that the histories contain records of other starfaring races."

"But they were all peaceful." Verren pointed out. "Humanity was coexisting in peace in the Galactic Federation."

Spiron raised his eyebrows at Verren, and Shanna was impressed that Verren had the courage to join the discussion. "That's certainly what the histories say but I, for one, am a student of our human nature, and even here we humans still don't always get along."

Allad nodded, his enthusiasm somewhat dampened by logic, but still intent on pursuing his point. "No matter what it may or may not contain, we still need to find out. We've been here on Frontier for over three hundred years now, and so far we've seen no sign of anyone searching for us. Now that our settlements are reasonably secure, we've begun to re-climb the technology ladder and properly explore our planet, but slowly, very slowly, and only as we have enough resources and personnel available. We know that we're still many many years from regaining the stars, and there are those few who say we shouldn't even try."

Spiron lowered his eyebrows and shook his head as Allad went on, "This may be our chance to take a leap forward, or to make contact with the civilisation that our forbears lost."

"We need to keep in mind the safety of the plateau." Sandar made a flat statement. "Our ancestors struggled to survive in that first hundred years. If this area hadn't been so isolated, they wouldn't have lived long enough to secure a future for us. Even now, there are only a few of us who can survive for long in the wilder areas, and only Scouts ever venture Below the plateau. You all know how relatively little we've managed to explore away from the plateau, and how few of us are equipped to do that exploration. We have with us right now one quarter of the whole year's intake of Scout cadets." The Scout Corps usually had two intakes of cadets per year and Shanna's group was the first intake of cadets for that year. "Do we have any real reason to put them at risk?"

Spiron looked at Sandar over the rim of his cup as Storm came and lay quietly next to Shanna's perch on a rock next to Allad. Twister rested his heavy head in her lap, and she patted it absently, engrossed in the discussion.

"I'm not sure that we have any reason not to. If we don't investigate immediately, we have several problems. Firstly, if there was a human or human beings in that craft, they may be injured, or if they've survived at all they're certainly in danger. Secondly, if it wasn't human, then the first point still applies. Our ancestors lived in peace with other species, we can at least try to do the same. Thirdly, if we find something that isn't friendly, then delaying may put the survival of all of us at risk. You've made the point well Sandar, the security of the plateau comes first." He looked around at the small group gathered in front of the fire, allowing his eyes to linger on the resting starcats, most now leaning some portion of themselves on their partners, while Fury sat sentinel-like on his perch.

Shanna realised with a thrill of fear, that Spiron was suggesting that the group might be about to venture Below - or at least down the side of the plateau. The Patrol First went on.

"We've forged special relationships with this planet. We know that the livestock that survived the crash has been altered and changed, and we know that Frontier's invasive genetic materials are beginning to change us as well. We only have to look at the starcats who surround us right now – they didn't even exist three hundred years ago. Our histories make these things clear. In addition, and this is not a well known fact," the cadets perked their ears up, "but our records show that we are becoming stronger and faster than our forbears and some of us have changed in even more unusual ways. Most Scouts show very strong empathic links with their starcats – when we communicate with them, they respond in much more complex ways than simple training will account for. Whether it's completely a result of us changing, or our starcats developing further, we don't really know, and that's only one example." He paused watching the others for a moment.

"I have one other concern to voice." Spiron looked at each of them, before returning his gaze to the fire. "If it is humans who have found us, then I'm not sure how they will regard the changes within us."

Shanna stared at him uncomprehendingly. Spiron's last statement was totally unexpected. The histories she'd studied as a much younger child all pointed to the moment of reunion with her forbears' civilisation as a joyful one – the lost child found, the unaccounted-for horgal returned to its pen. It had never crossed her mind that the people now on Frontier might be so different to the ones who had landed there, that the galactic federation might not want to reaccept them into their society.

"But we don't look any different to the pictures I've seen of the original settlers," said Ragar.

"We don't *look* different, because, outwardly, our features haven't changed particularly," Spiron replied. "But we are taller in general than was the norm, and we are much faster, and much stronger. Then there are those other 'little' things that I mentioned – empathy with animals, phenomenal accuracy, the ability to perform complex mathematics in our heads, affinity for weather changes, and a myriad of other tiny changes, that make us different to our ancestors." Shanna knew all about the accuracy that Spiron was talking about as she'd seen it in action, watching her brother with a bow in his hands. She hadn't thought that it was any great problem, simply an extremely useful talent – similar to many her friends had displayed. Gathering her thoughts together, she took a deep breath, and hesitantly ventured her own opinion.

"Spiron, I understand what you're saying, but we won't know if we don't find out."

Allad gave her a quick smile from under his moustache and Satin purred loudly, patting at her boot with a paw as if to agree with her statement. With a start, Shanna realised that the behaviour she took for granted from a starcat, was exactly the kind of thing Spiron was talking about.

"OK, Spiron, I see what you're saying," said Nelson, "So how do we go about it? And are we all in agreement here?"

"I have some reservations," said Sandar, "But I can understand your point of view, and I do see the need for immediate action." He nodded his head slowly. "Of some kind at least!"

"I think we need to begin to search below the rim of the plateau." Spiron had obviously decided to be blunt. "And I think we need to begin tomorrow. The cadets will come. Barron will be here tomorrow sometime, and we can rearrange our manpower then, but they've demonstrated enough skills to explore as far as we'll have time to get tomorrow." There were a few raised eyebrows from the other three scouts, which were then followed by thoughtful nods. "The watches will be staggered as normal tonight, and then first thing in the morning we'll begin rope construction. Sandar and Ragar found a stand of plybrush yesterday, not far from here. Make sure you all have your harnesses ready."

The cadets looked at each other, barely suppressed excitement visible. They'd worked on vertical rope skills from the beginning of their training, and had all looked forward to putting them into practice. There was one problem, though.

"Um, how will the starcats descend and ascend?" Shanna asked. Each time they'd worked the ropes recently, they had simply been advised to set their cats to a stay command while their human partners sweated up and down the ropes, developing their techniques. Starcat agility was legendary, but there would no doubt be overhangs to cope with the next day, and she'd never been shown any kind of cat harness. The other four Scouts all grinned in an amused fashion.

"It doesn't take long to teach them. Don't worry." Allad stroked the silky top of Satin's head, still grinning. Shanna didn't think it was any grinning matter, but decided against arguing just then as Allad was very obviously hoping that she would disagree with him, and pursue her questions.

"Anyone for marmal?" Nelson had removed the first marmal from the spit, and was dividing it into portions, "I didn't let Verren touch it, so it's completely safe. He did the veges tonight." Verren looked a little hurt at this comment until Ragar jabbed him in the ribs with his elbow, but then busied himself removing baked vegetables from the ashes. Shanna hoped fervently that they would not be completely charcoaled.

***

At the Garsal ship, the communications tech finally gave up trying to contact the missing aircraft. There had been no hint of a response, and the commander was resigned to the fact that the craft had perished in the cyclone. He would never treat the weather on this planet with such contempt again, recognising that the planet's storms reached a ferocity heretofore not experienced. The aircraft were irreplaceable until more sources of minerals were discovered. The Garsal would now have to rely on ground transport to seek out those precious resources. In the meantime, the slaves would be put to expanding the compound, pushing back the laser fencing piece by piece until there was a decent expanse of secure area inside. He directed the agronomists to commence preparing plans to subdue the inimical flora and fauna of this planet.

When they had left, he called in the troop commanders. They would now have the job of exploring on foot and by vehicle, guarding the scientists, without the advantage of aircraft, until they had located appropriate mineral deposits. He directed them to commence exploration north, towards the plateau where the signs of rudimentary habitation had been detected. First, they would need to rid the surrounding area of predators. The troop commanders inclined their heads, and indicated their requirements for slaves to attend to their needs in the wilderness. The commander hesitated, his supply of slaves was limited, and early losses had been high. A quick mental calculation and he agreed to send two slaves with each expedition. The rest would be needed for the expansion of the hive, and the Matriarch had requested his presence to discuss its progress. It was important that there were enough slaves to expedite the construction.

In the hold of the ship, Anjo huddled more closely into his ragged blankets. The ferocious sounds of the storm had penetrated even the spaceship's hull. The drive to escape burnt within him, but it was almost smothered by the apparent hopelessness of his captivity and the horror of an inhospitable world.

Chapter 13

PLYBRUSH vines were so tough that they were unable to be snapped, and required a very sharp knife to separate them from their low growing parent plants. Each vine would extend up to one hundred metres along the ground before terminating in a spectacular orange flower that became a seed head at the turn of the season. The orange flowers were the most reliable way to identify them, but the next morning, Nelson showed the cadets the typical foliage of the parent bush in order to make identification easier when the flowers were not evident. He also pointed out two other plants that often grew near the parent bush, and showed them how it often tucked itself away near rocky crevices. After locating and cutting the vines, they carted them back to the plateau, near where the artifact was embedded. The vines were then woven into surprisingly smooth ropes, which were enormously strong, yet extremely flexible. Each rope was then tidied into a neat hank, and placed near at hand at the campsite. Each Scout and cadet then donned and checked their harness, placing a number of karabiners on handy belt loops, along with well forged descending devices. Each also hung several lengths of thin but strong cord on the belt loops along with their knives. Shanna and her fellow cadets carefully fastened their packs, making sure the clips were well secured.

"Sandar, put the fire out and leave this note for Barron in a cairn near it. He'll have no trouble finding our campsite," Spiron said. "Meet us by the face to the west of the artifact." The patrol headed for the descent site, starcats in tow, and spent the next few moments securely anchoring a pair of the newly constructed ropes fairly high up on a well rooted tree. Nelson and Spiron tested the ropes, heaving together to ensure that they were securely anchored before.

"Allad, you're first," Spiron said. "Make sure you stop when you find a stable ledge. We'll send Satin as soon as you signal that you're down."

Allad nodded and casually tossed the ropes over the edge. Clipping his descender into his harness, he wove the rope through it. Sandar performed a final check of his gear then dispatched him over the edge.

There was a long pause when all that could be heard was the sound of Allad's descending transmitted through the rope. Sandar, perched on the edge but attached to the other rope, indicated when Allad passed out of his view into the vegetation on the cliff face. A few moments later, there was a whistle clearly heard and the weight lifted off the rope. A second whistle, and Satin's ears perked up. Spiron nodded and Sandar called Satin to the edge. The three cadets waited eagerly to see how they would attach Satin to the rope to lower her over, and were completely unprepared for what happened next. Green tidemarks glowing brightly with glee, Satin appeared to wrap her whole body around the rope, somehow managing to wrap her tail completely around the rope at least twice, and then simply leapt headfirst over the edge. They all gasped as Satin disappeared from view, listening in disbelief to the zipping sound as she slid rapidly down the rope. Shortly they heard yet another whistle from Allad indicating Satin's arrival and that he was ready for the next descent.

"Nelson, you next." Spiron was quick to get the patrol moving down the ropes. After Nelson and his starcat (rather appropriately named Glutton) had descended, Spiron had the three cadets ready themselves and their cats.

"Shanna, you go next, as we've to send two cats down after you. We'll get them to descend together on both ropes, so let Allad and Sandar know when you get down. And don't worry about them, we've never seen a starcat who couldn't do this the first time. In fact, it's as if they're born knowing how." And indeed, Storm and Twister were both leaning forward eagerly, almost quivering with the desire to follow.

Shanna clipped in and agilely backed over the edge of the cliff edge, and then slid neatly down the rope, carefully controlling her speed with her gloved right hand.

"Almost there Shanna." Allad's quiet voice sounded from below as she penetrated the vegetation, kicking the branches below her gently out of the way. She manoeuvred through them, and then gently came to a halt next to Allad. He, Nelson, Satin, and Glutton were safely on a wide ledge, which broadened again just to the east, and appeared to then descend for some distance on an angle. As Allad whistled, Shanna moved to the wider portion of the ledge, and then looked up as she heard the humming of the rope which meant someone was descending. Into view came two starcats, descending head first rapidly down the rope. Both had their tidemarks glowing brightly, and were shooting glances at each other as they hurtled down their individual ropes, using their tails to brake as they arrived on the ledge. They unwound themselves from the ropes and bounced happily to Shanna, violet eyes glowing, and tidemarks pulsing with glee.

"That's just wrong….." Shanna shook her head, thinking of all the sweat and effort she and the others had put into their rope training.

"See, told you they'd be no problem. Actually, now they've done it once, the hardest thing you'll have to do will be to contain their enthusiasm!" Nelson's grin was infectious, and Shanna grinned back as the two cats rubbed large heads on her hands, emitting loud purrs. She hushed them hurriedly.

The rest of the patrol arrived safely on the ledge, and then began to move along it, sending two starcats ahead in case of any unusual fauna on the prowl. The ledge took a sharp hairpin turn, angling downwards towards an area with a large gap in the foliage. They descended towards it, realising that the scar in the vegetation was recent, raw stems oozing sap, and branches freshly broken off trees clinging to the side of the cliff face. As they moved through the brush, Sandar in the lead paused suddenly, flinging out his arm to bar Ragar's way, then guided them carefully around a spiky plant with deep purple and green foliage. As they passed, he took a moment to point out the quivering spines deep inside the spiky fronds, tipped in a poisonous orange colour.

"This is the Barbed Palm – you may have heard of it. The spines shoot out when the foliage is brushed, and the tips of the barbs contain a poison that causes paralysis. When a victim is paralysed, the palm simply extends those coiled fronds onto the decaying flesh, which the plant then uses to sustain itself. When extracted, the poison can be refined to become a useful drug for the medics to use during surgical procedures, as it allows them to selectively paralyse and numb specific areas. In its unrefined form, it will simply kill within thirty minutes as it progressively paralyses the body. When we return, we'll show you how to harvest and package the spines for travel, as it's rare to find them, and the refined drug is so useful. Be careful now, as where there is one, there are often more."

"Look at this!" Ragar pointed to a long scar on the ledge where the edge had been scored away by something large impacting it. "I think it struck the ledge here, before falling further." He went to move to the edge of the scarred area, but Spiron pulled him roughly back.

"Never go near an unstable edge without properly securing yourself, Ragar."

Nelson and Verren made short work of attaching a plybrush rope to a stable outcropping on the face then attached themselves securely to it, before moving to the edge and peering over to try and ascertain the fall of the artifact.

"There are a few more pieces of the artifact just below the ledge and we can see where it's impacted a few more times on the cliff face. It looks like this ledge takes another hairpin shortly, and then peters out about two hundred metres further down. There's a pretty big abseil after that until we can land on a ledge," called Verren quietly.

"Right, let's follow the ledge down as far as possible, and then we'll see how far we can abseil down. Hopefully the craft may have stuck partway down, rather than be right at the plateau's base." Spiron directed the patrol to keep moving, while Verren and Nelson detached their safety rope. If they had to pursue damaged vegetation all the way to the bottom of the plateau, it would be a long, long hunt as the plateau was approximately fifteen hundred metres high. There would be stretches where they would be able to scramble down scree slopes and ledges, but the majority of the plateau was perched above sheer rock faces much like the one they had initially descended. They were a mixed blessing. It had been the sheer inaccessibility of the plateau that had sheltered the original settlers from the multitudes of dangerous fauna below, but it also made it extremely difficult for them to explore the surrounding areas. As part of her orientation training, Shanna had learned that the early settlers had slowly dug long subterranean tunnels from their original storage and storm shelter caverns from the major settlements to the bottom of the plateau, hoping to discover a predator free region, but they were heavily guarded and blockaded in order to prevent anything accessing the plateau from Below. Anyone who used such an access took care to erase all signs of their presence, in order to maintain the usefulness of the tunnels.

For several hours, they alternately descended on the plybrush ropes, which they left fixed behind, scrambled carefully down scree slopes, and cautiously stepped their way down steep sloping ledges, following the trail of debris and impacts that the falling craft had left, as it plummeted down the cliff face. It became obvious that if there had been any kind of life on board the craft, it would have taken a miracle for it to survive. Halfway through the day, Spiron called a halt to the downward descent. They had used nearly all the rope constructed earlier that day, and there was still no sight of the craft. He estimated that they had descended approximately half way down the plateau's edge, and there was still a visible scar in the vegetation approximately one hundred metres below where they perched on a wide ledge.

"We need more rope to descend further. I'd hoped to find the craft earlier than this, but I expect that we still have a considerable way to go, judging by what we can see," said Spiron. "Nelson, you and Verren will ascend to the campsite, meet Barron and the others, construct more ropes, and then descend again and rejoin us tomorrow. The rest of us will continue to descend until we have no more rope, and then we'll set up camp on a ledge. Don't forget to collect the Barbed Palm spines on the way back. You can show Verren how to collect and pack them. Next time we come across one, Verren can demonstrate to the others."

"Do you want anyone to wait above for word from the council?" asked Nelson. "Or do you want everyone to follow us back down?"

"I'd like at least two left above to wait for the council, and tell Barron he's to decide exactly who and how many. I'll trust his assessment of the other cadets. Tell him that if he's not sure of them and their cats, they can stay above." This was obliquely flattering to Shanna, Verren and Ragar. Shanna decided that the three of them must have passed some unwritten test of Spiron's if he was talking about leaving their fellow cadets above the plateau rim if they hadn't measured up.

"How do the starcats get back up?" Verren wanted to know.

"They climb, just like you do," was Nelson's reply with a grin. "You don't think we'd have let them come down if they couldn't get back up do you?"

In fact, Cirrus and Glutton made much lighter work of the ascent than Nelson and Verren. They simply seemed to flow up the ropes, much as they climbed poles, now that Shanna thought about it. She'd always admired how fast a starcat could climb anything, but she'd always taken it for granted that they used their formidable claws to assist them. Watching Cirrus and Glutton smoothly ascend the narrow rope showed her just how wrong she'd been, despite all her knowledge of starcats. It appeared that they almost suctioned their paws, bodies and tails to the rope, winding their lengths around the rope, and then flowing up it in a spiral.

"Just how do they do that?" asked Shanna. "It looks impossible."

"We're actually not sure," Allad replied. "But each successive generation seems better at it. Wish I could do it!" He was watching Nelson and Verren, ascending the rope steadily, while Cirrus and Glutton peered at them from above. Shanna was not at all envious of the climb ahead of them – she could almost feel the sore muscles Verren would experience the next day.

"OK, time to move on as far as we can today. Eyes out for a site to camp on, we'll stop as soon as we find somewhere suitable," said Spiron, "Allad and Shanna, send your cats on ahead."

An hour and one last long abseil later, they paused in a natural inset in the cliff face, which would be suitable as a safe campsite for the night. It was deep enough to provide some shelter from inclement weather, and far enough from the edge of the ledge that no-one should encounter any problems during the night. Allad, Sandar and Spiron showed Shanna and Ragar how to set a ledge camp up properly, with tie-ins to sleep connected.

"Never assume that a ledge will stay attached when you're asleep, no matter how big it is. I once saw a whole ledge come off the face, and it had been there for years – we'd used it as a training bivvy for final year cadets for about ten years," said Allad soberly. He continued building a small, smokeless fire and spitted the rock marmal over it. Shanna had stuffed the marmal with dried vegetables after he had skinned and cleaned it.

"Send your cats to hunt in pairs while we eat," ordered Spiron. "We'll turn in early so that we'll be fresh in the morning. Shanna and Ragar, you'll take individual watches tonight. Tomorrow we'll be descending lower towards the base of the plateau. The vegetation and animals will increase in numbers and ferocity. The forest, or more correctly, jungle, is much more dangerous than anything you will ever encounter above. I need to be sure that you'll obey any of us instantly should we so tell you. There are things you will have no idea about down there, and you need to react instantly. I also need to know that you can recall your starcats immediately should I tell you to."

The two cadets nodded soberly. Shanna was suddenly reminded of the injuries she'd seen on some of the Masters and their starcats, and a small cold chill gripped her. She suddenly felt uncertain, fearful of watching over her fellow Scouts alone with so little experience. So far, the post cyclonic trip had been an exciting adventure, slightly divorced from day to day life, but the reality of a solitary watch and then a dangerous descent into the complete unknown unnerved Shanna in a way she'd never experienced before.

Just before midnight she, Storm and Twister relieved Sandar from his watch. She set the starcats to lie beside her rock, tidemarks dimmed and heavy heads leaning on her feet. They appeared relatively unconcerned though alert, as the night time noises filtered through the scrub around the campsite. She concentrated on trying to identify the various creatures by their calls, to distract herself from self doubt, and that small tingle of fear that kept walking its way up and down her back bone, noting unfamiliar sounds to ask Allad about the following day. She could see the stars clearly in the cold night sky above her, and spent some time contemplating the idea of meeting someone from another planet. Although, intellectually she knew that her ancestors had also come from somewhere other than Frontier, it was bizarre to think of actually encountering someone who hadn't been born on her home planet; the idea had been purely abstract up until the day before. Would they like her? Would she understand them? Would they understand her? Questions buzzed in and out of her mind as she sat quietly on her rock, before being startled into goosebumps and a thudding heart by a quiet rustle nearby. Twister nudged her hand, violet ear tips gleaming slightly, and she recognized another rock marmal venturing down the cliff face. She stroked him, taking some reassurance from his relaxed stance, and he settled his large head on her right foot, weighing it down heavily. Every now and then she felt as if something was watching her, but one glance at her two relaxed starcats was enough to reduce the feeling to wariness. The watch passed in relative peace, until she was alerted by the approach of Fury, Spiron's blue tidemarked starcat. Spiron appeared noiselessly at her shoulder and she stood, whispered the all clear, and retired with her two starcats to her bedding, taking care to tie herself in carefully. It didn't make for the most comfortable of nights, and Storm complained slightly when he leant his head on her belly and laid it on the tie-in. A slightly disturbed several hours later, she awoke as the sun rose, with Twister purring loudly in her right ear.

***

Back at the Garsal compound, Anjo was jerked awake by the slave master, who commanded him to follow with a guttural bark. He joined Semba, one of the other slaves, and was taken to the outside compound. The early dawn light was filtering through the canopy above, as he was directed over to an assembled troop of Garsal soldiers. They were formed up next to one of the sturdy ground vehicles, which the Garsal had modified to cope with the unfamiliar terrain and wildlife. He and Semba were handed over to the troop commander, who indicated that they should begin loading the vehicle with supplies for a several week long journey.

"You will come with us on this patrol. We will be surveying and exploring, and removing as many of the large beasts as possible." The commander's insectoid face was completely expressionless as he gave his instructions to the pair. Anjo shot a frightened glance at Semba. She returned an equally terrified look, and as one they looked to the large clawed and toothed monster currently prowling outside the laser fence. He was brought to his senses by a stinging blow to his back, the commander growling angrily, and they hastened to begin the loading of the vehicle. He could see that the interior had also been modified to take the sleeping cocoons used by the Garsal – this was a well planned venture, and the commander was an efficient leader of troops, but he knew that his and Semba's chances of survival outside the compound were slim. They steadily packed the vehicle, until the commander was satisfied that everything he required was inside. The troops then climbed aboard, three of them manning offensive weapons from the interior turrets of the vehicle, and Semba and Anjo were then shoved into opposite corners of the sleeping compartment.

A quick command, and a section of the fence switched off and the vehicle surged forward. Anjo slid on the smooth floor, stopped only by the sharp corner of the galley area. There was a sudden jostling impact on the vehicle, and then they could hear the whine of the cannons firing from above. The heavy impacts ceased abruptly and there was a thud as the attacking creature struck the ground, dying under the concentrated fire from the cannons. The vehicle lurched forward again, carrying Anjo further into the terrifying unknown.

Chapter 14

SHANNA wriggled uncomfortably out from under Storm's large bulk, and pushed Twister's long whiskers out of her face, twisting around to unfasten the tie-in from her harness. The night had been full of many half awakenings, and she felt unrested and heavy headed. The whiskers approached again, accompanied by a loud purr, as Twister butted her with his head, attempting to smooch into her for some patting. Storm rumbled slightly as she wriggled further out from under him, sighing as she lowered his head off her belly and onto her bedding. Apart from Allad who was on guard, no-one else was awake. The light was just starting to pale over the horizon, tinted in pale purples and mauves with a few hazy clouds far to the south, showing the remnants of the storm steadily dissipating. With a sigh, she finished wriggling out of her bedding, and walked quietly to the rock where Allad sat with Satin lying quietly beside him.

"Quiet night, Allad?" said Shanna settling herself beside him companionably as the sky lightened in front of them. Storm and Twister settled themselves at her feet, Twister starting to purr as she scratched him behind his large, violet tipped ears. Storm nudged her other hand to encourage her to stroke the soft silkiness of his head, lapsing into loud purring as his eyes slowly closed in ecstasy.

Allad nodded absently and smiled quietly, as pink streaks began to colour the horizon.

"And a beautiful morning." Around them birds began their early morning chorus, and the cliff side vegetation rustled here and there as small animals made their way unseen through it.

The tall Scout turned his head to regard Shanna.

"When we start descending, you'll be in country you're not really prepared for, you know, and you'll need to use every skill you've learned in the last two days to conceal yourself. Stick very close to me at all times, don't touch anything you don't recognise, and keep completely silent. I expect we'll be here on this ledge until we're joined by Barron and the others, so there's no hurry to get going. I suggest you use the time to hunt your cats and reorganise your pack. We're on breakfast today too, so when you've sent Storm and Twister out to hunt, you can begin on that." He turned his face back to the surrounding vegetation, and Shanna turned towards the other sleepers to begin her tasks. With a sudden thought she turned back towards Allad.

"Allad, how many times have you been below the plateau?" asked Shanna. Allad turned his head briefly to look at her, and then faced forward again.

"In the last few years, probably three times a year. Our patrol has been almost exclusively on exploration for five or so years. When this cyclone arrived, we'd been returned from Below for two weeks, and were planning to sit the storm season out before resuming our explorations, penetrating further south. In fact, prior to our return to exploration, it would have been our patrol's task to take your class on its first foray Below – that's part of our role as well. We're just a few months in advance…" He smiled again. "Don't worry too much, there's no way Spiron would be taking you below if we weren't completely sure that you'll cope. We've learnt a lot about the three of you in the last few days. It doesn't take long to assess a new cadet when you're in the bush."

"You've certainly been drilling us vigorously the whole time we've been out here." Shanna grinned at him. "I'm still nervous about what we'll encounter though."

"And that's one reason why we we're confident that you'll be at minimal risk with us Below. Another is your starcats. You've done an excellent job with them so far, and you have a remarkable relationship with the two of them. I'm very much looking forward to seeing what you and they are capable of in the future." Shanna blushed slightly. "And of course we'll be in a well explored area - not *safe* mind you - but well explored. There is a difference." His eyes twinkled.

"Thanks Allad. I'd better get on with breakfast now." She felt a bit awkward about hearing praise for something her family took for granted and began quietly preparing breakfast, glad of something to do with her hands. She sent Storm out to hunt first, while she began to resurrect the remains of the fire, coaxing the embers into life and then carefully feeding it with dry wood so as to minimise any smoke. Slowly the wood caught, and Shanna put a pot of porridge with dried fruit on the edge to simmer slowly for when the others awoke. Twister nudged her gently, reminding her that his belly was extremely empty, and she quieted him, whispering gently to him that he would be able to eat after his brother returned. He rumbled back at her, clearly indicating that Storm had better be quick about it, or suffer the consequences. Shanna had to stifle a giggle at the ever impatient starcat, and then went to the small spring near the rock face to refill her water bottles and then start heating water for tea.

Storm reappeared shortly thereafter, licking his whiskers clean with a large pink tongue, and looking extremely self satisfied. Shanna sent Twister off to hunt, and he was gone in a flash as Storm settled down to wash himself thoroughly. It always amused her to watch Storm wash, as he was extremely finicky, spending inordinate amounts of time smoothing his fur and washing between his toes. When the others woke, they spent the morning having a leisurely breakfast and stretching the kinks out from the previous day, secure in the knowledge that Barron and the others would be some time arriving. They all rechecked their packs, while the Scouts gave Ragar and Shanna tips on handy stowage of useful items and instructed them in the proper application of the scent concealing paste and coloured pigments. They also foraged in the immediate vicinity for edible and medicinal plant life, Shanna and Ragar attempting to demonstrate the knowledge they had accumulated so far, and the Scouts tutoring them to fill in the gaps. Compared to the last few days, it seemed almost pedestrian.

As mid morning approached, the starcats all paused, ears pricked, and Spiron called a halt to the foraging.

"That should be Barron and the others. Make sure your packs are ready to go as soon as they arrive. Ragar and Shanna, clean up the camp area."

They bustled quietly about, quickly finalising their preparations to move out as soon as the others arrived and making sure all the starcats had drunk at the small spring. Shortly they were able to hear the sound of people descending the plybrush ropes above them, and within a few moments, Barron, Verren, Challon and Amma arrived, followed a few moments later by five starcats, and then Nelson. All their packs were festooned with rope hanks.

"You've left the other two cadets and Karri and Arad at the top?" Spiron asked Barron.

"Yes, they're coming along well, but they still need a bit of time to progress to the point where I'd be happy for them to go Below, so I've left them to wait for whoever the council sends back with Perri; I suspect they'll arrive sometime in the next day or two." He opened his mouth to add something else, and then shook his head. Spiron looked questioningly at him, but Barron simply shook his head again. "I'll discuss a couple of things with you later. Now is not the time." He looked around the ledge, which terminated another fifty metres or so further to the west. "We've about another five hundred metres of rope with us. Hopefully it will be enough."

"OK then, we've another six or seven hours of useful light, so let's see how much further we can get in that time." Spiron led the way to the point he'd designated for the descent, and without further ado, began fixing the line.

The pattern of descent changed as they entered subtly different vegetation, which was slowly conforming to what the cadets gradually learnt would be the bush of Below. The whole operation became quieter and stealthier the further they descended. There were frequent pauses as one or other of the starcats would freeze mid stride, and then slink forwards, ears flicking and tails held low. When this happened the patrol would conceal themselves as best they were able, sliding into the shadows of rocks, disappearing into hollows on the ground, or vanishing into the vegetation. Shanna was again awed by the ease with which the Scouts disappeared, their movements so smooth and quiet that it was almost like watching a starcat fade. At one point, just after the second rope had been rigged, Spiron tapped Allad on the shoulder and whispered into his ear. There was a nod from Allad, a quick hand signal and Satin leapt onto the rope in front of the Patrol, descending in advance, followed quickly by Allad. From then on, the starcats descended first, the Scouts relying on their superior strength, stealth and senses to give advance warning of any dangers. The descent seemed to go on for hours, as the stops to conceal themselves became more frequent.

Immediately ahead of Shanna and Allad at the head of the column, Satin, Storm and Twister froze, Satin turning her head to Allad and blinking with more alarm than Shanna had ever seen the cat display. Automatically, Shanna and Allad slid into concealment into a depression slightly to the left of them. The three starcats, began moving completely noiselessly, and very slowly, paw by paw, fading themselves at each step until they were completely unseen. Allad signalled with one hand to the patrol and it vanished behind them. There was silence for some moments, as the three lead cats slunk noiselessly into the cliff side vegetation. Shanna waited, heart thumping, trying to breathe quietly and stay completely still, as up ahead there came a soft slithering sound. Allad placed one hand on her arm, then placed his mouth directly over her ear.

"Do not move. It's a swarm of sliders. Even if they crawl in here with us, you must stay perfectly still, and make no noise." Shanna's heart almost stopped beating, and she felt suddenly frozen, her mouth drying. Sliders were almost unknown on the plateau now. It had been one of the settlers' first acts, wisely or not, to attempt to eliminate the serpentine creatures. As a result, there had been an increase in the numbers of some of the larger predators which had in turn threatened the colony's survival, but the sliders were so inimical to the human population that hysteria overruled reason, and wherever they were found they were destroyed. Sliders were shiny, black, segmented, serpent like creatures, with an extremely nasty habit of burrowing into the bodies of other living creatures, where they would then lay their eggs, allowing them to hatch and then slowly consume the host, before exiting in a swarm to begin the cycle all over again. Their one weakness was that they were attracted only to moving prey, relying on highly developed antennae that could detect movement on the ground from a quite a distance. The slider swarm must have sensed the movement of the patrol from further down the side of the plateau, and then come hunting for them.

The slithering noise became louder and louder, and Shanna fancied she could hear the sliders undulating all over each other as the swarm came through the vegetation towards them. She tried hard not to think about Twister and Storm, hoping frantically that they had made themselves scarce and would lie low and unmoving. The slider noise became more and more pronounced, and the first of the sinister black creatures slid into view, shiny segments gleaming in the dappled sunlight piercing the vegetation around them. Completely still, next to Allad, Shanna attempted to control her breathing, keeping her chest movement to a minimum, furiously attempting to ignore the sweat prickling her forehead and remain motionless, eyelids slitted. The volume of sliders increased, thronging past the depression that Shanna and Allad huddled in, the noise of them sliding over each other increasing Shanna's heart rate with every second. A questing individual broke off from the main group, making a dry slithering noise as it nosed around the depression in the ground. Shanna held her breath as it twitched its antennae, and then made as if to enter the hollow, lowering the first two segments of its shiny body over the rim, before it abruptly changed direction and rejoined the swarm. She breathed again, attempting to draw the gasping breaths she needed very slowly and gently.

Minute after minute went by, as the slider swarm continued past them. The endless slithering noise rasped Shanna's nerves to raw edges, and she began to need to clamp down on a slowly rising scream. Just when she felt that she couldn't possibly hold on any more, the stream of sliders began to abate. There had been no noise at all from the others behind them, and after the sound of the sliders began to fade into the distance, Allad and Shanna stayed huddled in the depression. Shanna knew that it was essential to remain still for long enough that the swarm would be out of range before they moved, or the sliders would return in a flash. Long moments passed one by one, which allowed Shanna's upwelling scream to be slowly pushed back down. She continued to sweat heavily, the stinging droplets slowly tracking down her face and into her eyes as they remained in their cramped positions in the hollow in the ground. After what felt like an hour, Shanna was startled by a sudden warm breath in her left ear – she caught a shudder almost as it began. Fearing the worst she remained motionless, sweat pouring off her until Allad chuckled slightly.

"It's OK Shan, you can move now," said Allad. "That was Satin, seeing how tough you were. She loves her little jokes with cadets." Shanna let out her breath with a whoosh, attempting to ease her stiffened limbs from their cramped positions, reflecting wryly that Satin had a very strange sense of humour, and then beginning to worry about Storm and Twister who had not yet appeared. She staggered slightly as she regained her feet, assisted by Allad's hand, realising that she was desperately thirsty and looking around frantically for her two cats. They appeared with that almost instantaneous ability that starcats often demonstrated, arriving soundlessly, and rubbing their long supple bodies down her in an excess of loving relief.

"That was…" Shanna was speechless, and Allad rested one hand comfortingly on her shoulder.

"It's OK, you did well – we're all still alive." He smiled slightly grimly at her.

Shanna and Allad then began slowly moving back towards the rest of the patrol behind them, Shanna hoping fervently that everyone had survived the swarm. There was no movement visible, and Allad told Shanna to send her cats to seek the others. He gave a quick command to Satin, and she headed rapidly into the distance in the wake of the swarm. Shanna sent Storm down on the cliff face side, and Twister on the edge side of the route they had just taken, while they waited close to where they had last seen Spiron and Fury just behind them.

Spiron appeared shortly, Fury at his side, then waited silently with them as the other Scouts and cadets gradually appeared, reassured by the presence of the three lead starcats. Finally the whole patrol was assembled in a ring of starcats, secure in the fact that after the passage of the slider swarm most creatures would still be in hiding. Satin reappeared to sit quietly with Allad, looking up at him with her great violet eyes, ducking her head in silent communication.

Shanna noticed that she was not the only one needing to wipe away sweat, and Amma was trembling openly, Spider leaning comfortingly against her. Most of the normally imperturbable Scouts were pale, and several were drawing deep breaths. Spiron looked around the group of Scouts and cadets, resting his gaze on them, noting their reactions.

"Hopefully that's nothing you'll ever have to experience again, but if you do, you'll know exactly what to do, cadets, and knowing you've come out unscathed you'll do so again." He paused, and then went on. "Remember to rely on your starcat's senses, and always wait until they let you know that you're in the clear before moving. The swarm should continue until they find something else to consume, or until they die of starvation. We'll not be returning this way after we locate the artifact, so don't worry about having to encounter that particular swarm again."

"If we're not coming back this way, then how will we return?" asked Amma, her voice still a little squeaky. She cleared her throat nervously.

"We'll return via the Watchtower tunnel. Most cadets travel it in the other direction for their first time," he smiled. "But we'll make an exception for you four. When we locate the artifact, we'll send a starcat with a message after we've reconnoitred the situation. For now, let's get going as we've only a couple of hours of daylight left."

They recommenced their slow trek, finally reaching yet another sheer face. Far below, there was a glint of metal visible amongst the shattered vegetation, broken stubs of trees poking through the greenery.

"At last," breathed Nelson as he peered carefully over the edge. "I can see it quite clearly just directly below us. It's big." He leaned further into the safety rope attached to a sturdy tree a number of metres from the edge.

"Time to double rope this one, so we can pull the final rope, and make sure nothing can access the plateau behind us. We also need to make sure we descend well to one side, just in case there are any problems." Spiron's voice was brisk and businesslike. "We'll send two of the cats first, and then follow as fast and quietly as possible. "Kalli, you and Allad descend first, after your cats, and make sure there's nothing unexpected waiting below."

The descent was accomplished rapidly, the many prior descents having produced a seamless smooth teamwork. As the experienced Scouts spread out cautiously, sending their starcats out to range through the adjoining jungle, the four cadets stealthily retrieved the plybrush rope from the anchor above, hanking it neatly before Verren stowed it on the outside of his pack.

"Move into the staggered formation," said Spiron quietly, "Barron, take the point with Allad and Shanna. I want the extra starcats to range ahead. No-one is to approach the craft until we've spent some time observing it. Set the cats to work an overlapping pattern while we move."

They moved out quietly, dull mottled khaki uniforms and face paint allowing them to fade more easily into the multicoloured vegetation, with the starcats weaving around them silently. As they moved, Shanna realised that they had actually reached the bottom of the plateau, and were moving through what she had learned as a child to think about as "Below". The thought was chilling yet exciting at the same time, the encounter with the slider swarm tending to colour everything she was experiencing. Somehow, after feeling more fear than she had ever imagined to experience, she felt better about the dangers she was sure to encounter here Below. Allad motioned to her to skirt a large clump that she identified as a nasty skin irritant, prone to leaving large itching lumps anywhere its fronds contacted bare skin.

The closer they came to where the artifact lay, the more quiet the jungle became, until only low insect noises were left, and all other animal and bird noises had died away. As the first glints of metal became visible through the surrounding trees, the patrol fanned out in a half circle around the area. Allad sent Satin slinking hidden, towards it, and Shanna sent Storm to circle the debris, while Twister silently scaled a tree, and then she sent him from tree branch to tree branch to peer down on what appeared to be some kind of craft from above. Barron sent Hunter in the opposite direction to Storm, and the Scouts waited silently, unmoving, concealed behind tree trunks and bushy shrubs. After ten minutes of patient waiting, Spiron motioned Barron forward towards the craft. He moved almost invisibly towards the glinting metal, Hunter joining him silently as Storm returned to Shanna. Storm was curious, slightly on edge, and watching Barron and Hunter sharply as they moved forward. There was no sign of movement around the craft, and Barron hand signalled the others forward. They flitted silently from cover to cover, even the cadets beginning to move more certainly as a result of the constant practice.

The craft was now clearly visible, and there was a gaping hole evident in the side of it. Challon, Amma and Spiron set their cats to guard the rear as Barron approached the hole from one side, cautiously angling his head around the edge, then recoiling slightly as he viewed the interior of the craft. Hunter produced a muted sneeze as he poked his large head inside, but was not visibly perturbed. Barron then beckoned the others over, and they all peered cautiously into the hole. Directly in front of them, was a large, apparently insectoid creature, appendages locked around what appeared to be the lifeless controls of the craft. It was clearly not human and bore absolutely no resemblance to the descriptions of the spacefaring races with whom humanity had worked in partnership, prior to the accident that had landed the settlers on Frontier. It was also obviously dead.

"Well, that doesn't look at all like any of the races our ancestors described in their original texts." Allad said bluntly. "What do you think it is?"

"I have no idea," Barron replied, his eyebrows drawing together, and an expression of distaste crossing his tanned face, as an odour of pungent decay wafted from inside the craft. "However, there's no doubt that it's dead, and that we're going to have to transport it back to Watchtower."

Shanna and the other cadets grimaced at each other, the whole idea of the grisly task ahead causing her stomach to heave in revolted anticipation.

"It'll be dark shortly," said Spiron, glancing at the canopy above. "We need to find somewhere safe to camp close by, and then tomorrow we'll begin removing whatever it is from the craft before examining it. Both the craft and whatever's inside it are pretty badly damaged, but we'll need to make as many drawings of it and its interior as possible before we return to Watchtower." He squinted at the light which was steadily fading, and then gestured to the others to get moving. "Whatever it is, has been here for several days already, and nothing big's bothered it so far, so I think it'll be fine for the night – it's a bit odd, really – perhaps it isn't tasty to the local predators. Our priority is to set up a secure camp to work out of. Scout in pairs, and we'll locate something faster."

The patrol spread out in pairs, starcats circling and gliding, while the aircraft sat silently amongst the crushed vegetation, its dead pilot still grasping the useless controls.

***

Two hundred kilometres to the south, Anjo and Semba cowered inside the exploration vehicle. The Garsal crew had already suffered several losses – one from some kind of plant that ejected spines at a crew member, when he brushed past it, and another had simply vanished when they had paused the vehicle to re-orient the navigation equipment. He had been standing guard one moment and gone the next. There had been no noise, and no apparent movement that any of the other guards had noticed. The commander had pressed on however, attempting to locate any of the three aircraft lost in the cyclone, and any significant mineral deposits that could supply the raw materials needed to synthesise new flying craft or the interior of the hive. The need was urgent, and his orders had been definite. He was to locate what was needed or perish in the attempt. He had no doubts he would succeed. The Garsal always succeeded. There was nothing else to consider.

Apart from a few troops detailed to be on watch from inside the vehicle, all the others were sleeping in their pod capsules. Anjo and Semba huddled together in one corner of the vehicle, knowing they would have to rise early to prepare the morning meal, and to anticipate any needs of the troop commander. They had learned early on that he would tolerate no slowness or hesitation. He expected to be obeyed instantly, and perfectly.

Now that they were outside the secure area, Anjo's fear increased. He and Semba were living one long, never ending nightmare.

Chapter 15

KAIDAN nocked the arrow, then drew and released in one smooth movement. It thudded home in the target that he had crept up on during the field exercise, then he immediately dropped out of sight and proceeded to navigate his way rapidly to the next one marked on the map. The exercise was in a patch of forest just outside Watchtower, which was sandwiched between the town and three other satellite settlements. He knew one of the Scout patrols had been through recently to confirm that no really dangerous predators had migrated in during the cyclone, but after the recent encounter with the staureg the back of his neck still prickled when he heard a strange sound in the bushes. It amused him that Shanna may have been part of the patrol that had investigated this area, as when enquiring about her whereabouts at Scout Compound he had simply been told that she was on post cyclone duties and had been temporarily attached to one of the Patrols. He was still calling at the Compound every couple of days to check on when she might be back.

He jerked his attention back to the job on hand. This was his first field exercise with the school archery team and he wanted to do well, and he really wanted to finish in the top rankings. There would be points awarded for accuracy, undetected movement and also speed, with a bonus for finishing ahead of the student behind him or in front of the student ahead. He knew he was an above average navigator, however the whole thing about being alone in even a relatively docile forested area kept distracting him from what he was doing. Ducking behind a large pardanus tree, he paused to check his bearings and calculate how far he should be from the next target. Reorientating himself, he realised that he was within one hundred metres of it, and that it was likely to be within view of the naked eye. He rechecked his bearing, and then stealthily peered out from behind his tree. Sure enough, the target was there, an orange splash of paint on another pardanus tree, dead ahead. Reminding himself that there would be extra points for speed, he unlimbered his bow, took a swift step out of cover, and aimed and fired in that same smooth movement. He disappeared behind the adjacent tree, hearing the solid "thunk" of his arrow embedding itself in the target. Quickly checking the map, he paused to listen for other competitors and then began to weave his way through the vegetation, flicking his gaze from side to side in an effort to avoid detection, and catch any other students out.

Behind him, he heard another "thunk" as a second arrow impacted the target he'd just left, and he picked up his pace, almost jogging, while rechecking his bearing. There was no way he was going to be passed by someone else. Only one target to go, and then a simple navigation back to the start point. The trees rustled behind him and he started slightly, the imprinted vision of the staureg replaying itself in his mind. Ruthlessly he pushed that thought back down and continued on, holding his course. He'd decided to take a risk in the interests of speed, and head straight into the target, relying on his pacing to be accurate, rather than pause, conceal himself, and suffer the risk that someone else might pass him. He sighted the small target directly ahead, increased his pace, and shot his arrow while on the run, continuing forward after he'd fired, diving into cover at the very base of the target, his arrow with its characteristic blue and violet fletching quivering above him.

Again he withdrew the map from his thigh pocket, and crouching, took his bearing, then set off at a stealthy run through the bush. He navigated uneventfully, and as the start became visible through the trees, threw caution to the winds and broke into a sprint. Just as he cleared the trees, he heard just the slightest sound, before a large body thudded into him, knocking him completely to the ground. He came up spitting dirt, raising his face into a smug bewhiskered visage.

"Socks! What are you doing?" Kaidan struggled to sit up, but was shoved back down firmly by a large paw. Socks then sat on him. "I've got to finish, let me go."

There was an amused laugh from behind Socks. Struggling to see who was laughing at him, Kaidan attempted again to get up from under the heavy starcat. Despite years of shoving starcats off his bed he was not successful, as Socks seemed to read his mind, and adjusted her weight appropriately as he wriggled from side to side.

"Come on Socks, hop off!" Kaidan was really past appreciating the big cat's sense of humour at this point. It was important that he finish the task and achieve maximum points, and every second he was pinned to the ground, was a second that counted against him.

"You've finished for now young man." Incredibly, the voice appeared to be Master Cerren's. Kaidan was slightly confused, as he realised that Socks would hardly be here without her human partner, but he had no idea why Master Cerren would take it upon himself to spectate so early in the morning at a field archery trial, and he had absolutely no idea why Socks was sitting on him.

"What? Sir? Finished? No I haven't, I'm not quite back at the start yet..." Kaidan trailed off as he began to understand that he probably wasn't going to complete the course, as Socks remained sitting on him, her weight becoming more and more uncomfortable as she shifted to wash first one side of her face, then the other. She seemed to be more amused by the second. He could hear a hint of a purr, and feel the vibration through Socks' feet.

"Yes, quite finished for now." Master Cerren moved into Kaidan's field of view, surprisingly clad in the mottled clothing of the Scout Corps, which made things all the more confusing for Kaidan. Without his scholar's robes he moved somehow differently, with a silent grace that was oddly deadly, given his cheerful nature. "You and I have a couple of things to discuss, young man." His tone was sober, and Kaidan felt a dawning realisation that the next few moments were probably not going to be the words of praise he had imagined after finishing the field course. Socks made herself more comfortable on his middle, draping her whole body over him, as Master Cerren seated himself on a convenient stump.

"Well, that was a very fast navigation around the course." Kaidan opened his mouth to reply, but was waved silent. "However," Cerren paused as if gathering his words carefully, "If there had been a predator loose in there with you, you'd be very, very dead. I followed you around the complete course." Kaidan's heart sank; this sounded very much like the beginning of one of his mother's lectures. He had been focussing more on speed and accuracy, and only paying lip service to the need for stealth and secrecy, reasoning (despite the ever present staureg image in his mind) that there would be nothing in the bush that could pose a threat he couldn't overcome with his bow, and that no-one was going to let any student be injured. Obviously he had been wrong.

"It was no trouble at all for Socks and I to track you, as you left a wake like a staureg. Every time you fired your bow, you were fully visible from the point of view of the target. We could have tracked you by sound alone in fact, if we'd wanted to. And you travelled in a direct line between targets, with no suggestion of concealment, or stalking up on something from a different angle." Master Cerren paused here, cleared his throat and went on, as Kaidan started to feel the red tide of a blush rising from his toes and begin to head for his face. "You are an excellent navigator, Kaidan, it would have been child's play for you to take an indirect route and be more creative about working your way through the course. Why didn't you?"

Kaidan realised he was expected to answer this question, and opened his mouth then shut it again, realising he didn't really want to admit that he'd wanted to show off, getting round the course faster than anyone had ever managed on their first try. Cerren cleared his throat noisily. "I'm waiting young man."

"Yes, Sir." Kaidan realised that the Master already knew why Kaidan had been ignoring the need for stealth, but it didn't help that he was going to have to say it out loud. "I was trying to break the speed record for first time field course participants, Sir." As he finished this agonising statement in almost a whisper, the blush hit his face like a tidal wave.

"Well, today you'll finish last. You will be awarded no points, because if you had taken this test in any wilderness area but this safe preserve, you would probably have been at the very least severely injured, if not dead. I would not relish being the one to take the news of your demise to your parents. Today, you're in an archery team, but what you do here with that bow isn't just for fun. One day, your life and the lives of your fellows may depend upon you. You must leave behind the desire for personal glory and put the needs of your society ahead of your own. What we're doing here is deadly serious. You left games behind when you moved into this specialised course. You may only be thirteen, but with great gifts come great responsibilities, and you must assume some of those responsibilities." Master Cerren's eyebrows were drawn together as he frowned down at Kaidan, "You and I and Socks will now repeat the course. You'll be following me, and you'll need to work hard to keep up and keep hidden." Kaidan was surprised at the change in his generally genial teacher, and was having difficulty reconciling this new aspect of Master Cerren with his previous experiences.

"Yes, Sir." Anyway, how difficult could it be to keep up with someone the age of Master Cerren? "Ummmm.... I'll need Socks to move before I can get up." Socks pricked her ears, and leaned a little heavier on Kaidan's middle. Master Cerren watched, the first signs of amusement glinting in his eyes.

"She's such a lovely starcat, my Socks. She reads my mind. Your family breeds wonderful cats." He smiled slightly, "Socks, leave him." The large starcat slowly heaved herself to her feet, then making sure that each paw landed on Kaidan's abdomen, strolled off him and over to her partner, to receive her due caress. Kaidan drew a large breath, rolled over and pushed himself up onto his feet, making sure his bow was not damaged, and that he had adequate arrows in his hip quiver.

"All right, young man, let's see if you can keep up." Master Cerren called Socks to heel, and then began to stride into the trees. As they thickened, Kaidan hastened to follow, suddenly realising the elderly Master had subtly accelerated and had begun to weave smoothly and silently through the trees, appearing to vanish as Kaidan hurried after. He stopped, looking around perplexed then checked his map, oriented himself, and then decided to remember what the master had said and act upon it. He set off, attempting to emulate Cerren's smooth gliding walk. Sliding behind a tree, he almost fell over Socks, who gave him a whack with a paw that staggered him.

"Do try and keep up with me, Kaidan." Master Cerren stood, hands on hips watching Kaidan attempt to regain his balance. He turned, adopted his gliding movement, and vanished into the thickening brush. Kaidan again followed, attempting to copy the smooth movement of the aged Master.

"Oh, and there are two other students and Masters out here right now. They will be attempting to catch us, and will signal that they've found us by shooting an arrow into a tree above your head. Mind you, if we find them, you can do the honours." With this matter of fact but somewhat surprising statement, he moved onwards.

Kaidan was pushed to the limit trying to keep up with the seemingly inexhaustible Master, attempting to remain hidden while trying to move quickly, and then remembering that he was expected to be able to accurately strike a target while remaining completely hidden. He became sweat soaked, covered in scratches and mud, and finally quivering with exhaustion. Master Cerren seemed to manage to move with no real effort, occasionally stopping to allow Kaidan to catch his breath, while Socks amused herself by popping up unexpectedly to breathe heavily in his ear just when he was most tense. He almost exploded at one point when she appeared, dangling her head, upside down from an overhead branch. Unfortunately this episode also coincided with the sudden "thunk" of an arrow in the tree trunk above his head. Kaidan sighed heavily, but gritted his teeth and continued in Master Cerren's wake, heading for the second last target, which they snuck up on from the side, Kaidan having to then shoot at it from a very oblique angle. As his arrow struck the target, his attention was suddenly diverted by a glimpse of something moving through the vegetation on the other side of the target. He paused, looked hard, and managed to discern the outline of another archer through the vegetation. He nocked another arrow, sighted carefully and sent the arrow to slam into the tree behind the other archer, just above head height. Master Cerren placed a hand on his arm, indicated his approval and beckoned Kaidan on. He followed the Master, glad there was only one more target to go, as he was more tired than he had ever been in his life.

Twenty minutes of stealthy concentrated movement later, and he sent the final arrow thudding into the target, then attempted to force his exhausted body after Master Cerren on the homeward run. As they arrived back at the start of the course, Kaidan stumbled to a halt and bent over, propping his hands on his legs. He was sweating, gasping, trembling, filthy, and covered with scratches and abrasions. Socks eyed him with some humour, then slid her long length luxuriously along his exhausted body, tidemarks flickering with amusement as he staggered slightly off balance.

"Better... better, young man; a pity about being spotted out there, however, nice shooting when you spied the other archer at the second last target," said Master Cerren, with a proportion of his normal twinkle returning to his eyes, "Now go back into the Records Precinct and take a long hot bath. You're excused from classes until after the noon meal. I expect to see you prior to then in my office. We have a few things to discuss." He strolled off completely relaxed, all his clothes in neat order and not a hair out of place. Socks strolled next to him, occasionally butting his hand with her large head, tidemarks glowing softly.

Kaidan walked his hands up his legs, straightening with some difficulty, and staggered off, slowly unstringing his bow and sliding it back into its cover before slinging it across his back. The hot water was extremely enticing, and he was thoroughly chastened by the Master's effortless display of woodcraft. There was definitely a lot more for him to learn.

***

At the downed aircraft, Shanna had been set to guard the perimeter with Allad, sending her starcats in ever changing patterns around the ship and the encampment. As the more experienced Scouts performed the grisly task of removing the dead pilot's corpse from the control seat of the craft, Allad continued her education about the creatures and plants below and quietly quizzed her about topics they had covered on previous days.

As Verren and Nelson finished weaving a stretcher envelope for the corpse, she recalled Storm and Twister before once again sending them out on a complex weaving pattern through the trees. Satin sat and watched her as she interacted with her cats, ducking her head as if in approval, occasionally glancing towards Allad.

***

In the exploration vehicle, Anjo sweated over the commander's noon meal as Semba tidied and cleaned the sleeping pods. At a guttural command, they dropped prostrate on the floor and the commander swept through, collecting his food along the way then seating himself in the forward cabin of the vehicle. It lurched suddenly into motion, as a roar sounded from outside and the vehicle shuddered under an impact from whatever nightmare had chosen to attack them this time. Progress would again be slowed, as another roar sounded from in front of them and the vehicle shook under the concussive force of the weapons firing.

Chapter 16

SHANNA heaved her end of the stretcher up as the patrol made its first change of bearers, and she and Allad took over from the heavily sweating and rapidly breathing Verren and Nelson. The sweat had made run marks through the paint on Verren's face. Spiron held a hand up and the patrol paused, listening, as he pointed slightly off to the right. There was a loud crunching of vegetation clearly audible, and Fury was sniffing the air with some distaste. Another quick hand signal and the patrol faded as fast and quietly as possible into the thick undergrowth, Shanna attempting to manoeuvre her end of the stretcher quietly, wondering whether the smell of the decomposing corpse was attracting a predator, while leaves and thin branches seemed to twine themselves around the roughly cut poles.

They had left the downed aircraft earlier that morning after two days of thorough investigation. Nelson had made detailed sketches of the interior and then the patrol had camouflaged it with undergrowth, covering as much of it as possible in order to preserve the machine for further investigation. Each of the patrol carried as much of the loose equipment and items found inside the aircraft as possible. The previous day, Spiron had directed Barron to dispatch Hunter with a message for the guards who manned the subterranean access to the plateau, to update the Council with the latest details.

Depositing the stretcher on the ground, Shanna and Allad made sure the woven covering was blending in well with the surrounding greenery and then concealed themselves quickly. Well accustomed now to the patrol's routines, Shanna then sent Twister up the nearest tree, and Storm arrowing out with Satin to check on the source of the noise. Both Satin and Storm faded completely into the vegetation, and Twister began moving agilely from tree branch to tree branch above their heads.

Fury returned, and Spiron murmured quietly in a just audible tone. "It looks like a staureg."

Shanna's mind was suddenly full of the memories of the staureg on her parents' property, its long tail swinging threateningly and its slashing claws and teeth scything through the air.

"Let the cats see if they can head it off. Allad, let Satin direct." He, Challon and Sandar were unlimbering small bows cased on the outsides of their packs. Nelson, Barron and Allad all had their knives in their hands, and motioned for the cadets to do the same. "If not, then we'll have to deal with it. I'd rather not though, as it's not doing any harm at this point and something that big and dead will attract more smaller carnivores into the area."

The crashing grew louder, and Shanna began to have glimpses of the staureg's hide through the trees, then the telltale signs of starcat tidemarks began glowing from all around it. Nine of the ten large cats were circling the huge reptile on the ground while the tenth, Twister, was leaping from branch to branch and then suddenly onto the staureg's back, digging his sharp claws in briefly before leaping back into the trees. The staureg bellowed and changed direction, the starcats under Satin's direction leaping and circling to push it away from the patrol. Twister sprang again as Satin hummed, appearing from a different direction as the other cats continued to drive it onwards. It moved to the south of the patrol, intermittently snarling and roaring at the circling cats. At Satin's command, Twister sprang again onto its haunches from above, slicing his foreclaws into the tough scaly skin. The large beast began to gain speed, obviously desiring to put a substantial distance between itself and the needling starcats, and gradually disappeared through the trees. Five minutes of quiet waiting later, the first of the starcats reappeared by its partner's side, followed quickly thereafter by the rest. Twister gave Shanna a horrible shock by dropping out of the tree above her, landing silently and immediately in front of her. He was looking rather pleased with himself, lazily picking a few of the staureg's slightly tattered scales from his claws. Storm smooched her leg apologetically, sniffing in disgust at his brother before circling off to his guard position.

"All right, let's move on."

Shanna hoisted her end of the stretcher. Whatever unknown species the pilot was, it was very heavy. Being so much shorter than Allad made the carry awkward, but she was determined to do her part of the job ahead as she knew that the entrance to the plateau access was still many hours away and that the whole patrol would be rotating as carriers. Soon she was sweating as heavily as Verren and Nelson had, and the rough wood of the poles had become uncomfortable even through gloves. Shanna had also discovered that attempting to glide noiselessly through thick undergrowth and around massive trees while carrying a stretcher was extraordinarily difficult. Her arms began to ache and her legs to tremble, after what seemed a very short time. Sweat kept dripping in her eyes and she had to keep shaking her head to try and clear her sight, and her braids were beginning to tickle and wisp. Fortunately Allad had the front, so she just followed her end of the stretcher. She couldn't imagine attempting to steer in her state of trembling exhaustion. Just when she felt like dropping the horrible, heavy thing, Spiron signalled another change of bearers.

As she handed over to Ragar and Sandar, Hunter appeared abruptly beside Barron, a note attached to his harness. Shanna took the opportunity to take a quick swig from her water bottle, pushing her braids back over her shoulders, and the wispy bits of hair out of her eyes, using the sleeve of her shirt to blot the sweat. As she did, her legs slowly ceased their trembling.

"They've received our message, and will be waiting for us at the entrance – usual signal. They'll also send for two more patrols as you requested, and have forwarded our information to the Council." Barron rubbed his hands down Hunter's sleek sides as the cat purred gently.

"Excellent news. Now all we have to do is to get all this lot safely to the entrance." Spiron was very pleased and moved the patrol on with alacrity, sending Barron out with Hunter to take the point.

The rest of the trip went relatively smoothly, with only a few encounters with some of Below's more interesting wildlife, none as large as the staureg, but all dangerous in their own right. When they were not heaving the stretcher containing the corpse, Allad continued to quietly lecture and test Shanna on all the flora and fauna they encountered.

"Look at this Shanna, see how the underneath of this leaf is covered in fine hairs? We don't get this particular species on the plateau, but it's a relative of the frondan tree – see how the shape of the leaf is the same? The hairs are the problem though, brush against them and you'll itch for a week." Shanna committed the strange stumpy looking plant to memory, as she had absolutely no wish to itch for a week. "Mind you, it's pretty useful – you can scrape the hairs off the leaf and then if you have a convenient pitcher plant around, tip them into the cup, and use it later to throw at something you'd rather not have chasing you – and that'll distract them nicely." He grinned, and Shanna was tempted to ask when he'd had to use that particular trick. She tucked the thought away for a more suitable moment and bent her mind to the matter on hand.

"How do you store it?" The idea of something like those hairs loose inside her pack with her spare clothing almost set her itching just thinking about it.

"Oh, you just snap the lid of the pitcher plant over, and the sap seals it nicely – but do check before you put it anywhere near your gear." Allad smiled reminiscently, "One of the cadets from our last group tried that, but didn't check – she was bright red within seconds of donning her wet weather gear.......took ages for the itches to go." Shanna's shoulder blades began to twitch immediately at the thought.

Sometime after Shanna's second shift on the stretcher, Spiron brought the patrol to a halt, directing them to place the stretcher on two convenient rocks while the rest of the patrol drank from water bottles or stretched tired arms and legs, rechecking packs and attending to their starcats. He then strolled over to the adjacent cliff face and used a small rock to tap a complicated rhythm on a protruding portion. Shanna, Verren, Ragar and Amma watched in amazement as a dark hole appeared next to him, and a face peered out at them.

"Hello Spiron, Barron, good to see you again! And I see you've not managed to lose any of your cadets either – always a good thing!" The tall smiling woman beckoned them to move inside the dark hole in the cliff face. "We need to get this shut down as fast as possible as there's little daylight left, and we've had a few unwanted guests wandering around since the storm." She moved aside to allow Amma and Challon to move the stretcher inside. "I take it you have something interesting on there." She wrinkled her nose.

As the patrol and the weary cadets filed through into the rocky interior, Spiron nodded. "Interesting is probably an understatement but we won't open the cocoon, it's pretty decayed and you may not like the odour in such an enclosed space. It's bad enough packaged as it is!" Spiron smiled to show that he was serious and not just fobbing her off. "Cadets, this is Feeny. She's also a Scout, but currently attached to the Gate Guard, as her cat, Gem, is about to give birth to her cubs. If you're between cats, or you have one with a litter, then you'll either be attached to Scout Compound as a teacher, on the Gate Guard, or be pursuing further studies. Some of you may even attain the lofty rank of "Master" one day, and be on the Council." Feeny gave a small whistle, and a very pregnant, deep grey, violet tidemarked starcat appeared from a doorway showing warm cheerful light. Behind the rearguard, the counterweighted Cliffside door closed.

The gate area was simply that, an interconnecting series of chambers around the main gate chamber, and a dimly lit tunnel ascending behind it. Shanna gave a sigh as she realised that even with the lack of inimical wildlife inside the tunnel there would still be a long trek back up to the plateau. Up until that moment, she hadn't thought about the homeward trip.

"Leave the stretcher in the second chamber, and then you can all proceed through decontamination," said Feeny. "You'll find Damar waiting for you inside, and he'll have fresh clothing for you. He'll run the cadets through the drill and show them what to do with their cats."

They passed through two chambers, Amma and Challon thankfully depositing the heavy stretcher on a side bench in the second one and then walked into another cheerfully lit room. An older Scout waited for them there, greeting them warmly.

"You can go through into the baths if you want, Spiron, I'll tend to the cadets."

"Thanks Damar, we appreciate that." Spiron and the other Scouts collected neat piles of clothing from niches set into the walls, and then, gathering large towels, and calling their starcats after them, vanished into what appeared to be two bathing rooms.

Damar placed his hands on his hips and regarded the four cadets sternly. "All right you four. Before ascending to the plateau, you need to decontaminate, to make sure that you don't bring any unwanted vegetation or wildlife back with you. You'll also need to decontaminate your starcats."

"What kind of decontamination are we talking about here?" Amma was clearly puzzled.

"You may have seeds attached to your clothing, bugs in your personal belongings or various parasites that you've picked up without noticing. Your studies have already shown to you that life on Frontier has changed many of the animals and plants that came with our original colony ship, well beyond their original forms." The cadets nodded. "Well, the only reason we haven't changed as much as some of them, is because we've kept ourselves isolated and protected. The wildlife on Frontier as you know, is very fond of merging with other genetic pools through a combination of symbiosis and parasitism. This is the only way we know of trying to keep our changes to a minimum. So far, in three hundred years, we've managed to keep the changes only minor – and nearly all those changes seem to be beneficial – we're taller, stronger, and faster than our forbears and we've developed empathy with some living things – starcats being the most obvious. But you've probably all met people who are a bit more different – you know what I mean – the ones who have extra toes or fingers, or who need to hibernate for part of the storm season." The cadets nodded, those people weren't talked about very much,. "As Scouts, you're much more at risk of collecting something that provokes that kind of change, as you'll move around Below during your careers and will be constantly in contact with Frontier's native wildlife. Most of the changes on the plateau seem to have been stable for the last hundred or so years, but there is still the odd change occurring, usually within those of us in the Scout Corps, and the only thing we can put it down to is our encounters with the life here Below. Occasionally we bring back a new parasite – there's a theory that they act as carriers of a viral vector for change."

That was not something that the Scout Corps had mentioned on entry. Shanna noticed the others looked more than a little dismayed at this information.

"Don't worry too much – that's why we decontaminate, and nothing drastic's occurred for years now. Have you noticed any extra arms or legs in Patrol Ten? No? Well don't worry, just follow what I tell you." Damar grinned with complete unconcern at their facial expressions and handed each cadet a large towel, directing them to the niches to select appropriately sized clothing. With an inward sigh, Shanna realised hers would again probably be too large and that she'd have to roll up the excess.

"Now, men to the right and women to the left and you'll find the baths. Empty your packs first, and then spray them with the green bottles. Sort out any clothing that you've worn and place it in the green bins. It'll be returned to you washed. Open, shake, and empty any other containers or pieces of unworn clothing and spray all of that with the green bottles too. Immerse yourselves fully after removing your current clothing. Check each others' hair for any insects, parasites or vegetation and wash it thoroughly with the soap provided. Check all body creases, and make sure you've not carted in any passengers. Encourage your starcats to hop in and bathe too, then go over them completely, making sure that nothing is attached to their coats or in their ears. Don't forget to check between their pads."

This last made Shanna smile, as she knew that the cats would relish all the attention and adored bathing. She mentally prepared herself for constant dunkings and shakings, and grinned at Damar as he mentioned that last bit.

"When you get out, spray your hair and your starcat with the blue bottle." Damar paused, and then counted the cats. "We seem to have an extra here..."

"I have two." Shanna decided to keep the explanations to a minimum. Damar raised his eyebrows and then as Shanna remained smilingly silent, visibly decided that it would be better if they just got on with the decontamination.

"You can tell me why during dinner, then. Off you go." He indicated the steamy doorways.

Shanna and Amma, with Spider, Twister and Storm, entered the steamy room as indicated while Verren and Ragar walked towards the other one. Deciding that it would be easier to get the worst of the starcat splashing out of the way before she and Amma hopped into the large warm pool, Shanna told Storm and Twister to go and bathe. They complied eagerly, sending fountains of water up into the air as they leapt into the pool. Amma sent Spider in after them, and the two young women emptied their packs companionably on a low bench near one of the green bins.

"Well, that was a trip and a half, not quite what I expected after a storm," said Amma as she removed socks and underwear from her pack, dropping them into the green bin. "What do you think will happen next?"

"I don't know, but I'm sure that there'll be more patrols sent out, looking for whoever or whatever sent that craft. What do you think that thing was?" Shanna was not sure if she could refer to the black insectoid creature, as a person. "I mean, I've learnt heaps on this trip, but finding an alien species wasn't exactly what I was expecting – and this could change absolutely everything for everyone!" It was a relief to be able to speak in normal tones to someone who had been thinking the same things and puzzling over the same questions. The older girl nodded soberly, as she began to spray down her pack and belongings. Loud splashing and hums of delight sounded from the warm pool behind them.

"I have no idea what that thing is, but it has to be intelligent, because it was flying that thing we found." Amma pulled the final bits of her gear out of the pack and picked up one of the spray bottles. "I really don't know what to think at the moment. I expect we'll simply get back into the regular training program when we're back up on the plateau. We probably won't hear another thing about it, I expect – not at our lowly cadet level." She smiled. "I had no idea really about the nitty gritty of what Scouts actually did when I applied to join the Corps. It always seemed to be great that I might be one of the elite, but there's a lot of grubbiness to the eliteness." Amma pushed dirty, curling black hair out of her face, brows quirked over her brown eyes and a wry smile twisting her lips. "The longer I've been with Patrol Ten, the more I've realised I didn't know. Were your first couple of days a constant quiz?" She smiled wryly as Shanna nodded, and began to disrobe, chucking her dirty clothing into the bin.

"They made us navigate without telling us if we were going wrong for two days as well! *And* we had to eat Verren's cooking one night...!" Amma grimaced, and then shared a grin with Shanna, making a retching noise.

Shanna finished removing her clothes and walked to the steps of the pool, testing the water temperature with one foot; fortunately the worst of the exuberance in the water appeared to be over.

"Hey Shan, you've got a glowstone!" Amma pointed to the blue stone glowing gently on its chain around Shanna's neck as she pulled off a dirty sock.

"It was my mother's – she gave it to me after the storm." As Amma removed her shirt, Shanna was surprised to see another glowstone glimmering around Amma's neck.

"Mine was Dad's, he gave it to me when I was accepted into the Corps." They smiled companionably, and Shanna realised that she was chatting to Amma easily for the first time since their class had been formed, and felt more relaxed that she had finally found the beginnings of a friendship as a result of their shared experiences.

"You know, I don't ever want to meet a slider swarm again." Amma's voice shook slightly as she slipped into the water and submerging up to her neck.

"Me neither, but at least we know that we can actually survive one." Shanna felt cold despite the heat of the water, as she relived those moments of motionless fear. They shared another companionable yet relieved glance, and the fear of the moment was broken as Storm surfaced next to Shanna with a loud hum, spraying water all over her. She grabbed the soap, and began to scrub her greasy, dirty hair. After washing thoroughly, they checked each other for passengers, with both of them finding a number of insects in the other's hair, and carefully discarded them into a container at the edge of the pool. The starcats thoroughly enjoyed the attention of being checked from head to toe, humming and purring as the two girls ran their hands all over the big dark bodies, tidemarks gleaming with pleasure.

After finally heaving their water wrinkled bodies out of the pool they proceeded to spray the cats and their own hair with the blue bottle, all five of them sneezing at the fresh but slightly medicinal smell the spray exuded. Finally dressed, they exited through the far door, packs bumping behind them and damp hair carefully braided back.

There was a hot meal on a large table waiting for them and the patrol spent the next hour filling Feeny and Damar in on their find, while intermittently stirring Verren about his cooking skills, advising him to listen carefully to any tips Feeny and Damar might choose to give. The starcats draped themselves comfortably on the large cushions placed conveniently about the room.

"You've not noticed or heard anything out of the ordinary since the storm?" Barron asked Damar and Feeny. Feeny shook her head. From what you've told us, we'll be needing to double the patrols though."

She looked at Damar who nodded. "I'll set up the extra living quarters after we've finished eating."

"We'll set out for the top in another hour or so, after the cats have fed," Spiron said. "We'll use the trolley to take the corpse up, but do you have one of those airtight crates to transport it in until we can get it to Healers Precinct? Wish it was light enough to send on the message lift." Spiron was keen to finish his patrol's task as soon as possible.

"Already done," replied Feeny. "Damar and I did it while you were bathing. This has enormous implications doesn't it?" She paused and voiced the constant thought, "Maybe we've finally been found?"

"But by whom?" Allad said. There was a long period of silence before the Patrol stirred themselves to start the ascent of the tunnel.

***

It had been a long, slow day. The exploration team had spent hour after hour digging the vehicle out of bogs, felling trees with the energy weapons, and repelling a wide variety of inimical wildlife. At times, Anjo and Semba had been pressed into service to assist with the most awkward tasks, passing chains under rotting logs and trying to place vegetation mats under the vehicle's mud mired wheels. They were terrified, exhausted and filthy. Semba was clutching her right arm to her chest, a large red lump increasing rapidly in size, after she had brushed a broadleafed plant while attempting to heave a chain around a tree trunk. She was moaning as the redness spread, complaining of an unbearable itching. Anjo hurried to her aid, noting a number of fine hairs protruding from the lump.

"We need to get those out." He pulled her back into the relative safety of the vehicle, prostrating himself and begging permission from the guard on duty to access medical supplies. Fortunately, the commander had recognised that if he killed his slaves by preventing them from doctoring small hurts, he would be deprived of his creature comforts, so the guard merely waved them towards the appropriate cabinet. Locating a pair of fine tweezers, Anjo removed the hairs, and then gave Semba a large dose of antihistamine; she sighed in relief. He regarded the hairs thoughtfully, and then packaged them carefully in a small sample container from the medical kit, concealing it furtively inside his ragged clothing.

"Can you remember what plant it was?" he queried Semba quietly. She nodded uncertainly, as he smiled slightly in what seemed the first hopeful moment for months. "We need more of these, but we need to figure out how to collect them without having a reaction ourselves. Keep an eye on the Garsal – we need to find out if they react like us."

He dropped his eyes hurriedly as the commander strode in, dropping to the floor in the customary abasement, Semba beside him. "Feed us. Now." They hurried to obey as the vehicle was locked down for the night.

Chapter 17

IT seemed to Shanna that she'd been walking in partial darkness for an eternity. Occasionally one or other of her starcats would brush against her leg or her hand, as the patrol moved higher and higher inside the plateau's subterranean access. Every couple of hours or so, she would take her turn at pushing the trolley on which the stretcher containing the corpse rested. There had been a few pauses in rest areas while the Patrol had slept for an hour or two before resuming the relentless climb. Shanna's best calculations suggested that they had been walking upward for close to thirty six hours. The access tunnel was set at a fairly regular slope, carved with smooth stone walls in places and in other areas the builders had taken advantage of natural cave formations, and the walls were of rugged stone. The constant upwards movement was placing quite a bit of strain on her legs. She could feel her calf and thigh muscles beginning to fatigue and burn and gradually tighten with the constant upward grade, and her brain felt hazy with exhaustion. She hoped she wasn't weaving as she walked.

"Will we be transporting the corpse to the Healers Precinct?" Shanna asked Allad, talking partly to try and keep herself alert.

"No, we should be met at the top by a group from there, and we'll simply give them the corpse and then go straight to Scout Compound for debriefing," replied Allad.

There was a slight pause as they continued upwards. Then Shanna was compelled to ask the question foremost in her mind for the better part of the dark journey. "Will you be going straight out again?"

Allad considered the question as they rounded a turn. "I'm not sure. We'll be debriefed fairly thoroughly, which you will also be involved in I might add, and then it will be up to the Council to decide whether they send our patrol out again, or a different one. We'll need a few days rest whatever they decide." He grinned, teeth glinting in the semi darkness, "And you look like you'll need about a week. By the time we're debriefed, the other two patrols they sent for will have been examining the artifact for a few days. I expect that they'll be escorting some of the other specialists and guarding them, rather than actually heading the investigation. Our expertise as Scouts is much more linked to the world of living things than two downed artifacts." He grinned and gave her a light rap on the shoulder. "Are you looking to go back down Below with us?"

"I don't think that's going to happen anytime soon, but I'm really glad we got to go this time! I think I know what you were trying to tell me when I asked you about Below that first time now." She smiled regretfully. The time Below had been full of tension and had been the most frightening thing she'd ever done, yet it had been strangely fulfilling. And although every trip would be perilous, she looked forward to exploring the most amazing landscape she'd ever experienced. She firmly placed the thoughts of being changed physically by the experiences to the back of her mind.

There was a long time of silent walking then, until there was the sound of multiple pairs of feet from up ahead. Into view came two full Patrols of Scouts, and a number of men and women accoutred for travel Below who were very obviously not Scouts. It wasn't simply the fact that most of them were not accompanied by starcats, but the way they moved that made them stand out as different. Shanna had become so accustomed to the smooth gliding walk of the Patrol she had been travelling with for so many days, that the lack of grace stood out like a large pimple on otherwise smooth skin. She also noticed that all of the Scouts carried some kind of weapon. Keeping such a contingent of people who were so obviously unsuited to wilderness travel would be a difficult prospect, even for the highly skilled Scouts. The cadets might have been inexperienced, but they were at least partially trained, and accustomed to a high level of physical activity.

Spiron waved the Patrol to a halt, and indicated that they should take a brief rest. Shanna lowered her tired body to the ground, resting her back against the tunnel wall next to Amma, as the Patrol First conferred with the other two leaders a few metres away. Shanna could hear the low rumble of fragments of their conversation as she rubbed her aching thighs.

"No, not human......"

"Uncertain where it came....."

"Scout HQ...." She leaned her head back against the rock, and resisted closing her eyes, trying not to eavesdrop. Spiron returned to the Patrol as the other group moved off.

"We're almost at the top," he said. "There's only another hour or two to go before we exit the tunnel on the plateau. When we exit, we're to go straight to the main conference room in the Compound, they'll be debriefing us as we eat." Shanna was glad to hear that there would be food involved in the debriefing, for apart from the meal with Feeny and Damar, they'd only snacked briefly during rest stops while moving up the tunnel.

She dropped back through the patrol to chat to Amma, Ragar and Verren who were conversing quietly.

"So what do you think will happen when we get back up? Do you think Zandany and Taya are back yet, or do you think they'll still be at the rim?" Shanna asked.

Amma grimaced. "I'm hoping they tipped Taya over the edge. You should have heard her when Barron told her she wouldn't be going Below."

"You're kidding?" Verren said. "You mean she actually argued with Barron?"

"Absolutely! Zandany was fine about it, he'd been having quite a bit of trouble with his navigation, but Taya was furious. She ranted – that's the only way to describe it. She'd been fine up until then, but it's obvious that Spinner needs more time before he'd be ready to go Below – Taya's till having to reinforce all her commands verbally." Amma shook her head in disgust. "I suspect the four of us will get the rough side of her tongue when we see her next."

Ragar was openly incredulous.

"I can't believe she'd be so stupid. I was surprised they took us, to be honest. Let's face it, we came close to death on the second day, when we met those sliders." He shuddered. "And I was terrified for almost the whole time we were below, every time there was a rustle in the bushes, I thought something else was going to leap out and eat me!" He laughed dryly at himself as the others nodded their heads in agreement.

"Hopefully we'll get used to it with time – I'm sure half the battle is learning to know what you're looking at and understanding how to cope with it. Most of the time Below I had no idea what I was looking at..." Verren's tone was rueful. "So much of it looked and sounded like things we've met up here, but everything was just that little bit different. And recognising the 'different' might mean the difference between life and death. And because of what we were doing, there wasn't enough time to consolidate what we were seeing."

"Yes, I know exactly what you mean. Scouting isn't quite what it appears on first glance is it?" said Amma.

The others murmured their agreement, and then they all returned to the steady upward trudge. Their starcats paced steadily beside them, occasionally humming gently and swiping their large heads on their partners hands and bodies. Now almost home and safe inside the subterranean tunnel, they were completely relaxed, their tidemarks glowing brightly, providing a dim illumination of their own.

An hour later, up ahead a dim light became visible, and the four cadets realised they were finally about to exit the long dark climb. Entering an apparently dead end room lit by a number of lanterns, the patrol was met by another two Scouts; this time both were older and lacking starcats at their sides. They greeted Spiron, then checked the stretcher perched on the trolley, spraying the outside thoroughly with yet another of the spray bottles, then the patrol and starcats who stood stoically if unenthusiastically under the fine mist.

With a quick sequence of movements, the two Scouts swung a lever and a section of the wall moved silently sideways, allowing natural light to penetrate the room. It was a relief to the cadets to smell the freshness of the breeze and allow their eyes to relax in the early dawn light. They had travelled upwards for over a day and a half and were, to Shanna's surprise, emerging from the wall of the Scout Compound arena. She was having trouble reconciling the distances, but then realised that with no need to be careful, the patrol had travelled much faster than they had been able to in the wilderness regions. The starcats were stretching in the early morning dawn light, yawning and rippling their skins with enjoyment. Outside the arena awaited a contingent of green garbed staff from the healer precinct, who took charge of the sealed stretcher without comment.

"You're all to go straight to the second floor conference room, Spiron," said the greyer of the two Scouts. Spiron nodded his thanks, and the Patrol headed for the stairs to the main building.

Waiting inside the conference room, were Taya, Perri, Zandany, Kalli, Arad and Karri, complete with starcats reclining on cushions around the perimeter of the room. As the weary travellers took seats, dispersing their cats to the cushions to curl up for a rest, Masters Lonish, Peron and Kenwell entered the room, and sat around the large table with the others.

Shanna yawned, suddenly aware of just how tired she was, hoping fervently, but she realised, completely unrealistically, that the debriefing would be a short one. There was a quiet rumble, and Perri moved quickly to open the door of the dumb waiter just behind her in the wall and began to remove steaming dishes and covered pitchers. Jerked out of tiredness by her rumbling stomach, Shanna decided to take a more active interest in the proceedings. Master Lonish gave a brief thanks, and they commenced their meal as the Masters began to quiz them about their trip, and individually about their observations of both the craft and the creature inside it. The group pored over the diagrams of the interior and the pilot, speculating about the creature's origin and exactly what it might be.

Several hours of discussion and description later, Shanna's eyes began to droop despite her best efforts to keep them open and to follow the discussion. She was abruptly jerked awake as the sound of chairs scraping on the wooden floor penetrated her somnolence.

"Go and rest for a few hours. We'll need to speak to you all individually again sometime today, but we'll send for you when we need you. Until then, get some sleep. You've done a very good job, and you are all to be highly commended." Shanna heaved herself upright, limping slightly as her feet throbbed inside her boots. She called Storm and Twister to her, and the two starcats levered themselves up, obviously regretful to have to move from their comfortable cushions.

"Come on boys, we'll be back in our room shortly and we can all collapse." Shanna staggered down the stairs to the ground floor, almost oblivious to her surroundings, intent only on one thing – her bed. The heavy pack she had reslung on her back seemed to be weighing her down with every step. Just after she had opened the door of her room, she was surprised by a sudden violent push from behind, staggering her off balance. Storm and Twister turned as one, hurtling back through the door through which they had preceded her, growling softly. It was a mark of their exhaustion that they had failed to notice Shanna's assailant coming up behind her. Shanna caught herself on the door frame and turned. Taya stood behind her, fists clenched and eyes blazing, yet warily regarding Shanna's now extremely alert starcats. Spinner sat behind her, head down in the face of Storm's growling regard.

"You think you're so good, don't you, Little Miss Starcat Trainer! Well, I'll sort you out one day! I'll make sure the Masters realise that you're only a silly little trumped up girl who shouldn't be anywhere near the cadet program." Her tone was bitter and she was almost spitting with fury.

"What's your problem, Taya?" said Shanna tiredly, she couldn't believe this was happening now, her mind was working too slowly to cope with this sudden aggression.

"*You're* my problem, subverting my friends, gaining the Masters' favour by sucking up to them, pretending you're special by bringing two cats, and weaselling your way down Below. *I* know the truth, you're just a spoilt brat!" She gave one more wary look at Shanna's cats, both growling more and more loudly, and turned tail, marching off towards her own room, Spinner trailing disconsolately behind, his tidemarks muted and his tail dragging.

Shanna leaned back against the door frame of her room, sighing heavily. She had hoped against hope that Taya would have given up on her animosity, but if anything it seemed to have grown out of all proportion during the recent operation. Storm nudged her comfortingly, and she sighed again, and entered the room. She dumped her pack on the floor and staggered over to her waiting bed, and despite the turmoil in her mind her body took over and she plummeted into exhausted sleep.

A loud knocking at the door penetrated the fog of sleep that wrapped Shanna snugly. She attempted to ignore it for a few moments, but it grew louder and more insistent.

"All right, all right, I'm coming!" She dragged herself off the bed and wriggled out from between the two large cats on the bed, shoving Storm's tail out of the way and Twister's large back paw. Storm twitched one ear and opened one eye before closing it firmly again, and Twister wriggled slightly, flicking the tip of his tail, as she staggered over to the door, her feet and calves still aching. She opened the door to find Allad standing there.

"Time for you to go and chat to the Masters up in the conference room." To Shanna's disgust, his large frame was clothed in an immaculately turned out fresh uniform and he looked completely refreshed. His eyebrows twitched slightly as he regarded her distinctly bedraggled appearance. "You've been asleep for about five hours."

"How long do I have?" She yawned loudly, and brushed hair out of her eyes. Somehow most of her braids seemed to have come undone, and all her hair was sticking out in different directions.

"You've got about fifteen minutes, so you'd better get a move on. You can leave the cats here. They deserve a rest." Apparently she didn't. He turned and left, pulling the door shut behind him.

She hurtled around her room, hastily washing herself, brushing her hair and replaiting her braids, while dragging a fresh uniform out of the cupboard. She dressed hastily in the clean, pressed uniform, straightening her clothes and doing one last check in the mirror over the bathroom sink, and kicking the discarded, overlong clothes she'd fallen asleep in towards the washing basket. Just before she departed the room, she ran an appreciative hand down the two sleek cats snoozing happily on her bed. Both lifted enquiring heads, and she smiled at them, and told them to stay where they were. There was a volley of loud purrs and the two black heads settled themselves comfortably back on the bed. Twister rolled contentedly onto his side into the depression her body had left on the covers. She envied them.

In the conference room, Shanna was greeted by the five Masters and invited her to take a seat with them at the table.

"We'd just like you to give us a brief summary of your impressions of the artifact and the creature within it, Shanna," said Master Peron. "We've spoken to everyone else, and yours is the last testimony we need to gather." Perhaps Allad had been kinder than she'd realised – she must have slept much longer than some of her classmates.

Shanna gathered her thoughts, and attempted to give a succinct account of her impressions and thoughts. She thought that it was rather kind of the Masters to include the recount of a first year fifteen year old cadet in the formal record. She finished with one thought that struck her towards the end of her recital.

"Whatever that thing is, close contact with both it and the aircraft made the starcats sneeze. I've no idea why, but every single one of them reacted the same way. Apart from that, I'm just wondering where the aircraft came from and what it was doing flying around in a storm like that." She sat back in her chair as the three Masters made a few final notations. For a few moments the room was full of the sound of scratching pencils as Shanna's thoughts were recorded for later consideration.

"Shanna, you can go down for the evening meal now; your classes will resume on the normal schedule tomorrow morning." Master Peron smiled at her. "I also need to congratulate you on the thorough job you've done so far with your starcat training. We've been very impressed with the way the young cats have come along, and both Spiron and Allad were effusive in their praise of your two. We'd like you to continue working on more complex skills over the next few months with the class. Make sure that if you have any particular needs for equipment or aids that you let me know."

He stood and gestured for her to precede him out of the room and down to the dining hall.

The other cadets were sitting with Patrol Ten around a long table, and Shanna joined them as they greeted her cheerfully. All except Taya, of course. She was seated next to Verren and Perri, carefully placed at the opposite end of the table to the only vacant seat, and avoided greeting Shanna by devoting all her attention to her plate of roast meat and vegetables.

"Hmmm, smells really good tonight. I take it the kitchen staff have been ignoring your cooking tips, Verren?" Shanna said, sitting herself at the vacant seat and trying to ignore Taya, who was glowering at her plate. Verren wagged his finger at Shanna in mock anger.

"So you've finally got out of bed, slacker!" Ragar nudged Shanna as she took a plate, loaded it with food and began to eat. "We thought you were going to sleep the whole day away!"

"I reckon I could have, I'm still really tired. How long have you all been up? The boys are still snoozing away." She replied, noting that there were very few starcats in evidence around the room. "So, back to normal lessons tomorrow for us, I've been told. What's Patrol Ten going to be doing? Are we allowed to know?"

"The Masters have decided to keep us around for a while apparently, and for the next couple of weeks we'll be assisting them to tutor your class." Allad's eyes twinkled, and his moustache twitched. "We've all noticed a few of your individual deficits over the last week or so, and we've volunteered to address them...." Spiron snorted and there were quiet chuckles all around the table, and a few sighs from the cadets. Shanna had a sneaking suspicion that the next couple of weeks would be one constant drill. "Apart from that, we believe we'll be sent Below again, when the Masters have decided we've addressed all your faults. But that won't be until the current crew Below have returned with as much information as they've been able to glean from the craft."

"Yep, lots of rest for us this next week or two, and not much for you lot." Nelson grinned at them. "Just wait until you find out what we've got for the six of you to do!"

The discussion then proceeded into a rehash of the expedition's finds and the possible implications. They pursued these topics for a considerable time, while consuming a remarkable quantity of food. Shanna learnt that Allad was not only an amazingly competent Scout, but had an appetite for fruit pies, second to none. They then spent time discussing the vagaries of their starcats, and learnt some fairly scurrilous tales about a few of the Masters they had yet to encounter.

Despite the relaxed enjoyment of the evening, which added a new dimension to life in the Scout Corps, Shanna could not help but suffer intermittent pangs of anxiety each time she encountered Taya's gaze. The older cadet spent little time interacting with the others, but remained quietly on the edge of the group, offering few remarks and only joining in the conversation when asked a specific question. Intermittently during lulls in the conversation, Shanna would catch Taya in an unguarded moment, her eyes fixed unblinkingly on Shanna. The looks were making Shanna more and more uncomfortable and she finally stood when Verren declared his intent to return to his bed, in order to prepare himself for what was most probably to be, as he put it, a week or two of absolute nightmare. There were appreciative grins from the members of Patrol Ten.

"I'm off too. Night, all!" Shanna paused, waiting for the comments about her affinity for sleep. She wasn't disappointed, and exited the room grinning as a cascade of comments followed her out. She and Verren said goodnight at their respective doors, and Shanna thankfully closed the door, looking for the sanctuary of her soft bed. She opened the outside door slightly in case the two cats needed to pop out during the night, then rejoined them on the bed, snuggling in between the two large bodies. They were warm and comforting and she again pushed Taya firmly to the back of her mind.

***

The Garsal vehicle had managed to move only ten kilometres over the course of the day. It had been attacked repeatedly by two large scaled beasts, which had learned quickly to dart and duck under the gun fire, taxing the Garsal gunners to their limits. As the sun dipped below the horizon, Anjo and Semba listened to yet another impact of a heavy body on the exterior of the vehicle. They had spent the whole day incarcerated in the vehicle, constantly collecting equipment and restoring it to its racks as the impacts of the large creatures shook the vehicle enough to jar things loose. As yet another strike rocked the vehicle on its heavy wheels, the Garsal commander issued an order to continue to move during the darkness in an attempt to lose the canny beasts that had been so persistent in their attacks.

Chapter 18

KAIDAN completed the final section of physical exercises Master Cerren had given him after the field exercise. It had been just over two weeks since he had sat chastened in the Master's office, Socks relaxed on the hearth rug. His teacher had worked exhaustively through each step of the field course - examining options for navigation at each point, use of ground features to assist stealthy movement, various methods of camouflage and other skills with the bow - that Kaidan had only dreamed about. He had spent a considerable amount of the time wondering if Master Cerren had forgotten that he was still only at the beginning of his senior schooling, and why he merited such detailed coaching. In the end, he'd decided to take it a compliment, but somewhat of a backhanded one. He'd learnt the hard way about having a swelled head. He gathered his breath and stretched himself slowly, then brushed dirt and twigs from his clothing. He had been moving his way slowly around the Hillview property, attempting to remain concealed at all times, pretending that he was sneaking through predator laden country.

He wasn't sure how well he'd done, as his only audience had been Boots and Moshi and he was sure he hadn't been able to fool them one bit. Particularly as first one, then the other would sneak up on him, either poking him with a paw while he attempted to conceal himself in a tiny hollow, or peering suddenly down at him from the branches of the tree he was attempting to hide behind. It had been somewhat off putting, to say the least.

He returned to the dwelling to eat his breakfast before walking into town for school with his father and Boots. He was hoping to be able to catch up with Shanna before his lessons started. He'd managed to see her briefly only twice in the past two weeks, but apart from saying that she'd been on a field mission after the cyclone she had declined to go into details, which struck him as somewhat odd as Shanna was certainly not known for her reticence. Boots and Moshi bounded through the door Kaidan held open for them as he entered the main living area. On the table was a warm bowl of porridge. His mother was sitting at the table drinking the end of her morning tea, while he could hear his father humming as he washed his breakfast dishes.

"Morning Kaidan. We didn't see you at all that time, so we're assuming that you're improving," said Janna, pushing his bowl of porridge over to him and pouring another cup of tea.

"Well, I'm hoping I've improved, but Moshi and Boots kept finding me pretty easily," he replied, shrugging his shoulders and smiling. "I'm not sure if anyone can be good enough to fool a starcat." He smiled.

"Hmmm, I suspect not," said Janna, her eyes twinkling, "I've never been able to hide from one, anyway, particularly if it's wanting its dinner! Do you think you might catch up with Shanna today?"

"I'm hoping so, Mum. You know, when she started this Scout stuff, I had no idea she'd be away so much. I actually miss her – and you know what she'd say if she heard me say that!"

Janna chuckled, "You're right about that. We're missing her a lot too, Kai, and I've a letter for her that you can give to her if you see her, or at least drop it off at Scout Compound."

"I'll do my best, Mum. I can at least drop it off." Kaidan said applying himself to his porridge with enthusiasm and then after washing the bowl, diverted to the bathroom for a good wash and a change of clothing before meeting his father with Boots out the front of the dwelling.

He put the letter into his pack after leaving Adlan at the gate of Watchtower and walked up through the town, through the Records Precinct to Scout Compound. He had an hour before his classes started and he was hoping to be able to have a reasonable chat with his sister. He'd been in the Scout Compound a couple of times now, looking for his sister, and after reporting to the administration officer, he went straight to her room on the ground floor, passing a few of the older students and Masters along the way. He was greeted by a couple who he'd spoken to on previous occasions, and nodded in return, finally knocking on his sister's door.

"Just a moment!" Her voice rang out and he heard the sound of running water, followed by the sound of a closing door inside the room and then the door in front of him opened, and Shanna smiled happily to see him.

"Kaidan, come in! I haven't seen you for at least a week, and I've finally got about half an hour free, so we can chat for a bit."

"Hi Shan, good to see you too." Kaidan surprised himself by actually hugging his big sister, noting new muscles through her uniform as he wrapped his arms around her.

"Well, absence has certainly made your heart grow fonder!" Shanna punched him affectionately in the shoulder as he let her go, and then perched himself on her bed. Twister wandered over and nosed his hand, angling for a head scratch as Storm purred a greeting from behind Shanna. "What do you think of the boys, little brother?"

"They've grown again, actually I think Storm might end up larger than Boots!" Kaidan replied as he obligingly scratched Twister's sleek head, the young cat's tidemarked ears glowing gently with pleasure. "So, what are you up to at the moment?"

"Well, we've been pretty busy with lessons since we got back – the Patrol that we were with has been assigned to work on our shortcomings, so we've been studying and practicing heaps of extra hours. I just seem to fall into bed exhausted every night. That is, the nights that we don't have night drills... when we actually get to sleep." She grimaced, and began to brush and braid her hair. "How's your archery going?"

Kaidan related the tale of his field exercise, as he'd not had time to describe it at their previous meetings.

"So Master Cerren was wearing Scout gear? And he could move like that? He must have actually been a Scout – I wonder why he's teaching at Records Precinct?" Shanna's voice was quite puzzled, as she knew by now that most of the older Scouts were employed in some capacity around the Scout Compound. "Oh well, there's probably some reason – and you say he's getting you to work on concealment and camouflage? Wonder why....?"

"Well, I'm not really sure, but it's very interesting and rather fun, except when I'm getting really tired and muddy, and my muscles get pretty sore at times. Boots and Moshi think it's really fun to sneak up on me when I'm practicing." His sister laughed at that.

"I just bet they do! How's Socks going with Master Cerren?"

"Well, sometimes I'm hard put to decide who's having more fun – Socks or the Master. You know, she's turning out to be one of the best cats Mum and Dad have ever bred. Master Cerren's besotted with her." He smiled. "Anyway, enough about me. What did you do after the cyclone?"

Shanna paused, and finished braiding her hair, knotting the last tie slowly, then turned away from the mirror and leaned on the dresser behind her, hands in her trouser pockets.

"We were assigned to assist Patrol Ten to do a check around Thunderfall Cascades." She called Storm over and began to check his feet out, asking him to extend his claws one by one.

"And?" Kaidan prompted.

"Well, we did a lot of bush work and I learnt heaps about surviving out there, and they made us navigate without any help in an area we'd never been in."

"Yes, you told me that before, Shan, but what exactly did you do?" Kaidan said irritably.

"Look Kai, there are some details I'm not allowed to tell you. And you'll just have to be happy with that. The field work was pretty intense, and some Scout stuff stays Scout stuff." Shanna's voice had that "no nonsense, don't mess with me tone" that struck fear into younger brothers' hearts all over Frontier. Messing with older sisters was usually a prelude to some kind of sibling violence, and Kaidan was mindful of the new muscles he'd noted on his sister. He'd previously been on the receiving end of some of her new wrestling tricks.

"OK,OK, but I'm still curious... Oh and Mum sent this." Drawing the letter out of his pocket he pushed it to the end of the bed towards her.

"I'm sorry Kai, I know I'm driving you mad," her tone became mischievous. "But that's just how it is." She picked up the letter and placed it on the dresser behind her. "Tell Mum and Dad I'll write back, because I don't know when I'll get home next, and tell them to drop in if they're in town too. I miss them." She looked suddenly wistful. "You can tell Mum and Dad I've seen a starlyne, though."

"You're kidding! You really saw a starlyne?" Kaidan was stunned, and he knew his parents would be thrilled to hear that news. "What was it like? Where were you?"

"It was one of the nights that we were out from Thunderfall Cascades, checking stuff out. I was on watch with Allad." Shanna related the story of the starlyne, answering Kaidan's many questions as thoroughly as he wished. After he finally ran out of steam, Shanna pushed herself off the dresser.

"Kai, I've got to go, and you'd better get to classes. Come and see me again when you can, and I'll try and drop by the archery field some mornings." She called her two cats to heel. Storm regretfully left Kaidan's scratching hand, rubbing his head appreciatively against the boy as he fell in behind Shanna. Kaidan got to his feet, preceding his sister out of the door, and surprised himself again by hugging her for a second time, then waved at her as he set off down the corridor. Two doors down from Shanna, a tall girl exited another room, a red toned starcat following her. Kaidan nodded at her, and was surprised to receive a glare in return, but shrugged mentally to himself and continued on his way. He wondered if this was the Taya who'd given Shanna so much difficulty in the beginning of her starcat training – she and her cat certainly fitted the description. As he exited the building, he caught a glimpse of the timepiece above the door, realised he was going to be late if he didn't hurry, and broke into a run towards the Records Precinct. He also had another meeting with Master Cerren after the first break. He was hoping that his practice had paid off, as the Master had arranged to meet him out at the field archery course with his bow, and he was fairly certain that there would be a practical test involved in the meeting – or why would the meeting be there?

When he arrived, his heart sank as he saw that the Master was dressed in his Scout fatigues. Socks hummed a greeting as Kaidan approached, and he hummed back politely.

"Now, Kaidan, have you been practicing?" Master Cerren got straight to the point.

"Yes Sir." Kaidan nodded.

"Well, we'll just see how you're coming along then, shall we?" The grey haired Master handed Kaidan a map with a course delineated in neat pencil strokes, targets defined by diamonds on the page. "On my command, you'll commence this course. I'll give you fifteen minutes head start, and then I'll be hunting you." Kaidan noted with a slight surge of alarm that the Master was hung with a variety of missile weapons. He counted a light bow, a blowpipe and four throwing knives hung at his belt. "If I sight you, I'll notify you with one of these." He indicated the weapons slung around his waist. "Now, off with you."

Kaidan gathered his thoughts as he checked the map. He realised that the first point on the map was some distance into the forested area, and taking care to begin his stealthy stalking immediately, began to calculate an appropriate course to take him to the first target. Glancing once behind him as the foliage concealed him from view, he glimpsed Master Cerren perch himself on a convenient rock with surprising agility, and begin to scratch Socks' ears. Her eyes were fastened on Kaidan.

As he slunk through the forested area, he found himself on a knife edge of tension, heart racing and small quivers shooting through his limbs. The whole concept of being hunted was disturbing to his sense of equilibrium. It made him even keener to conceal himself, using every skill he possessed and every method he had attempted to master over the past two weeks. His neck pricked.

Five targets later, there was a hiss, followed by a small "snick" and a feathered dart hit the tree two centimetres in front of his nose. He dropped immediately to his belly on the ground, realising that Master Cerren had located him, thought frantically and rolled himself into a depression, where he began to crawl rapidly backwards and down into a small gully. He then moved silently behind a large tree and began to work his way through the thick undergrowth. Five minutes later, he realised that he had moved without any thought of where he actually was. He spent another five minutes relocating his position on the map, before daring to move again. Wiping the sweat out of his eyes with his sleeve, he recommenced his stealthy progression. Another two targets later, and a throwing knife pinned the edge of his pants to the tree behind him. He had to tear his trousers to enable himself to move, the ripping noise sounding abnormally loudly as he dropped into a thick patch of scrub. Keeping his mind on his navigation, he scrambled silently over the top of a small knoll, and then backtracked by walking up a small creek bed.

Another three targets on, an arrow thudded into the ground between the fingers of his right hand, just as he prepared to crawl forward on his belly. Without thinking, he rolled to the left, into a small thicket. Thirty seconds later, he realised what a bad plan that was, as the thicket began to drip sticky, brown sap onto him – he'd rolled right into a thicket of wait-a-while trees. He exited from there as fast as possible, trying to avoid the large droplets of gluelike sap, but still managing to end up with a considerable portion of himself coated in the extremely adhesive brown liquid. This made things much more difficult. It would be thirty minutes before the sap dried and he would only be able to remove it effectively with the aid of a hot soak. In the meantime, anything that he brushed against would adhere to him. He consoled himself with the thought that his camouflage was going to be much more effective now, if somewhat difficult to remove.

Kaidan grumbled softly under his breath and attempted to avoid touching anything while alternatively crawling, slinking, and concealing himself in the bush. It didn't work, and he began to look a little like a moving shrub himself, as more and more vegetation and dirt attached itself to him. He looked at the map – one target left. He navigated confidently, but was more than a little hampered by the various bits of the local flora attaching themselves to the wait-a-while sap, which then began to catch on other things. Surprisingly, he was able to hit the final target without Master Cerren pinpointing him, and navigated his way confidently back towards the start point. Just as he exited the bush, Master Cerren tapped him on the shoulder, nearly causing him to collapse from heart failure. Socks purred and bumped him with her paw to keep him upright.

"Well done Kaidan, you really have practiced. I do think the camouflage, although creative, is a little overdone." The Master's eyes twinkled and Kaidan realised that he had probably seen him roll into the thicket. "I would suggest avoiding protruding additions if you want to blend in properly. It prevents noise, you see." Kaidan glanced up and saw a smile added to the twinkle.

"Yes sir. That was the part of the plan that didn't work." He grinned as he realised that Master Cerren was indeed quite pleased with him. "It's also hard to remove."

"Off to the baths now, and then meet me back in my office. We have a few more things to discuss this afternoon. You are excused from afternoon classes."

Somewhat elated, Kaidan shouldered his gear, and walked back towards Watchtower, only then realising that he was going to have to walk all the way through the main building covered in vegetation. He was going to be ribbed about this for weeks unless he could come up with a plausible explanation. Perhaps he could claim that it was deliberate camouflage, he thought.

***

In the previous two weeks, the Garsal ground vehicle had managed to travel a paltry seventy kilometres. Between the constant assaults from the planet's large predators, the thick vegetation, and the obstacles created by watercourses and rocky outcrops, the movement of the vehicle had been slow and tortuous. On the thirteenth day, sensors inside the vehicle had indicated traces of a valuable mineral deposit and they had paused to investigate further. Preliminary sampling had shown encouraging signs, and the Garsal commander had sent the information immediately back to the hive ship.

He had been instructed to make a thorough survey of the deposit before continuing towards the plateau. As a result, Anjo and Semba had been forced to begin erecting a smaller scale laser fence around the vehicle to create a compound safe enough to allow the detailed exploration. The task was fraught with danger. Large predators were regularly attracted to the vehicle area, and the two slaves would have to make a sudden run for safety while the Garsal soldiers attempted to fend the creatures off. On the second day, Anjo had been injured by a pretty, pink flowered plant, which turned out to be carnivorous, closing its concealed jaws with a snap on his left arm, deeply lacerating it.

That evening he sat in his corner of the vehicle, cradling his throbbing arm, now dressed cleanly by Semba. He had been heavily dosed with painkilling medication and antibiotics, and the commander had relegated him to onboard duties until his arm healed. He had then delegated part of his troop of soldiers to finish the fencing. Work continued to be slow and it appeared they'd be in one place for several weeks.

Anjo was depressed. He was hurt, and exhausted, and felt extraordinarily alone. Semba was good company when they were close enough to talk, but those moments were relatively few. In some ways life was better in the exploratory vehicle; there would have been no medical treatment back at the ship where slaves were much more expendable, and the food was better, but on most days, Anjo was in constant fear for his life. This was a strange planet – wildly beautiful but constantly deadly, with vegetation that camouflaged itself in bright colours and pretty foliage to conceal its murderous tendencies, and a huge variety of dangerous creatures constantly attempting to prey on any unwary traveller. There had also been a number of other bizarre occurrences during the journey. Two of the troopers had presented after night watches with strange debilitating illnesses, both requiring placement in hibernating pods, for further investigation on return to the mother ship, as the testing available on board the vehicle had shown no pathogens of any kind in the milky fluid that passed for Garsal blood.

Lapsing into a restless sleep disturbed by pain, fear, and formless nightmares, Anjo slumped onto his pallet, arm cradled on his chest, sweat popping out on his forehead as yet another dream wound its way through his unconsciousness.

Chapter 19

"RIGHT cadets, let's try that again!" Allad sent the six cadets back to the beginning of the obstacle course, while Spiron stood observing at his side. "Call your starcats to you, and on my command, send them through first as though you were sending them out to search the area for anything dangerous. When they return, go through the course allowing them to assist you. This time, it's a race." The cadets lined up near a flagged line, each sitting their cat by their side, or, in Shanna's case, one on each side.

"Ready; go!"

Shanna sent Storm and Twister off with a hand signal, and watched them leap to the top of the first obstacle, slightly ahead of Verren's Cirrus. Using her silent whistle, she directed one to each side of the course, and then signalled them to fade while doing the obstacle course at speed. With that uncanny starcat burst of speed, they seemed to blur just as they faded before her eyes, and she began to wait impatiently for the two of them to return.

Dust swirled shortly in front of her, and the two cats materialised in front of her, although she noted that Cirrus had actually arrived fractionally in front of the two males.

"Good boys!" Shanna bolted for the first obstacle, sending Storm to crouch in front of it and Twister to leap to the top. She used Storm as a foot stool, signalling him to boost her as she leapt lightly onto his sleek back. As she reached the top of the obstacle, Twister led the way across a narrow plank which sloped upwards, helpfully extending his tail to allow her to move faster. Behind her, she could hear the others scaling the first obstacle. She increased her pace and arrived at the top of a pole which had loops of rope suspended from it, leading to yet another pole. Twister wrapped himself around the rope, and Shanna began to swarm after him, aided by Storm who slung himself below her, preventing any chance of a fall. At the top of the next pole, Twister spiralled about half way down, and then paused as Shanna simply slid after him, cushioning her with his body to arrest her slide. Storm spiralled after then continued past, flowing over his litter mate, and stopping just above the base. Twister then simply removed himself from the pole, allowing Shanna to slide onto Storm before rejoining Shanna and Storm at the base of the pole.

They all dropped to their bellies, Twister preceding Shanna into the cloth covered crawl course as she grasped his rear end, wrapping her legs around Storm's front. The two cats then simply ferried her through the winding course at starcat speed. After the crawl, they were presented with a series of obstacles to move over and under, before a final climb up a wall from which hand and foot holds protruded. The starcats flanked Shanna as she climbed, before leaping down the other side as Shanna descended with the aid of a knotted rope.

The three of them then ran through a flagged finish line where Allad, Barron and Spiron awaited them. Shanna panted and rubbed sweat out of her eyes as the other cadets finished behind her, Taya and Spinner straggling in last.

"That was much better cadets!" Allad's tone was approving. "Interesting move through the tunnel Shanna, we may have to handicap you by sitting one of your cats out next time. Verren, I'd like you to work on your wall scaling; Ragar – nice moves on the horizontal ropes; Amma, just try and increase the speed of your descents – Spider *will* catch you, don't worry; Zandany, good crawl that time; Taya, you need to work on Spinner's moves – he's a great cat, but you've got to refine that partnership much more; Shanna, you'll need to do some one on one work with Taya and Spinner." Shanna's heart sank. More time with Taya was not what she wanted to hear. The antagonism radiating from the other girl was almost palpable, and Shanna was less than pleased at the idea of spending large amounts of time tutoring her. So far she'd managed to avoid any close contact with her, unless they were partnered in an exercise under the watchful eyes of their teachers. In those rare pairings, Taya had been at least civil, if not exactly helpful.

The past several weeks had been harder than anything Shanna had so far experienced in training, but still lacked the intensity of the time travelling Below. There hadn't been a whisper about either the corpse or the aircraft imparted to the cadets from any of their instructors. Shanna was becoming more and more curious about both – it seemed like such an anticlimax after the tension filled days of the initial discovery. Each day, Shanna spent time contemplating how her world might change in the next months and years, and every day she would finish with her thoughts in a complicated whirl, feeling almost let down.

"All right cadets, classroom three. Verren, you'll be taking over the lessons on wound care from Challon this afternoon, and you'll continue your class's education for the foreseeable future," said Spiron. "Amma, you'll be commencing instruction in weather systems and forecasting tomorrow." Both Amma and Verren looked a little taken aback, but nodded firmly.

"Dismissed." Spiron was obviously not going to impart any extra information to the cadets.

"Where do you think they're going?" Shanna asked.

"Below?" Zandany suggested, as they entered the ground floor of the main building.

"Perhaps they'll be checking out the origin of that aircraft." Amma was thoughtful.

"Maybe they'll be searching for more of those creatures," speculated Ragar.

Verren was practical. "Or maybe they're just having a few days off?"

There was a general laugh, as the six of them hadn't had a day off since they'd returned from Below. The last few weeks had been constant lessons, drills and assessments. Climbing the stone stairs to the first floor classroom, the students passed Masters Peron and Lonish descending. They all moved politely to one side to allow the Masters room.

The problem of Taya continued to plague Shanna throughout Verren's class on wound care. She was intermittently distracted by chills of anxiety about the upcoming work with Taya and Spinner – she was well aware that she could train Spinner to do anything, but it was the worry about working with Taya to develop the appropriate partnership that was the problem. She would have to try to impart the emotional cues necessary for Taya to sort out the underlying problems that were preventing her from developing her relationship with Spinner to its fullest. The other cadets had all bonded well with their cats – certainly there were a few training techniques to sort out, but the relationships they had developed would mature well with time and it was obvious that they shared a deep emotional bond with their young cats. Taya continued to be the problem. Shanna sighed quietly, and attempted to bring her attention back to the slightly grisly description Verrren was giving.

After the class, Shanna gritted her teeth and approached Taya, having decided that an approach with others around might be a better strategy than searching Taya out alone later.

"OK Taya, when do you want to start working on those extra training sessions?"

The other girl grimaced, but with the other cadets around was not about to make a scene.

"Whenever you wish, I suppose." Her tone was less than enthusiastic. Shanna decided to put the best face on the situation.

"How about we meet in the arena each morning, an hour before our first class, then?" She figured that she'd prefer to work on something difficult when she was fresh rather than when she was fatigued by the demands of the day. She'd always been more of a morning person anyway.

"All right." Taya flipped around and immediately commenced a loud conversation with Verren about one of the dressings he'd recommended for lacerations. Amma fell into place beside Shanna, Spider pacing placidly beside her.

Amma turned her head and in a quiet voice said, "Good luck with that one! I swear she's becoming more and more difficult to live with and I don't envy you your task at all. She's always been a bit intense, but I just don't get why she won't get over things!" Amma put a companionable hand on Shanna's arm as they descended the steps to the ground floor and the dining hall.

A week later, Shanna was ready to scream with frustration. She had met with Taya every morning in the arena to work with her and Spinner. The red toned cat was such a lovely softy that Shanna couldn't understand why Taya refused to allow herself to fully bond with him. Spinner was performing his tasks adequately, but without the extra verve that a starcat would normally have when working with a partner who shared and returned his affection, as well as his loyalty. How could she tell Taya that what was missing from her partnership with her starcat was fun, and affection? The problem plagued her constantly, and she seemed to be in a constant state of distraction, trying to fathom some way of getting those simple facts across to Taya, in the face of the other's constant disdain for any information that had Shanna as its source. Taya had not exactly been overtly rude to Shanna during their sessions, but there was a constant, silent, unspoken struggle going on between them.

Taya's animosity was slowly and subtly beginning to affect the whole cadet class. There was an undercurrent of discord that began to infect every activity that the class performed as a group. It was a relief for Shanna to resume her individual lessons in physical conditioning and the combat moves necessary to survive close up contact with some of Frontier's more aggressive predators, which she was taught by Master Peron every couple of days. There was almost a kind of peacefulness about thudding heavily to the mat that seemed to help her to restore her equilibrium. It was hard to stay preoccupied when not paying attention could actually result in minor injuries. Those classes were the one time when the question of Taya was able to be pushed out of her consciousness.

After one of Master Peron's sessions, Shanna headed to the bathing room for a hot soak. Shedding her clothing, she slipped into the hot bath in the locker room, sighing with relief. There had been a big session of strength work during the preceding session, and she was tired and sweaty, the quadriceps muscles in her thighs twitching as they slowly relaxed in the warm water. She was joined five minutes later by Amma, who was also looking very sweaty, settling into the hot water with a loud sigh.

"How's it going with Taya, Shan?" Amma raised her eyebrows in query as she began soaping her hair. "Don't worry that she'll burst in on us – I saw her dressed and heading into Master Yendy's office. She shouldn't bother us."

Shanna sighed heavily. "About as well as could be expected I suppose."

"You mean she's being awful still." Amma's tone was flat. "And she's doing everything she can to spite you. You know, I thought she'd gotten over it all, after you sorted her out earlier on, but since we went Below, and she didn't, she's just got worse. And it's not just you now, we're all starting to suffer."

"I know," replied Shanna. "But I'm not sure how I'm going to sort this one out. And poor Spinner just doesn't understand how he can do anything else to please her. I mean, how do I tell her that she has to love him, and give him affection, make things fun? It's like she just doesn't get starcats, and I thought that one of the prerequisites for Scouting training was an empathy with them." All her frustration poured out in a torrent to the other girl, as they soaked in the hot water.

"I know Shan, and it's making it really hard for our class to progress in the group exercises. We all seem to be doing really well as individuals, but our group exercises are very ordinary, and that's because we all know we can't rely on Taya - and we don't." Amma was openly frustrated. "I just can't imagine life without Spider now; she's my friend and my mate, and I just don't get why Taya can't or won't understand that!"

"Maybe she'll get her act into gear when we go out Below again." Shanna was hopeful that more contact with Patrol Ten and their obvious inclusion of their cats as full patrol members might rub off on Taya.

"If we don't start performing as a group we might not get to go Below for ages," said Amma gloomily, "and although it scared me witless last time, I can't wait to do it again."

"I know what you mean," replied Shanna, a grin breaking through the worry lines on her face, "It's so amazing down there. Hey, have you seen anyone from Patrol Ten around lately?"

"Not in the last week," said Amma. "Maybe they're back down Below. Wish we were too."

They both heaved themselves out of the water, drying off and dressing themselves in clean clothing. Three starcats padded into the room, Spider nudging Amma's hand for a head scratch, as Storm and Twister rubbed themselves luxuriously on Shanna's clean clothing.

"How could you resist something as cute as this?" Spider had leaned her long length on Amma so firmly she had inadvertently pinned her against the lockers. She gestured for her to remove her weight, which she did with a reluctant rumble, which lapsed into a purr as she scratched the cat's chin.

Shanna giggled, "I have no idea, although 'cute' is not the word most people use about starcats." Signalling their cats to follow they strolled off to their rooms together, chatting companionably about anything but Taya, Shanna smiling at the easy companionship she now shared with Amma.

The next morning, the tell tale signs of another storm were visible in the sky, tattered streamers of clouds indicating that yet another big blow was on the way. The cadets were detailed to assist with Scout Compound preparations and then those whose families lived in town were dispatched home. Those who lived out of town were to stay in the compound for the duration of the storm this time, and so Shanna found herself stowing loose equipment in the storage areas under the arena seating with Amma and Ragar, after Verren, Taya and Zandany had left to go home to their families. Two hours into the task, they were surprised by the subterranean door in the arena wall opening and three patrols exiting through it, one of which was Patrol Ten. They were accompanied by the experts who had been sifting through the wreckage of the aircraft, all of whom were looking extremely weary and bedraggled, and two who looked so frankly relieved to be back on top of the plateau that they looked almost ready to collapse.

Nelson waved to them, and the three responded. The rest of the Patrol looked tired but the scouts in the other two patrols looked exhausted, and all were carrying very heavy packs. She would have liked to ask what they'd been doing, what was in their packs, and whether they had come to any conclusions about the origin of the craft and its pilot, but decided that she was unlikely to receive anything but a smart reprimand should she do so.

The winds had begun to pick up in speed as the three cadets finally stowed the last of the equipment safely under the arena, and secured the doors with their heavy locking bars.

"I suppose we'd better let Master Lonish know we're all done," said Ragar.

"Hopefully he'll have run out of things for us to do by now," replied Amma, as she pushed back her windswept hair, and the three cadets left the arena together. "I'm dying for a hot drink, and maybe we can dig some information out of Challon and the others."

Master Lonish nodded, ticked a box on his checklist, and then reassigned them to conduct a final grounds check. Accompanied by their starcats, they completed a circuit of the Compound as the first raindrops began to fall, and darkness began to colour the grey clouds indigo. After reporting in to Master Lonish again, they fed their cats and then entered the dining hall to catch up on some much needed food for themselves. Shanna was sure the others could hear the loud rumblings from her stomach.

Much to their delight, Patrol Ten was seated around one of the long dining tables, Allad beckoning the three of them over to join them.

"So, finished for the day?" Perri asked them as they seated themselves after filling their plates with a savoury stew and dumplings from the warming dishes. Blowing out after a particularly hot mouthful, Shanna nodded.

"Yep, finally," said Amma, chasing a dumpling around her plate to coat it with gravy, "I don't think this storm will be as bad as the last one, though. Wetter maybe, but the winds won't be as bad." She trapped the dumpling and impaled it on her fork.

Spiron did a bit of a double take at that statement.

"And how do you come to that conclusion?" he asked. Amma glanced up at him in surprise.

"Well, you can just tell, can't you?"

"But *how* can you 'just tell'?" asked Challon in a puzzled tone of voice. He put his mug down on the table, and leant his elbows on the wooden surface. The whole Patrol had stopped its varied conversations to listen to the answer. Shanna was intrigued. She could usually tell that a storm was coming, but certainly couldn't tell whether it would be large, small, long or wet, which was apparently what Amma was taking for granted. The other girl had proved a good lecturer on weather systems, explaining that her mother taught meteorology over in Scholar's Precinct.

"Well, I can just tell – all my family can do it – doesn't everyone's? Can't you?" Amma looked up, slightly startled, and licked a little gravy off her chin. "It's sort of a feeling, really, I don't know how to describe it particularly, but I just know..." She trailed off looking around at the Patrol, who all had their eyes fixed on her, and blushed. "So none of you can tell?" She broke off looking around.

"Well, I can usually tell when one's coming, but not what it'll be like!" said Shanna, and most around the table nodded in agreement. "It sounds like a pretty useful ability – I bet it's one of those 'differences' that you were talking about Spiron."

"All right, let's take bets on whether Amma's right or not!" called Nelson. "It'll be a good way to pass some of the time until we're able to go outside. Amma, we'll need as many details as you can give us, and then we'll take bets on all the variables, and compare them against the reality at the end of the storm!" There was a chorus of cheers, and Amma looked a bit flustered at all the attention, but then began to issue more details. Shanna sat back with a smile and prepared to be very amused. A number of starcats began to wend their way into the dining hall as the winds outside began to rise, seeking out their human partners for a little love and patting. Storm and Twister appeared at the door, tidemarks glowing with the contentment of full bellies and post dinner relaxation. Nelson was sitting at one end of the table, taking bets about Amma's predictions and there was quite a queue in front of him as Scouts and older cadets wandered over to see what was causing all the fuss.

After the meal debris was cleared, most of the Scouts in the dining hall settled themselves in the large comfortable chairs arranged in groups down at the other end of the communal area. Shanna curled herself up in one near Allad and Barron, with Twister recumbent on the floor in front of her and Storm seated at her knees, his head lying heavily in her lap. She wondered how her family was doing at Hillview, taking comfort from Amma's predictions which she privately thought were probably pretty accurate. The dwelling in the hillside was one of the most protected in the Watchtower region and rarely suffered damage, and it had been years since any lives had been lost in one of the big storms that so plagued the region.

Barron and Allad were discussing their recent trip below, and Shanna attempted to listen without looking like she was listening, as Storm butted her hand with his head to remind her about the more important issues in her life – such as patting him. She stroked the soft silky fur of his head, while trying not to lean closer to hear more clearly. She felt slightly guilty about eavesdropping, but her curiosity was getting the better of her, and it wasn't as if they had really wanted to be private, she reasoned, or they'd have gone somewhere else.

"Well, our group saw no sign of anything on the ground at all," Allad was saying, "what about you?"

"We found nothing at all either, but that doesn't necessarily mean that we won't find anything when we go back down again. Maybe we were looking in the wrong direction, or maybe we just didn't go far enough this time. Perhaps we'll find some traces of where it came from next time we're Below."

Shanna was intrigued at the direction the discussion was taking.

"Have you heard whether the medics have identified the corpse or discovered anything about it?" asked Allad.

"So far they still don't know what it is exactly, but they've discovered a few things about it that are quite interesting." Barron said. "It is apparently male, as far as they can determine. It appears to be bipedal, with two sets of manipulative appendages, although one set is very small and probably only useful for fine motor activities. The creature has mainly insectoid characteristics, with a few hints of possible reptilian influences. It's an odd creature. It appears it probably communicates verbally, and judging by its structure, is probably very fast and quite strong."

"Does it bear any resemblance to anything in the archives?" asked Allad.

"Apparently not. It's completely different to anything our ancestors recorded, so it's likely that they never encountered this particular species. It's only speculation of course as to whether our fellow human beings have encountered this species in the last few hundred years. Let's face it, we've only got a basic idea where in the galaxy our ancestors ended up when it all went wrong for them." Barron cocked his head as the rising wind howled around the building, and the storm shutters rattled. "And if we're the first humans to encounter them, I wonder what their reaction might be. Or ours – that corpse gave me an uneasy feeling..."

Allad nodded and he and Barron sat quietly sipping their hot drinks as the wind rose. Shanna mused over what the two men had discussed. Most of what they had talked about she had already considered, but hearing other, older Scouts, seriously considering her thoughts made them somehow more real. She absently patted Storm's head and he rumbled a deep purr through her legs. Twister had gradually wormed his belly under her feet, and she realised she had been unconsciously rubbing him with her toes. She gave him a fond smile.

Outside, the rising winds howled and shrieked as the sound of heavy rain against the storm shutters securing the dining hall increased. Shanna contemplated wandering off to bed, but decided that the relief of uncomplicated company, lacking Taya, was what she felt like for a bit longer. Not necessarily talking company, but at least the feel of other human beings around her.

***

Inside the exploration vehicle, Anjo and Semba huddled together as the wind began to rise and the rain began as a gentle patter on the outside of the vehicle. The perimeter fence was protecting them from the suddenly vanished predators, but both the humans remembered the previous storm all too well. The Garsal commander had ordered a tie down of the vehicle, and then commanded all of the troops to shelter inside for the duration of the storm. The vehicle began to sway slightly under the larger gusts, and the two humans nestled closer together.

Chapter 20

IN the aftermath of the storm, the class had again been sent out with Patrol Ten, this time to assist with the smaller communities north of Watchtower where Amma's predicted rain had indeed eventuated. It had caused the creeks and tributaries that eventually joined to form the river that flowed past Watchtower, before plunging in a series of waterfalls over the edge of the plateau, to flood. Shanna noticed that several other patrols had departed almost immediately for Below, through the arena access, and the group of cadets had speculated privately about what they might be doing. For several weeks the Scout Corps assisted local authorities to deal with communities and isolated farm steadings coping with flood damage, using their starcats to search for missing people and lost stock, while constantly patrolling for more dangerous creatures brought in by the storms.

While the problem of the creature in the aircraft was still sitting heavily in everyone's thoughts, the survival and succour of the human population of the plateau was a much more pressing issue. Years of hard experience had taught the settlers that post storm activities were more important to survival on Frontier than almost anything else. Years of hard work and development could be washed away in the floods without a rapid response, and the gradually increasing population was still vulnerable to natural disaster.

Shanna pushed back a few strands of sweaty, dirty hair and directed Twister to run in a wide half circle around the large herd of horgals that the patrol had finally located approximately forty kilometres from where they had begun. Storm was at the far side of the herd with Satin and Hunter, driving the horgals steadily south, back to the settlement they had come from. Shanna had a new appreciation of just how fast and far a panicked herd of horgals could manage to move, and how stubborn the beasts were when you wanted to turn them around and head them back to where they'd come from. Not far from Shanna, Twister cut off a horgal as it attempted to make a run to the side of the main body of animals; the large creature turned back into the herd demurely batting its eyelashes, pretending it had never contemplated any escape manoeuvre.

Twister paused, just to make sure the horgal would not recommence its escape bid, and then continued his half circle. Around the herd the patrol's starcats were constantly circling and driving them onwards. They had now been on the road with the herd for five days, and hopefully today they would finally arrive back at Northall, the settlement that the horgals had broken away from during the storm. Apart from the logistics of moving such a large body of animals, there had been the constant difficulty of making sure they didn't end up dinner for the other denizens of the plateau. There was a shout from the front of the herd, where Spiron was walking ahead.

"Northall about thirty minutes ahead." There was a general sigh of relief from the Scouts within earshot of Shanna. None of them had felt they were really cut out as herdsmen, but they knew that the job was one that needed doing, and that they were the available competent labour. However, it didn't stop them being happy about the end of the onerous task.

As Shanna's portion of the herd crested the final hill, she could see the buildings of Northall spread out below, tucked just below another ridge line – a placement designed to mitigate the fiercest storms, and provide a natural barrier on one side of the settlement against any roving predators. It was a beautiful setting, particularly as the sun set over the wide expanse of farming land spread out below the settlement. Most settlements on Frontier were situated similarly – a congregation of buildings situated in a defensible position which used the geography of the land to protect those buildings from the cyclonic storms that regularly assaulted them during the storm season, or any passing dangerous wildlife.

As the last of the horgal herd jogged through the gate in the repaired fence near the settlement's stockyards, Shanna called Storm and Twister to her. The two starcats were dusty and had demonstrably had enough of herding horgals to last them a lifetime. Storm flicked one disgusted look at the shuffling herd of animals, now happily making inroads on bales of hay set out in the paddock or burying their noses in troughs of fresh water. Twister hummed in a fairly resigned tone as he looked towards Shanna enquiringly.

"All finished, boys!" Her tone was determinedly cheerful as she brushed dust from Storm's head with one hand and removed a couple of burrs from Twister's ears.

"Patrol, fall in!" Spiron's voice rang out from outside the paddock. He waved a hand at a young man, who nodded and walked off towards the nearest building. Shanna hastened to obey, her two cats heeling obediently, as she lined up with the others. She was pleased to note that she wasn't the only one looking as filthy and dishevelled as she felt. Even the normally immaculate Scouts of Patrol Ten were looking somewhat the worse for wear, with thick, reddish brown dust coating faces and clothing.

"We've just received word to go straight back to Scout Compound tomorrow morning. Northall has fresh supplies for us, and there's a soft bed for tonight in the community hall, and the public baths are available, so load up, get clean and be ready to leave at first light. Dismissed."

"Well, at least we'll get one night's sleep without the need to take a watch." Verren's grin was wry as he shouldered his pack and walked with the other cadets towards the building indicated by Spiron.

"Maybe we'll be back to normal after tomorrow," said Amma hopefully, as she dropped her pack on the floor inside the building, noting the neat pallets laid around the outside walls of the hall, now turned into a makeshift barracks for the night.

"In your dreams, Amma! Since when has anything been normal since we joined the Scouts?" Ragar laughed at Amma's hopeful expression. "We'll just be back to constant drills and sweat, right up until the next storm arrives..."

"Well, I'm for a wash before I restock my pack," said Zandany, "I reckon I've swallowed about ten kilos of dust in the last five days." The others laughed, and the six of them walked out together in search of the hot water. There had been what Shanna privately referred to in her mind as 'a cessation of hostilities' from Taya, during the post cyclone activities. Practically, it meant that she and Taya operated in an atmosphere of false camaraderie, getting the task at hand done, but making sure that they spent the minimal time possible in each other's company. It was partly a show for the Patrol they were working with, knowing that despite the storm recovery, they were still being scrutinised by the experienced Scouts, but Shanna wasn't sure that their act had fooled anyone in Patrol Ten. One thing was certain though, she knew that as soon as her private starcat classes recommenced, the animosity would flare unchecked again, and for that reason alone Shanna hoped that there would be more post storm tasks waiting for them when they returned to Watchtower.

The following morning, the patrol resumed its standard travelling formation for the tip back to Watchtower, each cadet paired with a Scout, who constantly quizzed and educated while on the move. Each cadet took a spell navigating with Spiron. Shanna no longer felt as intimidated by the Patrol Leader as she had been originally, having come to realise he was a fair if hard taskmaster, with a true gift for leadership. His patrol was a smoothly oiled machine, the individual members working together with a minimum of fuss, as they performed their tasks.

Allad called Satin to him as he and Shanna moved into the point position, and the two of them sent their starcats out in their now customary three pronged formation. The two youngsters had almost reached their full growth, both close to Satin's size, but they deferred without question to the older starcat as she adjusted their positions precisely to her liking.

"She still has them totally under her paw, doesn't she Allad?" Shanna was a definite fan of Allad's starcat.

"Yes she does – and they're wise enough to know it too." Allad smiled back at Shanna from his lofty height, moustache crinkling as they walked around a long bend in the road.

Thick vegetation sheltered the road in this vicinity, its greenery fresh and clean after the recent heavy rain. Storm was flanking the head of the patrol on the left, Twister on the right, and Satin was a hundred metres in front, working her way straight down the middle of the road. Shanna could see a few tracks and wheel marks in the road surface, which meant that life was beginning to return to normality in this region at least.

"Has she ever had any cubs, Allad?" Shanna was curious, because she imagined that cubs produced by Satin would rival Sabre's, and they were widely acknowledged in starcat breeding circles to be the best.

"Not yet," he replied. "She's never met a male starcat that suited her, really. Most of them just roll over and behave like cubs when she's around." He smiled briefly, as if those thoughts amused him greatly. "The patrol generally sits round watching when I try and introduce her to males, they take bets on how long it'll take her to intimidate them – it's become a kind of sporting event for them."

"Has she met Boots or Moshi? They're two of my parents' breeding males. Moshi is actually Storm and Twister's father, so he's off the list, but it wouldn't surprise me if Satin and Boots got along rather well. They've got some very similar traits, and Boots isn't yet mated." She grinned as she recalled Storm and Twister's first meetings with the two male cats.

"Not that I'm aware," Allad said, "But it might be worth an introduction one day. I'd trust your opinion any time where starcats are concerned, given the way that your two are turning out," Shanna blushed and ducked her head. "So if you think Boots might be the love of Satin's life, then it's certainly worth a try. I'd like to see what kind of cubs that lady of mine might produce." He smiled at her from under his bushy eyebrows.

Shanna nodded as they continued down the vegetation shrouded roadway.

"Let me know when the time might be right and I'll arrange an introduction for Satin."

At the end of the day, as the sun began to lower itself towards the horizon, the patrol reached Watchtower's gates. As fortune would have it, Shanna spied Adlan by the gate waiting for Kaidan, with Moshi and Boots sitting neatly at his heels. She nudged Allad, waving her hand at her father.

"You know that introduction I promised? It's going to happen without any planning at all. That's Boots up there, and Satin's about to walk right past him. You might want to ask Spiron if we've got time to pause for a few moments." Allad nodded, a smile spreading over his face, and after telling Shanna to remain on point, made his way back to Spiron, speaking quickly to him. There was a nod and a reply from Spiron, and then Allad was back with Shanna.

"Patrol, form into ranks for entry to the town." Spiron's voice rang out from behind Shanna. They complied, neatly forming ranks of four, starcats precisely at their heels. Spiron brought them to a formation halt, just in front of the gates, where Adlan waited for Kaidan. He gave them a welcoming smile and greeted Spiron, admiring the seventeen starcats ranked with their Scouts, with a professional eye, before winking at his daughter. Boots and Moshi sat obediently behind him, although both were openly appraising the other starcats.

Spiron moved out of the ranks and chatted briefly with Adlan out of earshot of the rest of the patrol, gesturing with his hands and motioning towards Allad and Satin. The green tidemarked starcat was the image of perfection, sleek, gleaming, and with her tidemarks glowing steadily. Adlan grinned and nodded. Spiron motioned Allad forward with one hand and then returned to the patrol.

"Make yourselves comfortable. We're just going to finish off our patrol with a light entertainment – we've made good time, so we can pause for this! Allad's going to attempt to introduce Satin to another eligible male." There was general laughter from the Scouts as Spiron ordered them to fall out and find somewhere comfortable to sit for the next few minutes. The Scouts began taking bets on how long the male starcat would last at Satin's velvet paws. Shanna thought for a few moments, and then casually strolled over to Nelson, the money holder.

"I'll bet on her taking to Boots." Nelson looked up, surprised, at her bet, which was completely contrary to everyone else's.

"I'll give you good odds on that one," he said, "You've not seen Satin with a prospective suitor yet, have you?"

"No," replied Shanna, "but I do know Boots!" She handed her small amount of coinage over to Nelson, and he noted her stake on a small notepad. A couple of the other Scouts looked speculatively at Boots and then began negotiating with Nelson. They all settled down in a clear space to one side of the main gates to watch the fun. Introducing prospective starcat pairs was an oddly formal procedure when the starcat was trained and partnered, as a partnered starcat was a very loyal creature, and required tacit permission to seek out a mate. Rejection or acceptance was an engaging procedure. The patrol, all of whom had previously spectated at no less than eleven prior introductions for Satin, looked eagerly towards what promised a very entertaining few moments.

Adlan put Moshi to a stay in a dropped position near the gate waiting for Kaidan, and then brought Boots over to the cleared area. Allad and Satin were already waiting for them, standing near Shanna who had found herself a vantage point on an old tree stump to watch the ensuing drama.

The two men stood about twenty metres apart, each calling his starcat to stand forward. Satin strolled forward, lithe strength in every line of her bearing, and a certain aura of aloofness. Boots strolled forward to stand in front of Adlan, displaying his smooth coat and tidemarks to best advantage. He was a particularly large cat and walked with a studied insolence that made Shanna giggle, until the two cats were about ten metres apart. Adlan took several steps back, and then made a complex gesture to the big male. Allad mirrored his actions with Satin and the two cats began to move slowly in a circle. There was an excited murmur from the Scouts – this was usually the moment that Satin tended to humiliate her potential suitors. They looked forward to seeing what she might do this time.

The two starcats circled slowly, their tidemarks glowing and pulsing in varying patterns as they eyed each other. There was a sudden flurry of movement and everyone leaned forward, intent on the action, only to discover that both cats had spun as one to circle in the other direction. Shanna caught a few murmured comments that indicated surprise from most of the Scouts. Boots hummed a challenge at Satin who stared unwinkingly at him, tidemarks gleaming brightly. She blurred into top speed directly at Boots, who seemed to vanish from view, reappearing where Satin had begun from. Satin glided to a halt, tidemarks rippling in surprise, the first time Shanna had ever seen her even slightly discomfited. She smiled quietly to herself as the murmurs from behind her escalated slightly. Even Allad was slightly taken aback, judging by his expression, which then quickly melted into delighted surprise.

Boots hummed again, this time his tone was deeper, and his tidemarks began to glow more brightly. Satin regarded him with a different expression on her face as the two began circling each other again. She hummed slightly, her tone enquiring, and Boots hummed back, with a slightly mocking tone to his hum. He blurred suddenly into action, spinning on the spot and leaping towards Satin in a graceful move, as she again mirrored his actions. There were louder murmurs from the patrol, and Adlan was nodding his head steadily, almost in rhythm with the circling cats. The two cats began a graceful circling dance, each alternating with a blurring speed movement which was immediately mirrored by the other. Finally, Satin hummed loudly, with a challenging tone to her voice, and faded rapidly, to vanish from view. Boots immediately followed suit, and then all that was visible to the watching patrol, was the odd puff of dust, signalling the presence of the two starcats, still within the cleared area.

There was a sudden intense flurry of dust, and the two cats abruptly popped into view, leaping and feinting at each other, tidemarks flashing and flicking in complex patterns. There was one last sudden flash of movement, and then sudden stillness. Satin was purring loudly, and Boots was pressed firmly up against her sleek side, his tail wrapped firmly around Satin's, and with one paw neatly slotted between her front two. He was looking almost unbearably smug, and Satin gently whacked him with one of her paws to draw his attention to her, green tidemarks glowing very brightly as she continued to purr.

"Well, I think I'll collect my winnings now." Shanna broke the silence with an uncharacteristically loud and satisfied statement. Allad's head flipped around and he laughed uproariously at the stunned expressions on everyone else's faces.

"So how much have you won?" he asked, as the two cats continued to purr at each other, and Adlan walked across to greet his daughter.

"Yes, how much did you win, Shan?" Adlan was quite amused as he hugged his daughter. "Boots looks pretty happy with himself."

"Yes he does, doesn't he? I was pretty sure Satin would like him, but you never know, really. She's a lot like him, same kind of attitude, same sense of humour, same quirky kind of personality. He's also got an enormous quota of self confidence, and I thought he'd probably be one of the only starcats who could ever stand up to Satin." Shanna was rather happy with herself as well, and her monetary wealth had increased substantially in the last fifteen minutes, although she wasn't about to mention the total amount – Nelson's odds had been very generous, and he was looking slightly green. "So, Allad, it looks like you'll be able to find out what kind of cubs Satin might produce now, all you have to do is notify Dad when a good time might be."

Allad nodded, his eyes on the two happily glowing starcats, his expression delighted.

"I'm glad she's finally found someone to match her. I think the cubs will be spectacular. We'll need to think about the timing, because she'll be out of action for field work for a bit, until the cubs are born and weaned, so I'd say maybe towards the end of storm season. I'll find out where we're to be assigned, and then we'll make some plans." He grinned ruefully. "I'm not sure how we'll go separating those two right now, though, what do you reckon Adlan?" Adlan grinned back. The two starcats had now wandered over, tails still linked, and the purring was deafening.

"If she's waited a while to find the right mate, a little longer won't hurt her. She may be a little tetchy for the next day or so, but she'll get over it as long as you convey to her that it's only a brief time until she can be with Boots for much longer. When you're ready, you and Satin can stay with us for the duration. We've a guest room you can have."

"Thanks Adlan, I'd like that." Shanna thought she could detect a slight mistiness in Allad's eyes beneath the bushy eyebrows. "She deserves time with her mate." Starcats mated for life, which was one of the slightly complicated aspects of partnering one, as their love lives needed to be catered for.

"Patrol, form up." The patrol fell in, and Allad called Satin to him. She looked at him with unblinking eyes, tail still entwined with Boots' and then slowly let the contact lapse, strolling slowly over to Allad with many looks back to Boots, who hummed softly at her and made as if to follow her, then halted at Adlan's hand signal. Shanna had to stifle a giggle as Satin deliberately stepped heavily on Allad's foot as she positioned herself beside him. She leaned her whole weight into her right front paw, and Allad grunted slightly, his expression becoming resigned. Boots was looking somewhat annoyed too as Adlan called him over, just as Kaidan appeared at the town gate. Boots gave Adlan a hefty whack with his tail as he strolled over to Kaidan, turning his back and completely ignoring Adlan, lavishing loving attention on the surprised Kaidan.

There were muffled sounds of amusement from the patrol as they marched through the gates, and started the trek through Watchtower and up to Scout Compound. Shanna chanced a quick wave to her father and brother as they started down the road towards Hillview. She noticed that both Boots and Satin were shooting longing glances towards each other, the normally graceful Satin occasionally thumping into Allad, who sighed, as he realised that there would be large quantities of patience required to get over the next few days as he coped with his suddenly lovesick starcat.

***

The Garsal exploratory vehicle had been situated over the mineral deposit for the last month, trapped by the flood waters generated by the recent storm. Gradually they had receded, and after relaying information to the colony ship, the troop commander made preparations to continue his search north towards the plateau. As soon as the relief vehicle arrived, they would be on their way, searching for more minerals, more resources and the life signs noted on the plateau.

Anjo's arm had finally healed, and he and Semba were back on normal duties, still secure inside the laser fence. He wasn't sure if he dreaded the coming resumption of the journey northward more than the enforced imprisonment inside the small compound. The Garsal troop commander entered the galley of the vehicle where Anjo laboured over a tray of food, motioning to Semba to remove his weapons belt and utility pouches. She jumped to do his bidding, as he picked up the tray of food and stalked towards the vehicle communication centre.

Both Anjo and Semba listened carefully as he plotted their course for the next day's journey. He was less ambitious about how many kilometres he would cover each day, but they could tell he was anticipating reaching the base of the plateau within the month.

Anjo brought his mouth close to Semba's ear.

"Maybe there'll be somewhere to go if there are some inhabitants on this planet. There's no hope they'll be human, but they can't be worse than the Garsal, can they?" There was a slight hope in Anjo's tone. Semba looked frightened, but nodded slightly and the two of them pretended to clean the already spotless galley, continuing to eavesdrop while the commander planned and communicated with the large ship in the jungle far to the south.

Chapter 21

THREE weeks later, Shanna returned to the Scout Compound accompanied by both Allad and Kaidan. There had been a two day leave at Hillview. Allad, also with two days free, had bowed to pressure from his starcat, who had somehow fathomed that Shanna, Storm and Twister would be returning home – home to where Boots was. She had abandoned Allad to shadow Shanna around the compound, refusing to leave her side and even accompanying her to her room to pack, while casting coy looks at Allad. He, along with the rest of Patrol Ten, had again been spending time tutoring the new cadet class in various skills, this time in preparation for their first formal trip Below which was to occur after the two days leave.

Boots and Satin had spent a blissful two days in each others' company. Shanna didn't think she'd ever seen two starcats so completely besotted with each other. Fortunately Allad, Janna and Adlan had formed a fast friendship over the weekend. The behaviour of the two cats had clearly shown that they were going to spend a considerable amount of time together over the next few years, and that Allad would need to be a frequent visitor to Hillview to accommodate Satin's love life.

Kaidan had enjoyed meeting the big Scout and had badgered both Shanna and Allad into working with him on his woodcraft skills, as he had noted that Shanna had begun to move with the same gliding grace demonstrated by Allad and Master Cerren. Storm and Twister had enjoyed the time at Hillview, and had been much wiser in their approaches to the older cats. Satin, in the company of Boots, had been inspected but accepted immediately into the inner circle of adult cats, Sabre clearly approving of Boots' choice. She continued to treat the two younger cats with her customary firm paw.

Leaving Kaidan at the Records Precinct, Shanna and Allad, accompanied by two happy starcats and one slightly grumpy one, entered the Scout Compound and parted company to finalise their packing for the trip Below. It had been made clear to the cadets that the field trip would be a mix of learning and assessment, and that their every move would be watched. The Patrol would not only familiarise the cadets with the area immediately adjacent to the access tunnel, but take them some distance from the entrance to improve their knowledge of the flora and fauna Below.

Shanna had become much more efficient in her ability to pack for an extended travel period in wilderness areas, and finalising her backpack took only a brief time. Then she and the two cats headed for the arena to meet with the rest of her class and Patrol Ten. Storm was particularly boisterous that morning, bouncing around her room as she packed, and whacking his brother intermittently with a large paw. Twister was more laid back, and had relaxed his long length luxuriously across Shanna's bed to have a last minute snooze, apart from the moments when Storm's paw intruded.

Shanna was first to the arena and sat down to await the others, propping her pack against the storage areas below the seating. It was quite peaceful sitting there, rubbing her two starcats' bellies as they sprawled on the ground at her feet. Her peace was disturbed about ten minutes later, as Taya and Spinner entered the arena, Taya casually dumping her pack in the middle of the arena and standing, back to Shanna, tapping one foot impatiently, and running her hand through her short, dark hair to fluff it up. The morning lessons had continued, but Shanna had still not managed to get her point across to Taya. Shanna shook her head silently, and continued rubbing her two cats' bellies. They were completely undisturbed by Taya's petty behaviour. Spinner ducked his head disconsolately, and Shanna looked at him with some concern. It was unusual to see a starcat sad, except at the death of a mate, cub, or partner. When Zandany and Amma entered, she got to her feet, waving at the others, and hefted her pack into the middle of the arena to wait with them. Verren arrived next, followed shortly by Ragar, their cats greeting the others with nose touchings and body rubbings. Spiron entered five minutes later, and formed them up.

"Cadets, you will now be formally going Below for the first time. I know that for four of you this will actually be the second time, however this expedition will be completely different. This time you're there to learn as much as possible, but also to be assessed as to your fitness for further trips. Apart from failing the probation period, if you are judged unfit by your assessors on this trip you will be required to leave the program. It's unusual to fail at this stage, but it does happen." Spiron took some time to eye each cadet individually as if beginning their assessment immediately. "This trip will extend for up to two weeks, dependent on your progress." Shanna wasn't sure if he meant that a longer trip meant they were not reaching the required standard or were actually doing well. She'd had a sudden pang of anxiety when Spiron had said the word 'fail' and she hoped desperately that Taya and Spinner wouldn't put her into that category. Becoming a Scout was now her whole focus. She thought a brief prayer of entreaty. Spiron went on, "You'll be paired as normal, with the same Scout you've been working with during the last few operations. Again, you will do nothing, touch nothing and go nowhere without the consent or instruction of your Scout." They all nodded their understanding.

"Make sure your starcats are in harmony with you at all times, they're your lifeline Below. A single Scout can survive quite happily with the aid of one starcat, but you must have implicit trust in them, and they in you. Whatever else you do, make sure the two of you work as a partnership," he paused and grinned.

"Or in your case, Shanna, the three of you. Remember that every member of the Patrol will have a say in your fitness for continuing on in the Scout Corps, not just your assigned instructor."

The rest of Patrol Ten filed in and lined up behind the cadets. Spiron gave a curt command and they all shouldered their packs.

"Watch carefully and remember, and *never* divulge this to anyone." He carefully pressed two points in the arena wall, and then pushed gently on the stone panel, sliding it to one side as it moved slowly under his pressure. The opening appeared, and the patrol filed through the hole into the semi darkness beyond, beginning the long trek through the subterranean access.

To Shanna, the trip seemed every bit as long and interminable as the first time they had travelled it - although in the opposite direction - but finally, after nearly a day and a half in the dark, they reached the more cheery confines of the quarters near the access hole to Below.

Here they were greeted again by Damar and Feeny, accompanied this time by a much slimmer starcat trailing six boisterous cubs who bounced and tumbled as they trotted after their mother on short chubby little legs, tidemarks flashing and gleaming in blue and violet patterns. After shooing the cubs back into her quarters, Feeny and Damar escorted the patrol to the access portal, demonstrating the technique to open it from the inside to the cadets, and rapping out the coded cadence that would signal the Scouts on duty inside to open it when they approached from outside.

After a brief farewell, the patrol ventured out into the green, rustling presence of Below. Spiron immediately formed the patrol into the now familiar standard formation, directing Barron and Hunter to take the point, and setting Allad and Shanna to the rear guard. He then moved the patrol south, away from the plateau base, directly into the wilderness.

Allad had Shanna quietly identify the various creatures of the wilderness by sound as their calls echoed through the trees around them. Behind them, Satin, Twister and Storm weaved their way silently through the thick greenery, making sure nothing circled behind them without their knowledge. To all sides, the patrol's starcats wove through the vegetation, silent in their watchfulness, each novice starcat shadowed by an experienced one. Shanna stopped Allad with a quiet hand on his arm as she noticed a mauve flash through the trees. She pointed silently and raised her eyebrows in query, and he flashed a quick hand signal to Spiron, who halted the patrol. Allad signalled Shanna to proceed through the bush to the mauve flower she had glimpsed. It was a beautiful flower, suspended about a metre off the ground from a tree trunk, with spectacular yellow stamens and a myriad of small blue fruit suspended just below the flower.

"Well done, Shanna," said Allad quietly, "we'll harvest this now. Signal the patrol to circle round." Shanna signalled the patrol and set Storm to circle behind the plant, as Satin paced a wide arc to either side of the plant and Twister went quickly up the nearest tree. As the patrol circled in, the Scouts positioned the cadets to the fore, and set their starcats in a circle around the group to watch.

"Watch this carefully, as it may be a while until you can see this again. This is what?" Allad looked expectantly at the cadets.

"It's a soothall berry flower." Verren's tone was reverent. "It's very rare on the plateau. All attempts to propagate them have failed, so the locations of any known plants are always carefully recorded and the area around is always searched, in case another plant is found, and a clue to their life cycle might be discovered. The fruit has amazing analgesic properties when rubbed on an injury, and it acts to halt almost any wound infection when taken orally as a tea. The taste is absolutely delicious, which makes it dangerous to work with, as it makes your tongue go numb and too much of it will make you fall into a coma..." He broke off, catching the expression on Allad's face and shrugged. "It's relatively simple to harvest, but the plant is usually accompanied by a nest of spooner spiders. Which are, of course, deadly." Verren's bronzed face was a study of concern mixed with humour. Frontier often seemed to pair amazing beauty and resource with the deadliest of companions.

"Well done Verren. All the facts neatly assembled and delivered, and I suspect you'll be able to demonstrate the correct technique for brewing the tea and seeding the fruit – and you will do so this evening when we camp." Allad's eyes twinkled. "Now, the spooner nest. Who can tell me how to identify if there is one?"

Zandany raised a tentative hand. "Check immediately below the flower for signs of webs, and then follow the strands to the nest."

Allad nodded. "All right Zandany, that's your job – off you go." Zandany gulped a little and then moved forward towards the plant, taking care to stop slightly in front of it, and crouched to peer cautiously under the flower.

"There are webs there all right, and they lead backwards around the trunk, then down to the ground; ah, there it is – a small mound of old berry pits held together with web." He drew a slightly shaky breath and moved back into the circle.

"Well done Zandany. What do we do next, cadets?" Allad looked brightly around the quiet circle. No-one really wanted to answer his question, as they were quite sure that they would then be asked to deal with the spooner spiders, so named because of their tendency to huddle in closely pressed groups, each neatly fitted to the other, which would then spring into a flying ring of deadly fangs when disturbed.

There was a moment of silence. Shanna sighed inwardly and opened her mouth resignedly to answer Allad's question, when Amma spoke up a second before she could get a word out. She shut her mouth thankfully.

"You need to carefully remove the pieces of web from below the flower, without disturbing the pile of fruit pits, and then use the web pieces from below the flower to anchor the fruit pits to the ground, effectively trapping the spiders within their nest." Allad nodded approvingly at Amma, and then gestured for her to perform the task. She nodded slowly and then carefully bent and looked under the flower, checking the location of the web strands and the spider's nest. Challon flicked an eyebrow upwards at Allad who nodded, and he moved forward to assist Amma. She gave him a grateful smile before extending slightly shaky hands underneath the flower. Carefully, the Scout and cadet gently detached the individual strands of web, and keeping the tension on the strands, took them across the fruit pits gently in a meshing weave, so that the pile was securely anchored to the ground and the small opening at the top was blocked.

Exhaling gently, the two moved backwards away from the nest, which quivered slightly as the spiders inside realised they were trapped. They would eventually break out, but there would be enough time to harvest the soothall berries.

"And the next step?" Allad was grinning this time.

"Simply pluck the fruit from the bush, and store it carefully in a secure place, then process as soon as possible." Taya was quick with the answer. "And always remember to leave one third of the fruit on the plant." Allad motioned for her to complete the task and she moved confidently forward, although she wasn't too keen on getting particularly close to the quivering pile of fruit pits that marked the spooner nest. After Taya had stowed the fruit in her pack, Spiron directed the patrol to spread out and survey the surrounding area, the cadets each with their attendant Scout overseeing their movements. Unfortunately there were no further soothall berries located, so they continued to move steadily south, occasionally pausing for another object lesson around either an exotic plant, or small animal or insect. Later that day, Barron directed them to a sheltered camping spot in a thick stand of trees, which had drooping branches that leaned towards the ground, making it almost impossible to push through them.

"Why did I pick this spot?" Barron swept his arm around in a semi circle.

"Because those are pungo trees, and nearly all the larger predators refuse to go anywhere near them because of the smell they exude at night, and that's even if we cook." said Ragar, pointing at the large trees. The pungent leaves were already beginning to waft their aroma on the slight breeze sighing around the thicket. Sniffing, Shanna recognised the aroma of the scent paste she'd been supplied with before that first post storm expedition. She wondered fleetingly if they would ever hear any more information about the downed craft and its inhabitant. Spiron then detailed the patrol to set up for the night, and directed Verren and Nelson to begin to prepare the evening meal from the collection of small animals that the starcats had brought in during the trek.

"Nelson, make sure you keep your eyes firmly on Verren at all times, we actually want to be able to eat our food tonight." There was only a slight hint of humour in Spiron's voice, and a large quantity of seriousness. Shanna devoutly hoped that Nelson would supervise Verren extremely closely, as she'd had too many of Verren's practice meals to be entirely happy about him preparing the whole meal by himself. Spiron must have decided that they needed to tough out Verren's learning process, but Shanna genuinely hoped that the patrol would survive it.

Fortunately for everyone's taste buds, Nelson must have been actively involved in the cooking of the small game collection, as the food was actually edible. During the customary hot drink after the meal Spiron took some time to quietly quiz the cadets about the fauna and flora observed during the day, before indicating that Verren should demonstrate the preparation of the soothall berries. Shanna always found it interesting to watch one of her classmates instruct the others. When he'd taught his first lesson in field medicine, Verren had begun by explaining his knowledge of healing.

"My parents, two brothers and four sisters are all healers – I'm the youngest and the black sheep of the family for abandoning the family profession," he grinned at the others and continued, "But you couldn't live in my family without learning a few tips, in fact there was almost no other conversation at the dinner table." Shanna grinned at the memory, and turned her attention to Verren.

He tipped the berries out onto a large leaf in front of him.

"My first tip, is to carefully remove the pits from the seeds while making sure you preserve as much of the flesh as possible. Don't discard the pits, as they're essential for making the tea. If you can't make the tea straight away, the pits can be stored for up to one month." His deft hands were making small incisions in the berries, and popping the pits out onto the leaf. As each pit was removed, Verren placed the berry flesh into a small cup he fashioned neatly out of another leaf. "Now, in the field in an emergency,you can rub the flesh directly onto a wound to relieve pain, but, if you have enough time, like now, you can make a really effective salve which keeps indefinitely, and is a much more efficient use of what is a very limited supply of medicinal plant life."

"Now, I noticed some useful plants earlier, and harvested them as we walked." He placed two large tuber like plants and several fine leafed plants on the leaf next to the pits. "This is oil root, pepperleaf and spiny mint." He pointed at each of the plants in turn. He handed each to Shanna, Zandany and Amma respectively, directing them to peel, strip and shred respectively. After the preparations were complete, he set the oil root to render in a small cooking pot on the smokeless fire, and then when the knobbly oil root had become a hot, thick, oily paste, he placed the pepperleaf and mint in it to simmer along with the blue soothall berry flesh.

As he stirred the pot gently, he said, "You need to simmer this until the berries and leaves have completely disintegrated and the mixture becomes quite thick and hard to stir, then take the pot off the heat, and pour it into a receptacle." He took the pot off the fire and poured it gently into half a dozen small leaf cups. "Make sure these little cups are made out of either pungo tree leaves or frondan leaves. Either of those will actually enhance the properties of the salve – the pungo will also aid in keeping any insects from an open wound." Verren grinned at Barron, who winked back. He then handed a leaf cup to each cadet, and demonstrated how to seal them with sticky sap from the pungo trees. He then showed the cadets how to brew the tea out of five of the soothall pits, reserving the other pits in small leaf packages, and handing them to all the patrol members to stow in their packs. He encouraged each of the Scouts and cadets to sample tiny portions of the tea, so that they would be able to identify its taste and strength easily at a future date.

"Don't forget, that if you over simmer the tea, you'll end up with a decoction that's toxic. You can tell that you've over simmered the liquid by its colour - it will turn a very dark brown." Verren finished by producing a small metal flask from his pack and pouring the tea into it, handing it to the patrol's official medic, Arad, who tucked it away carefully in his pack.

"Well, you're a much better medic than a cook, that's all I can say," said Shanna, stowing her soothall salve carefully in her pack with the berry pits. Verren grinned happily at her, as Cirrus smooched him with her head.

"My parents would be laughing their heads off right now if they could have seen me just then – poetic justice they'd call it. Mind you, they'd be pretty happy I suspect, that I'm not completely ignoring the family trade to 'run off into the wilderness, never to be heard of again'." Shanna laughed quietly as they carefully placed their packs neatly by their sleeping gear. The pungo trees were emitting quite a strong scent which fortunately Shanna quite liked, and they could both hear large creatures disturbing the undergrowth outside the ring of trees. Their starcats were listening intently as the undergrowth rustled just outside overhanging fronds, but appeared relatively unconcerned. Shanna could see Kalli the sentry, seated quietly nearby with her starcat, just under the circle of trees, staring intently into the darkness. She relaxed a few moments later, and her starcat leaned on her knees as she patted him gently.

Spiron quietly announced the watch roster, and Shanna decided she needed to roll herself up in her bedding immediately if she was to get any sleep at all, as she and Allad had ended up with the after midnight watch, and she knew from previous experience that it was an awkward one to cope with. Storm and Twister joined her, one on either side, snuggling their warm lengths against her, and resting heavy heads on her middle. She found their closeness comforting in the oddly scented air, and found her eyes closing as she regarded the stars flicking in and out of view through the gently swaying leaves above her. Sleepily, she again found herself wondering about the creature discovered in the flying craft, where it had come from, what it was doing here, and what it would be like when they finally found its compatriots. She imagined the universe opening up to the population of Frontier – not only a whole world to explore, but a galaxy out there waiting, full of exotic new experiences.

***

Less than forty kilometres away, the Garsal vehicle had stopped for the night. The commander had high hopes of reaching the foot of the plateau within the next few days, after which they would attempt to find a way up the massive sides to explore it and locate any native inhabitants who might prove to be another pool of slaves to help expand the Garsal empire. He had high hopes for the plateau. The Garsal were masters at subduing local populations and adding them to their pools of slave labourers. In the last two hundred years, they had enslaved six technologically advanced races and a lesser number who had only tribal cultures, and they were constantly searching for more as their rapid expansion drove an ever increasing need for labour to construct more hives. The upper echelons of the Garsal population had become accustomed to having their needs met by obedient and submissive slave labour and demand was high.

There was a small query in his mind as to why the life signs seemed to be located only in one area, but he dismissed it. There had been little time for a complete survey of the planet, just a simple scan as the ship passed over two of the major landmasses on the way to the landing site picked from far out in space as the colony ship approached. There had been none of the typical indicators of high technology, just signs of an emerging civilisation.

Anjo huddled in his corner, hoping against hope that this inimical planet had one safe place that the Garsal would be unable to penetrate, and that there were actually sentient inhabitants who might provide them some kind of refuge. Facing towards the vehicle wall, he checked yet again the container of packaged 'itchy hairs' that he and Semba added to as often as possible.

As the first impacts from the evening's quota of hungry carnivores began to rock the vehicle, and the weapon pulses commenced, he thought ahead to what might await him at the plateau. He desperately wanted to escape the Garsal, but was almost too frightened to hope that there might be somewhere to go. The planet itself seemed to be resisting the Garsal with all its might, and he held out to the remote hope that it might have some inhabitants who could shelter him from the nightmare of Garsal slavery. He plummeted from hope to depression in a rollercoaster of emotion from day to day. As he drifted into an exhausted sleep, huddled close to Semba's warm, human body, a tiny spark of hope refused to be smothered in his heart, no matter the practical realities of his situation. It was a very human feeling.

Chapter 22

AS Shanna sent Twister hurtling through the treetops ahead of the patrol, Spiron nodded in approval. While the patrol had carefully worked its way through the bush on its second day of travel, Spiron had used the time to fully explore the capabilities of each of the young starcats, and had so far worked his way through Spider, Cirrus and Punch. It was one thing to see them perform under ideal conditions in the arena, or the relatively tamed wilderness of the plateau, but the conditions Below were a whole different challenge. It was a much more demanding environment, with unusual creatures prone to pop out of the vegetation at any time, and plants that were a hazard all by themselves. Mostly, the patrol travelled in quiet, conversing only in soft tones, the human beings painted to blend into the foliage that surrounded them and with their scent covered by the paste Allad had provided Shanna on that first eventful foray. Several times over the past few days, they had halted to allow a large predator to pass without detecting them. The patrol's standard response on a normal trip Below was to avoid detection and to allow the native inhabitants to pass without disturbance or aggression.

Spiron had Shanna send Storm out to survey the terrain ahead with Satin, and he vanished silently and quickly into the greenery ahead, his blue tidemarked ears pricked and listening. Twister returned to the ground on Shanna's right side, nudging her with his paw and drawing her attention to the tree foliage gripped between his teeth. She thanked him, scratched his cheek, and looked at what he'd delivered.

"It's pungo. He must have found another grove ahead. It might make a good point to stop if we want a break," said Shanna, waving the twig of pungent leaves at Spiron.

"Thanks Shanna, tell him well done." Spiron signalled the rest of the patrol that a rest stop was just ahead. They had been on the move for about four hours, and Shanna's stomach was rumbling slightly, so she was pleased that they'd have a chance to stop somewhere relatively secure to pause for a break and a snack. Each pack contained easily accessible high energy snacks for consumption on the move, but a rest break was always welcome for the chance to consume something that hadn't been baked or dried to rock hardness.

As the pungo grove came into view, Spiron directed Amma, Taya and Ragar to set their cats to guard the grove along with their Scouts' more experienced partners. Shanna ensured that she made much of Twister's cleverness as she deposited her pack on the ground and accessed a piece of cheese to share with the two cats. Twister purred and nudged her hand, and she sat him down, placing the cheese on his nose. On her command, he flipped the cheese in the air and then swallowed it down with great pleasure. It was completely inadequate for a meal for the big cat, but he, like nearly all starcats, had a love affair with cheese, and Shanna used it for special rewards.

The patrol settled down to eat their small portions of food, while the six starcats circled around the grove, silently flitting through the bush, making sure their human partners were safe from any roving danger. Shanna caught occasional glimpses of tails or tidemarks softly glowing through the foliage.

Satin and Storm reappeared thirty minutes later, sliding gracefully into the centre of the grove of trees, both carrying a small quantity of vegetation, and depositing it gently at their partners' feet.

"Tell me what this vegetation means, Shanna," commanded Allad. Shanna bent down and carefully flicked through the pieces that Storm had delivered. Sometimes she felt like she was in the middle of a continuous exam.

"This is another pungo leaf, possibly from this grove but more likely from one further ahead. This one here is a piece of a short spined fern, which suggests a water source, most likely a small spring with a pool as the fern enjoys high humidity and constantly wet feet. The third piece is from another fern but a larger one, a quill fern, which also enjoys water but prefers a fine spray, so I'd think the spring tumbles down from a height into the pool to supply the spray for the quill fern. The last one is from a sugar fig tree which also grows near water, so this might be a good place to camp tonight, dependent on how far away it is."

Allad nodded, and then asked, "So how far would you estimate? Think about how long the cats were away, consider how fast they were moving, and translate that into walk time." Shanna pondered for several minutes, juggling figures in her head.

"Probably about three hours walk, I'd say."

"Close, but more likely four hours – remember how fast a starcat can move, and how much caution we need down here Below. You'd be right on the plateau, but down here you need to add an extra hour for about every three you'd estimate up there." Allad's tone was matter of fact. Spiron called the whole patrol in and reformed them, directing them to follow Satin and Storm as Allad and Shanna directed them to retrace their steps.

He then called Taya forward with Spinner, and requested her to send him up into the trees ahead. Shanna held her breath as she knew that Spinner, although much better than before, would still lack some confidence, and was not always reliable in performing all his tasks. Spinner gave a backward glance at Taya, before leaping into the trees, progressing steadily from branch to branch, but not moving further forward than the front of the patrol. Taya signalled to Spinner to move ahead, and he obeyed but distinctly reluctantly, moving more slowly than strictly required. Spiron shot a look at Taya, who was intently watching Spinner vanish up in the trees, her face expressionless. Ten minutes later Spinner reappeared, leaping down out of the trees to pace beside his partner. Taya continued to walk beside Spiron, looking steadily ahead. He requested her to send Spinner out in a circle around the patrol, and she complied with a quiet command and the sweeping hand signal that Shanna had taught all the cadets. Spinner again looked at Taya, and then moved off into the bush obediently, sweeping in the prescribed wide circle around the patrol. Several minutes later he reappeared silently beside Taya, who looked down at him and nodded. The large powerful cat paced silently at her side, his tail drooping.

Shanna looked at Spinner, he was doing his job the best he knew how, with little acknowledgment or affection from his partner, whom he clearly adored, and he was just as clearly disappointed with her responses. She chanced a quick glance at Spiron, whose face was impassive as he walked beside Taya, quizzing her on starcat commands, feeding and health checks. She answered correctly, demonstrating a large quantity of knowledge about the subject; she had at least, Shanna reflected, remembered all the completely dry facts about starcat care and handling. It was obvious to her, as it had been during all the extra lessons, that Taya was still refusing to love her cat, and try though she would, Shanna had been unable to convince the older girl to show more affection to Spinner. She simply didn't want to hear what Shanna was saying. Her basic training skills were now impeccable, and as they had just heard, Taya could spout as many facts about starcats as required, but she just wouldn't take that final step and commit her emotions. Shanna wasn't sure whether Taya's reluctance was due to the fact that the information came from her, or whether the girl was unable to commit emotionally.

Spiron's face continued to be impassive as Taya spouted fact after fact, until he stopped her with a sudden hand gesture.

"All right Taya, you've convinced me that you know a considerable amount about cat care and training, but you've left out the most important things. What can you tell me about your relationship with Spinner – what are his favourite rewards? Where does he like to be scratched? Where's his favourite sleeping spot? What's his favourite game?" Spiron turned a penetrating gaze on Taya, and she dropped her eyes slightly, then looked at the cat beside her for several seconds, before taking a breath and beginning her reply.

"Well, he doesn't have a particular favourite food, he generally likes the standard foods available, and he mostly likes to be just generally patted…"

"Enough!" Spiron's voice was louder than Shanna had ever heard anyone in the patrol speak while Below. Nearly everyone in the patrol faltered as his voice rang through the trees, and even Spiron appeared slightly startled at the noise he had generated. Taya stopped completely.

"Allad, how far do you estimate until we stop for the night?" Spiron's question was abrupt.

"I'd say we still have around three hours until we're at the spring." Allad's voice was quieter than normal, as if reminding his Patrol Leader of the requirements for safe travelling Below.

Spiron turned to Taya, a frown creasing his forehead, "Taya, we'll continue this discussion when we stop for the night. I'd like some more specifics by then. You can spend the next three hours with Spinner right by your side, contemplating the fundamental flaws in your most recent answers. You'll continue travelling in the centre of the patrol until we camp for the night. Move back now."

The patrol continued moving as Taya fell back to a centre position, Spinner pacing patiently by her side, her face confused and angry, then settling into an unhappy sag. Her starcat nudged her hand gently with the top of his head, and she looked momentarily surprised at his gesture but ignored him before setting her face in a tense miserable expression.

Shanna saw Spiron sigh and shake his head slightly, before calling for Ragar to come up to him with Sparks.

In front of her, Twister's tail was just slightly visible between the leaves of the nearest trees. Storm and Satin were slightly in advance of him, completely invisible to Shanna, but she had complete trust that Twister was following them accurately.

Just over three hours later, Allad tapped her on the shoulder and held one hand to his ear. Shanna concentrated on listening and was rewarded by the quiet sound of splashing water not far ahead. The closer they came to the sound, the more the vegetation began to change; small ferns, tree ferns and water loving plants became more prevalent. A rocky outcrop came into visibility through the trees, and Shanna noticed a number of small furred animals vanishing as they came closer, belatedly realising they were marpigs, which were very succulent eating. Fortunately Fury and Twister were considerably faster on the uptake, vanishing silently after the furry rear ends after quick glances at their partners for permission. Storm reappeared in front of Shanna at that moment, clearly beckoning the patrol forward. They moved carefully into the area near the base of the waterfall, spreading out to investigate what Shanna felt must be the most beautiful place she had ever seen.

A delicate waterfall floated down from twenty metres above, sending out plumes of spray into the air to water the ferns surrounding the clear pool below. The rock face towered two hundred metres above them, extending to either side for several kilometres forming a ridge line, and a kind of mini plateau rising from the forest surrounding them. The whole panorama was spectacularly beautiful. Satin was sitting like a queen on one of the rocks surrounding the pool, her green tidemarks glowing softly in harmony with her surrounds.

To the west, the sun was sitting low on the horizon as the patrol settled into a sheltered hollow in the rock face, an ideal spot to shelter from any of Frontier's dangerous denizens who might choose to stroll in for a drink at the pool. The patrol had identified a number of animal prints around the pool, mostly medium sized predators and mammals - nothing particularly large or overly dangerous - but it was always better to be prepared when travelling Below. Kalli sat just outside the half circle idly stroking her starcat as she kept watch while the patrol finished their evening meal.

"Shanna, a word please," said Spiron as he wiped his hands on a piece of wide leafed fern, and then discarded it into the smokeless fire. He walked with her to the edge of the circle of warm firelight. "Those lessons you were working on with Taya - about improving her partnership with Spinner. What exactly have you been teaching her?" This was exactly the question Shanna had been dreading, and she had spent part of the afternoon's journey trying to work out what to say, certain that she would be asked. She took her time to answer, searching for the right words.

"I've been trying to work with Taya on her communication with Spinner." She had decided in the end, to keep the conversation simple. "And trying to improve the way they work together."

"And just how have you been doing that?" Shanna sighed as she realised her attempt to evade the meat of the question wasn't going to work.

"I've been trying to teach her how to show him she loves him." That was the crux of the matter, really. Nothing she had tried had worked. In the last couple of weeks before leaving for Below, she had even screwed up her courage to tell Taya outright that the problem was her lack of affectionate response to her starcat. The older girl had simply laughed at her, coming the closest to scoffing Shanna had ever seen her during a lesson. "I've tried absolutely everything I can think of. I've been subtle, I've been blunt, and I've tried tens of different strategies."

"I would say that you have, so far, not succeeded." Spiron was grim. "It's not your fault, Shanna, the other cadets' cats are excellent – above average for this stage to be quite honest, but you probably should have brought the problem to our attention before we came Below." He rubbed his forehead. "Unfortunately, we're all here now, with one pair who are not truly a pair yet. Do you think the relationship between Taya and Spinner is beyond saving at this time?" Shanna was surprised that Spiron would ask such a question of her, but did her best to answer, Spinner's obvious unhappiness the catalyst to provoke her into spilling her most private thoughts.

"I think it's crunch time, Sir. Spinner's heart is close to breaking. He tries his heart out to please her, but receives no real response. He's a lovely cat, clever and loving, but she just doesn't seem to see it." All the bottled frustration finally boiled over. "I have no idea how to fix the problem. I've tried everything I know, and yet Taya won't listen to me and I just can't seem to get through to her, in fact, I think that she isn't listening because it's me telling her. I think she thinks I don't belong in the Scout Corps because I'm younger than she is, and her dislike of me is twisting everything. I was hoping that coming Below might make the difference, but it hasn't. I'm sorry I didn't come to you or someone else earlier." She was close to tears; Storm and Twister flanked her, sensing her distress, and gently nudged her hands with their silky heads in an offer of comfort. She allowed her hands to stroke the sleek fur, pulling the tidemarked ears gently. It was an enormous relief to finally speak her mind, but one source of anxiety still pulled urgently at her.

"Will this affect my future in the Scout Corps, Sir?" she burst out, suddenly. Spiron looked down at her in consternation.

"Oh, Shanna, don't worry about that. We know that you've done everything you could have. *Your* position in the Scout Corps is not under a cloud at all." He put a hand on her shoulder, and turned her to face the group around the fire.

"I want you to help me with the one last chance we have to get the idea into her head, Shanna. If things don't get sorted out this trip, then Taya will no longer be part of the Scout Corps." Spiron was still speaking grimly. "We'll begin tonight. Just follow my lead, and we'll see how far we can get." Shanna was aghast, she didn't like Taya, but she didn't want to see the other girl dropped because of her own stubbornness. She already loved the life she had tasted, and couldn't imagine how Taya would feel if she were deprived of it and, Shanna suddenly realised, most likely her starcat as well. The thought pushed a cold sinking feeling into her belly as she nodded at the patrol leader, and then followed him back into the circle of firelight. Zandany and Karri, accompanied by their starcats, relieved Kalli as the sun finally sunk below the horizon and the darkness fell like a curtain over the forest. The pungo tree scent rose on the slight breeze.

Around the fire, the other Scouts and Cadets had completed the evening cleanup and were sitting chatting quietly. Spiron and Shanna resumed their seats in the group. The embers were glowing quietly, bathing their faces in flickering, warm, ruddy light, and all at once Shanna felt a weight lift from her shoulders. Her nagging problem was now a shared problem, and it was an enormous relief. She felt stupid that she had not brought her issues with Taya to Master Peron, Allad or Spiron before the trip Below. Perhaps then tonight's uncomfortable conversation would have been unnecessary. She was intensely interested in how Spiron thought he'd be able to overcome Taya's resistance.

"Barron," Spiron spoke in a light tone. "How about you tell the cadets how you found out Hunter's favourite food was honey?" The patrol second smiled cheerfully and chuckled softly as he tipped the dregs of his cup on the ground.

"You remember how we'd been working on silent recalls?" The other cadets suddenly realised that Spiron and Barron had been in the same cadet class, and had probably been friends for years. It put a whole new perspective on their own futures, and the relationships they were developing now. "Well, I'd decided to hide myself in the dining room kitchen, and I'd ended up in the storeroom, under the bottom shelf at the back. The cooks knew I was there, but just kept on working." Shanna grinned as she realised she was not the first cadet to make the mistake of doing a recall exercise inside. "I whistled, and a couple of minutes later, I heard Hunter sliding around the kitchen bench, and the staff giggling as he cannoned into the odd stool or box – he always had huge feet, and was a tad on the clumsy side – and then he whacked into the door of the storeroom, and it bounced open. Well, he didn't stop, just barrelled on through the storeroom to the back where I was hiding... Straight into the shelf of honey above me. There were buckets and buckets of it, flying all over the place, and I think nearly all of them ended up on me – with their lids off, of course, and then a really full one landed on my head. The next thing I knew, I was waking up, covered in honey, on the floor of the storeroom. I must have been unconscious only briefly, but that didn't really bother Hunter, as he was too busy slurping the honey off my face, and it took me several minutes to extricate myself, and he wouldn't stop licking me until I'd had a shower after we'd finished the lesson – I was absolutely covered with honey and cat slobber. It took me a very long time to live it down." Barron smiled as he reminisced, and Shanna laughed to imagine Hunter as an engaging, big pawed, clumsy cub, with a honey fetish.

"Hey, do you remember when Spangles scoffed all the marmal sausage out of your pack six months ago? It was after we'd found that staureg harassing the farms out past Red Knoll..."

Perri nodded, "She loves marmal sausage – it's always one of the best rewards for her – although she's almost as partial to an armpit scratch. She just can't resist that sausage though, she even taught herself to undo the buckles to get into the pack. I've found it's a useful skill though, at times." She smiled as Spangles rolled over at her feet, presenting her with an armpit to rub.

"Storm and Twister are cheese freaks," said Shanna, who had finally caught on to Spiron's strategy, "They're absolutely addicted. I always try and carry a few bits in my pack for them. Storm actually got his head stuck inside my pack after the last cyclone operation – I think there was a tiny piece of cheese stuck right down at the bottom, and he was trying to lick it off the seam. He also likes to sleep with his head on my middle for some reason, and Twister's of the opinion that full body contact is the only way to go, and he takes up heaps of the bed."

"Do you remember when Cirrus kept leaping into my arms?" asked Verren. The other cadets laughed, trying to remember to keep the sound down, as the image of Verren crashing to the ground replayed in their minds and the Scouts asked for descriptions of the impacts. Verren described it from his point of view with enthusiastic input from the other cadets, who happily embellished his descriptions.

"So have you finally managed to stop her doing that?" asked Arad through gasps of quiet hilarity.

Shanna was surprised to see Verren blush slightly as he answered. "Well, mostly, occasionally when we've been roughhousing, she gets a little overenthusiastic and tries it again. I've had to get good at dodging, as I nearly keep getting crushed..." There was general amusement for his embarrassment. "It's getting much less though," he hastened to add.

"So Taya, how about Spinner?" There was a sudden silence in the circle and all eyes turned towards Taya, whose face was slightly in shadow. She got suddenly to her feet and walked to the edge of the circle of light, turning her back on the conversation. Spinner, who had been lying at her feet, stood immediately, and moved to sit firmly next to her. There was a sudden silence around the fire. Taya remained standing, staring out into the darkness that surrounded them, as the conversation slowly resumed in the circle behind her. Shanna noticed Spiron watching Taya covertly from his position near the rock face, and also turned her attention that way, trying to be inconspicuous about it. After a few uncomfortable moments, the rest of the patrol began to chat quietly amongst themselves, and faintly, she could hear the others continuing the conversation around her, discussing their cats' foibles and favourite foods.

Taya continued standing facing away into the darkness, with Spinner sitting at her feet, staring in the same direction. Half an hour later, Shanna saw Taya's hand slowly reach out to touch Spinner's head. He responded by leaning his cheek into it, tidemarks glowing gently, the gentle rumble of his purr reaching Shanna's glad ears. She glanced at Spiron, and saw a satisfied expression steal its way across his face. Normal group chitchat had done what weeks of plain speaking had been unable to achieve. Shanna only hoped the antagonism from the older girl would now slowly subside.

***

The Garsal exploration came to a halt for the day near what appeared to be a small version of the enormous plateau clearly visible to the north. The vehicle was carefully lodged into a crevice in the southern rock wall, the only vulnerable point now the very front of the vehicle, the other aspects securely protected by solid rock. As a special concession to their unusually secure positioning the Commander detailed only a forward watch, allowing the majority of the troops a full night's rest before they arrived at the base of the plateau sometime within the next two days. The small plateau was a considerable obstacle, but the commander was sure he would find an accessible point to go over it, or, if necessary, they would simply go around it, even if it took a day or two more.

Anjo and Semba collapsed exhausted into their bedding. It had been a long day of travelling through thick scrub and the final approach to the plateau had necessitated the crossing of a small watercourse, which had bogged the vehicle down in the mud. They had again been required to foray from the vehicle to feed cables around trees to winch the vehicle out. Semba had had a close brush with death, when she disturbed a nest of insects below a pretty, mauve flowered plant. They had come flying out in a ring towards her, as if fired from some kind of weapon. Only a fortuitous slip in the mud had saved her, the insects landing on the carapace of one of the Garsal troopers, attempting to bury their fangs in the chitinous shell-like exoskeleton. Two had penetrated the soft skin between the neck joint and the thorax, and the trooper had died screaming within a few minutes. The others had then scuttled back into a small pile of what looked like some kind of fruit pits, avoiding the still quivering form of the trooper.

So far the troop losses on this journey had been heavy. The commander now had only half of the troopers he had commenced the trip with. Anjo considered it a miracle that neither he nor Semba had yet perished. Both had been injured, both had come very close to death, yet somehow they still survived. Perhaps the planet would overcome the Garsal through sheer attrition, but somehow Anjo doubted it. If this colony failed, then another would come. The planet was in too critical a location in the Garsal expansion plan for them to bypass it. The garsal mantra – "We come, we hold, we breed" was like the sound of a tolling bell inside his head.

Chapter 23

THE morning dawned clear, as Shanna and Allad finished their watch shift and handed over to Nelson and Verren. They sent their cats off to hunt in the early light. As they returned to the sleeping patrol, Shanna could see Spinner lying with his head leaning on Taya's feet, one eye regarding her as the two of them began to stir the fire's embers gently, coaxing a small flame from the dry wood set aside the night before. Automatically Shanna reached out to place the billy on the fire, but was stopped by Allad's hand. He pointed inside the vessel, and Shanna could see that something small was swimming around inside it. On closer examination, she could see that it was some kind of tiny aquatic animal.

"Bring the billy very carefully over to the pool, Shanna," said Allad, rising to his feet. "Try not to frighten the creature, and keep your hands on the outside of the billy."

"What is that?" The small animal had webbed feet, a long, supple tail with a flattened end, and a sinuous body with a duck-like snout, that undulated quickly through the water left in the billy.

"It's a funny little creature," he replied, "We call it a flotter, and you'll see quite a few of them if you camp near still water Below. We've never seen them above, so either they don't like the altitude, or they just never made it up there. They've a few interesting tricks, but they can't jump, which is why that one's stuck in the billy."

He indicated that Shanna should carefully pour the creature out of the billy and onto the rocks surrounding the pond. She complied, being careful to keep her hands out of the way, just in case it had any ideas about biting the hand that was rescuing it. The little creature immediately began to change colour to mirror the rocks around it, almost melting into the crevices around it, so that within moments, Shanna had to work hard to see it.

"That's pretty clever," she said. "What else does it do?"

"This." Allad poked the camouflaged creature with a small stick, and it suddenly changed colour to a bright red, opening its mouth enormously wide before producing what appeared to be fog from it. He waved the stick through the fog, and the tip of the stick crumpled before their eyes, disintegrating into dusty particles. "And that is why you check carefully before you put the morning pot on the fire!"

He dropped the stick as the flotter recamouflaged itself, and then carefully keeping his hands away from the flotter, washed and refilled the billy before taking it back to the fire. Shanna joined him at the fire, noting with a final backward glance that the flotter had completely vanished from sight.

"So have you found any use for the flotter, yet?" Shanna asked.

"Not really, there's certainly potential in whatever it is that it produces from its mouth. If it contacts human flesh, a nasty burn results, and you don't want to inhale too close to one that's misting. We think that the fog is probably a kind of acid. The problem is, no-one's figured out how to transport any back above for testing without killing them, as so far they've simply fogged whatever anyone's tried to put them in and escaped," Allad replied.

After setting the morning ration of porridge to cook, Allad had Shanna cast around the pool looking for anything edible to add to their supplies. She managed to locate several nut bearing plants and harvested quite a quantity of nuts, which they then roasted in their shells on the fire, before putting them aside in neat piles for each of the Scouts to stow in their packs. Shanna took the morning meal over to Verren and Nelson, receiving grateful murmurs of appreciation as they sipped their steaming tea.

An hour later, the patrol formed up to resume their journey, regretfully leaving the spectacular beauty of the waterfall pool. Shanna was starting to feel much more comfortable about travelling Below. The unfamiliar was slowly beginning to feel less threatening, and she felt more and more that she could identify with the Scouts' philosophy of becoming part of the environment and working with it, rather than attempting to subdue it by force. The constant need to be watchful was wearing but also aided in heightening her appreciation of the wilderness, and she was beginning to understand just how difficult it would eventually be to expand the human settlement on Frontier to Below. Many more years of research by the Scout Corps would be required before the first tentative settlements were established.

"This small plateau extends for several kilometres to the east and west, and beyond it is a portion of Below that we're keen to resurvey for soothall berries, as many plants have been found there in the past. Part of our task during this trip will be to perform that survey." Spiron regarded the cadets one by one again. "Dependent on how you perform over the next few days, we may extend our time Below to push a little further south, so make sure you perform to the best of your abilities. Now, we'll actually be heading initially to the east, where there's a slope that's easy to ascend to the top of this plateau. It's much easier and faster to go over than around. Amma and Challon, you'll take point, everyone else, set yourselves as per the standard rotation behind them."

The patrol moved out, following the sure lead of Challon and Amma. Shanna was happy to see Spider moving confidently ahead with Challon's cat to take the lead. Nodding to Allad, she sent Storm out to one side, with Twister slightly behind him, to perform a lateral screening manouvre.

***

The Garsal exploratory vehicle lurched into motion, slowly trundling itself out of the crevice where they had spent the night. The commander issued the instruction to drive east, searching for an access point for the vehicle to climb over the plateau. Anjo and Semba clung to the galley fixtures as the vehicle swayed from side to side across the uneven ground, while attempting to stow the morning meal's debris in cupboards and pull out drawers. There was a particularly sharp lurch, and Semba cannoned into the sharp edge of the benchtop, hastily stifling a gasp of pain.

***

The patrol breasted the top of the mini plateau. Before them, to the north, the ocean of forest they had just traversed swayed in the edges of the breeze. Also to the north, Shanna could see the plateau rock faces obscuring the horizon. Turning her back on the stunning vista, she peered ahead into a stand of trees, looking for the southern edge of the small plateau. Trees grew thickly, and her eyes were unable to penetrate far into the green gloom.

"How far across is this plateau?" Shanna shaded her eyes with her hand the better to see further into the vegetation.

"About ten kilometres," replied Spiron, adjusting his pack straps slightly and sending Fury ahead of the patrol to do a quick sweep of the immediate vicinity. Shanna could see a number of marmals vanishing into the bush ahead, scattering rapidly in front of the starcat. A flock of small colourful birds spun out of the trees ahead, wheeling in a semi circle before coming back to roost. With a hand signal, he sent the patrol into formation and they began the traverse across the mini plateau.

***

The Garsal vehicle came to a halt at the beginning of an incline that looked as though it might be a suitable access to the top of the obstructing rock wall. The commander sent two of his remaining troops out to inspect the incline and they obeyed, shouldering their weapons and leaping down the access ramp to perform a quick scan around the vehicle, before hurrying up to the tree shrouded incline. One stationed himself at the base of the incline, watching the surrounding vegetation intently for any sign of hostile animal life. The other trooper shouldered his way through the overhanging trees, faceted eyes darting nervously from side to side, while advancing up the incline as fast as possible. He was gone for several minutes, before those inside the vehicle saw him return to the other trooper, gesturing that the incline was indeed a viable access. Just before he reached the other trooper, he appeared to stumble then caught himself, tugging frantically at a long vine that had snaked out from a low lying plant just to his right, and slung itself around his hind claw. The commander motioned quickly to two additional troopers, and they hurried out to assist the trapped trooper to slash the carnivorous vine away from his leg. After several minutes of frenzied hacking, they finally succeeded and all returned to the vehicle, the injured trooper assisted by the others.

As the three troopers dragged their injured crewmate into the vehicle via the access ramp, Anjo could see a line of punctures through the hard outer layer of its leg, inflicted by the vine. They were beginning to weep heavily, and the trooper was looking quite shaky, its normally black colour paling to a murky green. The able bodied troopers rolled the other into a sickbay berth. As the trooper was attended to, the exploration vehicle jerked into gear and began to grind its way up the incline.

***

The patrol slowly unwound itself from a freeze in the undergrowth as a large staureg stalked off behind a stand of trees. A few minutes later Storm and Twister reappeared, looking pleased with themselves, to brush past Shanna's hands in passing before resuming their survey of the surrounding bush. They skirted a colony of slinking snake vines, whose tendrils twitched as they registered the quiet vibrations from the passing patrol. Fortunately, the vines were easily recognisable due to their bright green foliage and azure flowers.

***

The large black vehicle ground its way over the crest of the incline, finally resting horizontally on the top of the mini plateau. The Garsal commander surveyed the surrounds and directed the vehicle driver to continue north towards the far edge of the mini plateau. The heavy vehicle bumped and thudded over the heavy undergrowth, weaving its way slowly through the trees, causing flocks of birds to erupt at intervals ahead of its slow passage.

***

Barron raised a hand and signalled the patrol to take cover. Quickly scanning the vegetation, Shanna dropped down behind a screen of palms, signalling Storm and Twister to hide. She watched as they faded silently vanishing from sight, and then focused forward, straining to see what might be up ahead. None of her companions were visible, and their starcats were likewise unseen. She watched and listened as hard as she could. And heard absolutely nothing. After several minutes, Shanna realised that it was the absence of sound that had bothered Barron enough to signal the patrol to take cover. There was a complete void of sound around them for some minutes, and then faintly, a low rumbling and crunching noise, which began to steadily grow in volume. It appeared to be coming from directly ahead. A quiet whistle sounded, signalling the patrol to move deeper into cover, and Shanna hastily dropped further back into the bush, secreting herself between a large rock and a frondan tree, noticing Allad vanish around the other side of the rock. Hastily checking her surrounds for signs of anything dangerous, she then froze completely, listening to the unfamiliar sound come closer.

As the rumbling increased, Shanna could also hear the sound of snapping vegetation and loud impacts of something heavy striking trees. A flock of stripy birds exploded out of the forest not far from where Shanna had last seen Barron, and she could see something black and shiny glinting through the greenery ahead. The rumbling grew to a throaty roar, and an enormous black metallic machine burst through the screen of vegetation, thrusting itself forward and over small obstacles in its way, light pouring from several sources into the dim greenness of the forest. Confused thoughts spun their way through Shanna's head, first of which was the thought that this must be yet another of the creatures found in the aircraft. Thoughts of finally contacting something from beyond the atmosphere sent goosebumps marching their way up her neck, and she fought a sudden desire to throw herself out of cover, and force the vehicle to stop in its tracks.

Rationally, she knew that the inhabitants of the vehicle were a complete un-known, and they didn't even know whether they would be friendly but the urge to stand up and flag the vehicle down was surprisingly strong. She pushed it down. The vehicle ground its way slowly over a number of fallen logs, rocking its immense body from side to side, the tracks and wheels sliding and slipping on the loose footing, and causing trees on each side to topple as it struck them with the protective barring around its sides. It left a swathe of devastated forest in its wake, fallen trees, crushed vegetation and deep scoring in the soft, fertile, earth.

As the heavy vehicle slowly ground its way north, vanishing at last as it turned to go around a small hillock the patrol had scaled, a second whistle sounded, and Shanna silently moved through the bush beside the trail left by the immense artifact. A quick signal and Storm and Twister appeared silently beside her, normally smooth fur bristling around their necks, tails held straight behind them, betraying their discomfort with occasional sharp twitches. The patrol gathered silently, moving as one to make sure no sign of them was visible from the trail of devastation left behind the alien vehicle.

Spiron detailed half the patrol to set their cats on a spiralling guard and then gestured them all to squat in a close circle.

"We'll follow whatever that was and see what we can discover about whoever is inside." He paused, "Assuming there is someone inside. Cadets, you will follow my orders or any additional ones given to you by any of the Scouts of this patrol. This is no longer a training exercise." Spiron turned his attention to the other Scouts. "We'll need to be extremely careful not to be seen until we choose to be. At this point, we have no idea what these things are like. We'll need to observe carefully until we have some kind of sense of them, and then we'll send a message to the tunnel. It's important that we notify the council as soon as possible but with as much information as we can gather. I'm not sure if we'll be able to keep up with that vehicle, but they may stop for the night." He paused, eyeing the whole patrol. "We travel completely silent, hand signals only. Taya, you and Spinner travel in the centre position." They all nodded, Taya, for once, completely non-argumentative at the curt placing Spiron had given her. Goose-bumps walked themselves down Shanna's back again. They formed up to one side of the vehicle trail, and began to silently and stealthily follow the receding noise and destruction left by the alien vehicle.

***

Inside the vehicle, Anjo and Semba clung to any available surface as they attempted to continue their cleaning of the sleep capsules and living areas. The troops were all secured in transit seats as the vehicle continued to bump and grunt its way across the mini plateau. They had made good time on the relatively level ground after cresting the incline, and most of the local fauna kept out of their way while they were moving. The commander had high hopes of descending before nightfall, and he was busily plotting a probable course to the base of the major plateau to search for some kind of access and his final successful survey of the life forms.

"Contact the ship and notify them of our location. Let them know that we'll be at the base of the plateau within two days. Tell them I will make contact again when we have an access point." The Garsal commander spun around from the communication centre, casually cuffing Anjo as he passed. "Provide food."

Anjo hurried to do his bidding, lurching as the vehicle heaved itself over a large fallen log.

***

Tracking the vehicle was not proving to be much of a challenge. Towards the late afternoon, the vehicle slowed and began to parallel the sheer edge of the plateau, obviously searching for a way down.

Spiron had the Scouts fan out and flank it, trying to observe if there was anyone within and if so, how many. Dimly lit windows lined the sides of the vehicle, but none of the Scouts had managed to make out more than shadowy figures. After an hour of slow progress, a slope was located with a gradient gentle enough for the massive vehicle to descend. There was a sudden cessation of noise as the vehicle ground to a halt, and a ramp extruded itself from one end. A large door slid partially open and two of the creatures from the aircraft descended it, carrying long objects which, from the way they were carrying them, Shanna concluded, were most likely weapons.

She watched fascinated as the creatures stalked warily to the front of the vehicle, noting that their walking limbs bent in the opposite direction to that of a human being, much like those of a bird. They approached the incline carefully, dark, multifaceted eyes glinting as they surveyed the terrain. One placed itself at the top of the slope, while the other proceeded cautiously down it, swinging its weapon ceaselessly around, jerking at the sound of its own footsteps on brittle shale. It was easy to see that the creatures had no idea what might be lurking in the bush surrounding them, and that they were unaccustomed to outdoor travel. They exhibited absolutely no wilderness skills at all, and despite their alien appearance Shanna could almost taste their fear. After a very short time the two creatures climbed the ramp and the vehicle roared into life again, and began to descend the incline.

A quiet whistle called the patrol in.

"We'll continue to shadow the creatures, but if anything goes wrong, make for last night's camp as fast and quietly as possible. Allad, you and Shanna take the point. I want the security of an extra cat out ahead."

They followed the vehicle down the plateau and into the bush at its base. Just as the sun set, the vehicle came to a halt not far from the slope it had just descended, backing itself towards a clump of rocks. Shanna decided that the creatures inside had learnt the hard way about Frontier's predators, and settled down behind a conveniently located pungo tree, stealthily plucking some of the pungo's overhanging leaves, crushing them silently and rubbing the resultant handful over her exposed skin and uniform. She held the handful out to Allad, crouched beside her. He took them with a nod of thanks. In the fading light, they settled in to wait patiently to see if any of the creatures would emerge from the vehicle.

***

Inside the vehicle, the Garsal commander was deep in discussion with the trooper in charge of the survey equipment. It appeared that yet again, they had stopped right over a deposit of a mineral necessary for the manufacture of some of the crucial components for the hive interior. Initial scans indicated that it might be quite sizeable and therefore a preliminary survey would be necessary. Anjo could see that the commander was in two minds about pausing now that he was so close to the plateau, but as with nearly any subordinate Garsal, the needs of the hive superseded any individual goal.

"Slaves!" Anjo and Semba hastened to report to the commander. "You will begin setting up the laser fence now." They dropped their heads to the ground, shaking as they realised that they would have to venture outside the vehicle immediately, just at the time that the large monsters would begin to zero in on the vehicle. The only redeeming thing was the vehicle's position – there would only be one line of fence to erect. With luck, they might manage it before something came. "Subcommander, take a half squad out to set up a guard until the laser fence is erected."

The Garsal subcommander bowed his head in acquiescence and deployed his squad down the access ramp, as Semba and Anjo began to heft the large poles of the barrier fence out of their storage compartments.

***

From their hiding place, Shanna and Allad had a direct view of the five creatures descending from the vehicle, each armed as the previous two had been, but apparently under the command of the slightly larger figure behind them who deployed them in a semi circle in front of the vehicle. Shanna watched as a small turret on the top of the vehicle swivelled from side to side, a tiny light blinking red on its roof. Then to their stunned surprise, two slightly smaller figures appeared from the vehicle's interior laden with large poles that they were struggling to carry. The two figures were very much human, somewhat smaller than the norm on Frontier, and clothed in a variety of ill fitting, ragged garments.

Shanna froze as she heard a sudden roar not far away in the bushes to the east. A wandering staureg, perhaps the one they'd seen earlier, no doubt attracted to the light and noise emanating from the now stationary vehicle. She looked sideways at Allad, who signalled her to remain completely still, and sent Satin into the bushes with one casual hand flick. She lifted one eyebrow at him, jerking her head slightly in Storm and Twister's direction, and he shook his head very slightly. She returned her attention to the drama unfolding in front of her.

***

Anjo and Semba both flinched as the roar of one of the larger beasts shook the air around them. They dropped their poles in a heap on the ground, and then returned quickly to the ship to collect more, along with the power pack for the energy beams. Anjo also slung the hole digger over his shoulder just before they began their trek down the ramp again, to make sure he didn't need to make another trip up into the vehicle. The faster the fence was erected, the better. The roar sounded again much closer than before, and the turret on the top of the vehicle began to spin from side to side. The sun had now fully set, and it was becoming darker by the second. Anjo began to dig the first hole as fast as he could, aware that his life hung by a thread. The Garsal guards were increasingly edgy as the two humans laboured to put the fence together.

***

Shanna watched as the two human figures began to place tall black poles into holes they had dug in the ground with some kind of mechanical tool. She could hear the staureg beginning to approach through the trees, its characteristic gait pattern thudding heavily through the undergrowth. Allad tapped her on the arm and indicated that she should now send Twister up through the trees towards the staureg. She sent him off, trusting that Satin would direct the action around the staureg and keep him safe.

As the sound of the oncoming predator increased, the creature that appeared to be commanding the others dealt a heavy blow to the smaller of the human figures, which staggered and fell to the ground, then struggled to its feet and laboured faster. Shanna almost gasped but caught herself, and looked sideways at Allad. His normally cheerful face was now set in lines, and he looked grim, an expression that did not go well with his bristling moustache and mobile eyebrows.

***

Anjo dared not look behind at Semba, despite hearing the heavy blow and the thud of her body impacting the ground. He dug yet another hole for the laser fence as he heard the heavy sound of the predator coming closer and closer. Despite his hatred of the Garsal, he knew the only way he would survive would be to get the fence up as fast as possible.

***

Shanna began to catch glimpses of the staureg through the trees to her left and directly in front of the vehicle. She could also see the dimmed tidemarks of various starcats occasionally glinting through the foliage. Her heart rate began to rise, and she hoped frantically that the cats would remain invisible to the creatures at the vehicle, who since the appearance of the raggedly clothed humans, were beginning to seem rather sinister. Storm, crouched beside her, was quivering slightly, as the staureg showed no signs of diverting away from the light and sound before it. The huge creatures were constantly hungry, their great size ensuring they were in a constant fury of predation, except for those few hours when they slept lightly after a large meal. Even asleep, a staureg was dangerous, jerking away in a flurry of teeth and spiked tail if disturbed.

***

The subcommander barked out a command to the sentinel troops who brought their weapons to bear as the thrashing branches in front of them signalled the imminent arrival of one of the spiked tail beasts they had learnt to fear so well. The gunner, high in the forward turret of the vehicle would be first to sight the huge beast, and was now training his sights steadily towards the disturbance, waiting for the first available second in which to take a clear shot.

The Garsal gunners had learnt by trial and error that hitting anything but the head, or a direct chest shot, meant an even more enraged beast.

Anjo and Semba now had the first line of poles settled in the ground. They worked frantically, the subcommander now standing directly over Anjo, while ceaselessly scanning the vegetation directly ahead. Anjo risked one glance towards the thundering footsteps of the oncoming predator, and received a stinging blow with the butt of the creature's weapon across his left shoulder. In pain, he bent to the task of lifting yet another pole into his finished hole, leaving Semba to align it with the preceding one.

***

What on earth are they doing? wondered Shanna, as she could think of no way that a flimsy line of poles would stop an enraged staureg. She could see the creatures lift their weapons as they prepared to defend themselves. Her emotions engaged as the larger human figure was struck by the tallest creature; although she had been repeatedly telling herself to think rationally that these humans could actually be criminals under sentence, not the captives her mind was suggesting. The blow struck her as completely pointless – there was no way that striking the two humans would increase their speed of construction, in fact it had exactly the opposite effect.

The staureg slowly but steadily began to change direction, as the starcats under Satin's control began to haze it away from the patrol concealed to one side of the alien vehicle. The huge beast veered to the other side of the vehicle, near where the two humans laboured over a final pole, frantically standing it upright and attempting to stabilise it. The tall creature was urging them on in a guttural tone, while swinging its hand weapon up as the trees directly in front of it began to sway and crack.

Shanna was surprised as Satin and Twister reappeared next to her and Allad, but then realised that they had done their job, turning the staureg away from their human partners, but wondered at the decision to allow the beast to attack the alien vehicle. She understood, then, just how bent on concealment Spiron truly was. Any sudden move away by the predator would have the creatures wondering why, and seeking a reason in the bush around the vehicle. By getting the starcats to just slightly divert the onrush of the beast, Spiron was allowing the patrol to remain safe, and providing an opportunity for them to continue to observe the alien creatures and their relationship with the human beings travelling with them.

***

As they struggled with the final pole in the line, Anjo heard the sounds of the advancing nightmare circle towards them. They worked faster, neither he nor

Semba lifting their heads from the task at hand. All thumbs, his hands shaking, Anjo began the final connections to the power supply as the beast burst from the trees directly in front of him. Beside him, out of the corner of his eye, he saw Semba slump to the ground, utterly spent or paralysed with fear, as the subcommander lifted his weapon. The last connection was proving difficult, his sweaty, dirty hands slipping on the plugs as he attempted to force them together. Above him, the pulse of the heavy front turret cannon sounded, and the area was lit with a sudden ruby light and the creature roared in pain, but continued to thunder towards them, swinging its spiked tail. The connection finally snapped together and he threw himself at the power pad as the subcommander fired repeatedly, joined by the troopers around the perimeter. The pulse cannon was firing rapidly and there was a cacophony of noise all around as his hand finally contacted the control pad. Red beams of light thrust out from each pole, forming a scarlet, many stranded bracelet that blocked the beast from the vehicle. It didn't pause in its charge, the many small injuries inflicted upon it driving it mad with pain and fury. It struck the laser fence and was burned repeatedly, throwing itself backwards from the agony reflexively, to be struck head on by a pulse from the front turret, convulsing in its death throes only metres from where Anjo was slumped against the control pad for the fence.

He dragged himself to his hands and knees and crawled over to where Semba huddled, shaking and white, her dirt stained hands covering her face as she shook in uncontrollable spasms. He gathered her in, cradling her shaking body to him.

***

From her position behind the pungo tree, Shanna had watched, heart pounding, as the staureg had begun its charge towards the vehicle. Ruby lines lanced out at it from the creatures' weapons followed by thundering pulses of light from the top of the vehicle, impacting repeatedly along the body of the beast as it drove itself forwards, tail swinging. She watched the smaller human figure crumple at the base of the pole and the larger one dive towards something several metres away, its hand outstretched, and then a cage of fine ruby lines strung themselves from pole to pole and the staureg crashed into them, instantly flinging itself backwards, roaring with pain, as one of the pulses of light engulfed its head, before thudding to the ground, thrashing.

In the sudden quiet, she saw the other creatures lower their weapons, and the larger human figure begin to crawl back to the smaller one. She let out her breath in a long sigh, as her two starcats settled down beside her, then drew it in sharply as the taller creature roared something at the two human figures, which at once dropped face down into the dirt in front of it. It gestured, and they struggled to their feet and turned to head back to the vehicle only to be struck by the butt of the creature's weapon, which knocked them both to their knees. Again they struggled to their feet, and again were knocked down, before another voice from inside the vehicle jerked the creature's head up and the two humans scuttled back into the craft.

Chapter 24

THERE was a small touch on her arm, and Allad signalled to Shanna to withdraw into the bush behind them. She nodded once and pulled back carefully, Storm guarding their retreat. They found the others gathered several hundred metres back in a small pungo grove. Shanna noted that Perri and Barron were still missing, and surmised that they were continuing to keep watch on the vehicle and its passengers. Without needing to be told, Shanna set Storm and Twister to a circling watch around the grove before joining the others crouched in the centre. It was now almost completely dark, and the only light came from the gentle glows of the circling starcats' tidemarks, and even they were subdued.

"I'm going to send our preliminary report to the council immediately. We'll make this grove a secondary camp for tonight, with multiple watches around the clock on that vehicle. I don't like the look of those creatures at all." There were nods from around the circle.

"I'm not yet sure what their relationship is with the two humans we've seen, or indeed whether there are any more, but this doesn't look like the friendly rescue mission we've all hoped for." There was a grimness to Spiron's tone that Shanna had never heard. "Arad, you and Taya, along with Karri and Zandany, will go straight to the access tunnel. It's imperative that you cover your tracks completely behind you, and that you get there as fast as possible. You will relate exactly what we've seen, and you will notify the council that I will continue to shadow these creatures and, if necessary, make sure they do not locate any access to the plateau. Tell them that we'll attempt to remove the humans from the vehicle if the opportunity arises." There was dead silence after the last flat statement, followed by slow nods from the surrounding patrol members. Whoever the two humans were or whatever they might have done, they were the only way that the patrol could get the information they needed. Assuming they spoke the same language.

The four named reshouldered their packs and under Arad's command left the shelter of the pungo grove, following Arad's starcat directly towards the plateau. Karri and Arad were conversing in low tones, but the four of them were already moving very quickly, the two cadet cats flanking the small group.

"Allad, you and Shanna will take the next watch on the vehicle. It's my guess they won't just sit tight all night, allowing that fence thing to protect them. There'll be some reason they went to the risk of setting it up this evening. That vehicle looked strong enough to protect them for the night, so there must be something they want to do right here. I want the two of you to attempt to get as close as possible without being seen, and see if you can get a cat into the compound. Your cats are young Shanna, but they're very bright and under Satin's direction the three of them should be a force to be reckoned with." Shanna was a little startled at that, but on reflection, knew Spiron was right. Sabre and Moshi constantly produced spectacular offspring, well known for their intelligence, and it was not lost on her that the remaining cadets all had starcats of the same breeding. Despite the gravity of the situation, she spent a moment to savour the compliment to her parents, and to almost salivate at the thought of Satin and Boots' potential offspring.

"Nelson and Verren, you'll go straight to last night's camp and begin to secure it. I want it to be as invisible as you can make it. If we do get those two away from the vehicle, we'll need a place to hide them, as I suspect they'll not be able to travel far or fast. Make sure you're ready in case of any injuries. Amma, Ragar, Challon and Sandar, you'll forage for more supplies, and transfer them to Verren and Nelson at the campsite, and then return here. Barron, Perri, Kalli and I will take rotating watches in pairs with Allad and Shanna. If the opportunity arises to remove the humans, then do not hesitate – take it. Alert the rest of us by sending a cat ahead of you. Any questions?"

There was silence and general head shaking. The instructions were simple and clear, with latitude left for independent action. Shanna felt very young all of a sudden, briefly wishing that she was either on her way to the plateau tunnel, or safely at home in the company of her family and not crouched in the wilderness of Below with part of the weight of her world's future resting squarely upon her shoulders.

As the patrol members set about their individual tasks, Shanna made sure that her two young cats were physically looked after, calling them in individually to check each over, spend a little affectionate time with them, and attempt to communicate the night's work to them.

"I want you to try and settle in for a rest for the next two hours, before you relieve Barron and Perri," said Spiron. Shanna and Allad nodded, and attempted to relax into a semblance of sleep, encouraging their cats to lie down with them, certain that nothing would get past the posted guard. Shanna was sure she wouldn't sleep at all, yet with the reassuring weights of Storm and Twister on either side, she found herself drifting off almost at once.

Almost instantaneously it seemed, she was woken by Allad, climbing out of what seemed like possibly the deepest sleep she'd ever experienced, stretching stiffened muscles and trying to make herself more alert. There were a few moments in which to eat some trail rations and have a quick drink, before the two of them called their cats and slid slowly into the forest.

"Shanna, we'll relieve the others, and then we'll circle around and check for any other access to the vehicle area. We need to find out exactly what they're doing, and where the humans are." Allad kept his mouth close to Shanna's ear as they moved carefully through the bush, making sure their passage was as silent as possible. Within ten minutes, they had made contact with Barron and Perri.

"It appears that they're looking for something here," said Barron, "Several of the creatures seem to be out at any one time, taking samples of the soil and digging in patterns, before taking more back inside the vehicle. We've been trying to tell them apart, so that we can get a head count."

"How many do you reckon so far?" asked Allad.

"We think we've been able to count ten or twelve different ones so far. We haven't seen the humans again, though. There have been a number of beasts attracted to the area, but they've contacted that fence and been frightened off or injured, and there are a few extra corpses around the outside which seem to be deterring more from touching the fence. There are a few on the prowl in the area though, so be careful."

"Any signs of another way in?"

"Not that we've been able to detect. Good luck." Barron raised one hand and he and Perri disappeared into the bush towards the pungo grove, each with a hand on the starcats pacing them.

"We'll spend a few moments just observing, and then we'll see what we can find." Allad and Shanna glided through the bush, and settled as close to the fence line as they could without being visible from inside. There were several of the creatures bent around a patch of disturbed earth, poking it with instruments held in their middle appendages and manipulating them with their upper ones. There were intermittent flurries of activity after which one or another of the creatures would vanish at a run into the vehicle via the access ramp. The creatures had placed lights around the perimeter of the fenced area to illuminate whatever it was that they were doing.

While they were watching, one of Frontier's medium sized predators, a razor-tail, attempted to pass through the fence line, shrieking and thrashing its sharp tail in agony after contacting the ruby wires of light. Shanna carefully directed Storm and Twister's attention to the fine streamers of deadly light, quietly using her word for danger to convey the deadly nature of the fence line, as prominent in her mind was the need to attempt to break into the compound, sometime in the next few days. Both cats gave her knowing looks, as if to remind her that they had fully functioning brains and that they were completely able to look after themselves. Storm followed up with a nudge at her hand with his large head, gently twinkling his tidemarks at her. She almost sighed out loud.

They took a circle as closely around the site as possible without revealing their presence to any of the creatures inside. Three quarters of the way around, Allad drew Shanna's attention to a soothall berry plant tucked away near the rock clump. Shanna ducked down to look at the plant, noting the telltale signs of a spooner spider nest just below it.

"We'll just note the position of this one, there's no time to harvest it. Don't forget the spooner spiders though, if we have to move out in a hurry." Shanna nodded and they continued their stealthy circle. The rock clump was composed of towering, steep sided rocks, like spires packed together, appearing to offer only sheer faces which would prevent even the most agile starcat from gaining purchase on them. They formed a V shaped niche into which the vehicle was tucked, with the fence forming a half circle around the front of it. Shanna surveyed the fence poles, which appeared to be made of some kind of smooth material. It was hard to see whether there would be any purchase points available for a starcat to climb, and there was no way either Shanna or Allad would be able to get any closer.

***

Inside the vehicle, Anjo and Semba had finally been able to collapse, huddled together in their bedding in the corner of the vehicle. Both were suffering from multiple bruises and had aching and painful joints and limbs, scratched and scraped by their digging and the brutal beating by the Garsal subcommander. Semba was still intermittently shaking as she huddled in Anjo's arms. They whispered together, simply glad to be inside and away from the nightmare that had charged out of the forest towards them. The Garsal commander was clearly excited about the mineral deposit so recently discovered beneath them, continuing to work the troopers through the night in order to attempt to define the quality of the ore and the quantity available.

There had been a flurry of communication between the vehicle and the colony ship, and judging by the comments that Anjo had caught, there would be another vehicle on the way very shortly to establish a mining camp. After the treatment that the subcommander had dealt out to himself and Semba, Anjo had become more and more desperate to escape as soon as there appeared to be somewhere or someone to go to. He had managed to catch a few glimpses of the sensor screen in the communications area; enough to show a large number of life signs in the immediate vicinity. The screen was only short range, showing life signs relatively accurately for only about two hundred metres around the vehicle before they blurred into the myriad of other life signs in the vegetation. Even within the two hundred metre radius, some of the signals appeared quite confused, splitting and merging continuously, making it hard for the operator to read accurately. Most of the time, the Garsal operator simply noted the presence of the signs, but only looked hard if there was an incursion by the larger predators. They glowed brightly and clearly.

Anjo was accustomed to glimpsing the screen as he passed the operator, while performing his allocated tasks, but during the evening meal preparation as he hurried to deliver plate after plate of food to the Garsal troops, he noted that there were a number of unusual looking life signs that seemed to be moving in pairs. While Semba was clearing up the galley area, Anjo had contrived to pass the communications station multiple times on the pretext of collecting plates and eating utensils. Each time he passed, he glanced furtively at the screen noting the continued presence of paired signals, each of which was associated with some of the splitting and merging signals, which was probably why the operator continued to ignore them.

Anjo began to develop a suspicion about those paired signals. He had spent enough time walking past the screen over the last few weeks, to have ended up with a kind of default version sitting in the back of his mind. The paired signals stood out as anomalies. The Garsal troops rotated through the communications centre every twelve hours or so, as there were no communications specialists on the vehicle, which meant their familiarity with what was on the screen was limited to the twelve hour shift, which repeated only every ten to twelve days. It was odd in a way, Anjo reflected, that he would probably have been a more effective reader of the display than the actual Garsal operator. However as the evening progressed, his suspicion began to firm that someone, or something, had the vehicle under scrutiny. Whether that someone or something was hostile or helpful or even sentient, was yet to be discovered. In his time on this planet so far, he had not seen anything that remotely resembled any benign creature. Remembering the life signs detected on the plateau that so interested the mission commander, though, he found himself slightly more hopeful, despite his exhausted and aching body, and utter lack of knowledge about what might really be outside.

***

Shanna and Allad had spent the better part of the first hour just observing the activities behind the fence, while attempting to assess whether there was any access for a creative starcat through the ruby fence. They had seen no sign of the humans again, and theorised that they were inside the vehicle for the night. They could see patches of vegetation and hollows in the rocks inside the fence, which would provide cover for getting closer to the vehicle. There were fewer incursions by predators as the night wore on, with the dead staureg as well as several other deceased predators, providing a warning that was beginning to repel other searching carnivores. A number of scavengers settled in to dine on the carcasses.

After watching for a while, Shanna touched Allad on the arm and suggested another circle of the area. They set off, moving silently through the bush, shadowed by their cats. As they reached the back of the rock spires, Shanna noticed that there were a number of large trees in relatively close proximity to the rock faces. She sent Twister up into them with a hand signal, and directed him to move as close as possible to the rocks. Allad nodded in the darkness, and Satin hummed quietly in approval as she watched the young cat moving sure footedly through the tree canopies. He crawled agilely out onto a branch and looked questioningly down at Shanna who after checking with Allad, signalled him forward. He backed up and hurtled himself down the branch, using it as a springboard to launch himself upwards towards the top of one of the smaller spires. He flew through the air, landing lightly on the edge of one of the very small spires, then, launching himself smoothly from one to another until he reached a high enough rock to give him access to the ring directly behind the vehicles. From observations taken from the other side of the fence, Shanna knew that descending and ascending on the other side would be child's play to a starcat. She chanced a quick whistle, which caused Twister to drop immediately to his belly, and descend silently back to the ground.

"Well, it looks like we might have an access point," said Allad quietly in Shanna's ear. "Now we just need to convey exactly what we need to the cats."

"Why don't we simply send them in on a silent hide command and ask them to bring back anything they can?"

"I think it might be wiser just to send the three of them up on the rocks, but not until we've some back up from the others. We'll need to make sure that our backs are well guarded, and that you and I are positioned where the cats can see us." Allad signalled Shanna to move around the rocks again, both of them surveying the terrain intently, looking for vantage points with a clear view of the rocks, yet still concealed from the creatures within the fence line.

"I have a silent whistle that Storm and Twister are accustomed to, and I've been teaching the other cadets to use them too," whispered Shanna, pulling the cord from inside the neck of her shirt, "Do you use one with Satin?"

"No," he replied, but grinned in sudden humour, "But if you can convey to Twister and Storm where they need to go, or what they need to do, I'm sure that Satin will pick it up. That'll make it easier, than just sending them in to do whatever they feel like..." There was a slightly mischievous glint in his eyes, and Shanna suspected that there had probably been occasions when he'd sent Satin in somewhere to do just that. She wondered if he might enlighten her at some point. It would probably be a good story.

An hour later, they were quietly joined by Spiron and Kalli, their cats stalking quietly beside them. Allad spent a couple of minutes quietly describing their plan of action, and Spiron and Kalli then began a circle patrol around the fortified area, as Shanna and Allad sent their three cats quickly into the trees again. Shanna felt suddenly naked, without either Storm or Twister at her side. She moved quickly to a vantage point where she felt that Storm and Twister would be able to see her while she remained hidden from the creatures inside, but would allow her a view of the activity inside the fence. She dropped into a crouch near one corner of the rocks that curved inwards slightly. Allad stood nearby ready to direct Satin, and to move quickly anywhere that might be required. Hopefully they would be able to watch the cats once they appeared at the top of the rocks. They both checked the site thoroughly for any dangerous fauna or flora.

Allad took a quick look around and then indicated to Shanna that she should signal the cats to begin to climb into the rocks. There was a small flurry of branches, and then she caught a glimpse of a faint tidemark vanishing behind a rock column.

There was a breathless wait, then Shanna saw a stealthy movement on the rocks closest the near side of the vehicle, almost directly above the creatures gathered around the hole they had dug into the ground. Shanna held her breath, and felt Allad stir slightly beside her, then realised that the cats would be completely invisible to the creatures on the ground as the angle was much too precipitous.

Allad's voice was soft near her ear.

"Have them circle around on the top of the rocks observing." Shanna complied, sounding the whistle silently, and saw three shadows move silently in two directions, no tidemarks visible, around the varied rock spires. She was reassured that she and Allad could barely spot the cats in the gloom, and they knew they were there.

"Have them fade, and then work their ways down if they're able. We won't be able to see them so give them a search and bring command while they're concealed." Even Allad sounded tense, and Shanna took a deep breath before nodding and sounding her "listen" call. Three shadows paused, and then she sent "fade", "search and bring" – the same command that indicated she wanted samples of whatever might be up ahead. Since that command usually meant vegetation, she was a little unsure what might come back. The three shadows disappeared completely. Now was the crunch time, hopefully the three cats would discover a way down into the secured area while remaining hidden. Shanna knew that starcat senses were much more acute than human ones, but those creatures were so far beyond anything familiar that she could only hope there were parallels with the human race.

The waiting dragged on for what seemed like hours, Allad and Shanna were concealed as best they were able, ever conscious of the noises in the bush around them, wondering if Spiron and Kalli would be able to see off any potential predators and fearful that their cats might be detected. Allad nudged her suddenly, indicating for her to look quickly toward the ramp of the vehicle. She caught her breath as a small piece of discarded equipment seemed to vanish, moving by itself behind the ramp. She squinted harder, but was unable to make out the figure of a starcat anywhere, yet there was definitely at least one, somewhere on the ground in there. She began to scan back and forth across the fenced area, knowing that her best hope of noticing a "faded cat" was to find a small movement flurry, and that was best done by visually scanning the area from side to side. She was rewarded shortly after, noticing a blur just behind where the creatures crouched near the hole in the ground.

She heard Allad suck in a quick breath, as he realised just how close the cat was to the creatures. She found herself gripping a small outcropping of rock in front of her, but was unable to make her fingers release it, holding tighter and tighter, while trying to continue her scanning. There was another slight blur, just in front of the vehicle ramp this time, and she felt Allad grip her arm tightly, almost cutting the circulation off. His moustache tickled her ear.

"Call them back, Shan. Or Satin will go too far." She didn't stop to ask why he knew it would be Satin prowling in front of the ramp, but fumbled the whistle to her lips and blew the recall as quickly as possible, her heart pounding. A few moments later, there was a quiet clatter from directly behind the vehicle, and the creatures around the hole looked up, appendages grasping weapons, heads spinning from side to side. Shanna's heart seemed to stop, and then began again with what she felt must have been an audible thud, as the creatures relaxed and went back to probing the hole.

Several minutes later, a silky head thrust itself under her hand as Storm materialised beside her. A few seconds later, Twister reappeared, sliding head first gracefully down a tree trunk. It was several anxious minutes though, until Satin reappeared near Allad. He put one arm around her neck and then moved off into the bush towards the pungo trees. Shanna could feel and see vaguely that the starcats all had things grasped in their mouths, but couldn't tell by feel what they were. The relief of having her cats back with her was almost exhausting, but she contented herself with putting a hand out to feel each soft coat as they worked their way back to the relative security of the trees.

Once inside the ring of trees, they found Perri and Barron resting on the ground, Spangles and Hunter taking turns to guard the grove, while their partners attempted to catch up on a little rest. With a sudden grateful thought for her parents, Shanna pulled her glowstone out of the neck of her shirt, allowing it to shed light over the objects the three starcats were depositing on the ground. The bluish light spread in a small pool around Shanna, illuminating the objects lying in a small heap on the ground. Neatly placed on top was a small pouch like object. As Barron and Perri came over to the two of them, Allad reached for it, and attempted to lift the flap on the pouch, which suddenly clicked open with a jerk. He closed and opened it several times, before realising that the pouch was actually held shut by a small, but powerful magnet. Inside he found a small artifact, flat and rectangular in shape, with a number of raised buttons on it and one small red light glowing steadily.

"I don't think we'll attempt to push any buttons here, as I have no idea what that is." Allad placed the object very carefully on the ground near the pile. The next object appeared to be some kind of footwear, which, with its long slim length, and lack of toe space, definitely belonged to the alien creatures. Allad sniffed it questioningly and then held it out to Shanna, who took a cautious sniff; there was a strange, almost pungent odour about it that made her nose tingle. She held it out for Storm to stick his nose into, and he promptly sneezed then shook his head.

"Well, that might be their dirty socks smell – what do you think?" asked Shanna. Allad smiled and picked up the final object, which turned out to be a piece of the same material that the poles were made out of. It felt slick and was shining faintly in the blue light, yet was marked by teeth marks from whichever starcat had brought it in. This meant that there was some hope that the starcats might be able to climb them if required. The object was about twenty centimetres long, and was something like a large comb, with widely spaced teeth.

"What do you think that's for?" asked Shanna, turning the object over in her hands.

"Well, they don't seem to have hair, so I've no idea, really, perhaps it does something else, and we're just not quite clever enough to figure it out," replied Allad with a small frown. He returned to the first object, handling it carefully, and running a finger over the red light thoughtfully. "Well, despite retrieving a few objects, I don't feel that we've really discovered much so far. And I nearly went grey in those few minutes before Satin returned - I'm not sure that I'd like to experience that again too soon."

"Well, we know that the smell of the creatures makes a starcat sneeze!" replied Shanna. "I'm wondering if we should send the cats back in during the day time, actually." Allad gave her an incredulous look, but then returned his gaze to the object in his hand and nodded slowly and thoughtfully.

"You may be right, but we need to let Spiron take a look at this stuff, and we need to spend more time observing those things. I'd like to see those humans again, and in daylight."

***

Inside the vehicle, the on duty communications trooper had just completed a routine check of the communications equipment, and discovered that there was one portable comm set unaccounted for. He began rechecking, marking each one off on the inventory and confirming with the survey crew exactly how many sets were outside the vehicle.

Semba had finally collapsed into an exhausted sleep, curled up in her corner, and Anjo was sitting, trying to puzzle out what had just happened. He had been in their corner, holding Semba's hand as she slowly settled down. There had been a moment when he was sure something had brushed against his leg, and he was convinced he'd seen something like the wobbling of a mirage near the ramp entry shortly after. This of course made no sense at all, but then he had noticed the sudden activity of the comms trooper as it frantically began to run through the comms set inventory again. The activity did not go unnoticed by the commander, who was beginning to shoot glances towards the communications section.

The trooper finished its third check through the comm sets and then began to surreptitiously hunt through the station, opening storage cabinets and lockers quietly and shuffling through their contents. A comb shaped long range antenna attachment toppled from the bench top and tumbled unnoticed, down the ramp. The commander stalked over and rapped out a query to the trooper, who fumbled its answer then simply indicated the missing set on the inventory. The commander's volume grew, and he gestured curtly at the trooper who made haste to explain that the set had been accounted for at the beginning of the shift, but could offer no explanation for its sudden disappearance. The commander ordered the trooper to perform a search of the vehicle, while he strode to the front of it, looking out into surrounding forest.

In his corner, Anjo wondered.

***

Up on the plateau, Master Cerren eyed the unusual looking arrows that had been delivered to him earlier that day by a team of innovative thinkers in the local militia. They had been working on a project he'd initiated after the discovery of the alien aircraft. He picked one up, its large bulbous head counterweighted by a small piece of lead crafted into the shaft near the fletchings. Cradling it in his hands thoughtfully, he looked out of his office window which overlooked the archery field, two stories below. The butts were silent and still at this hour. He stood, placed the arrow on his desk and paced over to the board on the wall, where he studied the list of names he had fastened to it several months ago. He tapped his chin with one long fingered hand, and Socks hummed and rubbed herself lovingly against his leg. He sighed, picked up the arrow again and weighed it again in his hands.

Chapter 25

AFTER a long tense night, interspersed with watch shifts, Shanna roused to muted sunlight slanting through the pungo grove. Her eyes felt grainy and hot, and she was very stiff. Apparently she'd not moved since falling asleep after her final watch, and she spent several minutes creakily stretching the kinks out before attempting to get up. Storm and Twister grumbled slightly as her movements disturbed their slumbers, Storm opening one eye as she extricated herself from under their relaxed heads. He closed it quickly as soon as he realised Shanna had noticed, and she chuckled quietly under her breath as she stretched one last kink out of her neck. Allad was still slumbering in his bedding, Satin asleep next to him with her tail neatly curled around her sleek body. Shanna decided to leave him asleep until she'd assembled some kind of breakfast.

She could see Spiron and Kalli nearby, tucked under separate pungo trees, which meant that Barron and Perri were currently on watch near the ruby toned fence. She wondered if it would be safe to make a smokeless fire, and then decided against it. She investigated the contents of her pack, weighing her water bottle in her hand to assess how much she had left, and had just decided that breakfast would be only dried trail rations, when all the cats lifted their heads and tensed for a moment before suddenly relaxing.

Shanna was somewhat surprised to see Spider slide neatly into the pungo grove just ahead of Amma and Challon, who were then joined by Challon's starcat, Dipper. Amma waved quietly to Shanna and began to unload a selection of leaf wrapped food from her pack as Challon carefully placed a billy on the ground. There were a few spirals of steam rising from it.

"How on earth did you manage that?" asked Shanna, raising her eyebrows in surprise at the pair.

"We managed to forage quite a quantity last night, thanks to Amma's glow-stone, and delivered it to Nelson and Verren in the early hours of this morning. So we slept there for a few hours and then figured you'd like a bit of breakfast." Challon poured tea into Shanna's proffered mug, and sent Dipper to poke the others awake. "We're about an hour from the other site in a direct line's fast travel so the tea's not really hot but it'll still be warm, and Amma's got some vaguely warm tubers and fruit." Shanna smiled in appreciation as she was joined by the still yawning Allad and then Spiron and Kalli.

"I'll take some food to Barron and Perri and then relieve them," said Challon, "Come on Amma. Oh, and Spiron; Nelson and Verren have managed to conceal the campsite really well, so if anyone needs to find it in a hurry they'll need to take direction from their cat." He gathered several leaf wrapped bundles from the ground, reshouldered his pack and jogged out, Amma just behind him.

Shanna unwrapped a leaf parcel, discovering one of the tasty tubers inside which had been baked in the coals. It was barely warm, but compared to what she had been expecting, absolutely delicious and she felt considerably more awake with it and a cup of tea inside her. After the brief breakfast, Ragar and Sandar appeared followed shortly thereafter by Barron and Perri. Shanna sent her cats off to hunt as Spiron detailed the day's plan.

"We continue to keep that compound under observation until they decide to move. I want as many eyes on what's going on in there as possible." He showed the others the objects that the cats had retrieved the previous night. They all handled them carefully, avoiding the buttons on the front of the flat rectangular one, and speculated over their function. "We'll encircle their encampment today and just watch until midday, unless they decide to move. After midday, we'll meet back here, leaving Ragar and Sandar to keep watch on the vehicle. I'd like to consider trying to get the starcats in during daylight this afternoon, to scout around carefully and see what they might be able to bring out this time." He considered carefully, and then tapped his jaw with one finger. "If we have the opportunity, I'd still like to see the humans extricated. If we can get them out, they're likely to be our best source of information about these creatures."

"Be careful today – the dead animals around the perimeter will bring predators in to feed off them. At all times, we'll have two cats circling, same rotation as the watch roster. Let's pack up and be ready to go as soon as possible."

During the short time it took her to reorganise her pack, Shanna was careful to review her geography, carefully plotting the course to the safe camp in her head to make sure she had a sure sense of direction in case they needed to move in a hurry. She carefully fastened her pack straps and made sure her knife, whistle and glowstone were secure on their various chains and belts. Storm and Twister reappeared licking their lips, looking satisfied with their morning hunt and she joined the patrol as they headed back to the vehicle.

Three hours later, she wriggled slightly to ease a small cramp in one foot, carefully keeping her eyes on the activity around the vehicle. There had been several close brushes with investigating wildlife, but by keeping still and concealing themselves, and the presence of thirteen starcats, the patrol had remained perfectly safe. A number of animals had perished from injuries inflicted by the fence, and many had simply hurtled howling into the surrounding vegetation without any consideration for what might be ahead of them. There had been a nasty moment when she'd almost been trodden on by a stampeding bokker. Shanna had a new appreciation of the bush skills that she'd learnt with Patrol Ten over the previous weeks which had allowed her to remain secure.

During the morning, the alien creatures had continued to dig up small sections of earth around the campsite, moving in and out of the vehicle frequently, often chivvying the smaller human figures to hurry them up, treating them with casual callousness. Shanna was able to discern that one appeared to be a woman and the other a man, both dressed in the ragged remnants of clothing. She attempted to identify individual creatures in order to make a count. The immense vehicle looked as though it could hold fifty or more but Shanna's best count was fifteen, although she was certain there would be more of the creatures on board.

Just after the sun signalled midday, Allad motioned to Shanna and they faded back into the bush, silently moving towards the pungo grove to regroup with the rest of the patrol. Ragar and Sandar remained on duty watching the vehicle.

In the pungo grove, Spiron turned to Allad and Shanna. "Do you remember the thing the human pressed to turn the fence on? I'm wondering what might happen if we managed to press it – whether the fence would turn off. We know from our archives that many of the devices our ancestors used were controlled very simply – and button pressing was a favourite method. It's a method that we've retained as we've slowly begun to rebuild our society's technological capabilities."

There were nods of agreement around the group, as both Shanna and Allad considered thoughtfully. She'd certainly taught her cats to poke things on command, as it was quite a useful skill in the context of search and rescue, to detect unstable ground or building structures, but they'd never pressed a button in their lives, and she wasn't entirely sure they'd know quite what to do.

"I'm thinking one of yours might do it Shanna. What about Storm?" Allad turned to Shanna, all seriousness now. "He's bright and a bit steadier than Twister, and I think Satin would be better off sneaking into the vehicle in the confusion."

Shanna considered. "Well, we can only try. I'll try and get Twister to run some interference if we manage to turn the thing off." Spiron nodded, pleased.

"The rest of us will run an encirclement pattern around the site. Now, how many do you estimate you've seen?"

"I reckon around thirteen or fourteen," said Kalli.

"About sixteen?" queried Amma.

"I'd agree, somewhere between fourteen and sixteen," replied Spiron, frowning slightly, "and however many more there might be inside. If we manage to turn the fence off, we're going to need at least half the cats to provide some confusion, and then Kalli, Perri and I will attempt to get the two humans out and into the bush. We'll have Amma and Challon ready to hide their tracks as I'm sure they've no idea what to do out here, and the rest of you will run interference behind them."

Again he paused, as he surveyed the patrol assessingly, "We'll make a run for the prepared camp, but not in a straight line. You're not to approach it unless you're completely certain that you're not being followed. Even if you have to walk circles all day, don't lead the creatures to it." There were assenting nods from all. "All right then, let's get to work."

They moved silently through the bush to the vehicle, Shanna and Allad peeling off together with their cats towards the rock spires. Shanna placed her hands on Twister and Storms' silky heads, staring into their violet eyes as she spoke to the two of them, entreating them to be careful, before sending them into the trees on the same commands as the previous night. Satin joined them silently and they faded quietly into the foliage. Shanna's heart rate began to increase as her two cats vanished into the danger inside the rock spires. She and Allad moved quickly to their vantage point to observe the ensuing activity inside the fenced area. There was a hint of movement on the spires above, and Shanna whistled her hide signal silently and then there was nothing to see. Shanna risked a quick glance to one side, and realised Allad's usually stoic face was mirroring her anxiety. Directly below where Shanna had glimpsed that half seen movement, two creatures patrolled. She held her breath, and then realised that they would have again seen nothing above them due to the angle. Allad tapped her on the shoulder, and she whistled the cats, keeping her eyes fixed on the area inside the fence.

There was nothing to be seen for some time, and then one of the creatures working at one of the holes, reached behind itself for something, and then spun around, searching the ground behind it frantically. Almost simultaneously, another creature on the other side of the fenced area groped at its utility belt, its whole demeanour indicating puzzlement, despite the unreadable alien facial features. One of the humans near the access ramp looked around in puzzlement as the two creatures continued to look for their missing equipment. Allad again tapped Shanna's shoulder, and brought his mouth to her ear.

"Ready?" She nodded again, and brought the whistle to her lips, signalling carefully to direct Storm over to the boxy object near the end fence post, not far from where she and Allad were concealed. There was a slight glint of blue as Storm allowed the tip of one ear to be seen, to indicate that he was positioned as requested. Again, Shanna held her breath, as she waited to see if any of the creatures had noticed the blue twinkle. Nothing inside the fence changed.

"Can you have him poke the thing with his paw now?" Allad requested.

"I'll need him to be able to see me, I'm afraid." Allad looked at her consideringly, checking the angle from their concealed position to the nearest creatures and then motioned for her to show a hand signal to Storm. She carefully parted a little of the vegetation in front of them, moving slowly and silently, trying to make it seem as though the branches were simply moving in the wind, whistled silently, and then signalled for Storm to paw at the box. There was a small shimmer in the air near the box, and Shanna knew Storm was attempting to do as she'd asked.

There was a sudden commotion from inside the vehicle, and two more of the creatures suddenly hurtled down the ramp gesticulating furiously at each other in obvious argument, while the two humans near the ramp cowered away from them. The commotion increased as the fence lights suddenly winked out and an alarm sounded. Every creature in the area whipped its head around quickly and the two humans huddled suddenly together. There was a sudden hush and two of the closest creatures began to stalk quickly over to the box. Shanna risked exposing herself to signal to Storm to remain concealed, but to make sure that he guarded the box from interference. Behind her there was a sudden flurry of silent movement, as a number of starcats sped into action into the fenced area, slowly fading into concealment before exiting the tree line. Shanna almost laughed as a number of the creatures fell heavily, apparently struck by nothing but obviously impeded by the hidden cats hurtling into the previously safe zone. She prepared herself for action as the cats began to herd the confused humans directly towards her and Allad.

***

Anjo and Semba watched amazed as the area around the vehicle suddenly erupted into chaos when the fence winked out. It was obvious that there had been some kind of malfunction, and Anjo felt a sudden thrill of fear as he realised that they were again vulnerable to the creatures in the surrounding vegetation and prepared to bolt into the vehicle. Out of the corner of one eye, he noticed a heat shimmer in the air just like the one he'd seen at the ramp inside the vehicle last night, and then something large brushed against him. He froze wide eyed, as Semba huddled closer to him, letting out a small shriek, which she tried to stifle with her hand.

"What was that?" her voice was a terrified whisper. Anjo, hushed her hurriedly.

Not far from them, two of the Garsal crew were approaching the control and power box for the fence, their heads turning constantly to ensure there were none of the large ferocious denizens of the planet homing in on them. There were startled shouts from inside the vehicle which Anjo couldn't make out, and outside it several of the Garsal troopers fell simultaneously to the ground.

Feeling panicked as the large something brushed firmly against him again, he moved frantically away from it just as Semba was doing next to him. Whatever it was, it was big, and he'd seen enough of the planet's fauna to spur him to greater efforts. He suddenly realised that the large nothing was attempting to herd him towards the overhanging trees at one end of the rock spires. Whatever it was seemed to be on every side of him at once and he became more and more panicked as the firm pressure drove him away from the relative safety of the vehicle. Around them there was chaos everywhere; Garsal troopers on all sides seemed unable to maintain their feet and Semba was now beginning to gasp and sob quietly as she and Anjo were chivvied closer and closer to the rocks.

***

Shanna kept a close eye on where she could just make out a cat shimmer in the air near the box. Storm was pacing the guard as the creatures attempted to get to it, their efforts becoming more and more frantic as they were repeatedly tripped and shoved to one side by yet more cat shimmers. It was usually impossible to see a cat when it was still, but during fast movements, the air appeared to shimmer like a heat wave to the careful observer – it was one of the things about starcats that no-one had been able to understand, but it was a very useful trait, when used effectively – as Master Cerren did with underperforming students.

She could see the two humans becoming frantic with fear as they were herded closer to the trees, suddenly realising that from their perspective they were not being rescued, but dragged off by unseen monsters; in their minds, monsters who would most likely then kill and eat them. Just as she turned to see where Spiron, Kalli and Perri were, they appeared at her shoulder.

Her attention was suddenly yanked back to the activity in front of her as one of the creature's weapons discharged with a humming pulse, sending a burst of light towards the vegetation, and she hastily ducked down behind the concealing rocks. Spiron spoke quietly next to her.

"We're going in there in a few seconds, and as soon as we have the humans, pull your cats out and begin to run interference. Move as fast as you can, as these things are getting pretty upset. Don't let them see you directly." Shanna took a deep breath and crouched, as more and more of the creatures sent bursts of light in many directions. There was a brief starcat grunt of pain from somewhere in front of her, and a shadowy form became suddenly visible near the humans before fading again. The two humans were now stumbling and moving frantically, heads whipping from side to side.

***

Anjo stumbled to his knees, hands contacting the dirt heavily as the invisible somethings pushed him hard from behind. As he staggered to his feet, he saw a weapon pulse flick just in front of him, and there was a grunt of pain followed by a partial materialisation of a huge feline form, which then faded again, right before his eyes. Thoughts of large predators with huge claws and teeth flashed into his mind and he redoubled his efforts to escape them, Semba now sobbing openly behind him. The tree line and rocks were now only about ten metres away, and there were multiple weapons discharging in all directions as the Garsal troopers attempted to fire at the invisible presences.

The trees directly in front suddenly rustled slightly, and three barely discernable figures appeared, their forms seeming to melt in and out of view. With a start, Anjo realised they appeared to be humanoid, although somewhat taller than both he and Semba. Semba's sobs paused, as the three figures appeared to beckon slightly. Before he could make up his mind about which way to run, the invisible presences around him forced him forward towards the figures, all of whom had begun to move swiftly towards him. There was no choice, the Garsal troopers were now firing indiscriminately all around him and the pulses were coming frighteningly close. The invisible presences were now pressing him constantly, and two of the figures were suddenly next to both him and Semba, grasping them firmly by an arm. A low voice with a slightly strange, but understandable accent was suddenly heard, speaking Standard in his ear.

"Move. Come with us quickly, before anyone else is hurt." Underneath the hood of what appeared to be some kind of varicoloured jacket, a human face with oddly coloured eyes was visible. Next to him, he could hear Semba gasp and with almost no thought he stopped resisting the force behind him, deciding that this was his only chance of escape from the Garsal, and if he died or was even enslaved by these people, at least they appeared to be human and not Garsal.

***

Shanna's heart was in her mouth as the ugly reality of an injured starcat thudded home in her mind. It was most likely Spangles, Flyer or Fury and her two were probably fine, yet the possibility that one of them might be injured was now not just a possibility, but a very real risk. The creatures in front of her were now continuously attempting to fire their weapons, but were being constantly flung off balance by a starcat. The three Scouts had now reached the two humans and Kalli and Perri were urging them forwards towards the treeline as Spiron circled behind them, hand signalling Fury to run interference behind them. There was another grunt of pain somewhere in the melee, and as the five finally reached the vegetation, she whistled urgently to her cats and moved directly behind Spiron. She could see that it was going to be a hair raising escape, and she could hear the rest of the patrol calling their cats from their various positions around the vehicle area.

As the starcat presence in the vehicle area reduced, more of the creatures inside began to regain their equilibrium, and began taking aim at the fleeing figures now beginning to vanish into the vegetation. Pulses of light began to spatter the bush not far from where Shanna and Allad crouched. There was another rustle and Storm appeared at Shanna's elbow, dropping a small object at her feet. Twister and Satin both appeared abruptly behind him, also dropping various objects. Allad and Shanna gathered them up quickly, fortunately none of them were too large,and fitted easily into thigh pockets. As the creatures became more confident that they were no longer going to be attacked they began to advance towards the fence line, firing their weapons towards the point at which Spiron, Kalli and Perri had taken their humans into the bush.

"Are your two OK?" asked Allad.

"They're fine," Shanna replied, having run her eyes almost frantically over the two large sleek bodies whose tidemarks were now glowing with exhilaration.

"All right then, we're going to need to send them on darting forays into that compound to make sure that the pursuit is delayed as long as possible. We'll need to start laying an obvious false trail for the creatures to pursue. Challon and Amma should be erasing the tracks made by our new guests by now, but in the meantime we'll need to draw them off and send them in the wrong direction." Shanna wasn't too happy about the need to send the cats back in, but could understand why. "Ready?" Allad's voice was low. She nodded, signalling to the cats to fade, and then sent Storm and Twister back into the fray. She could tell some of the other Scouts had come to the same conclusion, as chaos erupted again around the vehicle. She and Allad moved as silently as possible, keeping low. Pulses of light flicked above Shanna's head, and she ducked even lower as some of the vegetation exploded into shreds above her and a small branch crashed down just behind her, its severed end smoking.

There was more activity and she could hear the creatures behind her shouting in strange guttural voices, although she was unable to understand what they were saying. There was a sudden angry starcat hum, its volume and intensity rising rapidly, and she risked a glance behind as she ducked behind a tree trunk. She could see the faint form of Hunter fading in and out of sight as he blurred into high speed directly at one of the creatures. There was a sudden snap as his jaws closed on its arm and the creature and cat smashed heavily into the ground, Hunter losing his grip and then fading into near invisibility again. Shanna hoped frantically that Twister and Storm were all right, but was finding it hard to keep herself focused on the task at hand, as she and Allad began to set a trail leading away from the direction the other Scouts had taken, while at the same time keeping an eye out for her own safety in the absence of her feline partners.

The noises behind again increased in intensity; there were a number of starcats sounding off now, and more and more sounds of the weapons firing with an almost constant barrage of fire above their heads, sometimes snapping through vegetation on either side of where Shanna and Allad moved through the bush. After they had penetrated about two hundred metres into the vegetation, Allad signalled a stop and then drew Shanna into the shelter of a large tree, carefully avoiding a barbed palm close to the track they had made.

"I'm going to run back and show myself briefly, and then we'll draw them off after us. Can you cope with that?" She nodded, trying to remain calm.

"I think so." She nodded again, more firmly.

"Wait for my signal and then call your cats – I'll shout, and hopefully we'll draw not only the creatures after us but a few of the nasties down here Below to impede them as well. If I can I'll let some of the others know, and get them to assist." He vanished into the scrub, and Shanna suddenly realised that she was, for the very first time, totally and utterly alone Below. It was very unsettling, and she concealed herself quickly behind the tree, settling into a static posture to ensure her safety. She felt very alone without Storm or Twister, or Allad's comforting bulk somewhere in sight. There were loud noises from the direction of the compound, loud snarling hums from the starcats, pulses from the creatures' weapons and the guttural noises they made to each other. There was an abrupt shout from Allad and Shanna whistled Storm and Twister and then faced down the trail they'd made, waiting for the moment when someone might come into view. Within a few moments Twister appeared, hurtling down the trail, speed blurring his outline, and then Storm dropped heavily out of a tree just behind her. To her anxious eyes he appeared to be limping slightly, and as the two cats closed in on her she examined them hastily. Twister was unscathed, but Storm bore a small burn mark on his right front leg which was bleeding slightly. She checked it quickly, realising that there would be no time to tend it right then, as pursuit was likely to be imminent, relieved to find that it appeared to be relatively superficial.

She could hear pounding footsteps and snapping twigs; it sounded odd because Shanna had never heard any of the Scouts move anything but silently. It would act as a signal to anything inimical in the vicinity, and Shanna began to feel real fear. She had no idea how the next few hours would pan out - the creatures' ability to track was a complete unknown. Allad came into view, legs pumping, Satin pacing him, her usually immaculate coat streaked with dirt and grime. Behind them came two of the creatures in hot pursuit, both tripping and stumbling through the vegetation, but close enough to be dangerous should Allad pause at all.

"Come on!" Shanna gathered herself and joined Allad as he passed, carefully skirting the barbed palm. They began to run together, with the cats pacing them easily. Behind them Shanna could hear the creatures gaining slightly, and she sent Twister back to impede their progress. There was a sudden spate of guttural cries and she realised that Twister had cleverly diverted them towards the barbed palm. She hoped that the venom worked as well on them as on human beings, but could hear other creatures pursuing them from further behind and then a sudden roar from the clearing further back as the vehicle burst into life.

"Run for another couple of hundred metres and then we'll go bush and move quietly for several hundred metres. And then I think we'll need to let them see us occasionally to keep them following." Allad's words came out between breaths, but he was still running easily. "I managed to let Ragar and Sandar know what we're doing and they'll alert the others. They'll catch up with us in an hour or so, after they've made sure nothing stayed in the fenced area, and then we'll be able to catch our breath and begin to circle for the campsite."

"Is everyone all right?" Shanna continued to run steadily, feeling strong. Her cats were back with her and Satin was scouting ahead, while Twister kept the rear guard and Storm limped slightly but steadily beside her.

"I think so. There are a few injured cats, but all that I could see were moving OK, so hopefully any injuries are only minor." Satin hummed loudly from the front and Allad motioned to Shanna to begin to move to the left into the bush surrounding them. He led them steadily in a direction away from the campsite, moving silently but making little effort to conceal their trail. A sudden snarling grunt was heard directly to their right, which Shanna identified easily as a parquad, a moderate sized reptilian predator. It snuffled loudly and Shanna was glad that she was wearing crushed pungo. There was a spate of sound from the creatures behind them and a sudden cessation of their footfalls and she could hear their weapons pulsing loudly. Allad and Shanna slowed – it was important that they didn't lose their pursuers. Behind them they could hear the roaring of the vehicle approaching and continuing to move quietly, they drew the pursuit onwards.

***

Several hours later, Ragar and Sandar finally met up with them in another rock clump far to the east and south of their starting point. They had gone far beyond the small plateau, and Allad had made sure to lead the creatures well away from the home plateau while the sun began to lower itself towards the horizon. Shanna was reasonably sure she had a fairly good idea of where they were in relation to the safe camp, but she was glad to still be with the more experienced scout. They could still hear the monstrous vehicle in the distance, but knew it would take some time to traverse the tree studded rocky outcrop, where they had carefully left their trail. They had concealed their trail into the rock clump in order to take a quick breather.

"About time!" Allad's voice was tired, and he sat heavily on a rock. "Is everyone else away and safe?"

Sandar quirked one eyebrow drily at his fellow Scout.

"We've had a merry chase, although you left a trail wide enough for a staureg for us to follow. Sorry about the delay, but we had to deal with a group of the creatures left inside the fence – there were five, and they managed to get the fence back up again. We had to get a couple of cats back inside to drop it again and then we got them lost in the bush. It took a while. We've a few injuries, mainly to the cats and mostly minor, but Barron took quite a hit from one of those weapons on his left arm and it's not looking too good. Hopefully Verren can fix him up when he gets back to the waterfall campsite."

"They're pretty dismal at tracking, so we've discovered - hence the staureg trail. Can you lead them south for another hour or so? We need to rest up and Shanna needs to check out Storm's leg."

"Not a problem. We'll meet you here in two hours – you rest, and then we'll head back to the campsite together. From what you've said, losing them shouldn't be the problem."

Allad shook his head wearily, and waved one hand at Sandar and Ragar. They looked a little weary, but nothing to how Shanna felt. "Be careful as it gets dark. We've had less trouble from the creatures than we've had from the local wildlife." Both Sandar and Ragar nodded and then turned as one, heading into the darkening bush, Shanna could now hear the vehicle quite loudly. She sent Twister after Sandar and Ragar to begin a circle watch, and then removed the cat kit from her pack pocket, calling Storm to sit in front of her. He mutely lifted his right leg, now encrusted with blood and caked in grime. There was some mild swelling in the paw. As she cleaned it, he began to purr softly, leaning his leg across her knees. She carefully pulled out some of the soothall salve and plastered the wound with it, and Storm's purring increased in volume. Allad was carefully checking Satin over, brushing the dust from her silky coat and rubbing her ears gently as she laid her head in his lap.

"How's his leg, Shan?"

"Nothing particularly bad, but I'm not going to take any chances with all that dirt - hence the soothall. How's Satin?" Allad looked up from his stroking, and smiled tiredly at Shanna.

"She's fine. How are you?"

"Exhausted, And I think I've got a few spines from a cavechidna somewhere in my leg. Apart from that, and the fact that I've spent the afternoon scared witless, I'm starving. What about you?" Shanna gently removed Storm's leg from her knees and stood stiffly to replace the salve in her pack.

"About the same as you I'd say." There was a moment of silence. "Would you like me to take the spines out of your leg?" Shanna grinned, heaved a sigh of relief and walked stiffly over to Allad and sank to the ground with another sigh. She pulled up her blood stained trouser leg and rolled over on to her stomach.

"That would be a good start. Do you need the glowstone?"

"Yes please, and keep still, this will most definitely hurt." She pulled the chain over her head and handed the stone to Allad, who suspended it over her calf. "I see three, no four spines, and they're all nicely embedded." He probed carefully and Shanna tensed slightly as the embedded spines moved. "Sorry." He pulled a pair of tweezers from his field knife and held the glow stone's chain in his teeth.

Five minutes later the spines were removed and Allad was gently disinfecting the wounds.

"Time for a bit to eat and then we'll take turns having a sleep. It's going to be a long night I'm afraid. You sit still for a moment, and I'll sort out the food." Shanna rolled her trouser leg down and wriggled back to Storm, leaning her back on a convenient rock while gently stroking him.

She was comforted by his soft fur and warm bulk. "Call Twister back, I'll send Satin out for a while." Shanna complied and was soon running her hands up and down his long length, making sure he had come through unscathed. He purred and hummed gently, nudging her hand with his nose to encourage more patting then rolled on his back to allow her to scratch his tummy more easily. As she rested surrounded by her two loving partners, her breathing slowed and steadied, and when Allad next looked she had slumped down, head pillowed on Storm, one hand draped over Twister, fast asleep.

***

Master Cerren looked at the line of archers in front of him. They were a mixed group, from the venerable retired Scouts, called back into active duty especially for this task, to young Kaidan from Hillview - all of thirteen, tall, with gangly limbs, and brimming with enthusiasm. All their attention was directed towards him. He felt a brief pang of guilt for including Kaidan and the other students in the group.

He nodded to Master Dinian, who picked one of the bulbous nosed arrows from the carefully arranged quiver at his hip, and carefully nocked it.

"Please watch the demonstration." Master Cerren had pondered long and thoughtfully about the implications of the actions of the next few moments. With a firmness belied by his inward qualms, he inclined his head to Dinian. The master lifted his bow, drew and released, and the bulbous headed arrow flew through the air to thud into a target at the end of the archery range. A second later, a muted thump sounded, and the target exploded into flame, burning pieces of straw floating gently to the ground.

The line of archers stood, mouths open, watching the destruction unfold. One by one, they turned to look at Master Cerren, eyes wide and questions in every eye.

Chapter 26

SHANNA came to, feeling very ordinary and extremely thirsty. Underneath her head, the warm flank of a starcat rose and fell with a rumbling purr, and her right arm was propped on yet another length of silky fur. It was completely dark and there was little to be seen when she first dragged her eyelids apart.

"Glad to see you're awake." Allad's voice came quietly through the darkness to her, and she realised she must have dropped into sleep without any thought of his exhaustion. She shoved herself upright, reminded quickly of the puncture wounds in her leg by a sudden stab of pain.

"Sorry Allad, I hope I haven't been asleep for too long. " She rubbed sleep from her eyes and climbed creakily to her feet, still feeling exhausted, and walked slowly over to where he was seated on a rock. "Sorry, you must be done in."

"It's all right Shan, if you'll wake one of your cats, I'll call Satin in, and then you can wake me when the others return. You've only slept for about an hour actually. There's some dried food here, and I've found a small spring so we're right for water. Drink as much as you need." Shanna walked back to the sleeping starcats, regarding them fondly as she reminded herself of just how young they both were. She decided to wake Twister, and let Storm rest his leg for as long as possible. She gently poked him with her toe and he grunted slightly, raising one eyelid halfway to peer at her then shut it determinedly again. She sighed and poked him harder and he woke properly, eyeing her with some reproach and raised his head fully, before dragging himself to his feet and yawning widely.

"Sorry mate," she said with a smile, "But Satin needs a rest too." He perked his ears at Satin's name, and shook his head as if to wake himself up properly. She sent him off with a quick signal, and he vanished silently into the gloom. Satin reappeared several minutes later, strolling up to Allad, who lay down with a grateful sigh and cushioned his head on her black side, closing his eyes. She looked at his relaxed face, and carefully rearranged her long length to curl partially around her partner then lowered her head down to her paws and shut her eyes.

Just over an hour later, Ragar and Sandar strode quietly into the rock clump, Sparks and Gryphon accompanying their partners. Both were looking tired, and gratefully accepted the water that Shanna passed them. She woke Allad quietly and the four began to stride steadily along in the darkness, one hand on their cats, with Twister and Storm rotating on point on their way to the rendezvous site, as quickly and silently as possible.

"We left them trying to hide themselves from a herd of stampeding weldens and made ourselves scarce. I'm sure we've definitely lost them as we'd be able to hear that vehicle for kilometres," said Ragar as they moved carefully through a patch of clearer ground.

"Well, the sooner we're in a secure place, the better it will be. I'm looking forward to a hot meal and a decent rest." Allad urged them forward.

Several hours later, the four of them and their accompanying five starcats approached the campsite. Although the surroundings were familiar to them all, the approaches were subtly different, and a direct line into the campsite was no longer possible as deadfalls and creepers were everywhere tangled, obscuring the once easy access to the spectacular waterfall.

"Wait for a moment," cautioned Sandar as they approached, "Verren and Nelson were going to rig spring traps after we left, so let's just be careful." They approached with caution, Satin taking the point, and intermittently steering the group around certain areas. Shanna attempted to fix the sites in her mind in case of a hasty exit. Several hundred metres before the campsite became visible, Spangles appeared silently in front of them, her dark bulk suddenly visible as Satin gave a welcoming hum. Reassured by the big cat's relaxed stance, they followed her into the camp area, which was lit dimly by a small smokeless fire, passing Perri seated on a small rock beyond the reach of the firelight. She gave them a brief smile and a wave and then returned her gaze outwards, away from the dim light.

The others were all grouped around the fire, their cats in positions of repose, bellies turned to the fire. Shanna wondered how the flight from the vehicle had gone. The two humans looked exhausted, scratched and battered with their already ragged clothing now hanging in shreds, and again, huddled together. Both were casting intermittent nervous glances at the large reclining starcats. Glinting in the fire, Shanna could see what looked like vivid orange bracelets around their ankles.

"Welcome back," said Spiron.

***

From Anjo's perspective, the day had been completely bewildering. The chaos inside the fenced area had been followed by a hurtling flight through the vegetation, full of sudden stumbles and plummets to the floor of the forest. He and Semba had been dragged willy nilly through the bush, thrust bodily from one to the other of the strange humans who'd taken them from the Garsal. They'd been almost carried in parts, flung around some types of vegetation, and forced to lie motionless for what felt like hours at a time.

The biggest shock had come early in their flight when a multitude of enormous felines appeared to materialise from nowhere all around them. They were huge, dark, and coloured with glowing markings, as they stalked with a sinuous majestic grace through the forest. They were various shades of grey and black, their markings in tones of purple, blue and red that flowed and flickered in varying intensities. Occasionally he caught glimpses of huge sharp teeth and glinting claws as one or other of the huge creatures paced next to the strange humans dragging them through the bush.

The escape from the Garsal seemed to go on and on for hours, yet another never ending nightmare dished out by the planet. He was exhausted and stumbling long before the flight ended, as was Semba, their staggering forcing the pace to slow to a crawl. The strange humans seemed sympathetic but didn't cease their efforts to urge them onwards. They had finally arrived at the concealed campsite only about an hour prior, to be met by yet another pair of the strange humans and their enormous felines. They had supplied Anjo and Semba with food and drink before settling in around the fire, and Anjo had just braced himself to begin asking and answering questions, when they were disturbed yet again by the entry of another four accompanied by five more of the huge felines. They were a mixed bunch, he reflected, of varying ages and skin tones, but all were surprisingly tall and most had unusually coloured eyes. They had effectively ignored himself and Semba during the brief meal, preferring to tend their cats of whom several appeared to have been injured during the struggle with the Garsal, and assisted one of their own, a large dark haired man whose left arm had been severely damaged in the struggle. He had been settled comfortably on a quickly rigged pallet closest to the fire, his injured arm covered in some kind of pale blue salve, and a large black feline had wrapped itself protectively about him. Anjo was unable to keep himself from starting each time one of the large creatures paced past him.

***

As Shanna, Allad, Ragar and Sandar approached the fire, Verren handed leaf plates full of food to them and motioned to them to take seats around the fire as Cirrus presented a large marmal to each of the returning cats. They hummed gratefully.

"Thank you Verren," Allad said. "And Cirrus," he added quickly at a stare from the female cat, and taking his plate from Verren settled himself by the fire with a sigh.

"Are you all uninjured?" asked Spiron.

"We're fine," replied Allad, "Storm had a small injury, but it's been well doctored and should heal all right. How long have you been back? And how's Barron?"

Spiron grimaced slightly, and there were a few wry smiles from around the group gathered at the fire.

"About an hour. Our guests are not very fast on their feet, and it took us rather longer than anticipated. Barron's arm is pretty badly burned, but thanks to

Verren's soothall salve he'll probably do OK. He'll be out of action for a while when we get back, though." He picked up his cup and sipped slowly, eyes travelling over his patrol, and coming finally to rest on the two humans from the vehicle, who were seated on the opposite side of the fire. "We're just about to find out what we can from our guests."

Shanna perked her ears up, as she shovelled more savoury stew into her mouth. Her stomach was happily accepting each offering as she swallowed it, and her two cats were contentedly gnawing on their plump marmals, quiet purrs rumbling through them. She could see the two humans clearly for the first time, and was struck by how frightened they looked. Both were dark haired and dark eyed, and rather smaller than she'd originally thought. She could see both of them looking anxiously at Spiron. On the other side of the fire Verren paused by Barron, checking his colour and breathing and taking a quick look at the ugly burn on his left arm. Hunter raised his head and hummed gently at Verren, who nodded and replied soothingly to the cat, who then settled back down beside Barron.

"So, we have you here, where we can talk." His tone was gentle, but firm. "We need to know who you are, and where you've come from, and what those creatures are." The two across the fire glanced at each other quickly, and the woman dropped her eyes, letting out a muffled sob. The man sat taller, one arm protectively around the woman, and began to talk. His accent was strange, but Shanna could understand him quite well with a little concentration. Occasionally he used words she was unfamiliar with.

"I'm Anjo, and this is Semba and we're on this planet because we had no choice, because we are slaves of the Garsal. Who are you? And how did you get here? There are no humans in this sector." His voice was unsteady during the last questions and the woman finally raised her eyes again, trying to control her sobbing. There was a sudden mutter of voices around the fire as the patrol attempted to assimilate this astonishing information.

"What do you mean 'slaves'?" Spiron was incredulous.

Anjo looked confused, and exchanged another glance with Semba, who gestured at him to go on, rubbing her reddened eyes.

"You must know that we've been taken from our home worlds to labour for the Garsal. Everyone knows they're the overlords of the galaxy and that we exist only under their sufferance. Our families are safe as long as we serve - most probably safe that is, none of us really know for sure, but that's our hope. It's the only hope we have. But surely you know this. There are no free human worlds." The patrol sat stunned and motionless, as the horror of Anjo's words struck home.

"There are no free humans? What happened to the Galactic Federation? What's happened to the peaceful co-existence of alien races?" Allad burst out, verbalising the questions rushing around Shanna's mind. There were nods and murmurs of agreement around the fire.

"*Who* are you people that you don't know this?" The question burst from Semba in almost a shout. There were hushing motions from the patrol, and several sent their cats out into the bush to make sure nothing was attracted to the area by the sudden noise.

There was a period of silence, and Shanna felt more uncertain than ever about the future. She tried to imagine the universe without the distant but always present knowledge of the possibility of being found by benevolent, but welcoming human beings or their friendly alien allies. It was a strange, somewhat empty feeling. She snuck a surreptitious glance at the others sitting around the fire. Most were staring into the fire, with far away expressions on their faces, while a couple were studying Anjo and Semba thoughtfully. Spiron was one of them. He appeared to come abruptly to a decision, and stood up, pacing quietly around the fire to peer into Barron's face. Shanna realised that Barron was awake and listening intently to the discussion. There was a moment of silent communication between the patrol leader and his second, and then Barron nodded and Spiron inclined his head to the wounded man. He returned to his seat.

There was gravity in his voice, as he began to explain the situation on Frontier, and their history. He spoke steadily for about half an hour, outlining the relevant points of history,but, Shanna realised, giving nothing away about the population of Frontier or the intimate details of their existence on the plateau.

"So, as you can see, we're the descendants of the original colony ship, and we've been here for several hundred years, gradually spreading out and settling more and more areas. There have been some adaptations to the unique situations we've found ourselves in here, and as you are no doubt aware, the flora and fauna of this planet can be a little challenging." There were some quiet chuckles and grins from around the circle. "As for us specifically, well, we're a Scout Patrol out on a routine survey with a group of first year cadets. We found the remains of some kind of flying craft after one of the early storms, and we've been keeping an eye out for any strangers. For many years our people have been hoping for contact from the Federation. And now we discover it no longer exists…" He cleared his throat and his tone then became more businesslike and direct. "How likely are these Garsal to come after you? And how likely are they to find us?"

Anjo and Semba looked anxiously at each other, before Anjo again spoke up.

"They never let an escaped slave go. They will follow us until they retrieve us, and then they'll kill us slowly, in front of the other slaves. They can't track or find their way through the forest as you do, but when they notify the mother ship about our escape, it can activate these control bracelets on our ankles to stop us from moving and then locate us exactly. If we're to survive, then we need to remove them somehow and dispose of them far from here." He looked around the group, "The commander probably won't notify the ship for a couple of days, as to lose a slave is a shameful thing. He is also likely to be punished, most probably by revocation of his breeding privileges, and he has a full quota of pride, that one. We probably have two days at most, more likely one." Anjo held his breath. It was a calculated risk to let these 'Scouts' know about the tracking device, but he was unable to stomach the thought of leading the Garsal directly to the human settlements. It was now possible that they would simply abandon the two of them and they would perish quickly in Frontier's inimical wilderness.

Allad leaned forward and motioned to Anjo to lift his trouser leg.

"How do we remove them?" Shanna was able to see the bright orange brace-let clamped firmly around each of his ankles. There was enough laxity that they didn't rub the skin unduly, but there was no way the shiny material was going to slide off over his feet.

"They're very hard to remove, as the material is almost impossible to cut and the ends have been fused seamlessly. The Garsal use an unlocking device and the things simply separate, but without that, I'm not sure." Semba contributed her first coherent statement to the discussion and Shanna could see that the woman had finally gained enough control of her emotions to enable her to think more clearly.

"So, we have probably twelve hours or so to get them removed, before we're all endangered. We need to work on it immediately then. Amma and Challon, go and relieve Perri, and then we'll commence the normal watch roster. Allad, you begin trying to remove the bracelets by any method possible. The rest of us will sleep as much as possible. Kalli, you locate some spare clothing for Anjo and Semba, and Verren, consider whether Barron's going to need a litter for tomor-row." Spiron was typically decisive and the patrol moved into gear like a well oiled machine, the cadets moving as one with their patrol mates. Shanna walked stiffly over to Allad who was examining the bracelet around Anjo's ankle in minute detail. There were no seams visible on the orange band anywhere. It seemed to be a seamless flexible ring of shiny smooth material. He tried to slide it down Anjo's leg, requesting him to remove his footwear, but it was tight enough to make that impossible. Shanna could see that even greasing it would make no difference.

Allad sat back on his heels, moustache twitching thoughtfully, and his mobile eyebrows lowering. He removed his knife from its belt pouch, opening the blade and checking its sharpness before sliding it carefully under the bracelet and attempting to slit the shiny material. The sharp blade made no impression at all on the material, not even a scratch. He took the blade out from under the bracelet and checked its sharpness again, and then detailed Shanna to gather a collection of sharp knives from the rest of the patrol to try. Two hours later they had made no impression at all on the material. They had tried all the knives belonging to the patrol, they had heated the knives, they had carefully laid hot coals on the material, while protecting Anjo's skin, and they had even tried stretching the material as hard as possible, one on either side.

At the two hour mark, Storm appeared suddenly by Shanna's elbow, sticking his large nose down to sniff the orange material. He sneezed, startling Anjo who had frozen at the big cat's approach, very obviously fearful of the large feline.

"He won't hurt you Anjo," said Shanna smiling at the offworlder, "He's just curious about you and the bracelet. In fact, he likes to be scratched..." She demonstrated and encouraged Storm to lie down next to them, in reach of Anjo's hand. He tentatively reached out to touch the silky fur of Storm's head, relaxing slightly as the cat began to purr loudly and then smiling tentatively at Shanna who smiled back encouragingly. "See, he's really very friendly." Allad suddenly sighed in frustration, dropping the latest knife onto the leaf laid out for the purpose, and leaning back heavily on his haunches. There was disgust written all over his normally cheerful face, and a frown drew his eyebrows down over his nose.

"Well, that's the last of them. I'm not sure what else to try. Shanna, go and get another billy full of water, and we'll have a hot drink before we get back to work. I need to think of something else to try." Setting Storm to stay beside Anjo, who looked somewhat unsure of the arrangement, Shanna gathered the billy from near the fire and pulled her glowstone out of her shirt to light the way to the pool at the base of the waterfall. Twister joined her and paced companionably beside her as she walked towards the pool. She wondered if she could spot one of the little flotters camouflaged somewhere around the rocks bordering the water. She had found the quirky little creature oddly attractive with its amazing ability to blend into its surroundings, although she had a healthy respect for the corrosive fog it produced when startled. She came to an abrupt halt, as a sudden thought struck her. If they could somehow channel the flotter's spray of corrosion onto the bracelets, perhaps they'd be able to get them off.

"Come on Twister, let's see if we can find a flotter to take back." Shanna was halfway to the pool before she realised that carrying a flotter back to the campsite was going to be a bit of a problem, and did an about face to take her idea back to Allad. Perhaps he'd have a better idea how to go about it.

Several minutes later, they were carefully surveying the pool surrounds using the light from both Shanna and Amma's glowstones.

"Try and keep the light steady and then gradually move it across the rocks, looking for any signs of movement or colour change, and if you see anything, keep the light focused on it." Allad's instructions were fruitful, with Amma spotting a camouflaged flotter within the first few moments of their search.

"Now, Shanna you place the billy just in front of it – it is full isn't it? Now, Amma, take the light directly behind it and approach it slowly." Shanna felt a sudden slosh of the water in the billy and carefully and gently lowered it to the ground.

"I've got it. Should I cover the billy?"

"No, let's just take it very carefully back to the fire."

A few moments later, Shanna was gently tipping the flotter onto a flat rock near the fire, carefully sheltering it from too much light and then slowly watched it fade into the colours of the rock beneath it.

"OK, we've got the flotter, how are we going to get it to breathe on the bracelet without vaporising Anjo's leg?" This was the part of the plan that Shanna had not yet figured out. She was relying on the more experienced Scouts to come up with some ideas. "Is there anything that the flotter doesn't vaporise that we can use to catch its breath?"

"Well, it definitely vaporises anything vegetable, and it burns anything animal. We've tried metal, and it just corrodes away to almost nothing, and then we've tried cloth – no good; leather – no good." Perri recited the list of a standard Scout's pack in the negative.

"I think I might be able to help." Verren's voice came softly through the night. "I have some frondan resin in my pack – it's useful as a wound dressing, but my parents use it to acid proof stoppers for some of their flasks when they need to store acids that they use to render some types of plant. If we heat it, we might be able to coat both Anjo's skin and a leaf container."

"OK Verren, set up whatever you need, and then we'll try it – first on the leaf container and then on Anjo." Allad was much happier with the prospect of some success now appearing on the horizon. Shanna was still a little unsure about being able to get the flotter to perform on cue, but reckoned they'd figure it out somehow.

Some time later, Verren had a leaf container ready to go, coated thoroughly with warmed frondan resin. He'd coated Anjo's ankles as well, making sure that there were no gaps anywhere. Allad carefully positioned the leaf container, using two twigs to hold it in front of the flotter where it was crouching on the rock and then nodded at Shanna, who prodded the flotter gently with another small stick. It immediately performed up to expectations, turning bright red and emitting the small cloud of fog, which began to condense as it contacted the resin coated leaf container. There was a slight sizzle from one small spot at the lip of the container but the rest held nicely and Allad was left with a small puddle of slightly milky liquid in the bottom of the container. He swirled it around inside the leafy flask.

"Could you just check that resin's all over my ankles before you try that stuff out on me?" Anjo's slightly accented voice was a little quavery, as he eyed the sizzling portion of the leaf container.

"Verren, do a check of our guest's ankles please." Verren quickly checked over Anjo's legs, carefully adding a few drops here and there if he felt that the coating might be a little lacking and then nodded to confirm they were ready.

"Make sure you stay *very* still Anjo," said Allad as he carefully positioned the leaf container over the bracelet on Anjo's left leg. Anjo nodded, and closed his eyes, screwing up his face. Allad gently tipped the container over to drip the fluid onto the orange band. There was a sizzle, and the band began to smoke slightly, the acrid smell causing every cat within range to curl its nose up in disgust.

"I think it might be working!" said Allad excitedly as a small hole appeared in the material. He carefully used a leaf to tilt the bracelet so that the fluid began to burn a thin line across the width of the bracelet. He paused as a small rivulet of the milky fluid dripped onto Anjo's coated ankle. When the man didn't move, he carefully redirected the fluid back and forth across the bracelet until it suddenly dropped onto the ground beneath the man's leg. There was a sudden sizzle as the residual fluid contacted the leaf litter on the ground, and a small curl of smoke. Shanna hurriedly sloshed most of the billy water over Anjo's leg and the ground underneath it. Allad looked carefully into the leaf container, and then began to drip the fluid onto the other bracelet. Shanna bent to gently wake Semba, who had fallen asleep not long after they had begun to try and remove Anjo's bracelet.

"Wake up Semba, we need to remove those bracelets from your legs." Semba woke with a start, looking around wildy as Shanna tapped her gently on the shoulder, and then subsided with relief as she realised where she was. "Semba, we need to get your bracelets off now."

"You've figured out how to remove them?" There was disbelief on Semba's face which turned to joy as Shanna nodded and pointed to the two orange bands that had once imprisoned Anjo. "How do you get them off?"

Shanna explained, and Semba looked a bit uncertain, before nodding hesitantly and sat in front of Verren, raising her trouser legs to allow Verren to coat her legs with the warm resin he'd had sitting by the fire. A few moments later, with the somewhat grumpy aid of the little flotter, the two prisoners were free from their bands.

"Will they still be able to locate the bands?" asked Spiron, "Even though they're off?"

"I'm not sure," replied Anjo. "But it's probably a good idea to get them as far from us as possible."

"Kalli, I want you to send Flyer out to the east as far as he can get in about an hour, to drop the bracelets somewhere in the bush. We'll start for home first thing in the morning. It will most likely take us quite a bit longer to get home than it did to get here, but we'll have some support along the way hopefully. Arad, Taya, Zandany and Karri should have arrived at the tunnel by now, and there may already be some help on its way." Kalli picked up the now washed bracelets, called Flyer and then sent him off into the forest at a blurring speed.

"What *are* those things?" asked Anjo wonderingly, "I've never seen anything like them." His tone was wondering as Flyer vanished within a few seconds and he looked around the campsite, his eyes lingering on the cats relaxing in the dim firelight or being tended by their Scout partners.

"They're our starcats," replied Shanna, "And our partners. We choose each other and live and work together." She wasn't sure that her explanation was going to be adequate, but this was not the time to go into the minute details of Frontier's odd genetic quirks. It was also not the time to panic their two guests. Anjo nodded slowly and she could tell that he knew there was much more than her brief answer, but didn't ask any further questions. "You need to rest Anjo, as we'll be travelling as fast as possible tomorrow, and you and Semba are unaccustomed to this planet." She watched as Anjo settled himself with a sigh of exhaustion and moved over to Allad.

"We have the breakfast watch, so settle yourself as fast as possible to maximise your rest. Spiron tells me we'll begin as point tomorrow, and I'll be acting patrol second tomorrow while Barron's incapacitated. Verren feels he'll be able to keep up with our slower pace tomorrow, but he certainly won't be able to perform his normal duties so you and I will need to be covering more ground than usual and I need to know if you're up to it. I think you are, but I need to hear it from you – so tell me now if you can't and I'll assign you to Perri instead until we're home." Allad's tone was brisk, but Shanna didn't hesitate.

"I'll be fine Allad, just tell me what to do." Allad smiled, his eyes twinkling with their customary good humour.

"Get yourself to bed then, I'll wake you when it's our watch." Shanna smiled back and walked over to unpack her sleeping gear and get a bit of rest. She arranged her bedding neatly and then curled up with her starcats on either side, lulled by their soft purrs.

Chapter 27

THE return trip to the plateau began smoothly, with no sign of the Garsal vehicle. The patrol formed into its standard travelling formation, with Anjo and Semba placed in the middle with Barron, who despite his injury, coached them continuously in quiet movement and assisted them to avoid dangerous vegetation. Hunter paced steadily next to his partner, occasionally circling the group of three. Shanna found that working point with two novices in the centre of the patrol was much harder than she had thought. She and Allad had not only to navigate flawlessly and locate any dangerous animals, but scout a safe path through the vegetation, avoiding all the plants that might pose any kind of risk to the two offworlders, who would not know enough to avoid them. By the end of the second day, they had covered barely one normal day's distance, and it was clear that Anjo and Semba were at the end of their endurance. The injured Barron had easily managed the distance despite being in obvious pain, and that fact alone served to mark the difference between the offworlders and the Frontier Scouts.

After eating, the exhausted Anjo and Semba had simply fallen asleep where they sat, and Challon and Amma had carefully carried them to more comfortable resting places inside the pungo grove. The patrol gathered around the embers of the banked fire, sipping their drinks in companionable silence. Shanna stared into the glowing coals. For the first time since drawing the vehicle after them in the bush, she felt fully physically rested as though she'd simply been on a training march on the plateau. Emotionally she was on edge, knowing that somewhere behind them, were potentially the most destructive predators her people had ever known, and that those same predators would be hunting them ceaselessly. Predators were something every human being on Frontier knew well, but these were thinking, sentient beings, intent on domination, not animals following their inbuilt instincts. There was no doubt that they had been heading directly for the plateau - both Semba and Anjo had been very clear about that – and that the Garsal would view her people as yet another source of slaves for their ever expanding empire.

Her people had spent three hundred years remembering a golden age of galactic expansion for the human race, a federation that now no longer existed. There would be no "rescue" from the stars by a benevolent human and alien confederation of mutual fellowship. Instead, there was only a galaxy enslaved by a race of merciless slave masters, who would do everything in their power to add the settlers of Frontier to their collection of subjugated races. Shanna knew that there would be no choice for her people – they would resist enslavement with everything they had - yet how would they remain free from a race with superior technology and countless thousands of reserve troops?

At the edge of the firelight, Allad, Barron and Spiron were conferring quietly. Shanna wondered what they were discussing so intently together, as she idly ran a hand down Storm's sleek flank and he rolled onto his back to expose his belly, begging mutely for Shanna to rub it. She smiled at him and obliged as Twister nudged her other hand. Sometimes she felt as if she needed an extra hand for the two cats. As Storm rolled completely over, she took the opportunity to examine his injured leg, happily noting that it was healing nicely with no sign of infection.

As the three senior Scouts returned to the firelight circle, the others looked up intently; there was a sense in the group that a turning point had been reached, and that a decision of some kind had been made.

"We should be meeting up with reinforcements from the plateau sometime tomorrow I hope, and we'll then be handing the two offworlders over to an escort to take them back to the plateau. The rest of us will then go back to locate the vehicle, and see what we can do to locate this 'mother ship' that they've talked about so frequently." Spiron sat heavily on a stone, motioning to Allad and Barron to do so as well.

Barron sat carefully, cradling his arm carefully against jolting movements, and Hunter watched him anxiously, subtly supporting his partner as he bent his legs. Allad took up a position on the ground near Shanna, Satin strolling over to sprawl her long length conveniently close to him with a relaxed sigh. "It means that we'll not return to the plateau as planned, but we will gather important intelligence about these aliens. I've decided to send all the cadets back with the offworlders, however. Our peoples' future must be kept secure, and it's likely that locating the ship will take some time. You have all done well, and can be extremely proud of your achievements, but you can best serve our community by extending your skills in training on the plateau."

Shanna felt a sudden shock, as if she was suddenly a small child again, unexpectedly sent to bed during an important function. Her feelings were hurt, and looking around she could see that the other three cadets were feeling the same way. After the high intensity emotions and physical exertion of the last few days, the sudden prospect of going straight back to 'normal life' in a few days was almost unendurable.

"But Spiron, we can be useful to you. Haven't we proved ourselves?" Amma burst out suddenly.

"Yes, why send us back when we know what these creatures are like, and know how to cope with them?" Verren's tone was angry. Barron held up a placatory hand, wincing as the wounded arm jolted slightly.

"We're well aware of those things, cadets, but the patrol will be travelling faster and most probably further than anyone has yet penetrated into the country here Below. You and I are needed to take back first hand information on the Garsal to the Scout Council and indeed to the Watchtower Council, who will no doubt forward it to the other settlements as fast as possible." He cleared his throat and shifted his arm in its sling uncomfortably, before continuing. "You going back to the plateau is not 'babysitting', but instead an important step in beginning our society's defence against these creatures. It is imperative that you complete your Scout training as fast as possible. You and your older classmates are part of the front line of defence for our people and indeed it appears, our race, and we cannot risk our future prematurely. There is much for you still to learn about being Scouts. Normally your training would take three years, including breaks and family time. I am sure that the council will choose to accelerate the process as soon as they have our new information. Be prepared for this." There was a quiet murmur of voices as the Patrol mulled over these startling words.

Allad grunted as Satin shifted her weight to a more comfortable position, leaning heavily upon his crossed legs.

"Don't forget that we still have to get Anjo and Semba safely to the plateau and through the night. As we've all realised today, moving through Below with the offworlders is much harder than moving by ourselves, and it's absolutely imperative that they arrive safely."

The cadets were still somewhat disgruntled. Ragar nodded slowly, but still looked unhappy with Spiron's decision and Amma and Verren both looked unimpressed. Shanna could see the sense of the decision, but was still feeling as though she had gone from being regarded as an adult, to a small child who must be kept safe and secure. She sighed heavily, and Storm looked up with a small "Meh," as her hand momentarily stopped rubbing his belly, his eyes narrowing slightly in displeasure. Twister butted her other hand with his wet nose, momentarily jerking her out of her thoughts, before she resumed staring at the fire and stroking the two cats beside her.

There was a long period of silence before Sandar rose, beckoning to Ragar to join him and relieve Perri who had taken the first watch. Shanna decided to turn in as she and Allad were again on the final night watch, and the day had been a long one despite its slow pace. After curling herself up beneath a pungo tree towards the edge of the clearing, Shanna found herself unable to sleep immediately. She rolled over several times, disturbing her starcats each time, and found herself lying on her back with two annoyed faces peering into hers. Twister hummed plaintively as if to remind Shanna that his comfort was much more important than hers, while Storm simply grunted and then laid his body heavily across her middle, effectively pinning her to the ground. Twister then turned himself round several times before leaning on both Shanna and his brother with a satisfied sigh, then leaned his head on his paws and closed his eyes. She gave up, wriggled slightly to ensure she had breathing room, and determinedly closed her eyes.

The next morning, Shanna melted into the bush after Allad as Storm and Twister vanished behind Satin. There was a small flurry of activity behind her as the rest of the patrol settled into its normal formation, Barron quietly shepherding Anjo and Semba out of the pungo grove, his injured arm cradled carefully in a sling, and Hunter pacing close beside him gently rubbing his head on Barron's uninjured arm.

The early part of the morning passed without incident, and the Patrol settled into its smooth flow of silent movement through the bush, with only the occasional hiccough as the two offworlders stumbled or needed to pause for a break. Shortly after midmorning, Satin hurtled back to Allad and he signalled the patrol to stop and freeze in order to listen for whatever had alarmed the big female starcat. Twister appeared through the trees ahead, again moving through the topmost branches of the tallest of them.

Shanna listened carefully, ears attuned to the slightest noise from the foliage obscuring her view ahead. When Allad signalled her to move ahead she complied, sliding silently from cover to cover, with Twister moving noiselessly ahead of her through the tree branches. Just ahead, Storm was completely still, watching a herd of weldens in a small clearing. Shanna slid up beside him, being careful to make sure that she was downwind of the creatures, who were browsing on patches of salsa leaf bush. Mindful of the large omnivores' tendency to stampede, Shanna carefully counted, noting a total of fifteen adults and eight young weldens grazing peacefully, their double pronged horns pointing forwards as they grazed. She slid quietly backwards, leaving Storm on guard, aware that should the weldens elect to move, she would have advance warning from the reliable cat.

"Herd of weldens directly ahead – fifteen adults and eight juveniles. They're grazing peacefully at the moment and I left Storm on watch. I'd suggest we divert to the west and then circle back on track as soon as we're far enough down wind of them not to make them startle."

Allad nodded, signalling quickly to the rest of the patrol and then began to move off towards the west, motioning to Shanna to maintain a watch on the welden herd as the patrol passed. She nodded, and she and Twister returned to where Storm was waiting patiently beneath a tall frondan tree. Shanna carefully surveyed the herd and then sent Twister circling to the west in the tree tops.

With a sudden shivery thrill, she realised that she was now in a position of responsibility for the safety of the whole patrol, and effectively on her own. It was a mark of trust from Allad that he had delegated the task to Shanna and her two cats. Storm stayed in the drop position, his eyes fixed on the weldens grazing not much more than ten metres from their position. Twister was invisible in the trees to their left, and Shanna spent a number of minutes observing the weldens. The large omnivores were odd looking beasts, with long scything tails covered in tufts of coarse hair and lengthy, agile necks that browsed not only the ground plants but the taller flowering trees. They possessed a multitude of teeth, both grinders for vegetable matter and sharp ones for tearing flesh off anything that they decided to sample.

She watched as they continued to graze, the youngsters frolicking in the sunlight filtering through the canopy above. When she judged that adequate time had passed for the patrol to be far enough to the west even at the slow pace that the presence of Semba and Anjo had forced them to, she signalled Storm to begin to move in that direction and flicked a hand signal to Twister to maintain a hidden position in the tree tops as she and Storm quietly moved through the bush. They left without disturbing the creatures, and Shanna and Storm slunk quietly away through the trees. After they had circled to the west for about fifteen minutes, Shanna used her silent whistle to call Twister and then began to navigate towards the area where she estimated the patrol would be.

After a number of minutes, Shanna realised that the surrounding forest had fallen suddenly silent. There was no sign of the patrol as yet, and she was uneasy about the sudden absence of normal sound. The two cats had suddenly become preternaturally alert, their ears pricked and their heads turning from side to side as they attempted to identify the possible danger. Shanna went to ground quietly near a large rock conveniently located under a pungo tree, and sent Twister to circle around silently while she remained hidden. Storm dropped quietly beside her, his ears twitching ceaselessly and his tidemarks subdued. The silence continued with not a breath of sound anywhere, and Shanna felt her heart rate begin to escalate. Twister reappeared suddenly beside her and urged her deeper into the crevice behind the rock. It was unusual for him to take such a dominant role and she complied without question, trusting his instincts. He hummed quietly at Storm and the two starcats pressed her deeper into the crevice, covering her body with theirs. Their behaviour was so unusual that Shanna was unable to fathom a reason for it, and simply remained motionless, trusting to her cats' instincts as the oppressive silence seemed to press in upon her.

Moments of uncanny quiet passed, and Shanna remained still, the two cats completely silent and motionless, their heavy bodies forming a solid barrier in front of her and Shanna began to feel more and more uneasy. The silence was broken abruptly by a loud sighing, as if a sudden breeze was sweeping through the canopy, yet the trees were completely still and the dappled sunlight continued to fall steadily from above onto the forest floor. The sighing became louder and louder, the breeze-like sound increasing in intensity, and the tree trunks began to tremble and vibrate.

With a sudden shiver of horror, the truth dawned in Shanna's mind – somewhere close by was the largest danger known to the Frontier settlers. The early settlers had named the enormous snakelike reptile the 'tornado serpent', for the gale like sound of its approach, and because "snake" had seemed too tame for a reptile that grew to up to one hundred metres in length, was usually between two and three metres in diameter, and had a myriad of poisonous teeth in its large mouth. Fortunately they were extremely rare as their appetites were insatiable, and the vast snakes moved continuously from area to area in their constant hunt for food.

From the quivering in the trunks of the trees, Shanna was sure the serpent was close by, and would be upon her in a moment. Her only hope was to remain completely still, and hope that the reptile's poor vision would enable her to escape unscathed. The nearer trunks were now vibrating furiously and the leaves of the pungo tree above her quivered and rustled and some of the leaves drifted down onto the three huddled into the rock hollow. Storm and Twister pressed even closer, and Shanna was aware that they had begun to fade themselves. Strangely, she felt as though she too, was fading as she pressed herself deeper into the crevice. Two of the trees not twenty metres away swayed and then crashed heavily to the ground as the reptile's head appeared. It cast its scaly head back and forth, swaying its body from side to side as it undulated through the vegetation towards Shanna's hiding place. She was sweating and trying not to shake as the reptile's moss patterned scales came closer and closer and the noise of its progress became deafening. The pungo above Shanna vibrated furiously, showering Shanna and the two cats in leaves.

Storm and Twister were now no longer visible to Shanna, although she could feel their warm solid weights pressing heavily against her. She had curled herself into the smallest ball she could manage and was attempting to remain completely still despite the intensity of the fear that was passing through her. Her view of the oncoming creature was limited to a small gap between Storm's back and Twister's belly, otherwise she was completely concealed behind her two starcats. The reptile paused in its passage, head moving side to side as it allowed its thin tongue to sense the air, quivering as it paused and flicked it back and forth as if questing for Shanna and the cats. The seemingly endless moment finally finished and the great reptile resumed its passing, Shanna watching as metre after metre of patterned scales passed her by. The tornado serpent passed close enough that Shanna could have reached out and touched the mottled scales, had she not been so desperate to escape the reptile's notice.

As the final few metres of tail vanished through the bushes, the cats slowly reappeared, their tidemarks subdued, but rippling in muted blues and violets. Shanna silently unwound herself from their large bodies, running her shaky hands gratefully over the silky fur of their heads and necks and looking cautiously in the direction the tornado serpent had taken. She could still hear the sound of its passing sussurating through the vegetation interspersed with occasional crashing noises from falling trees. She calculated quickly, and realised it would be moving directly towards the point where she had expected to rendezvous with the patrol.

"Come on boys, we've got to get moving," she murmured quietly to the two cats and began the race towards the patrol, hoping against hope to get to the patrol to warn them about the tornado serpent. With two novices in the middle of the patrol, they'd be at much greater risk than if they had been travelling without them. Taking a few seconds to pencil a quick note, she tucked it into Twister's harness and sent him hurtling ahead towards the patrol and with Storm circling around, Shanna began a measured lope, trying to move silently but reasoning that the tornado serpent had probably sent most of the creatures around into hiding. Storm was completely invisible to the eye, but Shanna could feel him circling steadily around her position and increased her stride to a ground eating pace, trying to estimate exactly how far it would be until she might make contact with the rear guard of the patrol. As she ran she pondered, replaying through her mind exactly what had happened as the serpent passed. She remembered feeling as if she was fading just as the cats had, and kept running the sensation through her mind again and again, wondering if she was a little mad for thinking that perhaps she had faded too. She had no other real explanation for her survival, as usually the huge serpents had an amazing instinct for food sources, and it was extremely unusual for anyone to survive such a close encounter.

Again she ran the fading sensation through her mind, and was startled to realise that the peripheral vision of her hands that she usually experienced when she ran was suddenly absent. She did a double take and stumbled over a trailing plybrush trailer. She inadvertently slowed her pace and then redoubled it, while attempting to simultaneously visualise her hands and keep an eye on the vegetation in front of her. Abruptly her hands reappeared and she took a brief pause to reorient herself, making sure that she was navigating accurately in the hurry to reach the patrol.

Having reassured herself that she was still on track, Shanna decided to stay stopped for thirty seconds longer and ran the fade sensation through her mind again, while watching her hands. As she panted quietly, her hands began to shimmer and then faded almost completely from view. She was waving one in front of her eyes bemusedly when Storm sped to her side and nudged her as if to remind her of what was really important. She resumed her run, thinking furiously as she strode along. If she had somehow learnt to fade as did the starcats, then perhaps others in the patrol would be able to as well – it was now imperative for her to catch them as quickly as possible – her presence might mean the difference between survival and death for some of them.

She had been running for nearly thirty minutes, and was still able to hear the sound of the serpent in the distance off to her right. She was apparently just keeping pace with it, and not overtaking it at her current speed, however, she took some small comfort in the fact that she was sure Twister had now made contact with the patrol and that they would be doing their best to avoid the serpent by now. She decided to increase her pace in an attempt to catch up with them, hopefully without falling foul of the serpent to her right. Her breath began to come faster, and her legs began to burn as she forced herself to continue the rapid pace. The sound of the serpent began to fade slightly, and with Storm flanking her she continued to run silently as fast as she was able to maintain a steady pace, carefully ducking around and under any dangerous plants she recognised while hoping frantically not to encounter any dangerous vegetation that she didn't yet know about.

Fifteen minutes later, Twister reappeared by her side, another note tucked in his harness. Shanna paused to check it, quickly reorienting herself to proceed directly to the coordinates that Spiron had provided for her. She took a few seconds to jot a note about her bizarre fading ability and sent Twister off at a blurring run towards the patrol, which she estimated was now only about a half kilometre ahead. In the few moments she had taken to stop, the sound of the tornado serpent had increased in volume, so she decided that moving as fast as possible was the most important thing now. She hoped it wasn't tracking her by sound straight towards the Patrol. Shaking her head, she reminded herself that it hadn't deviated towards her as she travelled. Forcing her burning legs to more speed she loped through the bush, Storm now pacing rapidly not far from her. Within a few moments, Twister had returned and began to run on her other side. She knew their superior senses would take her more quickly to the others and stopped worrying about navigating, and just let the cats guide her. She must have tired more than she'd thought, as the sound of the serpent was increasing again, and she realised that she would have only moments with the patrol before it would be upon them.

As Satin emerged from behind a tree directly in front of her, Shanna almost let out a shout of relief but strangled it before it made it past her teeth. She pushed herself to one more effort and then Allad was beside her, signalling for her to slow to a more measured jog.

"We're concealed in a small pungo grove behind some rocks, just ahead. Try and explain what your note meant, as we run." His voice was a hoarse whisper. Shanna decided that actions would speak louder than too many words.

"Watch," she gasped, concentrated and then heard Allad's gasp as he saw her hand fade. "Was hiding from the serpent with the boys squashing me into a crevice." She paused and took a gasping breath, "When they faded, I must have too."

"But how?" Allad's whisper was incredulous as they breasted the slight rise into the pungo grove.

"No idea, but now all I have to do is remember the sensation and that happens." They slowed to a walk and Allad directed her into the trees. "I'd suggest everyone huddles as close as possible to their cats and then asks them to fade. Tell them to *feel* what's happening. Where are the offworlders?"

"They're in a small hollow. If you can do this, I need you to send one of your cats over to them, no, better still, come with me and you and I will protect them as much as possible. Do everything you can to keep them quiet – the woman's almost hysterical. You may need to control her physically – can you do it?"

Shanna felt exhausted, but nodded, knowing that she was most probably the woman's best chance of survival, and given her extra height she should be able to hold her down if required, and then followed Allad into the hollow where Anjo and Semba were huddled with Barron and Hunter.

"We'll help you Barron, just do what Shanna says." Barron raised his eyebrows but didn't argue with Allad's terse statement as the wind like sound of the serpent increased rapidly.

"Cats on the outside, all of us behind them, Allad, you lie on Anjo, and I'll cover Semba. Barron, get Hunter to spread himself across you and fade. While he fades, feel him fade." Shanna had no idea whether any of this would work, but could see Perri listening intently from behind a tree nearby, and felt rather than saw her vanish to pass the message on.

There was an uncomfortable moment when she laid her body over Semba's smaller one, and directed the willing Storm to squash them into the smallest possible crevices, while Twister covered any gaps over the four of them. As the cats faded, Shanna concentrated on the sensation and as she felt Semba gasp hurriedly covered the smaller woman's mouth with her hand, hoping she wasn't asphyxiating her. The Tornado serpent was almost on them, and the pungo trees had begun to shake violently. A terrified marmal bolted past them and Shanna concentrated even harder on the fade. The deafening sound of the serpent abruptly ceased, and Shanna tensed slightly, making sure that Semba was completely still beneath her while trying to control the heaving breaths that her oxygen starved body was trying to take. She felt Storm compress his body against her and saw that Allad had apparently vanished, while Barron's form was flickering slightly.

From off in the forest a sudden sound of movement came, along with a high wailing sound, and the serpent abruptly jolted into action, moving rapidly away from the hidden patrol. It disappeared into the distance, and Shanna relaxed herself slightly, but kept her firm hold on Semba. At last she allowed her body to take the huge breaths it so desperately wanted.

Chapter 28

IT had been a long day on the archery range. His group of five archers: Camid, Gwen, Horden, Tasha and himself, had spent half of it working hard on compensating for the balance and coordination issues posed by the new arrows. Camid, a physics teacher from Scholar's precinct, had been placed in command of the other four. Even nocking such a differently weighted missile had taken some time to master, and none of them were yet particularly accurate with them. All five had managed to hit targets ranged within forty metres, but not with their customary accuracy. Kaidan raised his bow again, feeling the tightness of his shoulder and back muscles as he drew the string back yet again. He sighted carefully, raised the bow slightly to compensate for the heavier arrow, and sent yet another practice missile towards the target. It struck the target, slightly closer than his other shots, but he shook his head slightly. Beside him, he heard the 'thrum' of Gwen's bow, and watched her arrow 'thwock' neatly into the centre rings.

"Yes!" She lowered her bow and grinned at Kaidan. "I think I've got it figured – just compensate a little more, and you'll be right." He fished another arrow out of his quiver and determinedly nocked it.

***

As Shanna slowly removed her death grip from Semba and eased her sweaty, fatigued body off the smaller framed woman, Storm and Twister loped off to circle the area. Next to her, Allad and Satin reappeared and Barron's form ceased its flickering. Around her, the other Scouts of Patrol Ten glided into view, preceded by their attendant starcats, eyes staring wonderingly at Shanna, where she stood brushing dirt and leaves off her front with one hand, while pulling the trembling Semba to her feet with the other. Sweat trickled down her face and she rubbed at it, smearing the dirt on her forehead across her face.

"What was that?" Semba's voice came out in a squeak, and she appeared to be completely breathless. Shanna ran her eyes over the woman to make sure she hadn't inadvertently injured her, and replied.

"Tornado serpent. We're lucky to have survived." She could tell that her information meant nothing to Semba, but the details could wait.

With a quick signal, Spiron sent Nelson and Verren to carefully follow in the wake of the departing tornado serpent and make sure it was continuing to move away from them. He then beckoned to the others to move further under cover into the pungo grove, sending Fury out to circle as several of the other Scouts did the same.

"Now, Shanna, we need to know exactly what you did and how you managed it." His voice was the nearest to stunned that Shanna had heard from the normally controlled Patrol Leader. "And then maybe we can figure out whether we can all do it, or whether like you, we can fade others as well."

"What?" Shanna was confused. "What do you mean fade others?" She was still trembling from the reaction of the run, the fade and the serpent.

"Allad told me – you faded Semba as well. Didn't you realise?"

"I could still see her, so she can't have been faded."

"Well unless Allad's going blind, you faded Semba too." Spiron's tone was now flat and he gestured for Shanna to keep talking. "Who knows how this might work?"

Shanna prepared herself and then took a breath and began to try and explain the phenomenon in more detail. Every now and then, one or other of her two starcats would brush against her as if to set their seal of approval on her explanations. She completed her explanation by fading herself.

Spiron looked around the group, and then asked.

"How many of you managed to fade using Shanna's instructions?" Allad raised his hand, along with Perri and Amma, Verren and Nelson, and Barron and Ragar wiggled their hands to indicate that they'd only succeeded partially. "OK, we can't stop here, because our priority is to get Anjo and Semba to the plateau. Each of you will spend some time with Shanna on the journey. Shanna you'll be in the centre of the patrol and you can start with Barron, and then work through the rest of us - alternate your cats – send one with Allad and swap them over intermittently. Allad, you'll continue on point and we'll keep moving until we meet the others. It shouldn't be too long now until we contact them."

The patrol formed up again, starcats circling, with Allad working the point with Satin. Shanna dispatched Storm to assist him, directing the cat to follow the older Scout's commands. Allad waved his thanks and then vanished into the scrub ahead in the wake of Satin and Storm, and Shanna turned her attention to instructing the injured Barron in the fade technique, while guiding Semba and Anjo through the thick vegetation without injury or risk. Barron proved to be an eager student and an adept questioner, his thoughtful queries eliciting information from Shanna that she hadn't consciously considered and allowing the two of them to build a much better picture of how the bizarre ability might work. Barron theorised that not all of the patrol would be able to fade, suggesting the ability to be similar to the genetic changes that allowed some of the Frontier settlers to have phenomenal accuracy or speed, and he also theorised that perhaps it was akin to the flotter's abilities. Shanna countered with the idea that perhaps the ability grew out of a person's innate empathy with their starcats, and that perhaps some would be better than others, but that most Scouts might be able to learn the technique. She also raised the theory that the flickering indicated a shift in vibration or phase. After some minutes of discussion, Barron waved his hands.

"Well, it remains to be seen whether either of us are correct, let's work on the technique now." Shanna nodded, demonstrating.

"So, you need to feel the fade…" Some time later, they had come to the conclusion that perhaps they were both right. Barron had been able to fade himself, but not hold the fade very long without flickering unless he was physically contacting Hunter, who had also faded.

"Well, enough of me, you need to work through the patrol now and then we'll figure out who can do this effectively, and who needs some kind of extra assistance or work," said Barron, "And I've ignored our guests long enough – they deserve more of my attention if we're going to keep them safe and get them to the plateau." Shanna nodded, and signalled Spiron to send the next Scout in.

By the late afternoon, Shanna had established that Perri, Amma, Allad, Spiron, Verren, Nelson and herself, were the only ones able to fade and remain so reliably. Barron, Ragar, Sandar, Kalli, and Challon were all able to fade but not hold the fade unless touching their faded starcat. She theorised that the cats somehow assisted the process through some kind of link with their partners. During the journey, she had had Anjo and Semba attempt to fade while touching Twister, but to no avail. Either way it proved neither theory correct, so she simply shrugged her shoulders and got on with practicing the technique, which was definitely harder if you were walking and navigating at the same time.

***

Anjo had spent the past few days in what seemed like a complete daze. The tall humans who had rescued Semba and himself seemed almost superhuman to him. He had slept the solid sleep of exhaustion each night, never ceasing to marvel that he was without the locator bracelets and that the other entities on this planet were actually human, although somewhat taller than he was accustomed to. He hadn't managed to get over the awe he felt each time he encountered the enormous black and grey starcats gliding past him, shining coats picked out with glowing colours that seemed to ripple and change intensity while he watched. He was slowly beginning to understand the hierarchy of the people around him as they worked their way towards their home area. These 'Scouts', as they called themselves, seemed almost uncanny in their ability to move so silently and confidently through the area they referred to as 'Below' – and he had come to realise that at least four of them were only trainees, apparently on a training trip when they had encountered the Garsal, although they still seemed remarkably able for youngsters and particularly when compared to himself and Semba.

He was bemused and still didn't know what to think about the society he was about to be thrust into, a society which had never heard of, or experienced, the marauding Garsal. It staggered him to know that these humans had spent the last three hundred years isolated, working on survival techniques, while imagining the rest of the human race to be living in a galactic utopia. He had been astounded at the resourcefulness of the group and their ability to problem solve while on the run from an inimical alien species, and had then been shocked almost senseless as he watched the youngest in the group demonstrate an apparently newfound ability to vanish before his eyes. Where and how she had managed to find this ability had completely perplexed him, although since his rescue from the Garsal, he had been aware that the huge cats around him could vanish on request. He had listened intently as Barron and Shanna had discussed the concept, discussing highly complex theories with ease, intermittently interrupting each other while talking casually about genetics, brain function and basic physics concepts.

Although these humans were technologically poor, they certainly didn't seem to be poor in terms of knowledge or intelligence, and the lack of high tech equipment puzzled him until he reflected on the skills required to simply survive on this planet, and reasoned that the settlers had jettisoned high tech fabrication in favour of being able to simply survive. And after surviving, to secure a small portion of the planet to feed and clothe themselves. Anjo wondered at the fortitude of those early involuntary settlers and the society that had subsequently rescued him from the Garsal. As he strode along, puffing, trying to move quietly enough that his noise would not attract the enormous predators that so frightened him, he marvelled again at the situation he found himself in. Next to him, Semba was sweating and staggering and appeared to be lost in a world of physical exhaustion. He touched her shoulder gently and she looked up briefly before returning her eyes to the vegetation in front, trying hard to place her feet carefully on the forest floor. She stumbled slightly and the injured Scout Barron, caught her elbow with his good hand without breaking a stride. He whistled softly and the leader Spiron, after motioning the patrol to move closer together, brought the group to a halt. Anjo took grateful breaths, and sipped greedily from the water container handed to him by young Shanna, aware that Semba was doing the same thing next to him.

"Are you all right to continue, Anjo?" Spiron's tone was slightly worried and he was squinting at the sun which was slowly lowering itself towards the horizon, judging by the slant of the rays through the canopy. Anjo took his time to respond before nodding. He knew the patrol had expected to rendezvous with additional people sometime today, and he realised that his and Semba's slow pace along with the pause required when the tornado serpent had appeared had combined to reduce their travel distance much more than the Scout Leader had hoped. "We're hoping to contact another patrol shortly, and it would be welcome news if the two of you can travel a little further before we stop for the night. There will be a secure campsite if we can travel for about another hour." Beside Anjo, Semba also nodded and straightened herself with some effort, but visibly began to steel herself for further travel.

They moved on as soon as the two offworlders had recovered adequately, and Anjo pushed himself to maintain the pace, which was obviously frustrating the Scouts with its slowness. Beside him, he could tell that Barron was practicing this new 'fading' skill, as the man's form flickered intermittently and occasionally vanished completely. Actually, Anjo corrected himself, he didn't really vanish, because if he looked carefully he could still see a slight shimmer in the air rather like a mirage on a hot day. Anjo began sweating again within a few moments, and found himself wishing that the campsite would come faster.

***

Shanna returned to the point position with Allad, greeting Storm who appeared by her side as Twister joined Satin in front. He poked her with one large paw as if to remind her that he had worked hard all afternoon without any affection available to him and she caressed his silky head as she followed Allad through the thickening vegetation. Behind her she was aware that the two offworlders were struggling to keep up, and noticed that Allad was choosing the easiest path through the undergrowth, managing to avoid most of the more dangerous vegetation. Several times, Storm, Twister and Satin saw off medium sized predators, and within three quarters of an hour they were greeted by a grey starcat bounding through the bush towards them. Satin hummed at the other cat, who hummed quietly back and then turned around, looking expectantly at them.

"That's Mist. Drop back and tell Spiron we've made contact with Patrol Four," instructed Allad, "And ask if he wants us to continue to make for the campsite, or whether we continue on when we contact the other patrol." Shanna nodded and turned back towards the patrol, flanked on either side by Storm and Twister.

Twenty minutes later, the patrol was settling into a sheltered camp area surrounded on three sides by rock walls, and covered by a large overhang. The other patrol set a guard, allowing Patrol Ten to finally relax properly for the first time in days. Spiron, Allad and Barron conferred with the Leader and Second of Patrol Four, while the others made camp underneath the overhang, starting a small, smokeless fire, and beginning the evening meal with game supplied by the other patrol. Shanna dumped her pack, set up her bedding and then spent some time with her cats, carefully checking Storm's leg, which had almost healed completely, and scratching under Twister's chin. Semba and Anjo were settled by members of the other patrol, after a brief explanation from Spiron.

Around the fire that evening, Spiron began to outline the plans for the next day. "The cadets, along with Anjo, Semba and Barron, will return to the plateau tomorrow. It's only a short march to the access point, and you should reach it by evening. After decontamination you will go straight to the Compound and the Masters, who will take Anjo and Semba to the Council. The rest of us will begin hunting the vehicle, and any more of these 'Garsal'." He paused and nodded to

Amma, who was signalling with one hand, while balancing a hot drink on her lap with the other, Spider lounging at her feet. She looked slightly hesitantly around at the group and then went on.

"Spiron, there's another storm coming." Some of the members of Patrol Four looked disbelievingly at her, but encouraged by Spiron's nod she continued. "I expect it'll be here by the day after tomorrow, and it should be much larger than the previous two. There'll be less rain but the winds are going to be a lot more violent and continue for just over a day."

Farron, the Leader of Patrol Four looked particularly sceptical, and seeing the scepticism, Allad raised a hand. "She's very accurate. I lost a lot of money betting against her during the last storm, and I'm sure that her lead in time will be as accurate as the description of the storm. We may need to reconsider our plans." Farron still looked sceptical, but her expression lightened as the rest of the patrol confirmed Allad's statement.

"Well, all I can say is that this year's intake of cadets is certainly packed full of surprises," Farron said straightening one long leg, and gently pushing her starcat over to make herself more comfortable. "Let me know when another one of them's about to demonstrate flying, or perhaps breathing underwater…" She finished with a wry grin at Spiron.

"Well, I'd suggest that we all make for the plateau together, if you're truly certain her weather prediction's so accurate. We'll be able to do nothing down here until the storm's gone, and judging from Anjo and Semba's information, the aliens will be considerably slowed as well." Farron's tone was definite if resigned, and she and Spiron began to revise their plans.

"Shanna, you can show Patrol Four how to fade for the next couple of hours, and then we'll stagger tonight's watches so that we'll be as fresh as possible for tomorrow."

Shanna nodded, feeling extremely fatigued, and began her explanations yet again, noticing that most of Patrol Ten stayed to practice their techniques. Her peripheral vision showed Anjo and Semba retiring to their bedding, and sinking into it with sighs of relief.

***

Anjo, lay back, his exhausted body feeling as though he was lying on the softest mattress. Beside him Semba groaned with relief as she lay back, wriggling to adjust her position slightly.

"Do you think we're safe with these people?" she queried, her tone tired and weary, yet not more than a whisper.

"I think we're much safer with them than with the Garsal," Anjo replied, "They've treated us with nothing but courtesy and politeness, and they rescued us when they could have just watched. The Garsal would have had no idea they were even here if they hadn't decided to pull us out."

"But they're 'different' to us, Anjo – and it's not just that they're taller – you know, this ability to disappear that they seem to be developing, knowing that a storm is coming, and the way they communicate with those cats..." Semba broke off shaking her head.

Anjo sighed, remembering that Semba had come from a world well known for its insularity.

"Just because they look a little different and have a few extra abilities doesn't make them any less human. They talk the same – albeit with a funny accent, eat the same and seem to have the same emotions. Remember that their ancestors managed to survive this planet after crash landing here three hundred years ago - and I doubt many of ours would have been able to do that. These people have created a whole new society here, while always believing that we would find them and lead them back into our civilisation. And now they find out that the very existence of human kind is under threat, and that threat is now directly affecting them, yet still they have the courtesy to be kind to us rather than ruthlessly pumping us for knowledge. I suspect that had the boot been on the other foot, our civilisation may not have been as kind."

Half way through Anjo's speech, Semba had looked up surprised, as Anjo's quiet voice had become almost impassioned, but at the end she simply nodded, slowly, and settled herself more comfortably.

"I'm sorry Anjo. It's just...things are so strange, and these people are so confident and decisive that I'm having trouble dealing with the contrasts. This planet has been just one long nightmare to me – and they seem to love it." Semba's voice trailed off as though she was completely perplexed at the incongruity of it all. "Before the Garsal brought me here, my life was predictable..."

"Remember Semba, they were born here. They have no other memories to compare this place to – no idea that there are places where the flora and fauna are not constantly trying to do them in, and where the only major hazards are the Garsal!" Anjo's laugh was short and ironic. "On the whole, I think I envy them their existence so far, however it remains to be seen how long they can hold out against the Garsal once they're located. I can't imagine that it will take long for the Garsal to overcome them and then we'll be back where we were. If of course, we survive."

He was silent for a few moments. "I plan to enjoy the freedom we have for however long we have it. I plan to offer all the information I have on the Garsal to these people in the hope that they'll be able to keep them at bay for longer than any of our home planets did. I hope you agree with me." There was no reply from beside him, just the deep breaths of sleep, and Anjo laid himself back onto his bedding, sinking quickly into sleep, despite his best efforts to remain alert.

***

By the time Shanna rolled herself into her bedding, she was completely exhausted, and so hungry she ate all the dried fruit and nuts she had left in her pack. She'd spent several hours demonstrating and instructing the Scouts in her fade technique, with varying degrees of success. Of Patrol Four, only one of the Scouts had managed to fade herself completely without the assistance of her starcat, while the others continued to flicker in and out of sight unless in contact with their cats. Farron was pleased with the progress however, and had complimented Shanna on her discovery, before asking her to demonstrate the technique just one more time.

As she relaxed, she felt Storm and Twister lean their heavy bodies across her, wriggling slightly to make themselves more comfortable. As young starcats, they had accomplished remarkable things over the past days, and she sleepily rubbed a hand over each silky head. She slept, lulled by the comforting rumble of the purrs through her body.

Chapter 29

THE Scouts emerged from the plateau access tunnel into an atmosphere already disturbed by rising winds and tattered clouds. The storm Amma had predicted was already beginning, and the first drops of rain were spattering the arena dust. They were met by two uniformed medics, and Masters Peron and Lonish.

"Anjo, Semba, welcome, please go with Ranna and Jame," Master Lomish said, indicating the two medics. "They will see to your comfort and allow you to rest for a time. We will talk with you when you are more recovered," He motioned for Barron to join them, and the Patrol Second followed with a nod, his arm cradled carefully in its sling, and Hunter trailing quietly behind. Shanna was struck by how tired he looked. Anjo and Semba smiled gratefully; they were clearly at the end of their endurance, and Semba had been close to tears for the final hour of the journey.

As Shanna filed into the upstairs conference room with the others the savoury smell of soup tickled her nose, and Storm hummed a plaintive query at her. Master Peron smiled as a number of the other cats also voiced their queries.

"Send your cats to the dining hall Scouts, the kitchen staff have meals prepared for them for today," he said, "They'll be as hungry as you are I'm sure!" There was a sudden blur of fur and rainbowed tidemarks, as 27 hungry starcats exited the room.

Down at the far end of the room, Nelson began passing out bowls of soup and chunks of crusty bread. Shanna cradled the warm bowl in her palms and located an empty chair at the far end of the table, hooking it out with one foot and sitting down before beginning to eat.

Master Lonish signalled for attention.

"All right Spiron, as soon as we've got everyone's initial reports we'll let you retire for a rest before the storm winds up too much more." Spiron got to his feet and began his lengthy description of their encounter with the Garsal and the subsequent actions. The two Masters listened mainly in silence, occasionally interrupting to clarify a point or ask a pertinent question. Both jerked their heads up with surprise when Spiron described Shanna's discovery of the ability to fade.

"Shanna, you actually faded like a starcat?" asked Master Peron, and then shook his head. "How did you do that?"

With an inward sigh, Shanna went through the whole thing yet again, and began to describe what had happened. She finished her description by demonstrating, and was slightly gratified to hear both Masters murmur in surprise.

"How many of the others can do this?" asked Master Lonish quietly, looking around the table. Seven Scouts and cadets including Shanna raised their hands, and Shanna hastened to explain that all the others were able to manage if a starcat was in physical contact with them, but that the offworlders had been unable to do so at all. Master Lonish shook his head, "You know, every time I think we've come to the end of discovering new things about our planet and our starcats, I'm surprised anew. I wonder exactly how much of this is due to the cats and how much is a normal adaptation to this planet, or perhaps as a result of contact with something from Below. Well, we can test the Below theory pretty easily anyway." He went on to question the individual Scouts from Patrol Ten and Four for more details for the next couple of hours, and then dismissed them for a short rest period. Outside, the winds were rising rapidly and Shanna was easily able to hear the impacts of flying debris beginning to strike the outside of the building.

She returned to her quarters to find Storm and Twister already curled up on her bed, and shoved them over so that she was able to stretch herself out. That raised a small chorus of sleepy starcat hums and Shanna giggled slightly at the two of them.

"It is my bed, you know!" She gave them both another push and they sleepily made room for her. Every time she returned to Scout Compound, the bed seemed smaller and smaller. The starcats were cubs no longer, their almost fully grown bodies taking up ever larger quantities of the bed, leaving Shanna to wonder if eventually she'd need a larger bed to cater for the three of them, or whether she should simply resign herself to sleeping on the floor. There were a few more sleepy grumbles from the two cats as she wriggled between the two warm bodies, attempting to gain as much personal space as possible without actually dumping either Storm or Twister on the floor, before sinking into a comfortably drowsy relaxed state.

Outside her room, the storm shutters rattled intermittently and the wind had begun to howl loudly, yet the familiar storm sounds for once lulled Shanna to sleep, secure in the knowledge that the Garsal would also be trapped inside a safe place for the duration.

***

Inside the Garsal exploratory vehicle, the commander finally gave in to the inevitable and contacted the mother ship with the information that he had lost his two slaves, and that there were definitely humans on this planet. As he communicated with his superior, he rolled the locator bracelets across his manipulator arms. They had finally located them on an outcropping of rock protruding from the side of a small cliff face. He had lost yet another trooper while retrieving them. He stoically relayed that he had yet to locate their settlement as he had been led far from the plateau by decoys, while the slaves made their escape. He noted that the plateau was the most likely location for a settlement, however. He had stood impassively as he listened to the news of his revocation of breeding privileges and his hope of offspring began to die. In the interim he was directed to rendezvous with three other vehicles before continuing on to the plateau to recommence his investigations.

***

In the Garsal ship the Hive Overlord sat in his command chair, pondering the implications of the message from the exploratory vehicle. As the commander of the Garsal incursion of this sector, he was technically an autocratic ruler with no need to report back to the central Garsal command. The implications of locating free humans on this planet could have major ramifications for his autocracy. There was a possibility that his Overlordship could be revoked if the central command so decided. He sat and pondered for some time, toying with the controls of the communicator.

***

Kaidan sat by the fire in Hillview, listening to the sounds of the winds howling around the front of his home. He wondered where his sister was – whether she was safe from the cyclone, or somewhere Below holed up with her training Patrol, and swiftly thought a prayer for her safety. He turned his attention to thoughts of his work on the archery range over the past few days. Along with the other students in the group, he had been excused his normal class work to allow him to master the new missiles. Absently patting Boots' silky head, he mused on the final session – each archer slamming practice shaft after practice shaft into the far targets, neatly grouping their shots. Then they'd each fired two of the real arrows.

The ensuing fiery detonations as the heads had thudded home had shocked the group to silence. Kaidan was unsure how he felt. Archery had mostly been a hunting skill to him. Mastering the physicality of the gymnastics had added spice to a new ability useful both to his family for their protection and succour, and to his society as a whole. It had also been fun. The explosive arrowheads had left Kaidan confused. The initial demonstration had encouraged all his teenage desire to put on a spectacular show, but actually firing something that destructive had awakened a sense of unease within him. Masters Cerron and Dinian had provided the arrowheads, the teaching and the demonstrations, but no explanations. They had also required a pledge of secrecy.

After musing for some time, Kaidan still had difficulty reconciling the destructive potential of the new arrows with the peaceful society that he had grown up in. He knew that there were criminals on Frontier, but the nature of a society that required constant cooperation simply to survive had indoctrinated its inhabitants with values that promoted a more selfless moral code than the one they had arrived on the planet with. Criminal behaviour was not unknown but was heavily punished when detected, and Kaidan was unable to think of many reasons to use such destructive potential – perhaps stopping a welden stampede or a staureg intruder – within the parameters of his society. He rubbed his forehead with one hand, frowned, and finally removed Master Cerren's letter to his parents from his pocket. It was sealed with the Master's personal wax imprint.

"Mum, Dad, Master Cerren wants me to stay in town for a couple of weeks for more training." He handed the letter to his parents.

***

The exploratory vehicle commander directed the driver towards the coordinates specified by his Overlord. His mind, behind the impassive Garsal features, worked through scenario after scenario where he might be able to redeem himself from the ultimate disgrace of no offspring. As the huge vehicle, now crewed by only the remnants of his original group of troopers, heaved and crawled through, around and over the obstacles in its path towards the rendezvous point, he reminded himself that the other vehicle commanders would have no inkling of his shame. Pride was essential, and he could bluff his way through until his return to the ship. Even then there might be some chance of redemption.

***

The Overlord decided. The communicator was replaced. He would conquer the upstart humans and then report his success. No intervention from central command would jeopardise his status, or his chance of future offspring.

***

A week later, Shanna was startled by the sudden loud hoots of the alarm claxon in the Scout Compound. It was the first time she'd ever heard the alarm sound anything but the drill hoots, and her head flicked sharply as she realised that this was not a drill. Responding as trained along with the other cadets, she headed at a run into the arena, Storm and Twister flowing along beside her.

She had spent the last week attempting to teach every Scout in the Compound how to fade. Fortunately she had had the assistance of Amma and Verren, though Spiron, Nelson and Allad had disappeared from the Compound. Neither Zandany nor Taya had been able to fade completely unless touching their cats. Shanna was certain that Patrol Ten had gone Below as soon as the storm had allowed, and she was secretly envious.

Shanna and Taya appeared to have reached an uneasy truce. The other cadet was certainly getting along better with her starcat, and Spinner was looking much happier and was responding better to Taya's teaching, but Shanna was aware that Taya's dislike of her was much deeper than just a simple case of envy. She had decided not to push the issue and simply treated Taya as she would any of the others, but without the easy give and take of humour and friendship. Both still avoided unnecessary time alone with the other, and kept any conversation to the essentials.

Forming up with the other cadets, Shanna turned her attention to Master Lonish.

"We've received a message from Patrols Ten and Four. The alien vehicle has been joined by another three, and they are heading directly for the plateau. The vehicles are travelling at a steady pace, and should now be within three or four days' travel of the base. Intelligence from the two offworlders has suggested that they have devices on board that can detect life forms. The same intelligence also suggests the possibility that our starcats mask us, making it hard for the devices to detect those with starcat companions. The Garsal know we are here, and we believe they will not cease looking for our settlements. We need to ensure that they never reach the plateau or any of our people. Messages have been sent to the other centres on the plateau. It is our task now to prevent them from accessing the plateau, and to then locate their ship and ensure that they are unable to communicate with their fellows in the nearer star systems." There was silence from the assembled Scouts, and Master Lonish regarded them steadily, eyes travelling across the Patrols. Quite a number of the Patrols were still out working on storm damage across the southern plateau, and only Patrols Three, Six and Eight were assembled in their entirety. The rest of the assembled Scouts consisted of the first to third year cadets and Scouts temporarily detached from their Patrols if they were lacking starcats, had breeding cats or were injured.

"Patrols Three, Six and Eight, you will equip yourselves immediately and assemble back here within one hour for a final briefing before you depart to rendezvous Below with Patrols Four and Ten." The named Patrols departed at a run. "Second Year cadets, you will depart in pairs to alert all our Patrols on damage control to return immediately. Report immediately to Master Peron for your assignments." The second years left quickly. "Third years, you will form a roving Patrol within half a day's travel from the access tunnel. Prepare yourselves now, and return here as soon as possible. You will be under my direct command." The third years nodded and bolted for the exit. "First years, you will be forming yet another Patrol under the command of Master Cerren and Master Peron. You will be escorting a company of archers from Scholar's precinct and deploying with them around the access tunnel. Move now and assemble in the dining hall in an hour." Shanna jogged out of the arena with the rest of the first years, mentally reviewing her list of gear while pondering the inclusion of Master Cerren in the command structure. It seemed a little unusual, although from

Kaidan's information Master Cerren must have been a Scout at some point, and perhaps still was.

The six cadets were grouped in the dining hall within thirty minutes, starcats prowling restlessly, infected by the muted agitation in their partners.

"How serious is this, do you think?" asked Zandany of the others. "I mean, you four have actually seen these Garsal in action."

Verren pondered a moment before answering. "I think it's extremely serious. Anjo and Semba were terrified of them, and their description of their lives under the Garsal was horrendous." Amma, Shanna and Ragar nodded in agreement.

"They're not bushwise, yet their firepower is frightening and we're unlikely to be able to prevent them from moving exactly where they wish, so we're going to have to be smarter than them if we want to stop them," replied Ragar. "The Scout Masters and the Council must have been preparing for something like this since we first knew that others had arrived on this planet. I've heard just enough snippets and ends of conversations to think that there's more to their plans and organisation than we're privy to. We don't have the technology of the Garsal, but we do have skills and techniques they know nothing about."

Shanna nodded again in agreement but Zandany looked worried. "But if we're unable to stop them and they manage to get up here somehow, who will protect our people?" he asked. "What happens if they have more of those flying vehicles?"

"Look," Shanna said. "We're obviously the first line of defence for the plateau because we can survive Below, but that doesn't mean our people up here are completely defenceless. There's still the militia corps and the town guards. And don't forget, the Garsal have to get up here first. They won't be able to do that in their vehicles." There was a chorus of agreement from her companions. "I see our task primarily as preventing the Garsal from gaining any knowledge of how to access the plateau, and to prevent them from contacting any other Garsal nearby for assistance. Anjo and Semba have said that they have no more flying machines unless they manage to mine the proper minerals." The others nodded again.

"I'll bet that the next part of our task will be to stop that occurring," said Zandany, "We'll have to stop the vehicles first and then some of us will have to find that ship."

There was a small commotion from the dining hall entry and a group of thirty archers filed in, carefully propping unstrung bows by the far wall, and dumping their packs next to them. Shanna noticed that they were all outfitted in shades of dappled green, with camo cloaks neatly tucked in their pack straps. She was startled to see her brother at the end of the line, looking a bit short compared to most of the others, and swivelling his head around nervously, but then smiling at her across the room. Before she could move across the hall to greet him, Masters Peron and Cerren entered, both in Scout field uniforms and accompanied by their starcats.

"Form up!" Master Cerren's voice was a far cry from his quiet teaching tones, and the cadets had automatically jumped into formation almost quicker than thought, flicking surprised glances at each other. The archers hurried into a neat series of ranks behind them. Seven starcats sat neatly at the heels of their partners in the cadet ranks.

"Cadets, you will each take a group of five archers under your guard Below. On the way down the tunnel, you'll attempt to find out if any are able to fade when in contact with a starcat. Instruct them in basic commands as well. Archers, listen to them. These cadets are young. In fact, most of them are younger than you, yet their knowledge of Below exceeds yours enormously and they've already journeyed safely there. Your survival will depend on them and how closely you follow their directions. Cadets, fall in with the archer ranks and make yourselves known to your group." The cadets each fell in with a rank of archers; Shanna as shortest, took the final rank, and found herself next to Kaidan, grinning quickly at him, before introducing herself and her cats.

An older man barely taller than her brother, looked at her with raised eyebrows, somehow seeming to peer down his nose at her, yet saying nothing more than a short grunt and his name: Camid. A young woman who appeared to be in her mid twenties was named Gwen and offered a quick smile, and the other two in her group whom she had known slightly through sharing occasional classes with them, Horden and Tasha, proved to be students just prior to choosing their specialty. Before she could do more than introduce herself, Master Cerren had the group underway towards the access tunnel. Master Peron led the group into the opening, while Master Cerren stood aside to review the troop, eyes narrowed as he observed each one moving past. There was a murmur of consternation from the archers as they eyed the dark entryway, which Shanna was happy to see her fellow cadets immediately soothed. She encouraged her group into the tunnel and was slightly startled when Master Cerren fell into step with her group, which was bringing up the rear. Socks gave a pleased hum, and nudged Shanna's hand as she walked in step with the Master. Storm and Twister gave her an assessing look before directing their attention forward. Shanna smiled at Socks, offering the obligatory head stroke, and eliciting a pleased purr from the female starcat.

"It is a difficult task we have, Shanna, and any advantage you can offer us is important. I would like you to first teach me how you fade, and then you can work with your group and catch up with that scamp of a brother of yours," said Master Cerren.

Shanna smiled, although with slightly gritted teeth, and began her recitation once more.

Several hours later, she had a few answers to some of her theories about fading. Master Cerren had been able to fade completely without contact with Socks after only one or two repetitions of the technique, and so to her surprise had Kaidan. He had begun by maintaining contact with Storm, but had then been able to fade without any contact. She experimented by moving him around the group, and found that he did need to be within a certain radius of a starcat, but was still able to maintain the fade at approximately ten metres. She and Master Cerren didn't seem to need the presence of a cat as far as she could tell. Of the others, only Gwen and Camid were able to fade at all and only while in firm contact with either Storm or Twister. After questioning them, Shanna was able to determine that both had regular contact with family starcats, but neither had ever had a starcat partner.

Just over halfway down the tunnel, the troop paused for a meal of dried rations and a rest stop. As she settled herself to sleep, Shanna finally had a few moments to talk to her brother.

"Do Mum and Dad know you're here?" She queried, looking at Kaidan in the dim light. Kaidan rolled towards her, smoothing his hand down Twister's front paw.

"They know I'm staying in Watchtower at Master Cerren's request," he replied, not meeting her eyes. "They don't know anything about the Garsal, or what we're doing. Actually, I didn't until yesterday either. In fact, I'm not sure about anything we're doing. Are the Garsal really that bad?"

Shanna nodded slowly. "I saw the way they treated Anjo and Semba, and I've heard their stories from their own mouths. Our hopes of a rescue are gone. Now, we need to survive, and whatever you're going to do to help is essential." Kaidan shook his head.

"Shan, the stuff we've been doing… I'm not sure if I can do it for real. I mean, I can hit anything I aim at but I don't know if I *should* do this." His hand slid up and down Twister's paw and the big cat nudged him gently with his head, purple ear tips glowing softly. He looked very young.

"Kai, if you'd seen what I had, you wouldn't have any doubts." Shanna reached out and touched her brother's shoulder. "You'll be OK when the time comes. And I'm here with you. And so are the boys." Both starcats hummed and Kaidan lay back, hand still on Twister's paw. As Shanna rolled over onto her back, she saw the grey shape of Master Cerren just behind her brother. He nodded quietly to her.

***

At the bottom of the tunnel, the Scout cadets prepared their groups of archers as much as possible, checking and rechecking equipment, scent concealing paste, and camouflage paint. Master Cerren reassured them that all the archers were trained in the basics of silent movement and bushcraft. Shanna smiled wryly, remembering her brother's last efforts well over a month ago. So much had happened in such a short time. She recalled Ragar's comments, and wondered a little more whether the Council had much longer reaching contingency plans than anyone realised. Master Cerren's position as a teacher made more sense in that context.

At the exit point, Shanna could see Masters Cerren and Peron conferring with Damar and Feeny. There was a quick exchange of comment accompanied by hand gestures and map referencing, and then Master Cerren had the troop form up into a standard patrol formation. There were only nine starcats for such a large group, which was when Shanna realised exactly how stretched the Patrol's resources were, and how seriously they were taking the Garsal incursion. To be utilising first years to escort such a large group into a potentially fatal situation must have required a lot of thought and even harder decisions. Her group was positioned on point, and she moved them up quietly, emphasising the need to remain silent and watch for her hand signals.

Master Cerren waved his hand for silence.

"Before we exit, remember two things. Archers, your cadet is your lifeline, do not hesitate to obey any command given to you by one of them. Cadets, your job is to keep the archers safe and protect them by any means possible."

He paused. "Today we begin to counter the biggest threat our civilisation has ever known. Damar and Feeny have received word from the advance Patrols. The vehicles are within a day and a half's travel of the plateau base, and coming directly towards us. None of them have stopped moving since the Patrols located them, and there has been no opportunity to sabotage their advance but only to slow them slightly. Spiron estimates that there could be as many as one hundred and twenty of the aliens, along with a number of human slaves, in each of the vehicles. The advance patrols are attempting to rig pit traps in front of the vehicles' advance paths, and we'll be stationed not far from them. It is imperative that the Garsal do *not* access our tunnel or even suspect that it's there. Damar and Feeny will bar it behind us, and attempt to conceal themselves from the vehicle instrumentation. From Anjo and Semba's information we believe that the presence of so many starcats may conceal us from their scans, but we are not truly sure how many starcats might be needed to hide so many people." He nodded to Feeny, and the woman opened the tunnel entrance, stepping out accompanied by her starcat and then signalling to Shanna to emerge with her group.

Shanna sent Storm and Twister out in advance, both sweeping the surrounding vegetation for any danger while she assembled the archers behind her.

"String your bows, and then form up in pairs." Kaidan gave her a shaky grin as he locked his legs and strung his bow before quietly taking his place. Master Cerren moved forward towards her, indicating a map reference. Shanna nodded: the spot on the map was the pungo grove of their first overnight stop of that last training trip. She flicked a hand at Twister who blurred up the nearest tree and began to move through the canopy, leaping silently from tree to tree, and then signalled Storm to begin a sweeping advance. As the others assembled behind her, she signalled her archers to follow while maintaining their formation, and began to sweep the vegetation herself, checking for anything that might pose a danger to the unwary.

Kaidan watched wonderingly as his sister so competently directed their advance. He was envious of the way she seemed to flow from place to place, moving silently across what seemed to him to be a minefield of noisy debris. He was extremely nervous to be so exposed Below, and he had to work hard to maintain his composure as they began to penetrate the vegetation. All his life he had been indoctrinated with the dangers of Below, and now here he was, attempting to hunt down some kind of nasty alien species in the most dangerous place known in his previously secure world, with only his sister and her two starcats to protect him. A year ago he would have scoffed at the idea. Now he scanned the greenery around him constantly, sure that some kind of nasty predator would leap out and eat him any second, finding his hands becoming sweaty and slippery on the smooth wood of his bow. He wiped them surreptitiously on his pants, hoping that no one would notice.

He was beginning to realise just how much Shanna's move into the Scout Corps had changed her. His older sister had always been good at nearly everything, but surprisingly had never really seemed confident in her own abilities. Now, she seemed to have the quiet self assurance that had always been missing, coupled with a new set of skills. The worry he had seen her exhibit about her problems with Taya had appeared to vanish as she submerged herself into 'Shanna the Scout'. He wondered what she'd be like after the full three years of training, if six months had changed her this much.

There was a sudden noise ahead and Shanna held up her hand, signalling the group to stop and hide. Kaidan pressed himself behind a tree, carefully scanning for any dangerous plants, his encounter with the wait-a-while clear in his thoughts, as his sister vanished into the vegetation ahead. Twister appeared, taking her place at the front of the patrol, imbuing him with a sense of security as the big cat paced silently across the front of their advance.

Within a few moments, Shanna reappeared, flicked a quick hand signal to Master Cerren and the other cadets, who passed it to Master Peron taking the rear guard. She signalled for her archer group to move into a tighter formation and then whispered.

"There's a small group of cantars ahead. Storm's seeing them off, but we need to move quietly to avoid attracting their attention." Kaidan was not reassured. Although cantars were only small reptiles, they were quite vicious and equipped with very sharp fangs which were able to inflict acutely painful wounds due to the acidic venom that they secreted from glands at the base of each tooth. Shanna seemed quite unconcerned though so he decided to trust his sister, in this instance at least. He was so preoccupied with these thoughts that he almost fell into a hole in the ground, recovering his balance clumsily while hoping again that no one had noticed his moment of incoordination. He could feel the blush starting to rise up his neck.

Shanna smiled slightly as her brother almost fell flat on his face, narrowly avoiding a nasty stinging plant, and then returned her attention to the job at hand, navigating towards the pungo grove while making sure that none of her archers were in any kind of danger. It was akin to the trip with Anjo and Semba but at least these people were natives of Frontier, with a keen appreciation of the dangers surrounding them and they were certainly much hardier physically. All of them exhibited at least a semblance of the skills that the Scouts took for granted.

After a day's travel, the group arrived in the pungo grove, and began setting up to ambush the oncoming vehicles. Shanna was puzzled as to how the archers would actually be effective, as the Garsal vehicle she had seen seemed as though it would be impervious to any kind of arrow fire. After the main base was set up, she noticed each archer unpacking a number of heavy shafted arrows equipped with large bulbous heads. After arranging the arrows upright in divided quivers, she noticed that the archers were carefully making sure that none of the bulbous heads came into contact with anything.

"What on earth are those?" she asked her brother. Kaidan carefully placed his sixth and final arrow into the odd quiver and looked up at her.

"They're new – a kind of exploding arrow head. Just before we make contact with the vehicle, we'll pierce the top of each one with a tiny tool to admit a small amount of air. When the arrow strikes a hard surface, the head will explode. It's full of a gel that ignites when provided with an impact force, and just the right amount of air. We've been practicing with them out on the range. The weight of the arrow head makes it more difficult to aim as you have to compensate quite a bit. They're what's been bothering me. The destruction..." He broke off abruptly.

"So you expect to be able to breach the vehicles with them?"

"We hope to." Kaidan replied, "And then we're to begin picking off any of the creatures that emerge, with normal arrows." He placed two full quivers of normal arrows by the other one. Kaidan lowered his voice and moved slightly closer to his sister. "I'm worried that I'll freeze when I see them and not be able to shoot. Apart from the staureg and a few marmals, I've never shot anything but a target. I'm worried that it's not the right thing to do."

Shanna regarded her brother for a few moments. His normally cheerful face was set in unhappy lines and he looked as though he had the weight of the world on his shoulders.

"Kai, it's not going to be easy for any of us. We've not even tried to communicate with these creatures, and we have only the word of two of their prisoners to go on. I'm confused myself, and I've seen them. All I can say to you is that the only thing we've seen from them is violence and ill treatment of our kind. Perhaps out there somewhere," she gestured towards the sky. "There are Garsal who don't hate or enslave humans. However, I have no doubt that these are not them, and I'm not sure that we could negotiate at all with the ones we've seen. They've invaded our world, sowing damage and destruction in their wake. This is not the way to live that our families have taught us. We know we survive here only by working with our world and not against it. We give thanks before each meal because of that truth, and because we know that this is how it should be. We're not perfect. Our society has many problems, and we have criminals amongst us, but we still have our dignity, our sense of worth, and our acknowledgement of what is right and what is wrong. I would much prefer to negotiate with these Garsal, but I see no way of doing that at this time." She paused and gathered her thoughts together. It seemed as if all her concerns had suddenly coalesced finally into coherent thoughts, and she was eager to articulate them and allay her brother's fears. "We need to stand firm right now, and protect our survival on this planet – do you realise that we may be the only free humans left in the galaxy? We may actually be at this time, the only hope that humanity has of ever regaining its freedom. I know that this sounds melodramatic but it's true. We've been waiting for three hundred years to be rescued from this planet, but it appears that we may be the ones who might one day rescue the rest of our race – if we maintain our own security first. And this is only the first step. After this, we've still got to deal with the ship."

Shanna paused. Kaidan was looking at her with an expression she'd never seen before, and she was suddenly aware that around her, all movement and activity had ceased. Her fellow cadets were looking at her thoughtfully, and the two Masters had paused in their instructions to a group of archers to listen. She felt herself blush hotly red. She hadn't meant to be so opinionated and she had meant only to reassure her very young brother, who was suddenly thrust into an immensely frightening position of responsibility at the tender age of thirteen. Through the blush, Shanna realised that her own sixteenth birthday had passed the week before without her even noticing. The changes that the Scout Corps, and the events that the last months had wrought in her, suddenly became evident to her. The Shanna of a year ago would have waited eagerly to see what kind of gifts her friends and family would provide, and there would have been little else in her head – certainly not the fate of her world.

Around her, the bustle of purposeful preparations quietly re-commenced. Kaidan hefted his quivers, checked his bowstring and equipment and began to finalise his preparations. There was a quiet purpose about his actions that had been absent prior to their discussion.

Chapter 30

SHANNA'S group of archers were secreted in a rocky eyrie about two hundred metres from the pungo grove. There was a relatively clear patch of ground before a number of similar outcrops and the Scouts had decided to attempt to draw the alien vehicles towards that spot. She had sent Twister on a canopy crawl towards the point at which the vehicles were expected to appear. About half an hour previously, a member of Patrol Four had brought news that the vehicles were continuing to travel on the same trajectory, and would be expected within the next two hours or so. A messenger from the access tunnel had notified them that two further Patrols would be available to reinforce the other Patrols in the field sometime in the next twenty four hours, and that the other four local Patrols were returning to Scout Compound as fast as possible.

In front of the rocky elevation, Patrols Four and Ten had planted stakes and plybrush rope obstacles at staggered distances in an effort to slow the vehicles' advance enough. They were hopeful that the archers would then have enough time to hit them with the explosive arrowheads. There was a quiet hum from Storm as he returned to Shanna's side from a circular sweep. From his relaxed demeanour, Shanna was sure that for the moment at least, they were safe from any native dangers. She ran her hand down Storm's sleek coat, checked once more that the wound on his leg had healed properly and then squatted down in her hide, checking the positions and attitudes of her five archers.

"Camid, you've got the locations of the obstacles clear?" Shanna asked the archer. Camid was perched at the top of the rock pile, his uniform blending so well with his surrounds that Shanna was finding it difficult to pick him out. Just below him, Gwen and Tasha were set slightly to either side with Kaidan and Horden on the same level as Shanna, still well above ground level, but nicely concealed behind rocky outcrops and bushy vegetation.

"Yes, we've a wide range of fire from here, so if the obstacles slow the vehicles down adequately, then we should be able to pinpoint them well. Can you run over the description again for me? I want to make sure we try and target any possible vulnerabilities." Shanna had noticed that the others all deferred to the older teacher, and had worked on developing a relationship with him, deferring to him in the placement of the group while ensuring that he respected her knowledge of Below. So far, after a slightly shaky start, they were developing a healthy respect for each other, if not the easy relationship that Shanna had with Allad. Her time attempting to sort Taya out had provided a number of techniques she was able to use to soothe the older man's distrust of a sixteen year old. She began to describe the alien vehicle to him again.

There was a sudden rustle from the trees near the front of the outcrop and Storm's head jerked up and his nose twitched, before he relaxed and Twister dropped out of the tree next to Shanna. There was a handwritten note attached to his harness, which she gathered and flicked open. Allad's scribble greeted her.

Four vehicles. They are down nineteen after obstacle stops. Prepare immediately. Casualties being transported to pungo grove. Send Verren.

"Be ready, Camid." The man nodded and alerted his archers.

Shanna whistled three high notes to sound the alarm and then sent Twister off in a blur towards Master Cerren. Storm she sent off at a run towards the point where she expected the oncoming vehicles to appear. She and the other cadets were angled in a semicircular field to allow their groups of archers the best pattern of fire. Each archer had the explosive head arrows arrayed carefully in front of them. She chanced a quick glimpse at her brother, wondering suddenly if her parents knew anything at all of the task that their offspring were about to perform.

Shanna gave a quick prayer and then turned her mind to concentrating on the task ahead as the soft wind brought the sound of the vehicles faintly to her. There were only a couple of hours of light left in the day, and she began to hope fervently that there would be enough light for the archers to be effective.

Storm reappeared, his form blurring with the speed of his passage as he bounded up the outcrop. Close behind him was Twister, returning with yet another note tucked in his harness.

Peron will replace Verren. Hold Storm in reserve for emergencies. Signal the sweep now.

Swallowing convulsively, Shanna signalled to Camid and he sent a whistling arrow into the air. Simultaneously, she sent Twister out on a sweeping run to direct the incoming Scouts safely between the set traps and to keep them out of any possible fields of fire. From her point to Amma's position directly opposite, she saw the sudden movements in the vegetation that indicated a starcat on the run towards where the six incoming patrols were expected. Each cat had a corridor assigned to them, and the cadets used the silent whistles to direct them down the safe areas. There was a commotion in the bushes where Twister had vanished,and Shanna saw the first of the Scouts appear, moving at a stumbling run, a far cry from the normally fluid movement of a Scout. She recognised Perri, one leg obviously injured, anxiously paced by Spangles, with Twister weaving in front of the pair attempting to keep them from straying into the set traps. More appeared, all seemed exhausted and a number were carrying minor injuries. On the breeze, the sound of the approaching Garsal vehicles now seemed a little louder.

Again she checked her archers, flicked her eyes across their fields of fire, and felt her heart thud with distress as she saw the number of already injured Scouts from the Patrols drawing the vehicles in. Her anxiety increased, but she kept her face as impassive as she was able, hiding her inner turmoil from the archers.

The ever increasing roar of sound that preceded the Garsal vehicles now seemed all encompassing, and there were Scouts flowing through all the safe zones towards the semicircle of hidden archers. Shanna anxiously watched the stumbling progression of Perri and Spangles. Spangles was attempting to prop Perri up to allow her to move faster, as she was gradually being overtaken by the other Scouts. Shanna whistled to Twister and he added his body to Perri's other side, allowing the pair to move more quickly. By her side, Storm quivered, but she held him next to her with a glance before returning her attention to the withdrawal. She began to see flashes of late afternoon sunlight glancing through the trees onto metal fittings as the monstrous vehicles announced their presences with crunching and crashing of vegetation.

Nearly all the Scouts were now behind the line of fire and Shanna gave one quick glance towards Perri, now vanishing into the trees with Spangles and Twister supporting her. With a bound, Satin appeared beside her and Shanna could hear the slow noise of an exhausted body climbing the rocks behind her. Storm relaxed and Shanna knew that Allad would not be far behind. She turned her attention back to sighting the vehicles as they appeared.

"They're coming fast! Are your archers ready?" Allad's voice was a hoarse pant in her ear.

"We're all ready, Allad. Sit and regain your breath." Shanna hadn't taken her eyes off the metallic flashes in the vegetation. There was a blur of starcat activity, and Twister was again beside her, rubbing Satin's nose with his own in greeting. The first thud of a falling tree penetrated the vehicle noise and a flash of red light was visible through the trees.

"They're felling the trees with their weapons as they come – that's why they've travelled so fast. They've learnt a few things since we last saw them." Allad's voice was less hoarse, but he was still taking the deep breaths of someone who had been in oxygen debt for some time. "We tried so hard to delay them, but they just kept coming. All we've been able to do is to draw them in the specific direction we wanted."

The first vehicle poked its nose out of the vegetation into the relatively clear ground of the ambush site, and lurched forward.

"You've done all you could, Allad. There was nothing else you could do unless they stopped, and at least they're where we want them to be." Shanna found it extremely odd to be reassuring the older man, but since her speech to her brother in the pungo grove, her thoughts had come together with surprising clarity. A second vehicle appeared, followed quickly by a third and then a fourth. As they exited the thicker vegetation they spread out, and then arrowed towards the final Scout fleeing into the bush ahead of them. Their path would funnel them through the middle of the semicircle of archers. Camid whistled quietly, and the archers checked their bows once more, then each deliberately punched a small hole in the head of the explosive tipped arrows. The lead vehicle suddenly slowed and its wheels began to grind heavily, and Shanna was able to see that several plybrush ropes were taut across its front end. The second vehicle immediately moved from directly behind to one side only to be mired in a nest of stakes, while the remaining two behind slowed and began to spread out.

On a second whistle, the archers raised their bows and took aim, arms drawing back, strings set to lips, and eyes intent on the vehicles below. There was a pause which seemed to stretch for an eternity, before a short, sharp whistle punctured the air, and five heavy headed arrows flew towards the tail end vehicle which was attempting to slowly manoeuvre around the others in front of it. There was a sudden snapping of bowstrings across the semicircle and other arrows arced in towards the vehicles. Shanna held her breath as the arrows struck, each igniting with a 'whoomphing' sound, sudden smoke obscuring the sight of the vehicles from view. As the smoke cleared, Shanna could see that although the vehicles were continuing to move, they all sported a number of dented panels. None of the arrows that she could see, however, seemed to have actually penetrated.

There was another whistle from Camid and the archers went through their drill again, arrows flying in with uncanny accuracy, yet still the vehicles continued to roll ominously forward. Camid signalled again and another flight arched out, denting and scoring the vehicles' sides yet not causing any serious damage. More problematic were the red lights beginning to lance out from the moving vehicles, their killing beams kicking up dirt and rocks around the archers' positions. Allad held up one hand.

"What's the lead archer's name?"

"Camid," Shanna replied.

"Camid!" Allad called in a low voice, "Have them all strike in one spot. Aim for the front of the vehicle!" The older archer's eyebrows raised and then he nodded once in comprehension as burning beam of light struck just in front of him. He raised his voice.

"On my command. Front of vehicle four and central, strike fifty centimetres below the top!" He whistled and the archers raised their bows. A barrage of beams struck the rocks around their positions, fragments of rock whining sharply through the air. There was a short cry from Gwen, but when Shanna's eyes found the woman she was still determinedly upright, her bow steady, as blood trickled slowly from her left side.

The short sharp whistle sounded again and the heavy arrows flew towards the tail end vehicle, all appearing to contact on the same point at the same time. There was a sudden barrage of sound and smoke again obscured the view, while the lancing red beams continued to cut through the smoke to find the outcrop edges. When Shanna next dared to raise her head, she could see that the end vehicle was stalled, smoke spiralling out of it and black insectoid forms swarming out of it.

Shanna slipped a note into Twister's collar, detailing the means of success and sent him off at a blurring run towards Master Cerren in the centre position, while trying to check on the safety of the archers around her. Gwen appeared to be slumped in a sitting position, while Camid was calling commands to the others.

"Normal arrows, pick them off now." Shanna began to worm her way upwards towards Gwen, fearful that the woman was seriously injured. Around her, beams of red kicked splinters off the rocks, and Storm growled deep in his throat.

"Fade, Shanna, fade!" Allad's urgent tones penetrated Shanna's ears, and she concentrated as hard as she could, feeling the now familiar sensation overtake her. She resumed her crawl towards Gwen, noting that the barrage of beams had suddenly stopped near her but continued to force the others down behind their cover. Reaching Gwen, she saw that the ominous trickle of blood from the woman's side had become a steady flow. Gwen's hand was clamped tightly over her side, yet the blood still flowed from between her fingers. Shanna fumbled her field kit out of a thigh pocket and slapped some of the soothall salve onto the woman's wound before placing a pad of bandage over the wound and bandaging it tightly to her side. Around them, the red beams of light played an ominous dance.

"Hold Storm, Gwen, and fade." The other woman lifted one blood stained shaking hand and placed it on Storm's paw, fading unsteadily from view along with the starcat. The lancing beams of light moved away and Shanna heard Camid urging the remaining archers to aim for the turret shooting back at them. There was a sudden 'whoomph' and the beams ceased altogether. The silence was now punctuated only by the sound of twanging bowstrings and soft moans from Gwen.

"Relax Gwen, we'll get you some help shortly," said Shanna, and signalled the now returned Twister to assist her and Storm to move the injured woman. Below her, black figures were falling, however, red beams were lancing towards several of the other archers' positions. There were cries from below mixing with intermittent shouts of pain and the snarl of angry starcats rising above the vehicle noise. As Shanna and the cats moved the injured woman into a more sheltered situation, she was able to see that two out of the four vehicles had been breached and that the other two were mired in a morass of plybrush ropes, their engines straining as the vehicles surged forward trying to break the restraining fibres.

There was another call from above her as Camid marshalled his four remaining archers for another shot with the explosive arrow heads. Another twang signalled the release of the bow strings, and there was another flash and 'whoomph' from the vehicles below although this time the angle made the arrows glance off, expending their energy harmlessly into the vegetation. Shanna carefully propped Gwen against a rock and checked the dressing which seemed to be holding firmly. She noted that the bleeding had slowed to a slow drip. Gwen was pale but conscious, and Shanna returned to the woman's previous position, collecting her bow and remaining arrows, placing them next to the injured woman.

"Give the arrows to Kaidan, he has the correct draw length." Gwen whispered, and Shanna crawled to her brother's position, placing two of the quivers in front of him. He looked down and nodded his thanks while simultaneously selecting another arrow and nocking it. She crawled back to Gwen, checked the wound again and resumed her position next to Allad, who had been watching the chaos below them. Socks reappeared, with a note tucked into her harness.

Prepare to sortie with your cats when you hear the second signal. Notify me of any wounded. Instruct your archers to lay down covering fire on the first signal.

Shanna scribbled Gwen's name, location and injuries on the back of the note, and then called the instructions to her group, loosening her knife in its sheath and nodding at Allad. Beside her, Storm crouched. The archers continued to loose shafts intermittently at the Garsal milling below but at the first signal arrow whistling high above, Camid signed for the archers to send their final explosive arrows towards the nearest heaving vehicle. They then began firing rapidly into the ensuing confusion as more Garsal boiled out of their burning vehicle. Shanna poised herself as Twister hurtled back to rejoin her, crouching next to his brother. She was trembling with a combination of fear and adrenalin, mixed emotions roiling around her head, yet anxious to get the moment of inactivity over. She could see Kaidan out of the corner of her eye, nocking arrow after arrow smoothly, his lanky form oddly graceful against the rocks behind him.

There was a sudden scream from the second signal arrow and Shanna leapt towards the milling Garsal, Storm and Twister on either side. The insectoid creatures had begun to organise themselves behind their disabled vehicles, while the last undamaged vehicle continued to fire its thick red beams into the rocks.

"Fade, Allad!!" Shanna shouted at the top of her lungs, doing so herself and flicking a signal to Storm and Twister to follow suit, then began to circle rapidly to the right. She could 'feel' Allad and Satin next to her, and the five of them moved quickly through the low vegetation towards the Garsal vehicles. To their left, a barrage from the Garsal weapons mowed down several Scouts and their starcats leapt, snarling with rage directly over the closest vehicle. Shanna could hear the rising screams of enraged starcats and could see a number of cats' tidemarks burning brightly with rage. Cooler headed Scouts followed her lead, and with a hand on their starcat partners faded from view. Allad began to signal whistle beside her, and there was a sudden lull except for the hiss and thud of arrows and the whining high pitched sounds of the Garsal weapons.

Following Allad's instructions, the faded Scouts moved into positions encircling the Garsal vehicles, crawling closer and closer, trying to remain below the archers' field of fire. Shanna was close enough to see the aliens crouched behind the huge bulks of their vehicles, taking turns at firing at the archers in alternating ranks. Another whistle from Allad signalled the Scouts to move closer, and then ready themselves and their cats for a sudden surge forwards. Shanna gripped her knife more tightly and prepared herself for action. There were fewer arrows hissing into the Garsal ranks, but there were many alien bodies littering the ground around the vehicles.

At Allad's whistle there was a sudden surge forward, and a number of Scouts flickered back into view as they lost contact with their cats. The howl of tens of enraged starcats escalated as physical contact was made with the Garsal. The rain of arrows abruptly ceased as the Scouts began to engage in hand to hand combat, struggling with the tall aliens. Insectoid eyes glittered and oddly jointed appendages grappled with softer human limbs, while howling starcats bowled full tilt into tall carapaced forms. There was a confused melee and Shanna found herself circling a blackly shining, fast moving figure attempting to bring a weapon to bear on someone behind her. She dodged quickly, rolling under a flailing appendage, as two starcats slammed heavily into the Garsal, extended claws ripping at the creature's soft jointed portions. Shanna rolled to her feet and followed the snarling, rolling heap of alien and starcats, preparing herself to strike at the creature with her knife. Before she could act, the two cats returned to her side, leaving the lifeless body of the Garsal trooper crumpled on the ground.

Shanna took quick stock of the situation around her and then moved to assist a Scout and starcat nearby, directing Twister and Storm to attack from either side. Around them the fighting intensified and Shanna and her cats dodged around the struggling pairs, their faded forms allowing them to attack with no warning at all, while Shanna made good use of the defensive takedowns Master Peron had imparted in her first few months of training. Gradually the intensity of the fighting began to diminish, and finally a small knot of struggling Garsal backed themselves towards the final remaining unbreached vehicle, which continued to pulse deadly beams into the fray, apparently uncaring of whether Garsal or human was injured. Shanna was fearful of the consequences should they not withdraw, when suddenly Storm and Twister began to herd her backwards towards the rocky area. While she frantically attempted to maintain her balance and equilibrium, along with her faded state, she could see starcats on all sides doing exactly the same thing with their partners, and faintly she heard a slithering sound and could see a dim glow approaching through the gathering gloom. The turret on the remaining vehicle continued to pulse as the final few Garsal ran through a suddenly open hatch into its interior.

The slithering sound became louder, and the top gunner in the vehicle swung the turret from side to side, his insectoid head scanning the panels in front of him. As the pulsing beams suddenly ceased, the starcats released their Scouts and stood awaiting the glowing creature that appeared from the thick vegetation. Shanna stood transfixed as the starlyne emerged from the green foliage and turned its head towards the Garsal vehicle.

A flurry of red beams lanced from the monstrous black vehicle towards the glowing creature, and then to Shanna's stunned surprise, simply vanished. The vehicle's engine died and the heavy Garsal contraption ceased attempting to move from the plybrush net. The artificial lights stayed on, illuminating the starlyne's immense body which seemed to glow even more brightly in the sudden silence. Shanna's heart continued to thud loudly, and her chest heaved as her body attempted to recover from the melee while sweat trickled down her back and stung her eyes. There was a long moment of silence, a silent 'thud' reverberated across the small clearing, and the air in front of the starlyne appeared to ripple. The lights on the vehicle died suddenly, and the group was illuminated only by the glow from the starlyne and the slowly rippling tidemarks of each starcat, as the sun finally sank below the horizon.

Shanna's eyes seemed riveted on the glowing body of the starlyne, wondering, as the creature turned its head slowly towards the group of Scouts and starcats. Storm and Twister hummed as the starlyne turned, and Shanna could hear the other cats humming as well, their deep tones vibrating through the air. There was another moment of silence and then an intense feeling of relaxation washed over Shanna's trembling, sweating limbs, and she knew she was now completely and utterly safe. The glow from the starlyne intensified slightly, and Shanna felt, rather than heard the words.

"Tend your injured, we will speak tomorrow." Then the glowing creature turned and vanished into the vegetation, and dusk descended upon the small clearing. There was silence and utter disbelief that the creature she had always thought of as an animal, special though it may have been, had spoken.

Around them, the injured and dead lay crumpled on the ground, starcat bodies intermingled with those of Garsal and human. Shanna paused, panting, and allowed herself to release the fade, blurring into visibility close to the vehicle that the remaining Garsal had retreated into. Storm and Twister reappeared beside her, both with hackles raised, and tidemarks burning brightly. There was a large burn mark scored down Twister's right flank and a slightly bleeding slash on Storm's nose. Shanna became aware of stinging sweat in a myriad of small cuts down one leg, and that there was a swelling lump on her right cheekbone throbbing in time with her heart beat.

The Garsal inside the vehicle were visible through the transparent ports in its side, urgently conferring. Master Cerren's voice rang out.

"We know you can understand us. You are defeated here today. We offer you a chance to come out and surrender." There was a flurry of activity and sound from inside the vehicle, and then there was a slow exodus of alien creatures from the dead mechanical contraption. Finally a group of fourteen stood in front of it, each creature dropping its weapons to the ground, and then standing with head bowed.

A grunting roar erupted from the forest behind them, and Shanna sent Twister arrowing towards her archer group with a flick of one hand, concerned for their safety. Half a dozen Scouts sent their cats in the direction of the roar, and then most of the others with uninjured starcats sent them circling the vehicle site in an undulating pattern. Shanna directed Storm to keep watch on the Garsal. He stalked menacingly towards the group of aliens, fur standing up on his neck and tail puffed out. He was joined by both Satin and Fury. Shanna picked out Allad and Spiron standing nearby, eyes watchful on the fourteen aliens. Both men showed the marks of battle on their faces and bodies, dirt and grime and sweat staining their field uniforms, mixed with patches of blood and stains that must have been the milky garsal equivalent. There was a deep tiredness exuding from both men that Shanna had never seen before, and she realised that she felt exactly as both of them looked.

Chapter 31

THE next morning dawned early, while Shanna was helping to look after a group of injured Scouts and archers. Her various cuts and bruises were stinging and aching, and she was as exhausted as she had been after the wild chase through Below with the original vehicle. In addition to the physical aches and pains, Shanna was wracked by the guilt of having killed another living being and stunned by the appearance of the starlyne. All her logical thoughts and reasoned arguments didn't assuage the guilty feelings for killing a thinking being unhesitatingly. Her statements before the battle now seemed hollow in the reality of what she'd done. She wondered if the lack of feelings at the time had been an indication that she was an awful, terrible, inhuman person. She had spent the remnants of the previous night having flashbacks and nightmares. By her side, the remnant of her group of archers was spaced around the wounded, Camid sitting grimly at one end of Gwen's stretcher while Horden sat poised to lift the other. Tasha and Kaidan stood beside Shanna, Storm and Twister alternating in circling the group, as the battered members of Patrol Ten and the Cadet Patrol worked together seamlessly, carefully guarding the wounded from any of Frontier's hazards. Several times during the night they had needed to see off various roaming predators. Fortunately the encounters had been low key; the commotion of the previous day's battle seemed to have warned off many of the normal denizens of the forest. The Scouts continued to move with their customary stealth however, the uninjured archers attempting to match them.

Shanna and Kaidan had spent some time talking together in the aftermath of the battle, while assisting with the treatment of the wounded starcats and the burying of the dead Garsal. The bodies of dead Scouts, archers and starcats had been gently laid out on the edge of the pungo grove. Shanna and Kaidan had treated nearly all of the surviving starcats, most of them sporting cuts or burns from the alien weapons. Sadly, a number of Scouts were now lacking their feline companions, and some cats were without human partners. There was a pall of sadness hanging over the pungo grove, almost visible in its thickness. There was something totally heartbreaking about a Scout sitting in the midst of the carnage, slowly stroking the silky fur of a companion who would never pace by their side again, whose tidemarks would never flicker and glow, or a living starcat curled by the unmoving form of their Scout partner, those same tidemarks dimmed to the dullness of grief. The now bereft halves of loving partnerships were left to grieve in quiet peace.

Shanna and Kaidan had laboured far into the night, soothing burns on injured paws and sides and carefully stitching larger slashes, while disinfecting smaller ones and smoothing on numbing salves. Both Storm and Twister had required treatment, sitting stoically as Shanna stitched and soothed their injuries. Both siblings thanked the training that they had absorbed from their parents.

The following morning, the cadets had been assigned to guard duty working with Patrol Ten again. The archery crew Kaidan was attached to was due to move out within the hour, to be escorted back to the access tunnel. Shanna had been assigned to remain Below, temporarily attached to Patrol Ten along with Verren and Amma, while Taya, Ragar and Zandany were to be assigned to Patrol Four. Nearly every Patrol had suffered injuries. Difficult times had made the previously unthinkable a necessity. Perri and Nelson were lying on stretchers nearby, while their cats sat or lay next to them. Both had suffered potentially disabling injuries; Perri's right knee was a massive swollen balloon, while Nelson had serious burns all down one side of his body.

Shanna kept trying not to look back to where Arad stood with his head down, his shoulders slumped and Kalli's arm around him, bereft without the companionship of his starcat. Every time she glimpsed him a shock of emotion coursed through her, and she was hard put to stop the tears that threatened to well up inside her, while she choked the ache in her throat back down. As she imagined how it would be to lose either Storm or Twister the unbearable feelings would well up inside her again.

In small groups within the clearing, the surviving members of each patrol laboured to assist their wounded and the archer groups. Several of the archer groups had already been escorted back, two fresh Patrols had arrived early in the morning and were now taking the brunt of the watch and escort duty. Masters Cerren and Peron had spent time in conference with the Patrol Firsts immediately after the astounding visit by the starlyne the night before. Shanna didn't know what to think, her head was so full of conflicting emotions that she eventually just concentrated on each task at hand, each injured starcat brought to her, before falling into her bedding near the rest of the cadets late that night.

Just before Kaidan's group was to leave for the plateau, the starcats all sat suddenly alert. There was a brief shaking in the lush greenness, and the starlyne emerged from the bush near the stilled Garsal vehicles. As soon as it appeared, all the starcats were immediately on their feet and flowing towards the great creature, rubbing their silky bodies along its great length and humming melodiously as they wove their way around it.

The starlyne seemed to be enjoying receiving the attentions of the starcats, returning their obvious affection with a rumbling hum of its own and rippling the tidemarks along its sinuous body. It wove its way past the silent black vehicles, and approached the waiting Scouts and the few remaining archers who scrambled somewhat nervously to their feet, the two Masters standing forth in greeting. Shanna felt her heart thud as the starlyne glided to a halt almost directly in front of her, its huge eyes glinting down at the gathered Scouts, several of whom took involuntary backward steps.

"Listen, watch and learn," intoned the creature.

The starcats returned to their partners, each huge cat sliding gently against their human partner's legs. Shanna felt Storm and Twister's humming as their warm bodies rested gently against her. She took a deep breath and raised her gaze towards the huge creature's face. The eyes gathered all her attention, dark pools with starry depths drawing her inwards, and Shanna was swept away on a tide rush of information, her mind swirling with starry vistas and multiple images – the sudden boom as the stricken alien craft appeared in her skies trailing smoke and debris, before crashing into the northern reaches of the Great Plateau. Her senses reeled as she felt the dying of huge minds along with the deaths of many smaller ones in the alien craft. Vast amounts of pain and great sorrow washed through her, as she watched not only her fellow starlynes perish, but realised that the smaller dying minds she could feel were the human passengers on the great colony ship. Shanna struggled to regain her orientation as she realised that she was viewing the memories of the great creature that had saved them the previous evening, and her awareness grew that the starlyne was many hundreds of years old.

Carried along by the rush of emotion as the starlyne continued to flood her mind with images and feelings, Shanna suffered through the sadness of the passing of four of the oldest of the starlyne community in residence upon the Great Plateau. She felt their great minds reach out and caress the others of their race as they died, and then slowly fade away towards the glory of eternity. She watched as the humans from the colony ship, afraid and lacking any knowledge of the great creatures, inadvertently murdered the young starlynes they encountered on their first forays away from the ship. Afraid, alone, and terrified by the inimical environment, the humans broadcast fear on a wide band that greatly distressed the remaining starlyne population. Shanna watched as the starlynes, grieving for their lost, withdrew from the area where the crashed colony ship lay amongst its devastation. For some years they observed from afar the struggles of the colonists to survive, watching as many perished, while others triumphed over adversity, watching and waiting to see whether the strange new species was worth any contact. Shanna grew to understand that the starlyne community was old beyond human understanding and deeply, compassionately empathic. She gasped in awe as the remembered history of the starlyne race unfolded for her to view. Their home planet had been green and lush, with multiple moons and high technology, and the starlyne race had been spacefarers. She saw the results of their first encounters with an inimical alien species, their subsequent confusion and predation by the alien species followed by the escape from their planet located on the Outer Arm of the galaxy, and their arrival on the planet she knew as Frontier some thousands of years before humankind. She saw the decision to choose to hide themselves from their foes by reducing their reliance on the higher technologies, choosing only to retain what was necessary for survival and to gently mould this new world . She watched as the starlyne elders conferred and decided to completely withdraw from any contact with the strange new creatures, fearful that predation of their gentle society might begin again – this time by a new race. Their gentle philosophy precluded eliminating them. For some years, no contact was had with the human colonists, until the inadvertent encounter of a youngling starlyne with a human child and its companion animal who had both strayed from the safety of the colony ship compound into the danger of the surrounding bush.

Incredulous, Shanna felt the astonishment as the young starlyne, child, and tiny black - Was it a starcat? she thought - played together in a dappled glade. No, not a starcat – in her mind she felt the amusement of the starlyne – just a 'cat', one of the domesticated animals brought by the colonists. She felt the startlement of the starlynes as they felt the beginnings of empathy between the small creature and its companion and the response of the starlyne youngling to the pair, a promise of joyful communion.

She watched as the starlyne elders sat again in council and decided to nurture the new creatures by subtle use of their biotechnologies, enhancing already present traits evident in both species. She saw the first starcats born, their tidemarks rippling on their small bodies, and she watched them grow in stature with each litter produced by the felines brought by the colonists, until she saw their starcat friends as they now were, reflected in the memories hurtling through her mind. Although still fearful of the destructive tendencies always present in the human mind, the starlyne race saw now the possibilities of eventual alliance. They recognised that in the tenaciousness of the human settlers and their ability to adapt quickly to a new environment was the hopeful promise that might one day protect both of them from the possibility of enslavement by the predators sure to have overrun their arm of the galaxy in the ensuing years. Shanna was stunned as she saw through starlyne eyes the shape of those predators form before her. They were Garsal.

Her senses were still reeling as the final images penetrated her mind. She saw herself, Storm and Twister standing before a vast number of humans, starcats and starlynes, and then all three faded, vanishing from view, except for an occasional ripple. There was a sense of great satisfaction as the last images left her mind, and she saw with her physical eyes again at last.

She blinked, trying to piece together what it all might mean. She felt dazed, as though she had stumbled from a dark cave out into the blinding midday sun and then back into the cave, the afterimages burnt into her retinas. Around Shanna the other Scouts were blinking their eyes and shaking their heads, all looking precisely how Shanna felt. She reached her hands out to steady herself against the warm bodies of Storm and Twister, seeking reassurance from their warm touch and soft fur. They both hummed reassuringly, ear tips glowing and twinkling brightly, and looked up towards the waiting starlyne again. Shanna realised that hours must have passed during the creature's revelations and that she was seated on the ground, and that the sun had plunged towards the horizon. Her stomach rumbled disconcertingly.

Next to Shanna Spiron struggled stiffly to his feet and took a step forward, hands out stretched, and lifted an eyebrow in query.

"But what does this really mean?" He cleared his throat and blinked as the great creature lowered its head towards him, tidemarks rippling softly along its coat.

The sensation of speech was clear, gently flowing from the starlyne with sorrow uppermost amongst a plethora of emotion. It unfolded small, many fingered hands from beneath its neck, spreading them expressively.

"It means that our nemesis has found us in our sanctuary but that there is hope, if our communities can join and work together as one. We lack the numbers and aggressive qualities that you have. Until now, your people have lacked knowledge of these invaders, and the skills and talents to defeat and put an end to the Garsal. In other words, we have always been strong, but few. In the old home the sheer numbers of Garsal always prevailed, taking all that they wished. When we resisted, they sent more and more until we were overcome, one by one. Your fellow humans are many but individually they are weak, lacking the ability to stand together against the Garsal." The starlyne ducked its head, and its colours rippled back and forth, as if for the first time, it was uncertain.

"You are different. This place has changed you. You know that – your own records show that you are no longer completely as you once were. We, the starlyne race, have subtly assisted that change."

The creature seemed almost embarrassed and hesitated briefly before continuing as heads all around it jerked up, "It would have happened in any case, as your own leaders knew from the beginning, when the first tests confirmed the presence of symbiotic viruses in the crash survivors. But we have accelerated the process so that now you stand ready at the time of greatest threat." There were murmurs from the gathered Scouts, confused sounds, and a number of uneasy rumblings.

"You mean that you have toyed with us for your own purpose?" Cerren's eyes narrowed, and his brows drew down. "You've changed the way we are to suit yourselves? You've hidden yourselves from us, when you could have helped – how many of us have died needlessly over the years as we struggled to survive on this planet? And you didn't tell us about these Garsal or even yourselves until they actually arrived? How will we ever be able to rejoin our fellow human beings as equals, if we're so different to them now?" His voice became louder with every question and there were angry murmurs of agreement from around her. Shanna's mind was confused, and her thoughts kept returning to the last image the starlyne had showed them – herself and her two cats, fading together from view, along with the great sense of satisfaction. She kept trying to reconcile what the creature was saying, with the picture her mind was constantly cycling.

"But what do you mean – ready?" She burst out suddenly, her question cutting loudly across the raised voices so suddenly that they ceased in shock. The starlyne again ducked its head, and she felt the impression of a sorrowful sigh from the creature.

"We knew that one day the Garsal would leave the home planets, and begin to spread across the galaxy. We knew that one day it was inevitable that our peaceful sanctuary would be disrupted by their presence. And when you arrived, and we discovered that you had the capacity to join with us, and possibly live in harmony, we knew that one day the Garsal would find your people too. As in fact, they have."

There was a pause. "We were unwilling to allow ourselves to become their slaves once again, and unwilling to leave you defenceless against them when together we might possibly overcome them. As you saw, initially we preferred to avoid you, fearful of the death and destruction you had brought with your arrival, but when we saw the potential in the human child and in the cat with the child, our minds were opened, and so gradually we encouraged change in you both. We have spent many years watching, waiting and hoping that you would prove to be the salvation of both us and of your own people. Now, you and your starcats have within you the potential for great skills - some of which you have already discovered - and great accomplishments." Again there was the faint overlay of Shanna and her two cats fading, along with the sensation of satisfaction.

"What do you mean, skills?" Master Peron's voice was almost accusatory "Yes, it appears that most of us can fade, with the help of our friends here, but what else do you mean?" There were nods of agreement from the Scouts around the starlyne, along with some closed faces, and still angry expressions, although a sense of anticipation now emanated from the starlyne, which had coiled its long length underneath it.

"There are more things you will be able to do with some training and with some assistance from us - and today I would offer that training to you. We are limited by our size, our shape, and numbers. If we can work together, we will be able to rid this planet of the foe, and then begin the work of freeing the enslaved peoples of this galaxy. We yet hold out hope that more of our people have survived. The changes we have encouraged within you are the skills and traits we lack. Together, we can make a greater enemy than the Garsal could ever have dreamed of."

Peron was openly incredulous.

"But we're so few in comparison to the myriads you've shown us – and we've already lost a considerable number of us against just a few Garsal vehicles, and you're talking about going to war against a species that spends its life warring. We're people of peace – explorers, colonists, farmers - and others who know nothing of war. We have a small militia and the Scout Corps, but we are not prepared for war!"

"You will have no choice," the starlyne said sadly. "Once the Garsal find a planet, they take it. You have defeated these few here, but once their commander realises that they have ceased communicating with the Ship they will send others to find out why and there will be other ships. You will have no choice but to fight or be enslaved like the rest of your race." Again the sense of sorrow was almost overwhelming. We will resist to the last starlyne youngling, and we pray that you will choose to stand with us – there is no hope otherwise." The starlyne slowly uncoiled its body and began to slide towards the vegetation. Its voice grew fainter. "I will leave you now for a time. Talk, think, and then when you wish to talk to me again, simply call. Consider our offer of training and alliance. While I am in this vicinity you are safe. No predators will bother you from now on." The starlyne was almost gone, when Amma called quietly after it.

"What is your name?" It stopped, turned its head back towards her and the thought came gently into all their minds.

"I am called The Keeper of the Knowledge. You may call me Keeper." The starlyne turned back towards the vegetation, quickly vanishing, and the gathered Scouts sat or stood in silence for some time.

Chapter 32

MASTER Cerron regained his wits quickly, and his voice rang out loudly into the silence in the clearing.

"We still have wounded to evacuate. Patrols One and Two, you will escort the evacuation parties to the access tunnel." He looked at Master Peron with a query in his eyes. The other Master nodded and took his place beside the two Patrol Firsts.

"I will take the message to the Council and return as fast as possible. Patrols One and Two will return as soon as the wounded and the archers are safe. I plan to bring the Council back with me as soon as I am able. Alternatively, we will attempt to make contact with any starlynes on the plateau. This will change everything." With that last cryptic statement, Master Peron indicated to the Patrol Leaders to call their Patrols in and to move off as soon as possible. Realising that Kaidan would soon be gone, Shanna whispered a quick permission from Spiron and went to her brother's side, hugging him tightly to her and feeling his long gawky arms tighten firmly around her in return.

"Tell Mum and Dad I'm OK please, and give them my love. I don't know when I'll be home." Shanna hugged her brother again and he nodded, each aware of the uncertainty of their futures in a way neither had had time to process.

"Shan, after what we've just experienced and seen, I can't imagine that I'll be allowed to walk out of that tunnel and back home straight to Mum and Dad. They still think I'm on a training exercise." Kaidan paused, his face serious. "As soon as I can, I'll tell Mum and Dad, but you saw it too – the image of you and the boys at the end there - it must mean something. I don't think you'll be home anytime soon." He shook his head sadly, "I hope I am."

Shanna nodded, understanding what her brother had left unsaid. That image of her with Twister and Storm kept intruding on her mind, and she was gripped with tension, along with wonder, that these suddenly sentient creatures knew of her – and also what they might want of her.

"Just tell them what you can when you can, and I'll be home as soon as I can." There was a moment of silence between the two siblings, and then Shanna hugged her brother again, tears prickling her eyes.

"See you when I see you. Love you little brother."

Kaidan looked at his sister, grinning wryly. "Love you too…mostly." He punched her arm gently and walked towards the assembling escort, bow in one hand, quiver of arrows at his hip, gawky and tall for his age, but somehow years older than when Shanna had left home all those months before. She waved once as Kaidan turned his head in farewell and then he was gone, swallowed up in the greenery. Twister and Storm each rubbed a large head on her hands, entreating her for caresses, and she looked down, smiled, and complied. Wondering.

***

The Garsal Overlord paced the command centre of the ship. All communications with the exploration vehicles had ceased abruptly two days previously. The last message from the Exploration commander had indicated that the human inhabitants had ambushed the vehicles sent to explore the plateau. The commander had assured his Overlord that there was no high technology to be seen and that the encounter should be brief and decisive. There had been nothing since, except for a sudden simultaneous cessation of the tracking telemetry that each vehicle had routinely sent back to the ship. For a full two day cycle, no communication had come from any of the vehicles. The commander paced back and forth, his black carapace reflecting the muted lights from the command centre displays and the comms tech on duty began to notice his agitation, shooting furtive glances towards him.

The Overlord was forced to consider that his vehicles had been lost. The dilemma returned: notify Central command, and perhaps lose his autonomy and the chance to hive build on a fruitful world – to establish his own gene line - or stand alone and possibly win or lose everything. He paced with intensity. As an Overlord, he burned to establish his own empire, to build multiple breeding hives to serve him alone, before launching his own pattern of interstellar conquest unfettered by the concerns of retaining his position and breeding privileges. His mind dwelt on the precious female enclave still sequestered in the safety of the ship. There had been a query from the senior Matriarch as to the status of the hive just that morning. Until now, the females had remained isolated in their secure accommodation on board the ship. Their numbers were few, the minimum necessary in order to establish a successful gene pool, and they had their own standards for accepting a breeding male. All of his status as Overlord would be nothing to them if he failed in building the hive to their satisfaction. Or if he admitted to them that the humans were here, free on this world, and had defeated the troops he had sent to enslave them. If he failed, no-one would mourn his death or mourn his lack of offspring. No Garsal female would consent to breed with a failure. If he reported the free humans and requested assistance, there was every chance he would be replaced and his own breeding privileges revoked. He would have done no less to an underling himself. Ambition burned within him. The decision was made - his path set. There would be no report to Central Command. There could be nothing less than total success on this world. Until that had occurred however, he must placate the sequestered females, hiding what he believed to be the destruction of the troops sent to seek out and enslave the human inhabitants of this planet. It was essential the hive was built, and essential that he conceal the Garsal enclave from the humans already here. They were a threat. But they would not prevail against him. This was a temporary set back.

***

Anjo sat in a comfortable chair near a fire, a hot drink at hand as Master Yendy began his queries again. Beside the Master Scout sat an older woman introduced only as 'Master Erilla'. She was an upright gray haired woman, straight bodied and fit, with piercing, vivid green eyes which contrasted strikingly with her dark brown skin. Clothed in a straight robe of deep green, she had a keen intellect and asked probing questions that drew more information from Anjo than he realised his memory contained. She was nodding quietly as he spoke and smiled encouragingly at him, and he racked his brains for more useful information. Anything he could do to help these people he would do. They were technology poor but very resourceful, and if he could assist in keeping them free of the Garsal, he would. They were his only hope.

***

Unusually for Below, no dangerous creatures had been sighted since Keeper had departed. The Scouts remaining in the area began to believe the starlyne's words - that they were safe while its presence was in the vicinity. Master Cerren conferred with the Patrol Leaders and the group set only a skeleton watch, urging the rest of the Scouts to rest. Cerren and the Patrol Leaders, and their seconds, held a small conference together under a spreading pungo tree.

Shanna took the opportunity to catch up with her cadet group, the six of them gathering together to one side of the clearing, all looking weary, Ragar sporting a bandaged forearm, Amma with abrasions all down one side of her face. Zandany was filthy but apparently unscathed, while Taya was limping and Verren's shirt showed burn marks across the back. Shanna realised she probably looked as bad – one sleeve was almost off at the shoulder and her trousers were stained with blood and dirt, legacies of treating the injured cats during the night. Her brother had informed her that her face was bruised down one side and an eye felt puffy. "Glad to see we're all still here." Ragar grunted as he sat heavily on a small rock, Sparks draping himself over his feet and humming at his partner. "I wasn't sure I was going to make it myself until the starlyne intervened." Amma put an arm around him and hugged him briefly which unleashed a small flurry of backslapping hugging amongst the six of them. Shanna even found Taya clasping her forearm briefly, not a tinge of animosity evident in the older girl's eyes for the first time in many months. She was able to return the gesture with a brief smile before Verren grabbed her in a bear hug. Finally, the group sat together on the rocks and ground, battered and worn but able to talk freely for the first time in what seemed days. It was odd to be able to converse Below without worrying too much about drawing in some kind of danger. There was still the odd piece of poisonous or carnivorous vegetation to keep an eye out for, but it was nice to have only one type of danger to consider.

"You know, I've been terrified for days!" said Amma, scratching Spider's ears as she purred loudly, "I'm tired, I'm filthy, and I don't know what to think. Oh, and I hurt all over."

"Me too," replied Verren. "I was scared witless when they gave me that group of archers and told me to look after them. I mean, we've had two trips Below but they've both not been anything like normal, and I felt that I could barely look after myself!"

There was a babble of conversation, each cadet describing their experiences during the battle, waving arms to emphasise points and detailing their perspective of the battle. As they wound down, Zandany ventured to say what was sitting in all their minds.

"So, what do you think about the Starlyne, and what it told us? What do you think the Council will decide?" His voice capitalised the word 'Starlyne.'

Taya nodded her head, a serious expression on her face. "Watchtower is still only one of three major towns. I don't think our Council can make any unilateral decisions."

"You're right, but it'll take days for the news to get to the other towns, and to their Councils. I don't know that we have the time to spare," replied Ragar. "In all seriousness, we can't leave that ship to dig in and build hives here on Frontier, or contact its allies elsewhere – if they haven't already. I think our Council may have to make the decision on behalf of us all."

"But what if the other towns disagree?" There was concern in Amma's voice. Zandany tickled Punch's belly as he looked up at her.

"In all our laws, there is latitude for one town to make major decisions should the circumstances warrant it. It was a proviso built into the law because of the dangers we face here just to survive, and a safeguard to make sure that if by chance a settlement or more is lost the rest of our society will continue to function." He grinned at around at the rest of them. "Most of my family are interpreters of the law or advocates. I suspect that at some point I'll be teaching you all law." He smiled. "Although I'm glad I didn't have to be the first cadet instructor! That must have been awful, Shan." Shanna smiled at the strongly built cadet.

"You've no idea! Try being considerably younger as well. And accidentally ending up with two starcats!" On the other side of the circle, she caught Taya's grimace.

"And what about that last image of you and the boys?" Verren was curious. "What do you think it means?" Shanna shook her head and sighed.

"I have absolutely no idea at all. I wish I could tell you, but I wouldn't have a clue." Twister hummed and Storm ducked his head gently against her hand, purring smugly. There was a chorus of hums and purrs from the other cats and the cadets shrugged bemusedly at each other, although Shanna noted a twinge of the antagonism returning to Taya's face.

"The more I get to know Spider, the more I think she understands a lot more than I originally thought," said Amma thoughtfully.

"My Mum always joked that I thought they talked to me when I was little," added Shanna. The others nodded, and she went on. "You know, it's not really in words, but you know they know what you're thinking, and you know what they mean…"

"Maybe we'll learn more when the Starlyne returns," put in Zandany.

Verren had been quiet for some time but now roused. "And when will that be, I wonder? You know, I really expected us to be sent back to the plateau with the wounded and the archers, but we're still here. We're attached to Patrols for who knows how long, and there's no doubt our training will be accelerated. But don't you think it's odd that the second years are still on the plateau and we're down here?" The tall cadet emphasised each of his points with a nod, finishing with a shrug of his shoulders. "I mean, I think there's more to it than we're seeing." Cirrus hummed at him and he resumed scratching her ears.

Ragar rubbed his chin thoughtfully, looked momentarily surprised at the amount of stubble on his chin, and then replied.

"You know, I didn't even think about it when we were detailed to bring the archers, but it would have made more sense if the second years had supervised the archers, and we were sent in search of the other patrols, yet the Masters still sent us. The question is – why?" There were nods of agreement around the group and thoughtful glances.

Sparks jerked his head up and then relaxed as Allad and Satin came towards them through the trees. The female starcat's tidemarks were glowing brightly, although Allad's expression was serious. He moved with his customary grace, although he like the cadets was filthy and his long sleeved shirt had a series of parallel bloodstained rips across the chest.

"Master Cerren wants to see you all."

The cadets looked at each other, scrambling to their feet and calling their cats to heel before following Allad, the oddly formal summons slightly forboding. Shanna sneaked glimpses at her fellow students as they walked together over to the informal headquarters established in one corner of the pungo grove. Spiron was standing with Master Cerren, several other Patrol Firsts and their seconds. Their cats were comfortably ensconced in various hollows and niches, all of them eyeing the young starcats accompanying the cadets. Satin hummed at Socks who replied musically, followed by a gentle chorus from the others, while the young cats' ears pricked up suddenly and their tidemarks became muddy uncertain ripples. Shanna looked at her two in surprise but their coats settled quickly into the regular pulsing patterns she was accustomed to. The cadets again eyed each other in startlement.

Master Cerren was tapping one long fingered hand on his thigh. Shanna noticed that he too bore the marks of the previous day's battle. His normally immaculate person was dirty, but he still seemed to exude the precision of the mathematical and navigational equations he taught with such enthusiasm. There was a toughness about the normally easy going and friendly Master that Shanna had never really noticed in all their previous encounters. It was the air of the wilderness Scout, she realised, someone completely at home in the wilds of Below - self reliant, competent and strong. While teaching, the Master had allowed that portion of himself to be almost completely concealed, although Shanna now recognised the odd moment when that part of Master Cerren had been revealed in glimpses to her now discerning eye. When she recalled lessons with him, she could see it in the penetrating questions that pushed a student further down an exploratory path than the student realised they were able to go, and the considering looks he used when examining .

She studied him warily as the sun glinted gently off the silvery fringes of his hair and Socks came to sit calmly beside him. He steepled his fingertips and regarded the group thoughtfully.

"Cadets, we'll be calling the Keeper within a few moments. Although you have until recently only ever encountered me as a teacher, you should have by now recognised that I was originally and in fact still am, part of the Scout Corps. I am also part of Watchtower's Council, and as such the greater Council of Frontier. Had your studies continued in the normal course, Zandany along with Master Lonish would have shortly begun lecturing you all on our laws and processes, and you would have more background for this discussion. As it is, suffice it to say, that I have some ability to make decisions on behalf of our community."

As Shanna looked around, she realised that all the Patrol Leaders must have already known these facts as none of them seemed at all surprised about the Master's revelations. Council Members were generally well known in their jurisdictions, and Shanna was surprised that she hadn't known that Master Cerren was one. "I was originally appointed in Skyfall some ten years ago, but was transferred to Watchtower almost immediately. The Council required that I keep myself relatively unknown, the better to observe our society without people reacting to me as a known Council Member. There are a number of us who have moved from town to town, to do this. It allows the Councils insight into areas we would otherwise not have. It also allows us to mentor those who may one day also fill a role in higher office. There are times when an unrecognised Councillor is able to gather information more easily than their public counterparts." There was a small pause after this statement.

"The events of the last few days require urgent attention. Our time is limited, and we may already be too late to react to the Garsal incursion, whatever our new Starlyne friends say. There is no doubt that we need to prepare as fast as possible to resist these creatures. We need to know more than we do, and explore anything that might keep us free of them." There were nods from all the Scouts assembled around Master Cerren. "To that end, we have made a joint decision, which now becomes my responsibility to act upon. When we call the Keeper of the Knowledge, I plan to offer the six of you, along with Patrol Ten, to the Starlynes to begin the training that the Keeper talked about."

There was complete silence from the group of cadets, and Shanna felt her jaw drop, hurriedly snapping it shut, before clearing her throat. Taya leapt in before anyone else could speak.

"You're going to do what?" Her voice was incredulous, and there was a heated expression on her face.

Master Cerren raised one hand. "I understand that the last few months have been unusual for you all, to say the least. In the normal manner of things, you would just now be venturing Below for the first time. For your group this is the third such trip for some of you – in many ways, you are the most unusual group of cadets we've ever begun to train. Put that aside, for now we have no time to waste. Even without the Starlyne's revelation, we'd be accelerating your training. As it is, we'll now have some of our most skilled Scouts and our newest, but very promising recruits, learning new skills and refining other ones together. You all saw the last vision – Shanna and her cats. She and all of you have already discovered how to fade. You are Shanna's cadet group – between all of you, the things you might learn and be able to do together are yet unknown, but where there is one prodigy," Shanna made a face, "There may well be more. I cannot imagine that she will be the only one of you to discover new things. I have watched you all for the last five years. There is more to you than you yet know." The cadets exchanged startled glances. "You will learn from and with each other, and with our new friends. Experienced eyes will see things young ones won't and the opposite will also be true. If we are to cement this alliance, we need to begin today. Our world is in peril – I say this not to be melodramatic, but as a bare fact. We *need* you to do this."

"Patrol Ten has agreed." Spiron's voice was firm, and Allad reinforced him with an emphatic nod. "We believe you are all suitable for this. You have proved adaptable," he smiled at Shanna and Amma, "Stubborn," he raised his eyebrows at Taya, who dropped her eyes slightly, and Shanna was surprised to see the older girl blush, "Steady," and he clapped Ragar and Zandany on the shoulder, "And teachable," he grinned at Verren, "Although some of us still have a way to go with culinary skills. We need your agreement. No-one who is unwilling will go. You may decide not to be a part of this should you so wish. Speak now. If you choose to go with the Starlyne, the Scout Corps will inform your families." Spiron was customarily decisive.

"I'll go," said Zandany. "I want to learn whatever it is they have to teach."

"Me too," Amma and Verren spoke in the same breath.

Shanna considered the image of herself and Storm and Twister then gave a nod. "I think I need to. I'm ready. Mostly."

"And me," Ragar smiled. "I'm curious. Perhaps I'm mad, but there it is."

The group looked at Taya. Part of Shanna wished the girl would say no - she still harboured some of the nagging hurt that the girl had inflicted on her, and was uncertain about any future relationship despite the recent amicability. The older girl looked torn, obviously uncertain about the step into the unknown. Spinner hummed softly, and she looked down at him. His red tidemarks rippled steadily and he ducked his head at her. Her eyes softened and she looked up.

"Spinner wants to go. So that's me in too." She sighed as if giving in to the inevitable, and her starcat purred loudly. Despite her reservations about the older girl, Shanna warmed slightly as she bowed to her starcat's wishes.

"In that case, Allad, call the Keeper." Master Cerren turned and faced the vegetation where the glowing Starlyne had previously disappeared. Allad took a step forward with Satin, looking slightly awkward and clearing his throat abruptly.

"Keeper!" His voice was slightly husky, so he cleared his throat again. "Keeper! We wish to talk again, please." There as a brief moment when the group felt as if nothing was going to happen, and then, faintly through the trees, was the sound of the Starlyne returning. A moment later, the great creature appeared between two pungo trees.

***

Arriving at the top of the access tunnel, Kaidan squared his shoulders, and gave a start as he realised there was yet another Starlyne crouched within the arena area. Around it, seated on long benches, appeared to be the full Council of Watchtower, as well as Master Peron, who had hurried ahead of the main group. The wounded were met by a crew of medics, who transferred them quickly to waiting horgal transports.

"Archers, you're to be quartered tonight in the visitors' barracks after debriefing," said Master Yendy. "There will be food in the mess hall immediately, so please follow the second year cadets." Kaidan's stomach rumbled loudly and he looked around hurriedly in case someone had noticed. He blushed as he realised that the normally taciturn Camid was attempting to quell a grin, feeling the fiery flush rise to the roots of his hair. Embarrassingly, his stomach gurgled even more loudly and there were a few stifled giggles from the group around him as they followed the cadet in front. Some sounded slightly hysterical. As he sat down to a full plate of roast dinner, Kaidan finally stopped blushing. He wondered how Shanna was getting along.

***

"Ask what you will, and I will answer as I am able," Keeper's voice without sound filled Shanna's mind.

"We have many questions, Keeper, however we wish to provide a gesture of good faith. These here with me will go wherever you wish to begin learning of the things you have offered." Master Cerren's voice was the measured tones of diplomacy. "Please take this as a sign of our intended cooperation."

The Starlyne dipped its great head. "We thank you Master Cerren, one will come momentarily and then you and I will talk. I am able to inform you that discussions have already begun on the plateau. My fellows there meet with your Councils as we speak to begin our planning. It is well though, that you wish to begin on the practicalities immediately. I have called, and I suggest that these collect their equipment as Teacher of the Young is within a few minutes of arrival." It (although Shanna had a suspicion that the Keeper might well be a 'he') glided forward a few paces towards Master Cerren. The Master nodded to Spiron, who gathered the cadets and the remainder of his patrol with his eyes, indicating that they should get their packs and return immediately.

Shanna and her fellow cadets collected their packs, hefting them to their shoulders, settling belts and water bottles without thought, habits of a lifetime formed within a few weeks, and returned to the Starlyne. Through the trees could be seen another glowing creature, even larger than the first.

"You may call my fellow 'Teacher'," said Keeper. "She is well skilled in all you will learn. Follow her, and when you return you will be ready." Keeper turned his head back to Master Cerren and Shanna looked forward to Teacher with some trepidation, her mind still whirling with all she had experienced. Despite having stated 'I'm ready' to Spiron and Master Cerren, she felt all at once very young again and much too inexperienced to cope with the fate of her world on her shoulders. There was the sudden pressure of a comforting hand on each shoulder and she looked up, surprised, to find Allad on one side and Verren on the other.

"We'll be alright. We're together, and our cats are with us – this is just the start of the next great adventure." Allad grinned. "And besides, we'll be back at some point. There's no way Satin will allow us to stay away from Boots for longer than she really has to."

"Follow your starcats. They will follow me." Her great eyes were kindly, though the depth of their knowledge was staggering if you looked for too long into their depths.

They moved into step, customary gracefulness in each stride, starcats roving in a standard Patrol formation, gliding through the greenness of Below as Teacher led them into the unknown.

List of Characters

Scout Cadets
Shanna – Storm and Twister
Amma – Spider
Ragar – Sparks
Zandany – Punch
Taya – Spinner
Verren – Cirrus

Patrol 10
Spiron (Team Leader) – Fury
Barron (Team Second) – Hunter
Allad – Satin
Nelson – Glutton
Karri
Kalli – Flyer
Sandar – Gryphon
Arad – Breeze
Challon – Dipper
Perri – Spangles

Other Scouts
Farron (Team Leader Patrol 4) – Mist
Feeny – Gem
Damar

Masters
Master Cerren (Teacher/Council) – Socks
Master Peron (Scout)
Master Lonish (Scout) – Samson
Master Yendy (Scout)
Master Vandon (Scout)
Master Kenwell (Scout)
Master Erilla (Council)
Master Dinian (Archery)

Archers
Kaidan (Student, Shanna's brother)
Camid
Gwen
Horden
Tasha

Others
Adlan (Shanna and Kaidan's father) – Boots and Moshi
Janna (Shanna and Kaidan's mother) – Sabre
Anjo (Garsal slave)
Semba (Garsal slave)
Hodan (Horgal wagoneer)

About The Author

GROWING up in Western Australia, Leonie Rogers was an avid reader from an early age. Her mother vividly recalls her stating "I can read faster with my eyes than you can with your mouth, Mum…" at around the age of six. Her parents and great aunt encouraged her interest in literature, providing her with books of many different genres. She began writing during high school, placing in the Western Australian Young Writers Award in 1980, and she fondly remembers several of her English teachers, who encouraged her to write, both fiction and poetry.

Leonie trained at Curtin University as a physiotherapist and moved to the remote north west of Western Australia, as a new graduate, in late 1986. She continued to write poetry for herself and for friends. Living in the remote northwest, she had the opportunity to work with camels, fight fires as a volunteer fire fighter, and develop vertical rescue and cyclone operation skills with the State Emergency Service.

After relocating to NSW with her husband and two children, Leonie continued to work as a physiotherapist while still dabbling with writing. Finally deciding to stop procrastinating, Leonie decided to write the novel she'd had sitting in the back of her head for the last twenty years. Her husband and two teenage children have been extremely tolerant of the amount of time she has devoted to writing in the last few years.

Thank you for reading Frontier Incursion. We hope you enjoyed it. If you would like to be kept informed of the further adventures of Shanna, the Scouts of Frontier, and their starcats, or other new releases from Hague Publishing, why not subscribe to our newsletter at:

www.HaguePublishing.com/subscribe.php

And if you loved the book and have a moment to spare we would really appreciate a short review. Your help in spreading the word is gratefully received.

Hague

Publishing

www.HaguePublishing.com

PO Box 451 Bassendean
Western Australia 6934

Made in United States
North Haven, CT
16 July 2022